Sacrificial Lambs

Keith A. Thomas, Jr.

Dedication

"To you, dear reader, thank you for making my dreams a reality. Thank you for giving my words a chance. Thank you for allowing me the opportunity to entertain you with my imagination."

K.T

Like and follow: @author.keitha.thomas

Contents

Chapter 1

It was midnight and featured overhead were typical characteristics of any ordinary night sky. With ease, the various Dippers could be seen twinkling amongst the familiar backdrop, and so did the chameleon reveal its full pale face. Yet, unlike any other autumn night ever recorded in the almanac for this region of Italy, there wasn't a breeze of any kind. Not even the mere chirping of crickets could be detected, nor could nocturnal predators be seen wandering or making a kill. Without question, something was brewing—something of historic proportion. Something which was maybe unexplainable in words, for all around, there was tranquility. It was almost as if the entire planet was totally deserted of life. However, despite this look of abandonment, somewhere, every creepy critter known to exist had to be waiting. They had to be awaiting in defiance, for tonight had all the prime ingredients for a revolt.

What could this be? It was the first telltale sign of movement in hours. Strangely, it was none other than a lone wolf. A lone wolf who was making its way with a businesslike approach up a steep but narrow cliff that overlooked a dark forest valley. From the start, the lone wolf had given the illusion as though it was lost, but one could almost sense by its stride that it had a destiny. An uncertain one. What was it, though? What purpose did the lone wolf have at the summit? Was the lone wolf maybe contemplating suicide? At first, there weren't any imminent clues as to these questions. Then, the lone wolf did something. The lone wolf sat on its hind legs and nodded its head twice toward the valley floor. That's when everything became apparent. That's when, from every cardinal direction, eyes of all sorts lit up like a wave of blinking Christmas lights.

Perhaps the creatures in the valley could see or hear something that had gone astray. Something like a cryptic message. Something only they could decipher. Maybe this was true, but it was most likely the lone wolf's responsibility to act as their medium. Since the lone wolf's initial arrival, it was obvious that it had many unique capabilities, but was it also somehow able to chart the stars? This could have been a possibility, as the lone wolf gave another stiffened nod to the creatures below just before it arched its head back and gazed aimlessly up at the heavenly sky.

How could a valley, which once looked so deserted and peaceful, now be luminous with the utmost of life? How could one valley alone possess so many mysteries? Yet it never revealed any of them. Nor did the lone wolf twitch or for once turn its devoted attention away, even though the pale moonlight was casting down upon its mangy coat as if it were center stage on Broadway. With this being the case, how could someone not deny that the groundwork wasn't being laid for something spectacular? Something which would soon serve a purpose in both the lone wolf's and the creature's universe to come. What was this something?

Within a matter of seconds, the answer had come. It had arrived in the form of three distinct blasts, which had torn open the night sky like a fire work show. From far away, each eruption appeared to produce a projectile in the form of a comet. Also as a direct result of this cosmic event, scores of rocks and debris had fallen towards the valley floor.

"Hear me, loyal guardians of the outer gates of divinity! A mischief has occurred in my father's house! A great treason, which would soon spell disaster for the children of Earth! Thus, I deliver ye forth, to return this sacred item which has uplifted itself! Now seize this property and serve thy Lord well! Seize every wicked seed which was also involved in this foul act so that I may render judgment on them or never return to my kingdom from whence ye were created!"

When the Lord had given this ultimatum to the two cornets, a change of event had occurred; the comets had transformed themselves into a pair of enormous white rams, which had taken off towards the third comet-like highway patrol officers. Around and around the paleface moon, the rams had gone. They were traveling at speeds and altitudes only dreamt of by man. However, when the third comet had stopped and changed its direction, the results were devastating. All three of them had burst into a bright ball of flames.

"*H-o-o-o-o-w-w-w-l*," screamed the lone wolf at the paleface moon.

"*H-h-h-o-o-o-o-w-w-w-l!*"

The second the lone wolf had turned its attention away from the moon, that's when the moon had taken on a grin of evil. That's when it started to change hues. In fact, the moon had turned so crimson in color that it had begun to rain down upon the creatures in the valley, faces like a squeezed orange. One after another, their throats could be heard gulping as they quenched down the delightful taste of wickedness like mad drunks. Something not of this world had just taken place. Something unholy, and for a split second, someone would have thought that they were witnessing the end of mankind. Especially when the third comet magically appeared in the sky opposite the moon. But what were the comet's intentions, and why was the Lord so opposed to it leaving his kingdom?

Rather oddly, the comet wasn't moving at all. It was just hovering in one spot, with its tail lighting up a vast portion of the sky. What was it doing? For several minutes, the comet had remained this way until it had made a play for the moon. There, it had made six complete orbits before it had returned to Earth's atmosphere. By the look of things, it appeared to be headed in the direction of the narrow cliff.

"H-0-0-0-0-w-w-w-l! H-H-H-0-0-0-0-w-w-w-l!"

It was too late for plea bargaining. The lone wolf never had a chance when the speeding comet hammered itself into the cliff. In the process, the lone wolf's burning carcass was expelled to the shimmering valley floor below, where the mute spectators paid no attention to its violent death. How was it, though, as the smoke and flames gradually began to fade away from the newly formed cliff, that there appeared to be a man standing about it? A man who was dressed in a full-length, dark hooded garment. He wasn't alone either. He was accompanied by a mystical beast called a griffin, which had the head, torso, and wings of a bald eagle but the body of a lion. Was this the same duo who had eluded the rams from heaven only minutes ago? If indeed it was, then what involvement did they have with the creatures in the valley?

The stranger appeared to be seven or perhaps eight feet tall, and he wore a hood that covered his entire face. Only his fiery reptilian eyes could be seen. With these eyes, he was in total control. With these eyes, he governed the creatures in the valley, and they did nothing to defy this truth. Except for his fireball-colored eyes and his tall but medium build, one was unable to depict any other characteristics of his figure fully. This was due to the moon's present darkness. Nothing at first glimpse appeared to be what it really was.

"Citizens under the new world regime and loyal workers of the uprising, ye are gathered here tonight by prophecy! Ye art gathered here from dimensions both far and near! Ye art also gathered here to take part in what will be known as the darkest day in man's suffering! I, Natas Christopher, salute thee, as does the fallen angel Nero!" Natas Christopher had shouted from the newly formed cliff. His voice was so massive it echoed off the high arching mountain walls, which in return had caused loose rocks to fall. "To all of my patrons who have kept the faith and fastened for generations, let my uncanny love for thee replenish thy wills and strengthen thy weakened bodies to full peak! For finally, I have arrived from light into darkness!"

These words alone were enough to send both the land and air creatures into a frenzy. They were celebrating Natas Christopher's escape from Heaven. Was it his arrival that had struck a nerve in the creatures, or was it the gratitude he had paid towards them? Something only that was driving the creatures insane. Some creatures had even taken the liberty to trample, fight, and eat the remains of the fallen. Then, some had seized the time out to engage in outer species sex and drink carefree from the still bloody moon.

"For speak, my beautiful followers! What have ye to say?"

"We are fed up with man, for he has invaded our way of life as we once knew it! Yes, for countless centuries, this has been the case!" The creatures had replied in a trance tone of voice. "Now we so eagerly thirst for revenge and human blood! For Heaven has turned their backs away from us for too long! Too long have we gone without any aide or welfare!"

"I say unto thee, rest assured and put away that explosive mind set until I tell ye when this day will come!" The creatures' aggressiveness had seemed to bother Natas Christopher. In a sense, it sounded as though their comments had made him nervous. "Yes, my followers, ye will have the chance to savage human flesh! Both Nero and myself will make thy desires a reality!"

Once again, the creatures had erupted into celebration. But when Natas Christopher had raised his hands, everything had ceased. Not even a single creature had dared to flex a muscle or bat an eyelid. Nor did a single creature dare to turn their face upwards at the moon for a drink.

"Listen to me! Until the true hour for redemption arises, the weak must lay low and prepare themselves mentally while the strong begin work on clearing the seventh gate!" He had over-emphasized. "Believe me, ye will have thy revenge! It will come!"

"But how shall we know when that day will come?" A creature from the valley had shouted.

"We are tired of waiting!" A second creature had heckled.

"Yes, we have been waiting in the cut long enough!" A third creature had replied. "We want a showing of force!"

"Damn it, now is the proper time!" A fourth creature had insisted.

"Yes!" A fifth creature had agreed. "Why wait when we can take action now!"

"No, let's hear him out!" A sixth creature had tried to be cautious. "This much we owe him! He has traveled too far and has risked so much!"

Growls, snares, and what sounded like a chorus of mixed boos

could be heard throughout the valley.

"Shit on what you say!" A seventh creature had become belligerent. "For my aging soul grows weary of waiting! I want to ride tonight! The survival of my species depends on it!"

"Yes! Let's terrorize man's cities!" An eighth creature had suggested.

Once again, the creatures had broken out into mayhem. This time, when Natas Christopher had raised his hands to stop them like before, nothing had happened. The creatures had simply ignored him. His presence had meant nothing to them anymore. It was almost as if he was nonexistent. Outraged by this, he hurled an unknown object toward the valley floor, which erupted like a hand grenade, killing many of the creatures at random.

"Hell has no time for failure! It will not be tolerated! Now, let this be a reminder! Ye will obey the rules set forth or else!"

"Forgive us, mighty one!" the creatures had replied in unison. "We are like fools waiting for a voyage, but we do not know when that ship will depart!"

"Imbeciles! Ye shall know this day when the sun will be hidden and when the moon will reflect the face of Nero for six nights! Then shall ye know this day! Ye shall know this day when the defeated angels from Heaven cry blood from their swollen eyes and curse the true name of the Trinity with their burning tongues of fire! Then shall ye know this day! And finally, ye shall know this day when all the events I have just mentioned come to pass! Therefore, I say unto ye, farewell! Farewell, and ready thyselves for the future battle!"

It was no surprise. The creatures in the valley were sold. Nothing could change this. They had their loyalty invested in Natas Christopher's promise to deliver them revenge against Heaven and humankind, as he had vanished on the back of the mystical griffin. Was he playing possum, or did he really decide to go elsewhere? If so, then where? Where would someone in his position take up refuge? How could he avoid the wrath of Christ? Still, this question meant little or nothing to the creatures in the valley, who continued to carry on as before.

Chapter 2

Now, for the first time in many hours, the sleepy sun has begun to peek its face over the brisk valley as it slowly but shyly lifted its dark veil, allowing bright speckles of eternal light to shine through cordially. This was the signaling of dawn, and along with this new occurrence had arrived a sky full of vultures who couldn't wait to make their debuts to the newly discovered animal carcasses. One after another, they landed until the ground was literally saturated with them. It was probably a slim chance that they could have filled a small football stadium. Was it the sight of blood or the aroma of death that had telephoned these flesh-eating birds from far and near? Whatever the case was, just their presence alone had seemed to drive some recipient jackals from last night's harvest moon in search of their homes.

From each corner of the valley's floor laid spoiled heaps of rotten animal flesh. However, when the vultures had begun to pick the meat from the bones of the thousand or so corpses, that's when the mutilated bodies gave off an eerie feeling of savagery. Indeed, all of these scattered bodies had come from the campsite of the night creatures who had dumped and left their toxic waste behind. Still, with all of these scattered organs and rearranged limbs, not once could a single creature be identified by its species. Not even one, due to the entire valley floor, looked as though it was burdened with the bloodshed of a bloody civil war. This is what had come to mind, as a couple of black birds had made their nest in some poor creature's hollow stomach cavity. This is also what had come to mind, as the lone wolf's smoldering carcass blocked the beginning of the only path that led to Vatican City from the valley.

"This is the will of thy Lord that ye be delivered unto this desolate world, so prepare thyself to do what He has intended for ye to do." This voice, which came from Heaven, was that of a young woman. Her voice was as pleasant as it was direct. "Remember as I purge thee on thy way to always serve thy Lord well and to protect thyself from the forces of evil at all costs. Go, great messengers, and do what ye are supposed to do! Go, but return quickly to our Lord's kingdom! Now, I will lead thee."

Without warning, the sky parted open, and in the midst of it appeared a ghostly image of a woman—a woman who was dressed in a long silk gown. However, in between this woman's palms, which she kept cradled, was a white ball of light. Was this woman the same woman who had spoken from Heaven only minutes ago? It had to be. Even though the woman's face was somewhat distorted due to its being transparent in color, it still depicted youthfulness and innocence. But the second the woman released the ball of light from her palms, she vanished altogether, and the sky was closed by the same supernatural force that had opened it.

The ball of light was so prodigious that even the vultures with swollen bits of flesh held tightly within their mouths paused to steal a glance. Yet where was this lightheaded? This question was somewhat answered when the light flew over St. Peter's Basilica and magically entered the Vatican Palace by way of the main entrance. Besides the Pope, some of his cardinals, who made up his cabinet, also resided there. Once inside, though, the light eluded the Swiss Guards on the first floor, who were dressed in their traditional Renaissance costumes, with its lateral movement. Then, the light employed the same technique to deceive the guards on the second floor. Legend has it that Michelangelo himself created these flamboyant-looking costumes with their puffed-out sleeves and knicker-bottomed pants that consisted of red, blue, and yellow stripes.

"Holy cow! Did you get a glimpse of what just whizzed past us?" The guard on the third floor had asked another guard. At the time, he and the other guard were both leaning over the banister smoking cigarettes.

"Are you serious?" The other guard had smirked. "I didn't see a thing."

"Well, I did." The guard had put his cigarette out while standing upright.

"Trust me, I saw something." He grabbed his long, pointed staff, which was a cosmetic instrument of his profession.

"Then where did it go? Where is this object you say that you saw?" The other guard was beginning to become spooked. "Do you know?"

"I don't know this very second, but I'm positive a ball of light about the size of a tennis ball had once traveled around that portion of the marble staircase." He had pointed with his weapon.

"Do you think it went towards the Pope's room?"

"Maybe."

"So, where is it?"

"It beats me." The guard had gone back to leaning over the banister. "The Pope will be up shortly. Anyway, our shift is almost over. I don't think the situation calls for disturbing him."

"If you say so."

It was true. The ball of light did seek invisibly through the Pope's door, but he had no recollection of this. He was still fast asleep on his plump belly with his nose pointed eastward, in the same direction as a narrow window. This window, which was parallel to the frame of the door, had its velvet curtains fully drawn. This had made the spacious room, filled with antique mahogany furniture, so dark that the only luminous objects were the ball of light, his radio/alarm clock on a nightstand, and a Holy Bible underneath. Directly west of the nightstand was a double wardrobe, and hanging from its two brass handles was a black cassock with red stitching – not to mention a silver cross on a thick silver chain.

One would guess that with the Pope devoting his entire life to the Roman Catholic order, he had very little need for any modern furnishings. He had very seldom watched television and was always on the move. The reason he had never stayed in one place was for safety purposes. Also, some nations were always requiring his religious advice, whether it was for a world hunger crisis, a war in the Middle East, or child molestation allegations. Besides his thinning gray hair, he had never shown his age publicly. He was either too proud or too stubborn to admit he had trouble seeing or remembering how to perform his ritualistic ceremonies.

"This is him," a voice had blurted out from the ball of light. "This is the Pope of Rome."

No sooner than the voice had spoken, something unique had occurred. The ball of light had drifted towards the Pope's face, where it had transformed itself into an angel from Heaven—an angel who had two heads and shared a single body identical to a human. This angel, which was also no bigger than a gnat, had one set of wings like a white dove. Without question, the angel's two heads represented unity and its honor to serve only one God. In no way was the angel's presence grotesque. On the contrary, the angel's gloves, tights, and boots, which were created from white linen, made it appear to be a character from a fairy tale.

"Time is of the essence," said the left to the right head.

"We need to progress."

"Then let us fulfill our quest."

Wasting no time, the angel leaped onto the Pope's earlobe, where it had begun its descent. The angel was moving very gingerly at first; then, it gradually picked up speed. It didn't matter which head did the communication. The angel still sounded as if it were a microcassette player being fast-forwarded with the play button held down.

"Behold, we have now entered the Pope's dream chamber," said the left to the right head. "Shall we advance forward?"

"By the will of our Lord, let us do move onward but with the strictest caution."

This was magnificent. Somewhere within the Pope's head was a movie-like projection screen, playing one of his dreams in which he was in a room surrounded by a thick cloud of whiteness. Oddly, only he and a redhead little girl with freckles were in this room. Still, he kept his distance from the girl, who was staring down at his white fiddle-back chasuble and up at his matching tiara. She would also, from time to time, gaze at his right hand, which clung to a silver crucifix. This crucifix looked exactly like the one hanging from the brass handles of his wardrobe.

"Shall we intervene?" said the left to the right head.

"No. Not yet!"

Everything seemed to match the room's color concept, except for the little girl. She was an outcast—an outcast who held a large circular sucker, which consisted of swirls of primary and secondary colors; an outcast who was wearing a black sun dress, a pair of red elbow gloves, a pair of red stockings, and a pair of black glossy shoes that had square buckles instead of laces.

"Don't be hesitant, child. Come to me." The Pope had suggested with a smile and a wave.

To make the approaching girl feel more comfortable in his presence, he kneeled until he was the same height as her.

"Why the sad face? You know, you can destroy the heels on your shoes if you continue to rock back and forth like that on them." The Pope had leaned forward. He had made a friendly grab for the girl's sucker, but she hid it behind her back. "I can see that we don't like to share. So tell me, what is your name?" He had tried his best to get her to smile.

"My name is Darkness."

"I'm terribly sorry." The Pope had tapped his ear. "Did you say your name was Donna?"

"No, my name is Darkness!" The girl rolled her eyes. "And I am a product of evil!" She conveyed in a demonic tone of voice.

"I see the problem here." The Pope stood up while staggering backward. "Your soul contains what is called a host. Well, let me speak to it again, child! In the name of the mighty Trinity, I command this foul life form which shares your body to come forth." He had dangled his crucifix before the girl's loony face.

"Take your bullshit elsewhere, gospel man! I serve neither Heaven nor Hell, for I am independent!" The spirit that had possessed the girl giggled. "This child belongs to me! She is tempting, but you will have to seek fruit from some other place!"

"What are you implying, demon?" The Pope pressed his crucifix against the girl's forehead, to the whining spirit's disapproval.

"Must you be so naive? You men of the cloth are all the same! You can't fight the urge to satisfy your boyish fantasies, so you take it out on the young and the weak-minded!"

"You have it all wrong!

I'm no monster! I don't prey on helpless children! I have spent my entire life being celibate. I know that Satan's veins run through the church, but it is my will and the will of other righteous people that this vessel be cut off! These evil-doers, which are few, will face judgment on Earth and in Heaven. The same applies to you, demon! I know your union is with Hell!"

"Fool, you leave me no choice! Now you must pay! You must pay with your soul for disturbing me with your religious hoopla!"

The Pope was speechless. He was appalled by the profane noises the transparent spirit had made when it had departed the little girl's body. He also didn't enjoy the fact that he was knocked to his knees as a result of the rush of wind generated by the supernatural act. To him, the spirit resembled a torn nightgown that was flying uncontrollably from side to side like a kite. To him, the spirit also smelled as rotten as sewage water. Despite these ills, he thought he had scored a moral victory over the wicked life form. Especially when the girl smiled for the first time and helped him to his feet, his initial reaction was that the worst was behind them both until the spirit returned from the cloud-covered air and took the form of an adult hyena.

"Greetings!" The two-headed angel had spoken in unison. Just with a single clap of its hands, the Pope was frozen in motion while the little girl and the hyena magically vanished in a puff of smoke. "We don't mean to trespass. Yet the Lord has sent us forth, to inform ye that his army is near and to deliver forth a golden scroll. Read it wisely, noble one, for soon, an unholy servant will pay Vatican City an unwelcome visit. When ye awake from thy sleep, ye will see the golden scroll to remind thee of our spoken words. Until this time, farewell and remember to serve thy Lord well."

In a reverse fashion, the two-headed angel had departed the Earth exactly as it arrived, in the form of a ball of light. Still, the question had seemed to be: what was written on the golden scroll? Another concern was how the aging Pope would react to this. Would he lose his mind, or would he faint? All was well, however, until he was awakened from his sleep by his radio/alarm clock. It was blaring a forecast of a tornado warning for Vatican City. As a result of this, many of the religious activities and tourist attractions were either closed or canceled. In other words, everyone was urged to seek safe shelter and to stay off the streets if possible.

"That was a rather peculiar turn of events." The Pope yawned while hitting the off button on his radio/alarm clock. I thought today was supposed to be mild and sunny?" He had gotten up from his bed, where he had nonchalantly walked over towards the window, wearing only his birthday suit.

With one hand, the Pope had tugged on the window shade until it went up about halfway. He was eager to contest the weatherman's forecast, but he had seen nothing to make him overrule what was already predicted for the region. From what he had observed, the wind was blowing paper through the air, and the sky was full of dark clouds. The sun was barely noticeable at all; he had snatched the shade back down.

"If those bright rays aren't coming from outside, then the main source has to be somewhere within this room." He slowly turned around. "Oh my! Oh my! What is that unbearable object up in my wardrobe? What could it be?" He grabbed his chest while stumbling forward to the edge of his bed, where his knees hit the floor.

The Pope couldn't tolerate the effects of the scroll any longer. It was beautiful in design but blinding as hell. The urge not to continue to look at it was too much for him to withstand; thus, he had whipped his head in the direction of his headboard and had begun to rub his eyes repeatedly with the backs of his fists. Even though he could sense that the scroll was put there by a divine power, he still hoped it would be gone once he had cleared the morning crust from his eyes.

"O Mighty Creator, who is in Heaven, what have you bestowed upon me? Please take back your precious scroll of gold, for I have a feeling of what its contents may allude to." The Pope had knelt in prayer. Although he was no longer facing the scroll, he could still see the silhouette that the bright rays had created. To his surprise, the rays were dancing on the ceiling and the walls as if it were a flickering candle. "Physically, I know I'm not the man I used to be. I know that age has distorted my vision and my hearing, but my passion for the gospel remains the same. I don't know, Lord. Maybe you see things the way the press or media does. Maybe I have become too unfit to lead the Catholic church, especially with its child molestation crisis. Maybe the time has come for me to step down and to appoint someone younger?" He wept in his palms. After all, he couldn't believe he was saying this.

Despite the Pope's somber mood, his tears were cut short by the sound of his radio/alarm clock. He thought he had turned it off, but naturally, he figured he had forgotten. Since he was in the later stages of his life, he knew his absent-mindedness was starting to become an everyday problem. Thus, he had leaned over and hit the off button twice, never leaving his knees. He couldn't believe it, though. Nothing could prepare him for what he was witnessing. He knew he couldn't explain this strange occurrence in actual scientific terms. However, the tuning dial from his radio/alarm clock seemed to be traveling up the station band by itself. He was so traumatized by this that he kicked his nightstand aside while snatching the power cord from the outlet.

"Why do ye weep?" A voice from nearby had asked. The voice was so fine-tuned and rich in bass that the Pope's clogged nasal passage was instantly opened. He didn't know why, but the voice had struck fear in him. His dilemma was so bad that he didn't even want to turn in the direction of the voice. "Get up! Get up! For haven't ye any faith?"

"Lord, is that you? Is that the sound of your voice that I hear?" The Pope had sprung to his feet. To his surprise, the Lord was using his radio/alarm clock as a transmitter. "I have faith, Lord! I have it!"

"Why have ye forsaken me, my child? Why haven't ye read my message brought forth by my messengers? How can ye now possibly be viewed as a high official of the Lord when ye have wept at the anticipation of my handwriting?"

"I was going to open the scroll, Lord. Honestly." The Pope darted over to retrieve it.

Once the scroll was in his control, it started to send tiny surges of electricity through his fingertips. Eventually, his hands became numb as he sunk his teeth into his bottom lip for comfort.

"Prove thy loyalty to me! Readeth that which is in thine grasp and prepare! Prepare thyself at once, my child!" The Lord's voice faded out.

"Prepare myself for what, Lord?" The Pope had directed his comment towards his radio/alarm clock. "What is it you want me to do? Lord, are you still present? I can't hear you. What is it you want me to do?"

The Pope was embarrassed. He felt awful that his stubbornness not to read the scroll right away resulted in the Lord questioning his honor. Did the Lord really want him to step down? He didn't know, but he knew the only way to be certain was to do as he was told. Thus, he placed eight of his fingers into the middle of the tightly rolled scroll. He was as excited as he was nervous, so he pulled the two rollers apart with care.

"By the time thy fingers caress this scroll, the angel Darr will be already standing amongst thee." He had read in a slow voice.

He didn't know if he was reading the scroll correctly on account of the Gothic lettering. The unusual-looking manuscript, which was written in the Blood of Sinners, was playing tricks on his eyesight. At times, the blood had appeared as though it was going to overflow the gold leaf paper but didn't. "Once in Vatican City, the angel Darr is to instruct and to send back information…"

"Concerning the sacred object which was uplifted from my kingdom."

"I take it you must be the archangel Darr." The Pope's heart was rapidly pounding away. "I'm honored to be in your presence." He pressed the scroll firmly against his waist.

"Likewise, Pope Pius the Fourth. Likewise."

The Pope was astounded, although he had refused to face Darr. For the time being, he was more than content, just staring straight ahead at the wall in the direction of his headboard. It was there that he had seen the shadow of this towering figure who had come equipped with a halo and wings. He couldn't believe it, but the angel was directly behind him. Since he was a kid, he had wondered how they looked and how they differed from men intellectually. "Tell me something, Darr. How tall are you?"

"Why don't ye turn and seek the knowledge which thou desire," replied Darr. His voice was deep, and the words would roll off his tongue like an English actor reading Shakespeare whenever he used emphasis.

The Pope didn't want to keep Darr waiting, nor did he want to give Darr the impression that he was being disrespectful. He had wanted to rotate his body and satisfy his curiosity. However, he couldn't hide the fact that he was hardly wearing any clothes.

"Ah, Darr. I think there's something I must do first."

The angel Darr, knowing what the Pope was thinking, spoke to him through his conscience. "Pope Pius the Forth, thy nudity doesn't startle me. When the Heavenly Father spawned Adam and Eve, he created them in their purest form to showcase the wonderfulness of the human body."

"I have no quarrel with this, Darr. But my body isn't picture-perfect either. I'm an old man with wrinkles and a pot belly. I would never turn and greet someone as prestigious as you this way. How would I ever live with myself afterward?"

"Fine." Darr had chuckled lightly. "I guess if ye feel that insecure about thyself, then ye may cover with garments."

"Thank you." The Pope showed his appreciation by bowing with his back turned.

He wasn't fooling around. He was headed straight towards his large dresser, which was located on the opposite side of his nightstand. The very top drawer itself is where he neatly keeps his underwear and T-shirts.

"Darr?"

"I'm listening."

"How were you able to do what you did about three seconds ago?" He had asked while dressing himself.

"It's a gift which I found came naturally. As thou would recall, Christ used this same method to read the minds of the multitudes when he had given his doctrine on top of the hillside."

"Yes, I do recollect this. That scene was out of the New Testament."

"Here. This should complete your attire."

"Again, thank you." The Pope reached over his shoulder to accept his white chasuble. He could also feel Darr removing the scroll from under his armpits.

Not once did he attempt to turn around. Indeed, Darr's telepathic ability made him feel like a valuable privilege was taken away from him—a privilege he had always cherished. It was his freedom of thought.

"Wait no longer. The time has cometh for ye to fulfill thy curiosity."

"Give me just a couple of seconds, Darr." The Pope wanted to gather himself. "Please." He could feel his heart beating faster and faster.

"Very well, and ye calleth thyself the Holy Father!"

Just then, the Pope had flinched as if he were expecting a slap to the back of his neck. This was the first time Darr's voice sounded unpleasant, and he didn't want to hear it again. Not in this lifetime. To him, Darr's angered voice had felt like a leather belt whipping against his flesh. He felt he would do anything Darr requested from here on out to keep the angel from speaking in that pitch again.

"I'm sorry, Darr." The Pope had stared down at his toes. "I didn't mean to upset you. It wasn't my attention. Please, no offense."

"None taken."

The Pope was worried. He knew the longer he had delayed things, the more hostile Darr could become. He felt it could even result in the Lord impeaching him from office. Thus, in a hesitant fashion, he spun around to his left, but Darr wasn't there. He could have sworn to himself that Darr was standing there no more than a second ago, as he had seen Darr's reflection on the wall. Not to be stumped by this, he turned to the opposite side, but still, there were no signs of Darr. Where was the angel? He asked himself this over and over.

"I said, I apologize, Darr." The Pope had cracked a smile. He had found Darr's behavior to be somewhat comical. "So why do you continue to play these cat-and-mouse games with me when I am prepared to meet you?" He had asked while spinning in circles.

The Pope let out a sigh of relief. His nerves were instantly calmed when he imagined that the angel Darr was probably just an invisible being with a shadow rather than a full-mass figure. But before he could complete his fourth turnabout, he was greeted by an individual who was taller than any man who had ever walked the face of the Earth—an individual who's facial and body features were molded from white light into a young man's image, but whose apparel was created from vast hues of colored light. This was also the case for Darr's long, sun-colored hair and matching eyebrows, which were a little on the bushy side. What impressed him the most was Darr's full-length robe, which was as blue as any cloudless sky. Attached to the robe by way of a black sheath was an exotic sword made from liquid titanium. Even though his brain had a hard time analyzing many things, he was positive portions of the robe would erupt into silent flames about every three seconds. He was also certain that Darr's wings weren't created from white bird feathers but rather from an assortment of floating cosmic pebbles.

"My word! You're astonishing! I would have never pictured you to appear this way. You seem to be the embodiment of our solar system, but your eyes are like they are glazing into it. Two topaz gems." The Pope dropped to his knees. He was so humbled by Darr's presence that he began to worship the angel's feet. In the back of his mind, he was expecting Darr to resemble the angels who are depicted on the ceiling of the Sistine Chapel.

"Greetings, Pope Pius the Fourth. I am Darr, a loyal servant sent to instruct thee and to inform the Lord of any worthy news. I am also here as a form of protection against those that may be harmful. With this being said, please taketh a hold of my hands and rise. Rise up, o' noble child of the Lord. Rise up."

The Pope couldn't help it. He was trembling with excitement the instant his hands had caressed Darr's. Initially, he didn't think Darr's grip would be so firm. From a logical standpoint, he was expecting his hands to simply vanish into Darr's body, which he felt was composed mainly of white light.

"Darr, what is this unusual power I feel sweeping through my body?"

"Do not be alarmed, for that which thou feel is the essence of the Holy Ghost. Ye must grow to embrace it, not to fear it."

"But I feel so alive. So refreshed. So content." The Pope explained while still holding onto Darrs' glued-together hands. It was almost as if they were crazy.

"The effects which ye feel aren't everlasting." Darr had informed while letting the Pope's hands go. "They will soon pass with time."

"But why?" argued the Pope. "I never felt better in my life. You haven't come to see that I step down? Have you?"

"No, the Lord adores ye, but thy patronage will soon be tested." Darr turned his back. "All of ours, for that matter." He mumbled before spinning back around.

"You seem really bothered by something. Does this have anything to do with the sacred key, which the Lord had mentioned in the scroll?"

"Certainly, but it also contains life on Earth as well. Behold, as I speak, he is prepared to unleash his destruction on the civilization of mankind."

"Who? Who is prepared to do this? Are you referring to the Devil? My word, Darr! Don't tell me that 'Revelations' is upon us already!" The Pope had grabbed his chest in anticipation of Darr's response.

"No. But there very well could be a holy war raging on this planet as well as in Heaven if the sacred key isn't found in time."

"What is this item? What does it do, and who do you suspect has it?"

The Pope was on a roll. He was too concerned to stop asking questions now. He had this burning desire to learn all there was to know, even if it meant he would have to pump more information out of Darr. His primary goal was to see if he could take the knowledge gathered and come up with an alternative resolution to finding the sacred key without the need for a bloody conflict.

"You ask, what is the sacred key? The sacred key is the Trinity's secret recipe for creating supernatural beings such as myself. It is no more than a genetic code; only it is destined for the wrong hands."

"In other words, y-y-you believe the Devil has it?"

"A soul by the name of Natas Christopher has it. He was once a follower of the fallen angel Nero. When the Trinity had cast Nero out along with the other rebellious angels, they locked Natas Christopher away until he was to be judged and sentenced to eternal death."

"So, how did he escape this punishment?" An awful feeling came over the Pope, which had made his stomach turn inside out.

"He had inside assistance. It is now his profit to gain if he can deliver the merchandise unto Nero, who has the knowledge to decipher it."

"I see."

"Thou doesn't see!" Darr had raised his tone of voice. "Ye have to realize that without the sacred key, the Trinity may become unable to campaign two separate battles. Man, as we speak, could become no more."

"How can I help?" The Pope had a look of seriousness on his face. "I may not have any supernatural strength, but I will give it my all! I will assist you in finding this lost property!" He clinched his fists into the air.

"Most excellent." Darr had nodded in approval. "First, thou may start by assembling some of thy finest clergymen. But only chose those who ye trust art worthy enough to see me, and art worthy enough to carry out the Lord's strict commands. Do I maketh myself clear?"

"Any particular number?" The Pope asked while searching under his bed for his black leather sandals.

"Nay. Therefore, go and doeth what ye were told to do." Darr dropped the Pope's sandals towards the floor. "For time is becoming extinct, and the Lord is growing more impatient by the minute."

The Pope couldn't believe his eyes, but he had watched his room door do something that he felt was haunted. He had watched it slam open on its own as if it were being controlled by some type of remote control gadget. Was Darr maybe at the helm? He didn't know because he was too shell-shocked. This condition had come about when the knob had hit the wall. It was true; it had given him a case of the jitters so bad he could hardly fasten the straps on his sandals. Still, despite the impact of the knob, the only noticeable damage he saw was a hairline crack to the molding, which had outlined the frame of the door.

"I-I-I will do as I was told, Darr! I will select only the b-b-best." The Pope had embraced Darr's hands before jogging towards the door.

He knew he had no time to waste. He was on a mission—a mission to assemble a team that he would use to confront this tyrant who had come to Vatican City. Yet before he could actually make his way over the threshold, the door had closed, just missing the bridge of his nose.

"There is just one more set of instructions I forgot to utter." Darr had expressed as he watched the Pope turn slowly towards him with his fingers in his mouth.

"There is?"

"When ye have chosen thy candidates, I will be waiting for them inside St. Peter's Basilica. There ye will sit them accordingly, and then I shall do the rest from that point on."

"But y-y-you will be seen." The Pope had removed his fingers. "Your presence will cause great panic in the streets."

"Haven't ye learned anything with my being here? Where is thy faith?

For St. Peter's Basilica and this palace will be invisible to all eyes, except for evil and the candidates whom ye will soon select!"

"Most extraordinary." The Pope had placed his hand underneath his chin.

He was thinking. He now knew he wouldn't have to worry about any chaos caused by someone spotting Darr inside the basilica or anywhere else for that matter. He felt this was a plus, given the seriousness of Darr's visit to Earth.

"O noble one, I must be on my way. I am needed elsewhere, still go. Go and doeth what ye were told to do. However, remember one thing as ye prepare to journey on thy quest."

"And what would that be, Darr?"

"To always serve the Lord with the utmost of honor and dignity. Serve him well, Pope Pius, for thou have no idea how much respect he has for thee."

"I promise, Darr. I will give my life for him." A tear fell from his eyes.

"By all means."

The Pope's visual contact with Darr was broken when he heard the door reopen and then closed as before. But when he had turned back around, Darr was gone. He didn't know where. He just knew Darr was no longer present in the same room. His only guess was that Darr had dematerialized while vanishing through the ceiling.

The Pope was skeptical if he had left a solid impression on the Lord and Darr. He swore his performance could have been much better as he sunk his teeth into his bottom lip. At the time, he was headed toward the narrow window in his room, where he had pulled the shade up about midway upon contact. He wasn't staring at anything in particular, just letting his eyes and mind wander aimlessly. He couldn't believe it. He had a hard time comprehending the supernatural acts which he had encountered so far. It was like he was living a lie, yet he knew he wasn't. He knew there was a real task at hand to complete – an important one. Personally, he thought he was going to become emotional by Darr's absence until he had started to feel about ten pounds lighter. This was because he no longer felt the need to be more than perfect when Darr wasn't towering over him.

"Ah, decisions. Decisions. There are so many to make." He murmured before turning his back towards the window.

The Pope was in a deep state of thought. He was thinking of candidates who he believed were worthy of representing the Lord and intelligent enough to be instructed by Darr. He also wanted to surround himself with candidates whom he felt had the credentials to maybe succeed in office if some misfortunes were to arise. Yet, out of his list of many cabinet members, only four names had stood out. They were Senior Cardinal Bishop Kelso O'Connor from Ireland, Cardinal Bishop Isaac Ivan from the United States, Cardinal Bishop Zutermier Sabatini, a native of Italy, and Cardinal Deacon Peter Nicholas from Russia.

"I need to get moving if I hope to find these four in a timely manner." The Pope exhaled while walking towards the front of the room.

He had tried to open the door, but it wouldn't budge. He figured something had most likely gotten jammed when it was forced shut. What he needed to do, he felt, was to reverse the process. With

this being the case, he grabbed the knob and began to twist it while pulling back with all his might, yet the results were the same. Still, he was unable to leave his room under his own accord, but why? Frustrated with his failed attempt, he began to pace around in circles. About a hundred thoughts per second were entering his mind when he stopped and noticed two brass objects of equal length lying on the floor.

"I know what these are. These are pins from the hinges." He grimaced as he bent to retrieve them. "I'd better put these aside in my dresser; that way, I know where they are." He went and did so.

With a new focus, he made another trip towards the front of the room. This time, instead of twisting the knob, he felt he would yank it in an upward fashion. Even though he was aware that his technique was somewhat primitive, he repeated the process until he watched the hinges separate and came undone. Satisfied with the results, he continued to inch the door to one side until it was resting in a slanted position along the inner frame itself.

"I can't believe it! Look what I've done! Look at this destruction I've caused!"

The Pope's cries were brief, and his adrenalin was overabundant. In an instinctive kind of way, he had felt the growing urge to shower the Lord and Darr with results. With this firmly implanted in his mind, his first order of business was to see if he could locate his four selected cardinals within the palace. He figured he would begin with Kelso and Peter since their rooms were located on the same level as his, but he had come up empty-handed. He couldn't even gain admittance. It was almost as if some unknown presence was presiding over all of the doorknobs on that level, including the library's. He had also determined this to be the case when he searched the second level for Zutermier and Isaac.

"That's odd. None of the doors will open for me. What's going on around here? Where is everyone? Where are all the Swiss Guards? Who's going to protect me?" He had complained as he made his way towards the first floor. He was curious if this phenomenon with the doors had occurred around the time he had become stuck. "Darr's right; the Lord has imposed his very will upon this palace."

The Pope was upset with himself. He felt as though he had accomplished nothing. To make matters worse, he knew he had wasted about an hour going from room to room. He figured if he couldn't find his cardinals within the palace, then he didn't know where else to search. What worried him the most was that they were spread-out all over town.

"I knew this wasn't going to be easy. Now I have to implore the services of Darr. I just pray Darr's inside the basilica." The Pope had mentioned before jogging off.

He knew he wasn't a spring chicken, nor did he believe he was in any physical condition to engage in prolonged cardiovascular activities. Given this, he had to occasionally rest and start again.

However, for the final thirty meters or so, he had maintained a jogging pace until he collided with Kelso and Peter. At the time of the collision, the two cardinals were just beginning to ascend a flight of stairs leading to a single push-door. It was through this side entrance that the Vatican chefs, maintenance, and various members of housekeeping had gained admittance into the palace.

"Good gracious, you nearly knocked us flat on our backs!" Kelso hollered while clinging to Peter's wrist for support. "Did you just see a ghost or something?"

"No, I didn't. Please forgive me, gentlemen. And top of the morning to you also, I must add." The Pope smiled. He knew this couldn't have been perfect timing for the two cardinals, who were both wearing black cassocks with red trimmings and buttons.

Kelso was one of the last dinosaurs who thought what the youth of today needed was more religion and strict discipline. He was a frail man, about five foot nine, with a buzz cut. If you could round off the wrinkles in his face to the nearest tenth, you could probably guess his age. To some, he had resembled Doctor McCoy (Bones) on Star Trek. The Pope had chosen him for the mission because he had stood for wisdom and tradition. Even though the two would often verbally criticize one another's views on society publicly, they had remained the best of friends for over four decades. The newspapers in Rome often referred to them as the dynamic duo. However, the only downside of the selection was the senior cardinal's ill health and quick temper.

Peter, on the other hand, had the appearance of a choir boy. He was about five foot six with curly red hair, freckles, and a fair-shaped body to match. He was one of the youngest members to ever serve on the Pope's cabinet. He also had the ability to adapt his intellectual skills to any situation at hand. His two pet peeves were that he was dedicated to serving the Lord and Christians. Due to his innocent nature, he seemed a little shy at times. Still, he always followed the Pope's commands without any backlash.

"Before you ran into us, Pope Pius, where were you headed?"

"Actually, Peter, I was trying to locate both Kelso and yourself. Now that I have found you, I would like the two of you to remain where you stand. Please, don't go inside. I beg of you."

"Here?" Kelso had asked with a confused look on his face. "You want us to remain here? But there's a deadly storm on the horizon! Just feel that wind and gaze up at those clouds!"

"I see the clouds, Kelso!" The Pope frowned as he made his way down towards the sidewalk. "Trust me, my eyesight isn't that far gone yet." He babbled with his back turned.

"But what's going on, Pope Pius?"

"I have no time to answer any questions, Peter. I'm in a bit of a hurry. I need to locate Cardinal Zutermier and Cardinal Isaac before I can begin to entertain your thoughts. Have the two of you seen them?" The Pope asked while searching in every direction imaginable. At the time, he was hoping that they would just spring up from out of nowhere or drop down from the sky.

"I'm sorry, Pope Pius, but I haven't seen them. Have you checked their chambers?"

"Yes, Peter. I have."

"Let me guess, Zutermier's probably out analyzing the storm, and Isaac's probably somewhere feeling sorry for himself. You know, Isaac hasn't been himself since his parents' tragedy. Someone told me he keeps blaming himself for everything that happened. If you ask me, I'm starting to believe he's nothing more than a big baby who still wants affection. I feel it's time we address his position in the church."

The Pope had paid Kelso's sarcastic remark no mind as he lazily swatted his hand in the air. He knew that this was Kelso's normal way of expressing his feelings with his mouth first rather than his brain. He was also aware that there was some bad blood beginning to stir between Kelso and Isaac on account of remarks such as those. Yet he knew now wasn't the best time nor the place to address it, so he turned his back and ran southward down the sidewalk. To his right was a forest of tall oak trees, and to his left was a steep hillside.

Nevertheless, he did notice a person several yards out in front of him. Just for a second, he assumed it was Isaac until he realized the person was too slender in build.

"That's odd. Where did that person get to?" He had pulled up in his tracks. He had traveled so far that Kelso and Peter were both nothing but a blur. "I only turned my head for a second."

He was so winded that he had difficulty keeping his balance. He couldn't understand how a person could vanish that quickly. At first, he thought he was hallucinating until he heard the voices of two male tourists in the woods off to his right. He could see them, but it was obvious that one of them had spotted something up in the trees of great importance. What was it, though?

"Look at that! Look at that!" one of the overexcited tourists had cried out.

"Look at what?" the second tourist had replied grumpily.

"Look at that spectacular source of light high above the treetops! Quick, get your camera out!"

"In which direction are you speaking?"

"Right there! Just follow the tip of my finger!"

"I am, but I don't see anything out of the norm!"

"Great God, I think it's an angel!"

"You do? Are we referring to that same tree over there, the one which is swaying back and forth?"

"Yes! Oh, God! I think the end has finally come!"

"Hmmmm." The second tourist had paused. "Let me smell your breath. It's just as I thought. You're still wasted! I believe you had a little too much wine at supper last night, my friend!" He was compelled with laughter.

"I did not! You can't possibly tell me that you don't see a figure of light up there! No, wait! Try the other tree! No, wait! Try the tree next to that one! Shit! I swear on my grandmother's grave that there was an angel up in those treetops just a minute ago! I'll kiss my own ass if there wasn't!"

"Maybe you did see something," the second tourist had kept snickering. "Maybe it was a large gull or some other type of bird. You know, the possibilities are endless."

"Tell me about it. I only wished you had taken a picture as proof."

"Come on, let's get back to town. The girls are probably awake by now. Don't worry, if you still feel that strongly about what you saw after breakfast, then we'll return."

"Sounds good to me. Hopefully, by this time, the storm will have passed us by."

The Pope had deemed the situation comical. He couldn't help but smile. He knew the whole time that the one tourist's account was anything but far-fetched. Even though he couldn't see the visual evidence, his gut had told him the being of light in the tree was none other than the angel Darr. From a physical standpoint, he had a suspicion that Darr didn't feel he was right for the mission. He also felt that Darr was probably grading him for how well he followed simple instructions.

Chapter 3

The Pope was doubtful if Darr was still around. A voice from within told him that Darr had taken flight when the commotion on the ground had begun. Naturally, he was hoping he could strengthen the bond between Darr and himself by accomplishing his primary objective, which was to locate and seat his selected cardinals within the basilica. Although he was still winded, he was ready to move onward down the sidewalk with a newfound passion. The only thing he felt needed to occur was for the tourists to exit into the woods. For safety purposes, he didn't want to take any chances of being identified. Thus, he continued to crouch while shielding his face with his fingers. Not until he had watched the tourists vanish over the hillside towards his left did he find the urge to stand upright once again.

"Just out of curiosity, I wonder if I could better my chances of finding Cardinals Zutermier and Isaac by following the path of those two?" He mumbled to himself. He knew he would only be wasting time if he were to continue to travel the sidewalk where he could visually see no one up ahead. "Well, here goes nothing."

The Pope didn't know what to expect as he approached the hill. He was just acting on his own intuition. This insight led him to three cardinals and to a tall but skinny man dressed in all black like a local priest from town. His first assumption was that they were having some religious debate.

"I guess one out of two isn't so bad." Even though he was still some distance away, he was certain that one of the cardinals was Isaac. The other two he had recognized were senior Cardinal Julias and senior Cardinal Vincent. Not that it mattered, but they were both as short and as old as he was.

Isaac was an easy target to notice since he was the only cardinal of Afro-American descent to serve on the Pope's cabinet. Like a stocky giant, he had stood about six feet tall with skin as dark as coal. Although he wasn't blessed with the physique of a world-class bodybuilder, he sure did have the strength of one. At times, he had a smile that could light up a room but a temper that could clear it in seconds. The fact that his bushy brown hair was beginning to recede was rumored to be the fuel of his rage. But the people who were closest to him knew that a personal tragedy was behind his deep depression and eating disorder. Before his traumatic setback, though, he was lobbying for the catholic church to break away from tradition and become more modernized. He had wanted stiffer sanctions imposed on clergymen who were knowingly involved in sexual scandals. He was also said to be in favor of stem cell research and some forms of abortion.

"Stop! Stop! What is the meaning of all this? What are you all doing?" The Pope yelled as he sprinted towards the four men. "In the name of the Lord, I command this activity to cease at once!"

He couldn't believe what he was witnessing. He couldn't believe that Isaac and the local priest were wrestling right in front of him. He was so preoccupied earlier with his thoughts he didn't even know how or why the skirmish had begun.

"Isaac, listen to me! You know this type of behavior is unacceptable!

You know it isn't right! No matter what your differences are with this priest, fighting is never the best solution!" The Pope was hoping he could break the brawl up from afar like the other two senior cardinals rather than risk getting tangled up and trampled over.

He was uncertain who had started the confrontation. He just knew that he had a better chance of getting through to Isaac. This was based on their father-son relationship.

"This is going too far now! Enough is enough!" The Pope had to hurry out of the way to avoid being hit. "Listen to me, Isaac! On my count to three, I want you to release this man! Do I make myself clear?"

"I'm trying to!" Isaac had conveyed as he applied a headlock from behind on the much taller priest. "But this devil of a character keeps coming back for more!"

"Well, who is he?" The Pope wanted to know. "Is he from town?"

"We don't know," replied senior Cardinal Julias.

"Yeah, none of us has ever seen him before!" Isaac had grimaced as he continued to toggle with the priest, attacking me from below the waist."

"He just came from out of nowhere."

"God as our witness, Isaac 's telling the truth." Senior Cardinal Vincent had tried to explain. "That crazy Arab did come from out of nowhere. Trust us, he did."

"Never mind his origin!" The Pope snapped. "What did he say to you, Isaac? What did he say?"

"He said I was the only questionable one."

"Was that all?"

"Not by a long shot." Isaac beamed at the Pope. "He also stated that he wanted me to prove I was worthy enough to serve a greater calling."

"Tell me, you're kidding."

"It's the truth, Pope Pius. Honest."

Bitter, the Pope had seen through Isaac's smiling face as though Isaac wasn't even there. He was more concerned with the misbehaving priest, whose whereabouts were still a mystery to him. Was this priest an angel in disguise, or was the priest the villain Darr had warned him of? If so, then he knew he had to do something. He knew he couldn't just let the priest walk away. What if someone in town got injured or even killed? Because he could see the priest was no physical match for Isaac, he was optimistic he could seize and drag the priest to the basilica, where there would soon be safety in numbers.

"I have an idea, Isaac. Try to hold him still so I may have a word with him."

"Okay. But I would advise you not to get too close, Pope Pius. He could turn out to be more than you bargain for."

"Isaac's right." Senior Cardinal Julias agreed. "You better watch yourself, for this man has a face that resembles Satan."

"I don't know about that." Senior Cardinal Vincent chuckled. "But his eyes are kind of weird looking. Maybe he just forgot to take his medication."

"Don't worry about me; just be quiet, you two, and stand back out of the way. Please, don't come any closer." The Pope had forbidden them with an intense sparkle in his eyes. "Isaac, can you hold his head still without covering his mouth with your hand so much? I know that this may sound or even seem. It's ridiculous, but I do need to have a word with this man. It's very important."

"It would be an honor." Isaac could be heard struggling. "There. How's that?"

"Much better." The Pope had moved into position. "Tell me, who are you, and why are you behaving this way? Can you speak?"

"I don't think he does." Isaac was being optimistic. "If he could, then it would probably be in riddles and not in a sentence."

"He speaks all right! You just have to know how to break his terrorist mentality! Watch and learn!" Julias had begun to approach the priest with his fists balled up.

"Stop! Remain where you are! Don't do it, Julias. I will deal with this situation at hand without resulting in any further violence!" The Pope said, pushing him away. "Don't make me tell you twice!"

"Okay, I will let you try your way." Julias could be seen back paddling. "Then, when all else fails, let me slap it out of him!"

The sight of visualizing this handmade Isaac burst out in laughter. "Silence! I can't hear!" The Pope had lashed out. "All right, let us try

these questions again! Who are you? In the name of Heaven, where did you come from, and why are you in Vatican City perpetrating a priest?"

"Answer him!" Isaac had tightened his grip. "Answer the Pope! Do it if you know what's best!"

"Tell me, what do you know about Heaven? And are you willing to sacrifice your life for it? This is my question to you."

"He speaks! He speaks!" Isaac had become excited.

"We know!" The Pope had responded. "Now loosen that chokehold of your just a bit so we can better understand him!"

"Is this better?" Isaac had asked. This time, he was applying for a police-style, double-arm bar.

"Yes." The Pope had nodded.

"Now, are you going to answer any of my questions, or do I have to report you to the proper authorities?"

"You know why I am here. And deep within, you know where I hail."

Out of anger, the Pope grabbed and squeezed the priest's nose.

"Don't worry, I am not he," the priest had said with a smirk. "However, he whom you seek is already amongst us! Waiting, he is for the perfect opportunity."

Once again, the Pope grabbed the priest's nose and squeezed it. He was furious. He was fed up with the priest speaking in what he felt were riddles. From what he had observed, the man perpetrating a priest was acting more like a drug-enraged lunatic rather than an archangel or some religious tyrant.

"I think you' re insane. I think you're just talking to hear yourself talk. I really don't believe you have a clue as to what you say or do."

"Is that so, noble Pope of Rome?"

"Yes!" The Pope had answered, stirring into the priest's eyes. He wasn't about to back down or be intimidated.

"Then take a look within my pocket! Not that one! The other one! Now tell me, what do you feel? What do you feel?"

"What does he have, Pope Pius?" Senior Cardinal Vincent was trying to steal a glimpse for himself. "Is it a bomb or a suicide note?"

"Why, it's just a mere skeleton key of some sort." The Pope held it up.

"So it may seem! But examine it much closer!" The priest had directed the Pope. "Go ahead; it's for your eyes only!"

The Pope was literally tongue-tied. He couldn't find the words to express what he saw. At first glimpse, the key didn't seem to be anything out of the ordinary. It was only about the diameter of his palm and was constructed from gold. However, upon closer observation, it had become apparent to him that the key had something of brilliant substance within its middle. He wasn't a biologist, and even he was certain it was a live DNA strand. One which he felt was composed of several different planetary gases.

It's beautiful." A tear fell from the Pope's eyes. "It's like something right out of a sci-fi movie. Only a master craftsman could accomplish such an amazing feat." He whispered to himself before closing his palm.

He had wanted to conceal the key's identity from the others. The key was unlike any other object in the world. Just the design itself had held a celestial value that he believed was so significant that he thought he could feel tiny pulses of electricity traveling through his fingertips. Yet when he had gone to re-examine the key a second time, it was gone.

"What did you do? Give it to me!" The Pope raised his voice at the priest. "Give it back!"

"If only it were that easy. That key was only symbolical."

"I don't care! Make it reappear!" The Pope became irate. He was hoping to present it to Darr. "Bring it back, I said!"

"I'm afraid I can't."

Isaac could feel the priest starting to resist again. Something was happening in front of him, but he couldn't see what. He only wished the Pope wouldn't keep provoking the priest. To combat this new aggression, he had switched from the police-style arm restraints back to a choke hold. Still, the priest was becoming too unbearable for him to contain. It was like he was battling a monster.

"This is my last request. I want you to make that key reappear before me." The Pope held out his palm.

"Unfortunately, my answer remains the same." The priest struggled to get the words out.

"Then you leave me no other choice but to contain you? Senior Cardinal's Vincent and Julias, you are to assist but only when asked!"

"Stop!" The priest yelled. "You'll have them stay where they stand!" "Please, do as he says!" Isaac warned them in a discomforting tone of voice. "He has my finger in his mouth!"

Despite the pain, Isaac had continued to apply his choke hold. He didn't know if it was the wisest thing to do, but he didn't want to let everybody down. Nor did he want to be known in the newspapers as the quitter who had let an insane priest free back in the society. He was tired of being criticized.

"Release me, and I will spare you this agony."

"Never! Not in a million years!"

"Listen to reason, Isaac, and do what's best. He won't get very far." To prevent an injury, the Pope was content with releasing and recapturing the priest later with the aid of Darr. "You don't have to be a hero, Isaac. You're no good to me all banged up."

"I will never surrender. I won't let you down like this, Pope Pius."

"Don't put your body at risk for me, child." The Pope pleaded with him. "You must listen to reason."

Isaac was beaten. He could barely hold on. It seemed the more pressure he applied to the priest's neck, the sharper the pain became in his finger. He knew if he wasn't careful with his decision-making, he could suffer a permanent injury as a result. He didn't want to admit it, but he was obviously in need of help. A miracle was more like it, and it had come in the form of Cardinal Bishop Zutermier Sabatini, who had snuck up from behind and jammed two fingers in the priest's eye sockets.

"Zutermier, that was very quick thinking on your behalf!" The Pope embraced him as he watched the priest stagger towards the ground. "I saw you approaching the whole time."

The Pope's emotions were at their highest. He predicted that he was only about a half hour away from seating his four candidates before Darr. Still, he was undecided about how to get rid of Vincent and Julius without them becoming too suspicious.

"I guess my first question to you is, who initiated this conflict?"

"That one did, Zutermier. The man disguised as a priest," the Pope pointed out to him.

"So, what's his problem?"

"Other than being an enraged madman, I haven't the faintest idea. All I know is that when I arrived on the scene, he was attacking Isaac. Speaking of Isaac, would you two go and check on his condition for me? Don't worry. Zutermier and I will keep a sharp eye on the priest."

"By all means," Vincent stated before strolling over to where Isaac was hunched over.

"Thank you." The Pope responded as he turned his attention back towards Zutermier.

"Do you know if this man is from town?"

"Neither of us has ever seen him before, Zutermier. Personally, I get the feeling that he's not from around here."

"Then, have you tried to communicate with him yet?"

"Sure. But he only speaks in riddles."

"That doesn't surprise me one bit."

On average, Zutermier stood about six foot two. He was, by far, one of the tallest and best spokespersons in the Pope's cabinet. He was a nature lover. He was a man who would periodically travel into the wilderness to read books on logic and physiology. He was in his mid-forties and had the body of a Greek god, which was obtained by a daily regimen of push-ups and sit-ups. Clothing-wise, he was dressed exactly like the others. Yet despite this, one could tell just by looking at his long white hair and his full-length white beard that he was unique. He truly was a people person, a native son who was often referred to as having the scientific mind of a genius but the humorous side of a comic. This alone had made him one of the most celebrated cardinals. It was like he was a movie star. Many were even content to believe he was a prophet who had returned from the grave.

"I have given it a second thought, Pope Pius. Do you suppose this priest is a member of a terrorist cell that may be operating in Rome?"

"Unfortunately, Zutermier, I am unable to entertain that notion. My response will be as good as your question. That's why I have elected Isaac and yourself to help me escort him to the basilica, along with Kelso and Peter."

"But why the basilica?"

"A visitor came to Rome. He was the answer to all our questions."

"Who is this visitor? What's his name? Is he some type of special agent?"

"Special? Yes, you could say that, Zutermier." The Pope chuckled. "However, time is working against us." He turned his attention to where Isaac was crouched over.

Zutermier was curious as to what was really going on. It was obvious the Pope was way over his head with something. It was also obvious the Pope was withholding vital information from him. He could sense it. He knew by experience that the Pope would become nervous and turn completely red in the face when a lot of stress was upon him. He felt such was the case now, with the misbehaving priest on his plate and the mysterious visitor in the basilica.

"How is he?"

"Isaac's finger is bruised, but I don't know how badly," Vincent had responded to the Pope's question.

"I'll feel a lot more comfortable once I have a look for myself. Step away from him, you two."

Concerned for Isaac's health, the Pope had rushed over with urgency. He was accompanied by Zutermier, who had also wanted to check the situation out for himself. At the time, they each thought that they were still within range to keep an eye on the priest, who had continued to lie face down on the ground.

"You'll have to meet me about halfway, child. Stand up straight so I can examine that finger of yours. Don't worry; I'm not going to put any pressure on it." The Pope ensured Isaac by grabbing his wrist instead of his hand. "You know, it's an absolute miracle that your flesh wasn't penetrated during the ordeal."

"Thank heavens for that." Zutermier sighed.

"So tell us, Isaac, just how does your finger feel?"

"The Pope's right." Senior Cardinal Julias had acknowledged. "Only you know your body best."

"Do you think you need a medical exam, Isaac?" Senior Cardinal Vincent thought he would ask. He was worried that Isaac had suffered a fracture to his finger.

"No." Isaac had winced. "Even though my finger is still throbbing like crazy, I think it should be all right in time."

"Wonderful!" The Pope had let Isaac's arm go. "Now that we're clear on this, I believe it's about time we escort the priest to the——"

"What's wrong? Why did you pause?" Zutermier tried to obtain his answers by gazing through the Pope's eyes. "Is everything okay?"

"He's gone!" The Pope had become irate. "The priest is gone, and I don't know in what direction he traveled!"

"Impossible!" Zutermier thought until he looked for himself.

"Don't just stand there! Come on! We have to cut him off!" The Pope had urged the others to follow him. "Heaven knows what he'll do next!"

One after another, the cardinals had followed the Pope down the hillside and onto the sidewalk. However, Isaac was the last to do so as he watched the group begin to distance themselves. Still nursing his injury, he knew it would be difficult to catch them. Yet he put his head down and gave it his all, but it just wasn't good enough. It seemed the more he had tried to assert himself, the greater the pain had become in his finger, which had eventually traveled to his lower back. He felt he had no choice but to hinder his movement, which had angered him to the point where he thought the others were criticizing him. Even though he knew it wasn't true, he couldn't help but think he was the sole reason why the priest had escaped.

"Wait. It's urgent that I have a word with you." Zutermier had brushed up against the Pope.

"Feel free to say whatever is on your mind." The Pope had never once turned to acknowledge him. He didn't want to lose his focus.

"I was hoping that it would be in private."

"Oh. I don't think the others will hear us as long as we keep our voices down." The Pope had glanced back to gauge where everyone was. "We still have them by several feet, so what did you want to say to me?"

"There was a great unease in the valley last night."

"Really." The Pope had paused to collect his thoughts. "What kind of disturbance?"

"One of death and destruction."

"Is this just an accusation, or do you have proof?"

"With my own eyes, I saw mounds upon mounds of dead animal carcasses. They were spread out and rotting beneath the newborn sun in pools of some kind of red substance."

"How terrible." The Pope had felt his stomach turn inside out. "So what do you suppose this red stuff was?"

"Blood, of course."

"Blood?"

"Yes. Although, I don't believe it was that of the creatures. You see, it was too much for their bodies to produce."

"Then where do you think it came from?"

"That's what was troubling me." Zutermier threw his hands up in disgust. "But if it were feasible, I would swear to you the blood had poured down from the moon itself."

"That may be a little far-fetched, don't you think?" The Pope tried to hide his concerns with a false smile. "Listen, Zutermier, I don't want anyone else to get news of this until I can have the matter investigated. Do I have your word?"

"My lips are sealed."

"I appreciate it."

The Pope didn't want to hear anything else. Zutermier's account of what had taken place in the valley was too graphic for him. He was ready to bend over and puke his guts out, but he didn't. Unlike Zutermier, he had firsthand knowledge of who was responsible for such a devastating act.

"Thank goodness Kelso and Peter are in sight," he mumbled to himself before turning and blocking the sidewalk with his outstretched hands. "Let's hold up until Isaac can join us."

The Pope could feel his heart starting to pound. He knew within a matter of minutes; his four selected cardinals would be sitting before Darr. Yet he was aware he would have to make a crucial decision before this could become a reality. That decision was to rid himself of senior cardinals Vincent and Julias in a manner that wouldn't offend or lead them to suspect he was trying to cover up something.

"I know what happened to Isaac was a tragedy. So, to prevent a widespread pandemic, I do not want what happened to him to leak out in any way. Gentlemen, this means no one is to go to the press. We will handle this affair privately. I'll ensure each and every one of you that the priest will be apprehended without further incident."

Nodding their heads, everyone complied.

"Excellent." The Pope had proclaimed but with a bewildered look. He just wasn't expecting his list of demands to roll over so smoothly with the others. To be honest, he was expecting more of a verbal confrontation. "Once we make our way towards Kelso and Peter, I will break the news to them myself. The two are to follow me to the basilica."

"But don't you think we could use some outside assistance?"

"I don't feel it necessary, Julias." The Pope wanted to guarantee him without giving away any information. "You see, someone is already here. Besides, he's the best in the business." He smiled as he proceeded to walk up the sidewalk.

"I guess we'll just have to take your word for it."

"That you do, Julias. However, there is something I would like to ask of senior cardinal Vincent and yourself."

"Anything, Pope Pius. We'll do it with honor." Vincent was quick to respond.

"Since you two know the priest's identity, I need you to search the palace for his whereabouts. What I'm asking is for you to keep a low profile. By doing this, you are helping me to ensure the safety of everyone inside the palace. Not by any means, though, are you to take matters into your own hands. Do I make myself perfectly clear?"

"Yes." The two had spoken in unison.

"Good. When I arrive at the palace with my entourage within the next half hour or so, we'll bring the priest to justice if you should happen to come across him."

"That sounds fair enough." Senior Cardinal Julias had shaken the Pope's hand.

The Pope wasn't concerned about either senior cardinal Vincent or Julia's warfare. He simply had no reason to be. He knew the odds of them entering an unsafe environment were slim to none. For one, he was confident that they would be protected under the spell which the Lord had cast over the palace. Although he didn't have any visual proof, it was a spell that he believed would subdue a person into a coma-like sleep.

"Vincent and Julias, this is where we'll separate," the Pope had informed them while continuing to walk straight ahead. In the distance, he could vaguely see the dome of St. Peter's Basilica, which was engulfed by a mysterious dark cloud.

Using sign language, he had motioned for Kelso and Peter. To his surprise, the two were quick to respond. In less than two minutes flat, they were standing on opposite sides of him at the front of the line. This was also taking into consideration the fact that the two had stopped to exchange greetings with the others.

"Kelso."

"Yes, Pius."

"I'm curious." The Pope had hesitated for a moment while glancing over his left shoulder. He was trying to make certain that Senior Cardinals Vincent and Julias had done what they were told.

"Did you happen to see anyone enter or exit the palace since the time I last left you?"

"No. There was no one," Kelso answered, sounding most certain of himself.

"How about yourself, Peter?" The Pope thought he would get a second opinion. It wasn't that he didn't trust Kelso. He just felt as though Peter's eyesight was a little keener. "Well, son, did you see anyone? Maybe a man dressed as a traditional priest?"

"We saw no one, Pope Pius."

"But why do you ask us this?" Kelso had become defensive. "What's on your mind? Are you troubled by someone or something?"

"What would lead you to ever believe this?"

"Like always, your body language gives you away." Kelso pointed out to him.

"Then I confess. I am troubled."

"Don't tell me that Isaac has gone and tried to harm himself?" Kelso whispered in the Pope's ear. "I always said that his depression was at a dangerous level."

"Isaac's fine." The Pope shoved Kelso aside. "There's nothing wrong with him mentally, and I'm tired of you making these lame accusations. However, he has suffered an injury to his finger. An injury that was inflicted by a man disguised as a priest from town."

"Around what time did all of this take place, Pope Pius?" "Roughly about ten minutes ago, Peter."

"Now it's starting to make sense." Kelso had begun to see the big picture. "So that's why you were grilling us?"

"Exactly." The Pope raised his eyebrows.

"You see, it's important that we recapture this individual before he has a chance to assault his next victim or victims."

"I don't mean to be frank, but isn't this a job for the police? I'm just an old man." Kelso thought he would remind him.

"An authority figure is already present. We just have to assist him." The Pope conveyed unto them all. By no means did he want to tell them that they were up against a supernatural being.

"So, who is this authority figure?" Peter was hoping that if he kept being persistent, the Pope would leak the information.

"Well, who is he?"

"When the time is right, you'll see who he is. He has been awaiting us."

The Pope was tired of repeating this. Even more so, he was tired of ducking and dogging the truth of what his cardinals were about to encounter. It was a role he knew he wouldn't have to play much longer, though, as he and the others had turned into St. Peter's Square. For preventive measures, he had a ten-foot iron gate constructed around the perimeter to ward off any would-be terrorists. It was through this main entrance, which was connected to a Corinthian-style archway that guests would enter and exit. The symmetrical beauty of the square was what he adored the most, especially how the statues of the various biblical figures and saints were arranged on top of the elliptical roofs, which were supported by multiple rows of columns. He didn't know why, but the statues had always given him the impression that they were escorting him into the Roman-influenced basilica, which was composed primarily of limestone.

"Isaac, how are you holding up back there?" the Pope felt a need to turn and ask.

"Trust me, I've felt better." Isaac could be seen biting his bottom lip. At the time, he was being consoled by Zutermier.

"Do you want to rest?"

"Not really. I can pretty much do that once we're inside the basilica, Pope Pius."

"Amazing!"

"What is?" the Pope wanted Kelso to be more detailed.

"In all of my years, I have never seen the square this vacant before. Not even at night."

"It's breathtaking, Kelso, isn't it? I mean, the sheer volume of this place when it's empty," Peter also observed.

"Yes," Kelso was quick to utter. "But where do you suppose everyone is?"

"Your guess is as good as mine." Peter had hunched his shoulders together. "However, the weather report did call for everyone to remain indoors until the threat of the storm had passed."

"Then what in God's creation are we doing in the midst of it? Just look at those clouds." Kelso had pointed toward the ever-changing sky.

The Pope knew the sensible thing to do was to simply bite his tongue. He was aware that Kelso was trying to provoke him into a bitter discussion, but he wouldn't feed into it. One reason was that he didn't want his voice to carry without knowing where Darr was positioned. The other reason was that he knew he was on holy ground, a site which he believed marked the spot where the chief Apostle Peter was buried.

"My beloved cardinals, please wait here until I summon you," the Pope instructed as he made his way up a large flight of limestone stairs that led directly to the basilica's numerous entrance doors. There were four, to be exact, but only the centermost one would open for him.

"But what about us?" Kelso had become irritable. "Surely, you're not going to just leave us down here. Well, are you?"

"No," the Pope had responded while trying to recapture his breath. "Come on. Come on up." He had motioned.

A look of excitement could be seen on each cardinal's face as they followed the Pope to the center door of the basilica, which was embedded with a solid gold cross. Even though they had no recollection of who was inside, this didn't stop them from detecting an unusual energy field. It seemed more prevalent the wider the Pope had cracked the door. They didn't know why at the time, but it almost felt as though they were about to be in the presence of royalty.

"Right here is far enough," the Pope had made them aware, blocking the door with his back.

"But we would also like to go inside." Peter had come forth, along with the others. He didn't know why the Pope was acting so territorial.

"Unfortunately, now is not the time." The Pope had gently brushed them back. "Trust me, your wait won't be a long one. This, I promise."

"But why can't we enter the shrine together?" Kelso stormed forward.

"Please, hear me out. I just want to spend a little alone time with our guest before I announce you all to him," whispered the Pope. "Is this too much to ask? Is it?"

"I don't think it is." Zutermier had pulled Kelso back by the wrist. "You can take all the time you need, Pope Pius. We'll be waiting right here for you."

"Thank you." The Pope had bowed.

Chapter 4

Zutermier's diplomatic qualities were already paying huge dividends; the Pope had let out a sigh of relief as he turned his back and proceeded through the narrow opening of the door. By no means did he want to ruin the element of surprise for his cardinals. From the start, he had wanted their initial encounter with Darr to be memorable, so he had pulled the door shut from the inside. However, it wasn't until he found himself alone in the hallway that he realized all the lights were out. He couldn't see a thing, and to make matters worse, he had numerous visions of the impostor priest sneaking up behind him. Still, he was curious as to what the others were saying. It wasn't important; he had just wanted to know how they felt. Thus, he had put his ear toward the crack in the door and had begun to listen despite the fact he had the shakes.

"Any guesses as to whom this visitor is?" The Pope had heard Kelso ask. "Unfortunately, the Pope never said," Zutermier had pointed out. "But I personally would suspect that this visitor is probably a special investigator from the United States."

"On what kind of business?"

"I'm not certain," Zutermier had responded to Peter's bombardment. "Maybe it has something to do with the impostor priest."

"Isaac, just how did he look?" Kelso was hoping to paint an elaborate portrait in his mind.

"I guess he was average height for a Middle Eastern man," Isaac had recalled. "Other than his demonic behavior, I would say he was clean-cut with a pointed goatee."

The Pope could tell by the way Isaac had kept pausing in his sentence that he was still in some discomfort.

"Was the impostor priest saying much of anything?" Peter wanted to know.

"He wasn't when I encountered him," Zutermier responded quickly.

"How about you, Isaac? Did you hear?"

"I don't know," said Isaac.

Kelso was anxious to find out.

"What do you mean you don't know?"

"It was kind of difficult—to understand him, Kelso, because he kept speaking in riddles."

"But surely, you must have understood something?" Kelso continued his interrogation. "Think back!"

"Well, I did hear the impostor priest utter to the Pope that he knew why he had come. And I did hear the impostor priest say unto me that I was the only questionable one."

"The only questionable one," repeated Kelso. "What do you think he ever meant by that?"

"Just watch yourself, Kelso! I know what you're trying to imply!" Isaac raised his tone of voice. "You might amuse yourself, but don't flatter me!"

The Pope was appalled. He couldn't figure out why Kelso was treating Isaac like the villain rather than the victim. In his mind, he wanted to open the door and let Kelso have it. Even though he had no visual proof, he was more than convinced Kelso was tickled pink by what the impostor priest had said unto Isaac. It was no secret that the two were feuding, but his own intuition told him their quarrel would soon cease once they were in the presence of Darr.

"My word, look how dark the sky is getting now!"

The Pope had heard Peter try to defuse the tension between Kelso and Isaac by bringing up a new topic.

"Yep. It looks like the brunt of the storm has finally arrived."

"I think you're right, Zutermier. I think the wind has picked up speed. I can feel it." Kelso had found it nearly impossible not to concur.

"Tell me, what do you think is taking the Pope so long to return?" Peter was hoping to be showered with responses.

"It's a good chance that we'll probably be swept away by the time he arrives."

"Maybe that will be the least of our worries." Isaac's voice sounded distant and plain.

The Cardinals were telling the truth. The wind was becoming a bit of a nuisance. This was also the case for the Pope, who couldn't make out anything over the top of its whistling arrival into the hallway. From what he had observed, the wind was making its way in through the crack of the door, which he had once held his ear to, yet he wasn't distraught. There was no need to be, for he had heard all that he wanted to hear anyway. But as he was making his way down the main aisle, a violent gust of wind shoved him forward until he fell face-first onto the decorative marble floor.

"Ouch. My head feels as though I'm suffering from a migraine. Who or what had the power to do this?" the Pope mumbled as he slowly came to his senses. He didn't know how long he was out but suspected it was only for a brief spell.

The basilica was too quiet for his taste. Not to mention, it was too dark for him to determine if the angel Darr was present. This alone was enough to drive him insane due to the weird sensation that he was being watched. This was evident, he felt, by the two eyeballs of white light he had seen over the top of the high altar in the direction where the newly life-sized replica of Christ was positioned. Were these the eyes of Darr? He wasn't positive. Yet the eyes seemed to be traveling towards him, even though he knew they were stationary.

"Bliss art those who serve their Lord in His time of need! For they art truly the heart and soul of His glory! Without them, His words would have no meaning, and His actions would have no virtue! Harmony is the strength and the key element for all societies, Darren, especially those who believe in Me!

"Amen!"

"So let it be!"

"Amen!"

"So let it be!"

"Amen!"

"So let it be as it was intended to be!"

One of the voices that the Pope recognized in the darkness was that of Darr's. By the sound of things, the angel was a few yards in front of him, probably near the high altar, to be exact. The second voice, which was rich in authority, he was uncertain of. However, faith had told him it was the voice of his Lord, but how could he prove it? Yet how could he be a hundred percent sure when he was too timid to even pull his face from the colored marbled floor?

"Darren, the hour will soon be upon us! So let there be light! Let there be light for all to stand witness to!"

Much to the Pope's approval, the basilica was automatically lit.

"I knew it," he had babbled to himself. "I knew Darr was knelt down in prayer by the high altar." He quivered with excitement. Out of respect, he thought it would be wise if he didn't stand or stare too long.

What had impressed him the most was how human-like the replica had presented itself from a distance. The thought of the replica being artificial no longer crossed his mind, as it had time and time before. He figured much of this had to do with the replica's facial expressions and robotic-style movements. To him personally, the replica had acted as if it were in agony while its eyes had periodically rolled back into its head. He had even noticed steady streams of blood coming from the replica's many wounds.

"Darren?"

"Yes, my Lord."

"Who do you put thy faith in?"

"You, my Lord."

"Then erect thyself."

"It is done, my Lord."

"Instruct my children well, Darren, for I love them dearly. At the time, be protective of their souls. Bliss art those who follow in the path of righteousness and brotherly love. One of them must be exposed to this ancient ritual but in short form only."

"Yes, my Lord. Thy request will be fulfilled, as it was fulfilled by those who served long before me."

"So let it be."

The Pope had noticed something different about the replica the moment it had spoken its final words. He had noticed that all life had vanished from it in the form of a brisk breeze. Nor could he detect any more traces of blood. In his mind, the replica had gone back to looking artificial as it did prior to the wraith of the Lord entering it.

"Humble thyself no more, for the kingdom of Heaven wills it!" Darr was referring to the Pope. "So rise thyself upwards, and standeth tall in the sky like the sun."

Even though several hours had elapsed since he was last in Darr's presence, he didn't show any signs of intimidation while standing there. He had only felt remorse, which had come about when he had replayed the haunting images of the replica's face. The image was like a symbol to him, containing a hidden message. It is a message that he and the others might have to sacrifice themselves to help save the human race from extinction.

"Darr was that the voice of the—"

"Certainly. For thou hast just witnessed the beauty and the mystery of the Lord. He has the ability to communicate through any object. But tell me, did ye notice how the replica's body and facial features had changed before thy eyes?"

"Yes, Darr. I was aware of the replica's height increase and the fullness of its beard. I was also aware of the replica's dark skin."

"Praise be unto ye, for thou art truly blessed. What ye have just witnessed, Pope Pius the Fourth, was the way Jesus of Nazareth looked when He had suffered for the sins of all mankind."

"I promise never to reveal what I have seen to anyone." The Pope had felt obligated as a tear had run down the side of his face. He couldn't believe how Bernini's bronze canopy had made Darr appear to be a dwarf.

"If there isn't anything else that thou may wish to bring before me, then ye may proceed with the seating of thy candidates?"

"There is something that I would like to discuss." Thinking to himself, the Pope thought it would be best if Zutermier and Isaac had also given their account of the impostor priest. "On second thoughts, Darr, I think that something can wait."

"Very well. Do as ye wish."

Out of respect, the Pope bowed before he turned his back and proceeded up the main aisle. He was headed to let his cardinals in, but the door seemed as if it was in another dimension. Aware that Darr was maybe evaluating him, he wanted to walk with a soldier's stride instead of his usual wobble. His only concern at the time was how long it would take for his cardinals to adjust to Darr.

"May I have everyone's undivided attention?" the Pope asked as he cracked and stuck his head through the small opening of the door. "As I have already told you, a very important figure has come to Vatican City. I'm aware that it will be nearly impossible for you to control your emotions at first, but just remember that he is here on official business. A lot is at stake, whether you know it or not. So, I will be counting on each and every one of you to approach this encounter with extreme professionalism. Any soul who wants to opt out may do so at this time."

He was deeply relieved when he saw everyone stay put. The last thing he wanted was to belittle himself and request that Darr give him more time to search for replacements.

"Well, are you going to show us in?" Kelso had taken control of the door. "Or are you just going to stand there?"

"By all means, do come in," the Pope had stepped aside. "Now, you may follow me towards the main altar."

Since Peter was the last one to enter, he had taken it upon himself to shut the door. Yet he was baffled. He kept fighting with himself as to why the Pope had summoned only four members of his cabinet to the basilica, which was commonly reserved for ceremonies. It didn't make any sense to him, not when it was known that the Vatican Palace contained several conference rooms suitable for a king. Thus, the only logical explanation he could come up with was that the Pope was going to announce his resignation.

"Pardon me, Pope Pius. I don't mean to be rebellious, but where is this visitor? I don't see anyone." Peter had already surveyed the basilica from top to bottom.

"If you don't mind my asking, I would like to know as well," Kelso had sped up his stride in order to get his voice heard.

"Oh, he's here," the Pope had turned and winked at them. "Trust me, our visitor has a way of showing up when you least expect him."

"Then he must be here by himself," Zutermier was first to point out. In his mind, he was expecting the inside of the basilica to be crawling with high-level security officers.

"Although I haven't been formally introduced to anyone else of our visitor's magnitude, it is my belief that he isn't alone." The Pope was speaking from experience. "Right here is where we'll be seated." He was pointing to the first set of pews on the left-hand side.

Acting like an usher, he had left the very first seat nearest the aisle vacant for himself. Then he had sat Zutermier, Isaac, Kelso, and Peter. The seating arrangement had held no numeric value or rank with him; it was based primarily on a first-come basis.

"So, this whole dilemma has nothing to do with you?" Peter was a nervous wreck and wasn't certain how much more stalling from the Pope he could withstand. He needed answers, and he needed them now.

"Well?"

"In an ironic way, the situation at hand has something to do with all of us." The Pope looked briefly into Peter's face. He wanted to be honest with him, but at the same time, he didn't want to slip and reveal any key information. "But why do you ask me this, Peter?"

"Because the butterflies in my stomach are telling me you're about to announce something of historic proportion."

"Can you be a little more specific?"

"I think you brought us here to tell us that you're going to resign as Pope." Peter put it to him bluntly.

"What about you, Kelso?" The Pope thought he would go around the horn with the same question. "Why do you think I brought the four of you here?"

"Obviously, it has nothing to do with you resigning as Pope," Kelso was more than positive. "For one, we go back too far for you not to have discussed the matter with me in private first. No. I think you brought us here on account of there having been another break in the Vatican's investigation into the child molestation cases."

"I think there has been a breach in security. In my heart, I feel the impostor priest was some icing on the cake. I think that there may be many more out there like him."

"I agree with Zutermier," Isaac said, standing up while still nursing his finger. He found it idiotic to be sitting in the basilica when they could be out searching for the impostor priest.

"Truth be told, there was a breach in security."

"But when did all of this transpire?"

"Last night," the Pope responded to Peter. "Gentlemen, I feel an all-out war is about to be waged upon this very planet if what was lost in Heaven is not found."

"What kind of war?" Kelso had a look of fear in his eyes.

"A holy war!" The Pope was careful with his choice of words. "A war against evil which mankind has never seen."

"But between what two factions?" Peter felt he deserved to know.

"Two, you happen to know very well."

"Great," Kelso chuckled in utter disbelief. "Your answer really narrows it down to about seven different nations."

"So, what was lost?"

"That I can't explain, Zutermier," the Pope said, averting his attention to the floor. "I feel our visitor can best do that."

There were mixed emotions among the cardinals as they struggled to make common sense out of the information given to them. They knew that the Pope was being partial with his responses, but what could they do? Little did they suspect, he just didn't want to let the cat out of the bag, so to speak, until they had encountered the sheer mystic of the angel Darr for themselves. In the long run, he knew that this would eliminate any chaos created by his speaking on a subject he knew little about himself.

"What now?" Isaac broke the silence. He was hoping to maybe converse on a strategy. "Any ideas?"

"I don't know," replied the Pope. "Your guess is as good as mine."

"Then should one of us go and seek this visitor out?"

"No. I don't think that would be a wise decision, Zutermier. Please, be seated." There was no way; the Pope was letting anyone roam freely about the basilica. Not when he had orders from Darr for everyone to remain seated.

"Just give it some time; our guest will show up. You'll see."

"I don't think we have a choice. I take it you want us to wait here for several hours, if need be, until this visitor decides to float down from the ceiling above and introduce himself to us." Kelso thought it would be humorous to twiddle his fingers in the air to simulate a spider descending down its web. "This guest of the Vatican can fly, can't he?"

The Pope could only sit and cringe at the idea that his cardinals were laughing at him. Like a champ, he took the humiliation on the chin. He felt he had it done to him, with the way how he was deliberately beating around the truth as to why he had summoned everyone to the basilica. He knew if the shoes were on the other foot, he would have displayed some of the same emotions of distress.

"Be careful how you choose your words, Kelso. Trust me, I don't want you to regret what you say later. That goes for all of you. This situation at hand is no laughing matter." The Pope thought he would forewarn them.

"Then be fair with us!" Kelso had become irate. "Tell us why we're really here?"

"Please, we want details!" Peter exclaimed while on his hands and knees. "What harm can this cause?"

"A lot if he was sworn not to do so!" Isaac had become upset. To him, Peter and Kelso were both behaving like spoiled brats. Not by any means did he want the Pope to be forced into making an unwise decision due to pressure.

"You know what, I think His Holiness can answer for himself." Kelso stood up and directed his comment in Isaac's proximity.

"So, why don't you swallow your own advice?" Isaac fired back.

"Gentlemen! You are going to drive me insane!" Zutermier threw his hands over his ears. "Please, we have to be respectful."

The Pope felt numb all over. It was almost as if he had fallen into a trance-like state. He felt that this reaction was most likely induced by his cardinals' behavior. He was so embarrassed that he wished he had the option of vanishing off the face of the Earth. Except for Zutermier, he was beginning to have second guesses about the rest of them carrying out the Lord's mission, but he knew he had to stick with his selections. He knew he had to snap back to reality and instill some discipline. But before he could muster up an attempt, there was a loud noise that had come from the back—a noise that sounded exactly like a heavy door slamming shut.

"What mysteries do ye mortal men of the Gospel wish to findeth amongst the stars? Behold, what gives thee the desire to act as pawns in a world full of dark royalty? Is it payment ye request, or do ye wish to ensure thy place in a kingdom which serves as a refuge to those who played accordingly to the rules and regulations? So again, I ask thee, what mysteries do ye mortal men of the Gospel wish to findeth amongst the stars? Seek no more I sayeth unto thee, for I am the angel Darr! Good evening!"

"And good evening to you also." The Pope had responded without glancing back.

Much to his cardinal surprise, he was grinning from ear to ear. But for what, they did not know. Initially, they thought Darr's accusations of being an angel were a figure or speech or a verse taken from a poem. Yet they wouldn't turn around. They couldn't. It was something about Darr that had made fear ooze from their pores. One, they felt that

Darr's voice had sounded too much like an android to be possibly human. It was this dilemma alone that had made them uncertain what to entrust.

"Really, who is that?"

"Kelso, he is who he said he was." The Pope had found Kelso's blank stare to be somewhat comical. He wished he had more time to play into it. "If you don't believe me, then you can always turn around and see for yourself. That implies to all of you."

"This is a practical joke, right?"

"Unfortunately, Isaac, I don't think it is?" Unlike the other three cardinals, Zutermier was the only one who wasn't smiling.

"Tell me, Zutermier, what makes you believe otherwise?" Isaac had tried to damper the tone of his voice with his hands. "What makes you so certain that there's a real-life angel behind us?"

"The voice, for starters." Zutermier had whispered back. "And the fact that there is an overpowering source of light reflecting high off the brass canopy." Although he was hesitant to point toward it.

"Come to think about it, I guess I can feel what seems like the sun breathing against my back." Isaac had revealed. "What about anyone else?" "I thought it was just me." Kelso had shaken his head in disbelief.

"If what you say is true, Pope Pius, then can you describe to us how this angel looks? Better yet, can you explain what this angel is doing here on Earth? Did we do something wrong as a society?"

"The angel 's name is Darr, and you should refer to him by such, Peter." The Pope thought he would set the record straight. "The Lord has sent forth Darr to deliver a message. A very important one."

"So, how long have you known about this?"

"For a good part of the day, Kelso. Now, I want everyone to be courteous and greet our guest from Heaven."

"Worry not, for I was created from all which is righteous," confessed the angel Darr. "Therefore, no harm will cometh unto thee if ye were to turn and pay homage."

"Darr's right. I know that your stomachs are probably tossing and turning as mine once did, but you'll soon overcome this anxiety. I will help. So, on my count to three, I want everyone to do as I do."

The Pope knew his cardinals inside out. He was most certain that they would never be disrespectful to Darr on purpose. Given the circumstances, he suspected they were probably just paralyzed from the neck on down in excitement or struggling to face reality. The reality was that they were about to come face to face with a delegate from Heaven.

"Get ready!" The Pope announced. "One! Two! Three! Now turn and greet our guest from——"

"But there's no one behind us!" Kelso was most certain of this. "Really, there's no one there!"

"I-I-I don't understand," stuttered Isaac. Clearly, we all heard the voice of this individual."

"Or did we?" Kelso raised the suspicion. "I think what we heard was the voice of a practical joker, and I feel the Pope was in on it. You sure had us fooled."

"I'm sorry you feel that way, Kelso." The Pope was trying to conceal his laughter. "But I can assure each and every one of you the voice you heard was no fraud. There has to be a sound explanation for Darr's disappearance." He knew from his own interactions with Darr that it wasn't beneath the angel to partake in a game of cat and mouse.

Convinced that the notion of an angel being present inside the basilica was nothing more than a hoax, the cardinals were ready to face the front. In their minds, they had heard enough bull. They were fed up and very anxious to leave. Yet what they encountered, floating in mid-air, lotus-style, was enough to make their tongues drop to the floor.

"Great heavens!" shouted Isaac.

"Who or what in blue blazes is that?" Peter was so uncertain of what was before him that he was using the backs of his fists to adjust his vision.

"If I didn't think I was hallucinating, I would probably tell you that there's an angel bathed in fire before us!" Zutermier was more than willing to share this information. "A rather tall angel!"

"But why have the heavens allowed us to see such a wonder?"

"Maybe it has something to do with the ongoing wars in the Middle East." Zutermier wanted to shed a little light on Kelso's question. "Maybe Darr has been sent to warn us of a nuclear outbreak."

"It's possible," Peter couldn't deny. "But I feel Darr has been sent to notify us of a cosmic disaster. You know, something like a large asteroid is about to come into contact with Earth's orbit."

"Highly imaginative," proclaimed Isaac. "Yet we all know from current events that Darr's appearance has something to do, in part, with the child molestation cases. I believe the Lord has become upset with the way the matters are being addressed by the Church."

"You make an excellent point," Zutermier was speaking from his conscience. "This ongoing scandal has definitely cast a dark cloud over the Church and humanity. But with all of this set aside for the moment, aren't you overwhelmed to be in the presence of this angel?"

"How could I not be?" Isaac smiled. "For I feel like a kid at Christmas."

"Quiet, everyone. You'll soon have your say." The Pope had become nauseous and had wasted a lot of time. "Darr, these are the candidates whom I have selected. The candidates whom I know can best serve the Lord in His time and need. All of them are members of my cabinet."

The Pope could literally hear his heart pounding as he watched Darr descend from the air in slow motion. "Should I have chosen more?"

"I feel thy selections should be sufficient enough, Pope Pius."

"I can assure you, Darr, that these cardinals will do whatever you demand them to do with great loyalty and honor. You have my word in blood."

"Only thy soul will be required," Darr explained. "All of thy souls, for that matter."

"If that's what it takes to accomplish the goal at hand, then so be it. And if any of you cardinals think I am speaking out of turn or putting words in your mouths, you may remove yourself from the basilica at once." The Pope didn't care whose feelings got hurt.

"Don't be absurd," replied Kelso. "The four of us would rather die a million times, and still, we wouldn't turn our backs on the Trinity!"

"We're in for the long haul," said a very passionate Peter. Just minutes ago, he was so bashful he could hardly find the inner strength to make eye contact.

"Darr, I would like to take this time to formally introduce you to my cardinals. This is Kelso, Peter, Zutermier, and Isaac."

"I am heartfelt by their words. Please, hold out thy hands so that I may fill the veins of thine limbs with the power of the Holy Spirit," Darr had announced as he drifted his way towards the Pope and the others. "Join me in the one place which I have set aside for thee," said the Lord. "Yea. For he who is willing to standeth in my shadow now, I promise, will walk in light of me later."

The moment Isaac made contact with Darr, his entire body began to vibrate. The effects were so overpowering that he could feel the wax in his ears starting to overflow. He also noticed that the bite mark on his finger had healed. No longer was he in pain; he gleamed as he gestured with a nod for the others to take notice. Initially, he expected his hands to vanish through Darr's body like a cloud, but they never did. Out of curiosity, he wondered if there was something like a translucent casing over Darr's body that had prevented this from occurring.

"Darr, we are enlightened by your presence. Just you being here makes us feel as though we're in Heaven."

"The feeling is mutual, Zutermier," Darr informed him as he removed his palms and took a seat on the floor with his legs crossed in the lotus position. This made him less strenuous to look at. "Please, feel free to relax thyselves in my presence."

"Yes, everyone, please be seated." The Pope was the first to do so.

"Darr, what are you?" Kelso sought to know. "I mean, are you a spirit?"

"Nay. For my body consists of various planetary elements, many of which can be found within a nebula."

"Were you always an angel, or did you once live as a human?"

"My existence has always been in my current form, Isaac. Unlike the angels of olden times, I have never been in the presence of man. Behold, this is my first voyage to this world."

"I guess this will be a learning experience for all of us." Knowing this information about Darr made Zutermier feel much more comfortable. It made him feel as though he was on an even playing field when it came to familiarity. Although he knew the Gospels, which made mention of angels, were different in many ways, he felt the stories shared one common fact: the angels would never reveal themselves unto mankind unless there was a historic crisis on the horizon.

"So, how much do you really know about man?" Kelso knew this was probably a foolish question to ask. "On second thought, don't answer that."

"My knowledge comes firsthand from the Trinity," Darr responded to the question anyway. "Do ye disapprove or have a problem with this?"

"No, by no means." Kelso quickly humbled himself, pushing his hands forward in the air. "Darr, I don't think it's possible for one to achieve an education more renowned than what you have received. Believe me on this, for it's straight from the heart."

"Amen to that," Isaac found himself in agreement. "Hey, Kelso finally said something worthwhile."

"Darr, how will we each appear in the afterlife?" Peter wanted to change the subject. It was quite obvious to him that Darr was more intellectual than any human could ever be. "Will we look as you do?"

"Thou will be in the form of a spirit—a translucent form of conscious energy."

"And will we have wings?"

"Unfortunately, ye will have to earn them."

"But how?" This seemed impossible for Peter to imagine.

"There are many ways to earn them. I earned mine by serving the Trinity in a time of war."

"Then I suppose you had to use that magnificent sword of yours in battle?" Kelso was somewhat reluctant to point towards it.

"This sword is an instrument of my profession," Darr made him aware by pulling the blinding blade from its sheath. "With it, I cast out those who seek to dethrone my Father or bring shame against His house."

"By all means." Kelso had sat way back in his seat until Darr retracted the lethal device.

"Listen, everyone, Darr is not here to answer random questions on spirituality." The Pope wanted to be upfront with his cardinals. "He is here on a sacred quest." He had gotten up to make this point clear.

"We do apologize," Zutermier stood up and bowed in Darr's direction after he watched the Pope be seated. "It's not every day that we get the chance to meet an angel of the Lord."

"No foul was committed," Darr assured him in a soothing voice.

"Great. Now that we're settled in, there's something I have to bring before you. Something of great importance, Darr."

"Go on, I'm listening."

"Do you recall when you first sent me to summon my candidates?"

"I have knowledge of that and much more, but why do ye ask?"

"It starts like this, Darr. As I was leaving the palace, I ran into two of my selections by coincidence." The Pope wiped his forehead. "So I asked them, meaning Kelso and Peter, if they had seen Zutermier or Isaac by any chance."

"But neither of us had a clue."

"Please let me finish, Kelso!" The Pope didn't like being interrupted by him. "That's right, they didn't have a clue, so I began a search of my own down the sidewalk. However, it was just over the hilltop where I located Isaac and a couple of other cardinals. They were all tussling at the time with an unknown assailant who was disguised as an impostor priest from town."

"He kept saying I was the only questionable one," Isaac had so bitterly recalled.

"The impostor priest had said something else as well, Darr. Something you ought to know. Something that the others should be let in on as well."

"Please continue, Pope Pius."

"When Isaac first subdued the impostor priest on the hilltop, he spoke to me in strange riddles. Then he revealed unto me an artifact." The Pope had closed his eyes while grabbing at his heart. "It was so beautiful in design."

"What was it?" Darr reached out and caressed the Pope's face.

"It was a key. A golden key embedded with genetic strands of different colored light."

"Unusual," proclaimed Darr. "I will have to research the matter in Heaven's archives when I go back at dark."

"Is this what we're looking for?" Peter wanted to be certain before he burned an image of the key into his memory bank.

"The Lord has blessed thou indeed, Pope Pius. Yet I feel what ye have seen was only meant to be symbolic."

"Believe me, Darr, I saw the key with my own eyes. I felt its power. I would have brought the impostor priest to you, except he vanished into the day while our backs were turned, tending to the wounded finger on Isaac's hand."

"I had him totally immobilized until he sunk his teeth into me." Isaac thought he could best tell the events from this point on. "The wound is healed now, thanks to your touch." He held his hand in the air to display to Darr.

"Then the stage is set! We must prepare ourselves, and we must do so in a hurry, for the fallen angel Nero may already have his evil pawns positioned before us in great numbers!" Darr had warned them all.

"But isn't the key probably out of reach by now?" Kelso scratched his head. "This impostor priest could be anywhere."

"Nothing is lost forever, Kelso, and ye needeth not think like that anymore," Darr had instructed him. "Behold, no secret shall remain untold, and no lie shall be kept from the truth."

"Then where will we need to look first?" Kelso was more than willing to start right away.

"Eager one who price questions for what they art worth, ye will needeth not to look very far or for very long. For whose flesh ye will seek, sins not below Hell's red creeks. Journey if thou must, but ye will findeth no hybrid reptilian there. Needless to say, he will findeth his way here."

"Does this hybrid have a name?"

"Natas Christopher is what he is called," the Pope had responded to Zutermier's question. "You see, it was he who looted and escaped from Heaven with the precious artifact."

"Let me guess, he is attempting to sell it to the fallen angel Nero?" Isaac had sounded a little disturbed by this. "But at what cost?"

"Natas Christopher is hoping to seek dominion over all mankind," replied Darr. "This is after he has helped Nero create a new master race and capture the throne in Heaven."

The Pope and his cardinals were speechless. They were deeply concerned for the welfare of the Trinity, not to mention their own and their planet at hand. This was a race for nothing other than first, and they knew there would be no margin for error on their behalf.

"I think we need to find both this key and this so-called Natas Christopher character."

"My words exactly, Zutermier." The Pope felt the same way.

Unlike the others, Peter could never come to terms with the belief that the Devil acted as the sole perpetrator of all society's troubles. He felt that society had only used the Devil's name in vain to excuse themselves of their wicked ways instead of holding themselves accountable for their own actions. Ten years ago, after his mother's death, he used to toy with the idea that Hell was meant to be a state of mind rather than an actual place. This concept, he believed, was occasionally echoed by religious figures from ages ago in order to keep man from straying or thinking outside the box.

"There is doubt among one of thee," Darr detected, placing his left hand over his temple. "I can hear thy thoughts lingering through the air."

"It is I," Peter confessed, shaking in his seat. "It is my negative energy that you sense, Darr."

"There is no need to feel threatened, for doubt is just one of many aspects of human nature. Although man creates the majority of his sins, the fallen angel Nero and his disciples have been known to influence and assist from time to time."

"I guess I was too stubborn to realize this."

"Look at me, Peter. The Trinity and I are fully aware that some of thy views on religion and life will change. For thy old way of believing will be true in many aspects, but in other instances, ye will need to abandon or alter the way thou once perceived things to be."

"Your being here is proof of that, Darr," Isaac admitted.

"Thank you, Darr!" Peter was more than gracious for the words of wisdom. "Thank you for explaining to me what I was uncertain of."

"When will this rampant manhunt for the key begin?"

"What do you mean?" The Pope shook his head. "It has already begun, Kelso!"

"True. It has already begun, but it must end swiftly if there is going to be any salvation," Darr had elected to tell them. "A lot is at stake."

"Pardon me," Peter said as he stood up. "But I must excuse myself for a couple of minutes. I won't be very long." He said, signaling that he had to use the restroom.

"Do whatever it is ye humans do, but return when thou hast finished."

"I will, Darr. I will."

"Go on, Peter! Go on!" The Pope fanned him away with the back of his hand. He was very upset with Peter's lack of timing.

Peter was so humiliated that he hid his face. There was no way he was going to make eye contact with anyone. The dirty stares he imagined he would receive from the others were punishment enough in his book. But as he made his way past Darr, he felt a jolt of raw energy shoot through his entire body. It wasn't painful, but it was enough to make him pause at the top of the altar's stairs, just behind the brass canopy. It was from this vantage point that he felt he got the chance to really hone in on Darr. From his own personal observation, though, Darr had the characteristics of an animated cartoon figure. He suspected that it was probably Darr's bright hues and 3-D appeal that made him feel this way.

"Is there something that ye wish to bring before me, Cardinal Peter Nicholas?"

"No, Darr. No, there isn't," Peter confessed. He couldn't believe that Darr had the ability to see without turning. This was remarkable to him. Yet it also left him contemplating if Darr had invaded his mind a few seconds ago.

Peter was really distraught by Darr's ability. It had troubled him so much that he had picked up speed and bulldozed his way through a single door, which, in detail, had intersected a hallway barely large enough for two people to walk side by side. His heart was exploding like dynamite as he stood with his hands stretched out over his face and his back against the middle portion of the door. He had only hoped and prayed that he hadn't offended Darr in any way with his sarcastic thoughts. The idea of the Lord reprimanding him despite this had made him nauseous, even though he felt he deserved to be punished for temporarily deserting the mission by excusing himself to the restroom. It was obvious that it was bad timing on his behalf, but after all, he was human, and this did give him the opportunity to put things into perspective. Up until his departure, everything was occurring too rapidly for him to comprehend in the way he had wanted.

"Wow! It's hotter than seven Hells in here!"

The hallway was considerably humid for this time of year, as Peter was made aware by his perspiring body. He also saw a weak source of light through the cracks of his fingers, appearing from the back wall. What was it, though? It was exactly as he had anticipated, snatching his hands away from his face. Someone had gone and left the door at the end of the hallway open. Someone had forgotten to close it on their way to or from the basilica, but it was no big deal to him. This was enough light to see what he had to do, he thought to himself upon entering the restroom and standing before the urinal. After letting out a deep sigh of relief, he made his way over to the sink, where he washed and dried his hands before leaving.

"Funny, I don't remember that door being open." He had paused, staring across the hallway. He was referring to the door connected to the storage room.

This door was always locked, and only a handful of people had the key that he knew of. Gold coins, jewels, vintage manuscripts, and priceless paintings were said to be in there, although he never had the chance to see them for himself. He had heard this by rumor, usually when Kelso was full of Russian vodka. Now, the urge was too great for him not to stick his head inside and see for himself, but he knew he had already wasted enough time. He had to get back. There was no way he was going to get caught in there without some form of permission. It was never in his nature to be sneaky, so he slammed the door shut without glancing inside, but somehow the door had managed to reopen. Thinking nothing of it, he had closed the door exactly as before, but again, the door had opted to reopen when his back was turned.

"I'll fix you this time," Peter mumbled as he slammed the door upwards while pulling back on the knob.

Still, the door wouldn't remain shut upon his releasing the knob. He was losing patience, and to add to his frustration, he thought he had heard voices from within making fun of him. But he had quickly substituted these voices for the squeals of field mice, who he believed could have come in through the open door at the end of the hallway.

"All right, the joke is over! I heard the footsteps! You got me! Now come out of there!" Peter smiled. "Didn't you hear me? I said, come out of there!"

There was no reply from within. There was only silence, much to Peter's distaste, as he stood frozen in the hallway with his hand under his chin. He was undecided if someone was actually in there, but the silence held too many mysteries. Yet he was well aware something had to be done on his behalf, but he knew peeking his head inside was not the answer. What if the impostor priest was lying in wait with a weapon? He balled his fists up as a precaution. He wasn't in the mood for this. He wanted to get back to where he felt he was needed. By now, he imagined the others were probably wondering what was taking him so long to return. What could he tell them? Was he held up by a haunted door?

"This is a restricted area—warning! If anyone is in there, I would advise you to come out at this time! You're not supposed to be in there! I repeat, you're not supposed to be in there!"

Again, there was no reply. Maybe no one was in there at all. Maybe the latch was broken, or the door was no longer level, he thought to himself. He knew the heat of the hallway could have also played a part as he reached out his nervous hand. This time, he only hoped the results would be much different, but before he could place his hand flush on the knob, he watched the door slam shut on its own.

"Oh, my!" Peter cried out, grabbing his ears and falling hard to the floor. "I think I've been shot! I think I've been shot! Save me, Lord!" he screamed as he held his rib cage.

For several minutes, nothing changed. He was still alive, so he carefully felt his body for blood. This was a good thing, but it didn't change the fact someone was playing him for a fool. He knew in his right mind that there was no way he could allow this abuse to continue. He felt he had to put an end to this childish game once and for all.

"I tried to be nice, but you leave me no choice!" Peter said with an attitude as he rose to his feet. "Now, prepare to pay the consequences for your unwise actions!"

Even Isaac wasn't stubborn enough to continue with a prank like this, he thought to himself upon flicking on the light switch in the restroom. What could he do? He certainly couldn't leave things the way they were. What if some valuables were stolen? How could he live with himself after allowing this to happen? It was obvious that he had to at least attempt to do something. The storm clouds were making it dark outside, and he was wasting time doing nothing constructive. Yet, even when he tried to open the door by force, he failed. God knows he wasn't a quitter, but the only reasonable thing he could think to do was to close both doors and trap the perpetrator in the middle until he had time to inform the others. He knew that this solution was sound, provided the perpetrator didn't have keys to any of the deadbolt locks.

"Fine! Have it your way, but the joke will be on you!" Peter had babbled while banging the door twice with his fist.

He was at his breaking point. He could sense that the situation wasn't going to progress. So, with his head down and his hands behind his back, he walked until he stood by the door at the end of the hallway.

"What's this?" he noticed while staring at the floor. "These look to be footprints, only they're not human. There's some there and some over there."

His body began to shiver the second he took the initiative to trace a random set of prints with the bridge of his pinkie finger. With the prints being so dry and faint, he wanted to be delicate in his approach. He didn't want to push down too hard or exhale directly on them. He wasn't an expert on paleontology, but he was most certain the prints were created by a creature with hooves—a creature he suspected was maybe held up in the storage room.

"That's odd; there are no stables around here. Why would a horse wander this far from town?" This was troubling to Peter at first, but then it dawned on him that the horse probably got spooked by the approaching storm and chewed its way free. He also didn't rule out the possibility of the horse belonging to the angel Darr.

"Since I'm already down here, I should explore how far these tracks extend outside."

With the tips of his fingers, Peter pushed open the door and crawled out into the fading daylight like an inspector on the prowl. He was searching for clues that supported his theory that the footprints he saw belonged to a horse. At the time, he would have been satisfied with some poop droppings. This was just so he could quickly close his investigation.

"Great." He had stood up. "The footprints seem to end right here."

Peter wasn't ready to throw in the towel just yet. He wanted to lurk around for another minute more. What had piqued his curiosity the most was the monstrous opening in the ground, only thirty yards in front of him. He was convinced no evidence would be there, but he thought he would check it out anyway before he returned inside for good.

"I don't believe it." He was stopped in his tracks. "Someone has created a mine shaft. From what I can tell, the entrance is very deep."

Peter was so petrified by what he saw that he began to feel light-headed. The hole was about as wide as an Olympic-sized swimming pool and was very deep in design. If was as if it had all ways been there, only covered up. But by whom? He had made his assumption based on the giant stairs which led downward into the darkness. On one occasion, he even though he has seen the upright image of a beast with horns standing in the mist. What also kept him at bay was an unpleasant aroma of burning flesh, which would soar out of the opening sporadically like a hot summer breeze. He wasn't a swearing man, yet he was positive the structure had never been unearthed until today. He had based this primarily on memory and the fact that there were mounds of freshly excavated soil off to the side everywhere.

"Wait a minute. What am I thinking?" he murmured himself. "This can't be the telltale sign of righteousness; it has to be the work of the underworld. I better notify Darr at once; for all I know, Natas Christopher could be held up in there."

Peter had seen enough. He was headed back inside, but before he could get a good distance from where he was standing, he felt the ground tremor. As a natural reaction, he took off running. His initial objective wasn't to reenter the basilica through the narrow hallway but rather to take the long route around to the front entrance. This was until he got the weird impression that something was in pursuit of him. Yet when he turned to see who or what it was, he saw nothing. He only felt a steady flow of air, which made him believe it was an evil spirit—one so powerful it had swept him off his feet before dumping him headfirst into the mouth of the hallway.

Chapter 5

"Wow! My head feels like it was run over by an elephant!" Peter complained as he massaged his temples. "I wonder how long I was out?"

He was disappointed that Darr and the others weren't standing over him. Surely, he thought they would have come to his aid by now. What were they waiting for? For some reason, he didn't quite feel like himself. In a weird kind of way, his body felt weak and lifeless. It was almost as if the entity that had left him laid out in the hallway had taken a part of his soul. He wasn't certain if it was still present, but he wasn't going to wait around for it either, so he pulled the door shut. Given the outcome of his first encounter with the entity, he knew he was fortunate to be alive.

"I better get up from here." Peter gritted his teeth before he stood up. To his displeasure, the hallway light flickered out after his first couple of steps. "That's just wonderful!"

He was a nervous wreck but wasn't about to turn back. He was prepared to walk through the darkness, even though he preferred to see where he was going. He never suspected foul play as the cause of the lights going out. For example, he didn't know how long it had been since the bulb was last changed. The last thing he wanted to do was create more drama than there already was, so he chalked the whole dilemma up as being coincidental—until he heard a door creak open.

"Who's there?" Peter paused. "Is that you, Pope Pius?" He was baffled.

He was undecided about which of the two doors he had heard open. He didn't want to put too much emphasis on it, but he wished he had paid a little more attention. Now, his error in judgment had made him more cautious than ever. It seemed he wouldn't take another step forward until he was assured it was safe.

"Come on, who's there?" Peter knew from experience that the Pope had the ability to remain silent and motionless for minutes at a time whenever he was extremely upset. "Please, this is no longer humorous. Why won't you say anything?"

Once again, there was no reply. Instead, he saw the silhouette of a figure emerge from within the darkness. Not by any stretch of the imagination did he believe it was the Pope. The unknown figure was too tall. To make matters more complex, the figure also had footsteps that were identical to how a horse would sound—a horse that smelled like a combination of month-old urine and stale beer.

"Pew! Back away, you filthy beast! Get! Go back to where you came from! I'm not afraid of you!"

He didn't want to harm the creature, especially if it was associated with Darr. Nor did he want to force it outside with the entity. He was willing to share the hallway, at least until he had a chance to sneak past.

"Don't do it! Don't you dare come any closer! You'll pay the price when Darr finds out what you tried to do!"

He was no dummy. He wasn't about to stand in the path of this raging animal. He had to protect himself. He knew his body was still too unstable to withstand a collision of any magnitude. Embracing himself for the worst to come, he sucked in his stomach and placed his back flush against the wall. He did this so he could reduce the odds of being trampled to death. He also elected to do this so he could use his left hand to shield his face while using his other hand to open the door as the creature galloped past. His plan was simple, but when he turned to execute the part of opening the door, he felt something jab him just below his heart. The pain was so overbearing that he was forced into a fetal position. It was in this vulnerable state that he heard and felt the breeze of the creature hurdling him.

"Why do these things always have to happen to me?" Peter had become irate when he felt his own blood. There was no way he was going to allow either the creature or the entity to harm him a second time, so he pulled the door shut while on his side. "Tell me, what did I do to deserve this?"

He was in need of medical assistance, but he knew he wasn't in the best condition to pursue it. He was too hysterical mentally, and the entire left-hand side of his body felt as though someone had driven a handful of railroad spikes into it. Despite this, he did not know how the projectile that had struck him looked. He only knew it was sharp enough to tear through his garment and penetrate his flesh. Yet when he tried to fumble around in the dark in search of the object, he came up with snake eyes. This left him with the belief that the object had become disengaged when he initially impacted the floor.

"Lord, I need You. I need You." Every time he tried to take a deep breath, he coughed up blood, which made him grasp his wound area even more. "Help me to stand on my feet, Lord. Be my guide as I walk through the darkness. Protect my soul from what may hide and wait at the narrow, for I am just a helpless child needing Your mercy," he said in a faint voice as he stood erect.

The sight of blood had always made Peter's stomach turn. It would also make him dizzy when he was a kid. Now was no exception, as he had begun to hallucinate. Out of nowhere, he thought he heard the voices of a thousand demons calling to him. He also thought he saw his deceased mother of five years in the form of a spirit. She appeared to be standing just a few yards in front of him with her head down.

"Peter." She looked up. "Peter. All roads must come to an end, but you haven't begun to travel yours yet."

"I hear you, Mother." He had walked straight through her. "Honest, I hear you." He didn't know what to believe anymore, even though she had looked and sounded genuine.

"Son, I am the light that will lead you through the darkness." She had reappeared beside him in a puff of wind. "Is that you, Mother? Is it really?"

"Yes, it's me. I have come to deliver you, but you must listen to me, my darling boy."

Although his mother used to always refer to him as her darling boy, he still wouldn't stop to pay homage to her. Her gentle voice was soothing to him. It was a luxury that he feared would abruptly end once he did turn.

"Son, soon you must temporarily give up the ghost. When you do, call on the Lord. Call on Him. He has been awaiting you."

There wasn't much Peter could say. He was too choked up as his tears had run the length of his face. His mother had struck a congenital nerve, and she had struck it flush. But when he had glanced over his shoulder blade, she was no longer present. This had left an empty spot in his heart, for he truly did believe her spirit was the lantern that had inspired him forward. Without her, he felt cold and unprotected in the hallway of darkness.

"I always loved you, Mother." He had dried his face with the sleeve of his garment. "I always did."

Peter wasn't about to hold back his emotions. He knew that as soon as he was safely through the frame of the door, he was going to spill the beans on what had happened to him. He had never thought of himself as a whiner in life, but today was an exception. He wanted Darr and the others to feel his pain. He wanted them to see that he was a victim of physical violence. In his mind, he was praying that Darr would waste no time tearing the hallway apart in search of a motive or an actual perpetrator.

"Help me! Help me! I think I've been attacked!" he hollered as he staggered over the threshold. Despite the way he felt, he was still focused enough to yank the door shut. "Do you see what they've done to me? Do you?" He had dropped to his knees while grasping his chest.

"Hey, it's Peter!" Kelso had happened to glance up. "He's finally come back! I was beginning to believe he fell in!"

"We see him, but what's he carrying on about?" The Pope could only pretend to know the answer. "I wish he would just come down from there. He's been gone long enough. Tell me, what do you think that red stuff is all over his hands?"

"It appears to be blood!" Zutermier had really wanted to be wrong.

"It is blood!" Isaac had alarmed everyone to their feet. "Look, Peter has been injured!"

"Peter! In the name of all that is holy, come to me! Come to me and explain the misfortune that has been dealt unto thee!"

"I don't think he's in any condition to do that, Darr." The Pope didn't comment until he had watched Peter fall straight back and hit his head. "I think it's best if we go to him."

A lot of negative thoughts were channeling back and forth throughout the Pope's head as he began his journey to where Peter was laid out. He had wanted to arrive first, but he physically couldn't keep up; thus, he settled for being last. He could tell by the way Peter was favoring his chest before collapsing that Peter had either been shot or stabbed. What he didn't know was whether Peter was alive or dead. The angel Darr's body language had never given him any implications. From what he had seen for himself, Darr didn't even acknowledge Peter's presence. Instead, he had watched Darr unveil his sword while opening the door that led into the narrow hallway.

"That was a pretty nasty spill Peter had suffered!" The Pope had snuck his head in amongst his three cardinals. At the time, the three were all positioned as if they were about to administer mouth-to-mouth resuscitation. "So, how bad off is he?"

"He's alive but unconscious," Zutermier had responded while checking Peter's temples for a pulse.

"Thank heavens for that bit of information." The Pope had crossed his heart as he moved his focus toward Peter's midsection.

"Yeah, it's amazing his head wasn't shattered open during the impact," Isaac ran his fingers through Peter's hair just to be certain. "He truly was lucky."

"Indeed, Peter was." The Pope had motioned for everyone to move back a few paces. "But right now, I'm more concerned with finding out where this blood is coming from." He had exposed Peter's chest to the thin air.

Pulling a handkerchief from his side pocket, Kelso had nervously applied it. But as quickly as he could dab the blood away, more had emerged. In a desperate attempt to control the bleeding, he had begun to apply more pressure to the wound area with the palms of his hands. It was a stressful process and more work than he had initially set out to do.

"Okay, Kelso. You can move that cloth away for a second or two so I can have another look inward," the Pope had suggested.

"Wow! Whatever struck Peter did so four times in an ever-clear line across his chest!" Isaac had used his index finger to showcase this.

"But there are only pinholes," exclaimed Kelso. "Peter's wounds aren't severe at all, so why is he bleeding so profusely?"

"I don't know," replied the Pope. "Just keep applying pressure like before. It seems to be doing some good." He was about to hop up and summon Darr when he noticed Darr walking back toward the group while placing his sword within its sheath.

"Who or what do you think could have done this to Peter?" Zutermier had focused his question in the Pope's direction. "You don't suppose Natas Christopher had anything to do with it, do you?"

"We must assume the worst," Darr was quick to answer for the Pope. "For only Peter knows what actually took place."

"That's true." The Pope had patted Kelso on the back before standing up. Darr's response had kind of caught him off guard. In a sense, it frightened him because he wasn't expecting Darr to arrive so suddenly. "Darr, do you think there is anything you can do to bring Peter along?"

"Let me gaze upon the matter for myself." Darr had removed the stained cloth from under Kelso's palms. Ironically, none of Peter's blood had ever made contact with Darr's finger. Instead, the blood had retracted away in the form of microbeads. "I'm quite taken. Never before have I seen something so deceiving in appearance."

The Pope was purely bent on reviving Peter; this was first on his agenda. Surely, he didn't want to linger around and watch Peter bleed to death. He wanted Peter's wounds healed. He wanted it done by the same magic that had cured Isaac's finger earlier. It was very vital to him that Peter gave an account of what had taken place during his time spent in the restroom.

"What's wrong, Darr?" Kelso could only ponder with a look of aghast on his face. "Why did you cease? Why did you give up on what you were doing when Peter was still bleeding?" He had stared at Darr while blindly reaching for his cloth.

"Stand back! Stand back!" Darr had jumped up. In a fury of rage, he had withdrawn his sword and began to chop away at the air surrounding Peter's body. "Do as I command!" He had insisted.

Out of respect, the Pope and his cardinals had wasted no time moving aside.

"Something isn't right! I can sense it, Lord! I know it to be, but I don't know how to respond to it!"

"What could Darr possibly be talking about?" whispered Kelso.

"I'm not certain." The Pope didn't want his voice to carry either. "But maybe the answer lies within the hallway."

"I think you're onto something." A light bulb went off in Zutermier's head. "It did seem as if Darr was expecting to encounter someone or something when he opened the door."

"Say what you like; still, I believe Darr is out of control. Just look at what he's doing when he could assist Peter."

"No, Kelso, calm down. I beg to differ. See how Darr swings and twirls his sword in perfect rhythm?" Zutermier allowed a couple of minutes to elapse to better get his point across. "Why, Darr's probably performing some type of ritual."

"I would sure hope so." The Pope was becoming restless. "We could have made two trips to the emergency room."

"Just give it more time," said Zutermier. "Darr knows what he's doing. Isaac can best attest to this."

"Then explain why Darr has Peter cradled in the air. And explain why Darr is pulling on Peter's tongue." Kelso momentarily diverted his attention. "I do believe Darr is going to rip it out."

"Well, Zutermier?" The Pope was hoping for some positive feedback.

"I-I-I don't know what to say," stuttered Zutermier. "At least Darr has put away his sword."

Kelso could only look on in horror. He didn't want to be too judgmental, but he didn't have a lot of trust in what Darr was doing. Better yet, he couldn't even begin to comprehend the notion of how Darr could heal Peter's wounds by yanking on his tongue. He didn't think it was a sin for him to be this judgmental, on account Darr wasn't his Savior. Even when he tried to find some logic in Darr's actions, he couldn't. This was until he witnessed Darr take a deep breath and exhale the air into Peter's mouth.

"Why do thou stand there like lost sheep?" Darr had raised the question as he laid Peter gently on the floor. "Go! Go unto thy fallen brother and console him!" he said while walking away. At the time, he was headed back towards the door, which fed into the narrow hallway.

"I don't believe it!" Kelso felt his jaw drop as he watched Peter sit upright and cough three times before lying back down. "Peter is alive and responsive!" He was the first to rush over.

"He's been saved." The Pope had thoroughly checked Peter over before making this comment. "It's another miracle."

"Yes, it is," Zutermier agreed. "Yes, it is."

"Did you see how the vapors from Darr's breath escaped through the pinholes as Peter's flesh was starting to mend together?"

"How could one not?" The Pope beamed at Isaac.

Isaac was rejoicing at the moment, but at the same time, he remained a little skeptical. In his mind, he was beginning to compare and debate his own supernatural experience with Peter's. What he didn't understand the most was why Peter's wounds weren't initially healed by the touch of Darr's hand. Surely, he knew Peter was just as good of a Christian as he was, despite the fact they didn't agree on a lot of urban subjects. Yet, after giving it some more thought, he realized there was a difference—a difference in Peter's being in an unconscious state, which he felt could have been the reason for him not being made whole by his own faith.

"Peter, are you all right?" Kelso wanted to be assured as he watched Peter's eyes open one at a time. "Please, speak to us."

"Who did this to you?" The Pope was ready to conduct his investigation. "Can you remember? Do you know where you are?"

"I saw its face," Peter muttered while closing his eyes. "I saw its face."

"Whose face?" The Pope begged him to repeat. "Whose face was it you saw?"

"Maybe it was the impostor priest's face that he saw," Zutermier drove home the possibility.

"Listen to him! He has a valiant point!" Isaac licked his lips.

He couldn't wait for a second engagement. "That savage impostor probably did inflict those wounds on Peter's body, but with what type of instrument?"

"If this is true, then we must find this devil at once!" Kelso leaped up while clenching his fists. "He has caused enough ill for one day!"

"No." Peter tried to warn as he reached out and took hold of Kelso's heel. "It won't do any good. It won't do any good."

"What won't?" Kelso stooped back down to be by Peter's side. "Tell me, what would you like us to do then?"

"You mustn't do anything drastic. You must all listen to reason," Peter communicated with his eyes shut. He was still too weak to stand on his feet or speak in a loud tone of voice. In a sense, he almost felt like a mummy trapped inside its sarcophagus. "Where's Darr? Darr, please come unto me." He stretched his hands upward.

"I am present." Darr folded Peter's arm back down.

"What do you ask of me?"

"Don't… don't let them do anything insane?" Peter had difficulty saying. "The impostor priest wasn't the one who did this to me."

"Then who else could it have been?" The Pope had turned red in the face. He felt irritable that there were more than two assailants on the loose and beside himself because a quick resolution didn't seem feasible. "Speak, son! For now, isn't the time to withhold information!"

"Bear with me, for my soul is tired, and my memory grows faint."

"Take your time, Peter. We'll bear with you." Kelso ran his fingers through Peter's hair.

"What I encountered wasn't human. It was a creature, and it wasn't spawned from this Earth either. I know you are probably laughing inside at me, but I know what I saw. I know what I saw."

"Thou hast suffered a great deal, Peter. Why wouldn't we put our trust in thee?" The angel Darr had wanted to reassure him.

"Peter, we are going to need to create a snapshot of this creature in our minds. Can you provide us with some distinguishing characteristics?"

"If you must know, Zutermier, the creature had the body of a stallion and the torso of a man. A barbarian-looking man with long, matted hair," Peter described with newfound life as he reopened his eyes.

"What in the name of evil are we up against?" The Pope had nearly fainted backward.

"Apparently, a Greek monster!" Kelso had stood up and had begun to pace around in circles.

"But that's impossible," Isaac had suspected Peter of being delirious.

"I thought only such a creature existed in mythology."

"Perhaps. But if what Peter said is true, then what will we do?" Kelso had become hysterical. "How will we capture such a beast?"

"Silence back there! I can't hear a thing!" The Pope had lashed out.

"Peter, what else can you recall? What else?"

"A mine shaft. A large mine shaft that breathed heat. Yes, intense heat."

"Where exactly was this mine shaft?" Darr had wanted Peter to be more specific.

"It was out back." Sweat had poured from Peter's forehead as his body started to tremble. "It was almost as if the soil was being excavated right before me."

"Stay with us, Peter! Stay with us!" The Pope had tried to hold Peter's eyelids open. "I think we're losing him!"

"I think you're right!" Zutermier had watched Peter fall unconscious. "I don't think we're going to get another word out of him."

"As much as we are in need of logical answers, Peter is in need of dire rest," Darr had informed everyone while standing upright. "If all is possible at the return of the next sun, ye may further question him.

By that time, I will have arrived from Heaven with the knowledge I obtained."

"Darr, don't you know your departure could spell the end for us?"

"Kelso has a valid point!" A tear ran down the side of the Pope's face. "Darr, what will my cardinals and I do? Who will protect us in the wake of a full-out assault?"

The Pope knew he was just wasting his breath by complaining. It wasn't in his nature to be aggressive, but he felt there probably would come an instance where he might have to do what needed to be done to protect others and himself, even if it meant wielding a weapon. He wished this wasn't the case, but he knew there was no one on Earth who could convince Darr to stay. He was saddened, yet he wasn't upset with Darr's decision either. He knew Darr was only following the Lord's itineraries, which he felt took precedence over everything else.

"Say you'll stay, Darr! Please say you'll stay!" Isaac pleaded while on his knees. He was trying to grab hold of Darr's robe, but his hands kept falling through to the floor.

"Worthy ones of the Lord, gather around me." Darr paused to allow the Pope and Isaac time to erect themselves. "My periodical visits to this kingdom are just as significant to this mission as my stay here on Earth. Ask yourselves, who or what can match the Lord's wisdom?"

"No one can, Darr." The Pope felt compelled to speak on behalf of the others. "No one can."

"As I leave, so does another assume my role in assuring the Lord of thy safety."

"But where will we go?" Zutermier wanted to know. He had no problem meeting new angels; in fact, he insisted on it. "Where will we be housed?"

"Say no more." Darr turned his back and proceeded up the main aisle. "Come. I will showeth thee."

"Wait a minute!" The Pope signaled for Darr to stop and turn in his direction. "What about Peter? We can't leave him. He's still unable to walk!"

"Zutermier or Isaac can escort him to our destination!" Darr responded without turning.

"Well, you've been informed what to do. One of you grab Peter's ankles, while the other takes his arms," the Pope directed them into motion.

"Hold it, Zutermier. I'll do it myself," said Isaac. "Peter doesn't weigh that much. Trust me, it won't be a burden."

"Fine! But will you do it now so we can catch up with Darr?" Kelso rolled his eyes before walking up the aisle behind the Pope.

"Nothing he says ever ceases to amaze me." Isaac became heated as he lifted Peter over his right shoulder like a sack of potatoes. "I guess we better get a move on."

"It's the pressure. Don't worry about him," Zutermier gave Isaac a pat on the back while trailing him up the aisle.

Isaac didn't like Kelso's snooty disposition. In his hindsight, Kelso was always trying to belittle or upstage him. Nothing he did ever seemed to be good enough, but he knew he couldn't let Kelso's juvenile antics cause him to blow up in front of Darr. The last thing he wanted to do was allow Kelso the privilege of seeing him stripped from the Lord's mission.

"Can I have a word with you?" The Pope sped up his pace so he could position himself alongside Darr. "Where are we headed?"

"To the palace," Darr paused in the hallway. He was just a few feet from the centermost door. "A feast has been prepared in the sick bay chamber in thy nor."

"That sounds wonderful." The Pope could feel his taste buds starting to awake.

"Is there an echo in here?" Isaac wanted to check. "Darr, did I just hear the word 'food' mentioned?"

"Ye have heard correctly."

"Then what are we standing idle for?" Isaac lightly chuckled. "Let's get out of this building."

Without anyone lifting a finger, the door miraculously opened on its own. Naturally, everyone assumed Darr had used some form of telepathic power unknown to man to accomplish this until they noticed that his posture was also affected by the two blasts of air that had ripped one after another into the hallway. The first blast was a little on the arctic side, but the second blast was as brutal as a desert heat wave.

"What was that?" Kelso became excited. "It kind of felt like gale-force winds!"

"You could be onto something," Zutermier half-heartedly agreed. "Still, whatever it was, it nearly took the skin from my face along with it!"

"Thank the stars, it's over," Isaac sighed. "I could begin to feel myself being swept upward."

"Isaac, I know it was pretty horrific for you," Zutermier observed. "Taking into consideration, you have the weight of Peter on your shoulder."

"Tell me about it."

The Pope could hardly breathe due to the amount of butterflies forming in his lower abdomen. Unlike his cardinals, he had a hunch about who was responsible for at least the arctic air. A strong vibe led him to believe it was the wraith of the Lord. Yet he was unsure of the

second blast.

"Pope Pius, there's something inside the basilica that I must attend to. I shall not be long."

"Don't worry, Darr. I have everything under control," the Pope winked. "We'll just wait for you outside." He had wanted to ensure him.

"By all means," Darr bowed his head before turning his back.

Chapter 6

"I know that ye are here! Where art thou?" Darr had called out while searching every inch of the basilica from a distance. "Speaketh to me!"

He had an uneasy look about himself as he made his way down the main aisle—one of distress. Not to mention one of caution, which was evident by the way he had kept his right hand positioned on the handle of his sword.

"Why are ye so silent? I know that ye are here! I can feel thy presence! Reveal thy wraith unto me! I demand it!"

At the drop of a dime, a tornado, which was the total height of the basilica from top to bottom, appeared just underneath the Christ replica. Unlike the usual tornadoes, which are composed of destructive wind, this one was made up of fire instead. The heat was so intense and the flames so blinding that Darr had to back away several feet while shielding his eyes with his free hand.

"No one has the authority to summon me, fool! I am here by my own free will and accord!"

"I summon thee, Devil! Return the sacred key back to its rightful place, or else!"

"Or else?" The angel Nero had repeated before erupting into laughter.

His voice was so pure in clarity and rich with bass that the basilica floor began to quake every time he used emphasis.

"Thou art no match for me, Darren! Ye are too weak due to thine choice to serve both Heaven and man!" Out of nowhere, a silhouette of a demonic figure with bat-shaped wings appeared from within the tornado of flames. "Trust what I say, Darren! I have been there and done that long before ye were ever created by the Trinity to which ye play puppet, and ye calleth thyself ancient? I should destroy thee with this fire demon, but there is a method to my madness!"

"The forces of righteousness have defeated thee on numerous occasions! Neither today nor tomorrow will be any different!"

"Runt, what makes ye believe Hell bears thy Lord's treasure?"

"Don't play games, Nero! I know that ye have thy pawns in position! If ye were so naive as thou would have me believe, then ye wouldn't be present!"

"If it is a second and final war that Heaven seeks, then from below awaits my finest fleets!" Nero erupted into laughter. "Many may hold their tongues in doubt, but ye watch and see as I methodically defeat thy Lord's armies and these so-called worthy men of the gospel! I am compelled with envy! Thy Lord has given them a gift I most adore, and soon it will be mine for the grasping!"

Angered by Nero's remarks, Darr hurled his sword toward the tornado of flames. However, the fire demon within intercepted the weapon with little difficulty. This was a humiliating defeat in itself, but when the demon began to brandish the weapon, Darr lowered his head in shame.

"Thy faith in the Trinity will prove to be thine greatest downfall!" Nero paused before filling the basilica with laughter. "Abandon them! Let me guide thee up the stairs, which thou needeth to climb!"

By some form of dark magic, Darr's sword floated in midair like a feather until it fell noisily by his feet. Still, he wouldn't apprehend or even glance at it for any lengthy period. Maybe it was pure pride or his instinctive nature.

"Pick it up and try again, I demand thee! This sword is twice as powerful as yours! With it, ye can rule over entire nations!"

"I won't be tempted by thee, Devil!" Darr had made this point known while blindly kicking the sword off to the side. "Ye move me not, for thy powers aren't everlasting!"

"Is that what they preach to thee?" the fallen angel Nero had asked as the demon from within the tornado of flames had vanished. "I have defied the rulers of Heaven since the days of old, and still, I survive to impose my will!"

"Ye only exist because they allow it! In a weird way, thou art like a form of amusement to them!"

"My tribulations have only strengthened me! In time, thou wilt bow to me along with thy former masters! This feat will be made possible with the use of the sacred key! With it, I will raise a hybrid army capable of doing battle in Heaven and on Earth!"

"You will never succeed in doing so!" Darr had pumped his fists in the air. "Thy forces will perish due to genocide long before they ever cross the threshold of the Trinity's inner chamber!"

"I beg to differ, imbecile! When the time comes, I will see to it personally that thou art the first to kowtow before my cock!"

"Be gone, Devil! Thou hast shamed this temple enough with thy tongue of thorns!"

As suddenly as the wraith of Nero had appeared, it had disappeared. This was not before transforming back into an invisible state—a form of hot air, which had opted to escape under the same door that had intercepted the narrow hallway. It was uncertain if this route was chosen out of guilt or to avoid a head-on confrontation with Darr.

"Revenge and lost dreams are what he only seeks, Darren," the Christ replica had explained as it once again came to life.

"I hear thee, Lord," Darr had come forward. "My faith is strong with thou." He had taken to one knee.

"Notice the sword on thine right."

"I see it, my Lord."

"Take ye that sword and govern over my interest with it! Strike down those who wish to defy and plunder my kingdom!"

"It will be done, my Lord!" Darr held the sword high above his face. This sword was exactly like the one he had lost, only it had a much greater aura about it. "Thy commands will be carried out, my Lord. The same way it was carried out by those who served long before me, so shall I grip this working tool in honor of the departed."

"Thy loyalty has never been in question, Darr. However, time is escaping us. Erect thyself at once, for my children are awaiting their instructions."

"Yes, my Lord." Darr stood up while placing his sword within its sheath. "I will guide them accordingly."

Just like earlier, all existence of physical life vanished from the Christ replica the instant it closed its eyes. Still, Darr wouldn't turn or proceed up the aisle. He seemed to be waiting for something. What was it, though? Ultimately, his cue to vacate came when sane artic vapors began to dissipate from the mouth area of the replica.

"It's time!" Darr informed as he stormed out of the basilica's centermost door. "Come! The way has been paved!"

"This is amazing."

"What is?" The Pope wanted Zutermier to be a little more specific as he followed Darr down a flight of limestone stairs. "What are you making reference to?"

"I am referring to the heavens," Zutermier pointed upwards. "Wouldn't you agree that the stars and the moon never looked so brilliant?"

"Stop! Be forewarned!" Darr spun around and held everyone at bay with his outstretched hands. "Within this tranquility lurks eternal darkness and murderous villains!"

"Where?" Isaac had tried to use the elevation of the middle stairs to look beyond. "I don't see any of those things." He had shifted Peter's limp body to his opposite shoulder.

"Do ye want to have thy spirit ripped from thy body as if it were soft linen?"

"No, Darr. I wouldn't."

"Then ye and the others must understand that this is a time for caution. A time to obey. For what may seem obvious at first may in some instances be counterfeit or fake." Darr had turned to proceed to the ground below.

"Please continue on, Darr." The Pope had followed behind him, along with his cardinals. "We want to learn more."

"Annihilation can be avoided if you'll all notice the divine light at the base of thy feet. Notice also that the light extends beyond St. Peter's Square."

"Yes. It acts almost like a paved walkway. A walkway which isn't made of brick or cement, but merely of white light and fog."

Zutermier couldn't believe how soft the walkway of light felt. It was as giving as plush carpet, he deemed. Yet, in the same sense, he couldn't believe how chilly and numb it had made his toes. It was almost as if a rink of ice were situated underneath.

"This is the light of the Lord! Ye are to stay on this prescribed pathway, no matter what ye hear or see around thee. Thus, I will advise that no one looks back or off to the side, for ye may inadvertently lose thy balance. Beware, there is no margin for error. Stay on the path, or ye will no longer exist in this world!"

"But what will happen to us if we don't?" Kelso had become horrified. "Will we be punished by death?"

"Ye will enter one of the countless dimensions. There thy fate will be determined by the ruling bodies of its domain."

"I don't think I would enjoy that too much." Just the idea of someone other than the Lord presiding over Kelso's fate was enough to cause him to blackout momentarily.

"Please, get a grip!" The Pope had bear-hugged Kelso from behind. The reason he had opted to use this much force was to prevent Kelso from banging his noggin. "Are you okay to stand on your own?"

"I'm fine! I'm fine!" Kelso had brushed the Pope away. "You can let me be!"

Kelso didn't like it. The task at hand had sounded too simple to be true. There had to be more complexity to it, he originally thought. If there was, then he felt he would rather know up front. The last thing he wanted was to be snowballed or blindsided.

"Isaac?" "Yes, Darr."

"Ye have carried the burden of thy brother long enough; hand him over and fall in place behind me."

Timidly, Isaac did as he was told. He relinquished Peter to Darr, who then cradled Peter within his mighty arms like a newborn child. He had only complied with Darr's demands, not because he was becoming worn down. It had more to do with his conscience. For the most part, he had wanted to be held accountable for his soul, not Peter's, if he were to have the misfortune of wandering off the walkway of light.

"What about the other two cardinals and myself, Darr?" The Pope still wanted to be included in the grand scheme of things. "What would you like for us to do?"

"Zutermier and Kelso can follow suit as long as ye make up the rear."

"By all means." The Pope had stood aside in order to allow the pair to maneuver into position behind Isaac.

"Remember, as we walk along this walkway, no bodily harm will come unto thee." Darr had turned to face everyone. "The images and voices that ye encounter will be fictitious unless ye stray off. Once more, it is wise to seek straight ahead. But if someone is careless enough to venture from grace, may the Lord and his Shepherd be with their soul! Do be warned. I will not stop until I am inside the palace."

"We can comprehend that," replied Zutermier.

"Good!" Darr had done an about-face with Peter still in his arms. "Let us begin."

"Don't follow him!"

"Leave the walkway!"

"Turn back now or else!"

"Who said that?" Kelso had tapped the Pope on the hand without ever turning to acknowledge him. "I could be mistaken, but the voices sounded like they came from over yonder." He had pointed towards his left.

"I don't have a clue where the voices came from." The Pope really didn't want to be involved in the discussion. His main concern was to stay focused so he wouldn't lose his footing. "Your guess is as good as mine, Kelso. The fog from the walkway is becoming so thick in some areas that I can hardly make out a thing."

"My sentiments exactly," conveyed Zutermier. "If I didn't know any better, I would think we were walking inside of a giant cloud."

"Fools, don't follow this angel! He'll lead you astray!"

"Save yourselves before it's too late!"

"Don't stop! Continue onward!" Darr had never broken his stride. "Thou must ignore the luring voices! They art of the sinister one! Their main purpose is to invite thee off the walkway to their world of mayhem!"

Darr's words were like a ray of enchantment. It was a glimpse of hope that the Pope and his cardinal had clung to inspire them through the rough time ahead, but this only seemed to anger the demented ones. In an all-out display of aggression, the towering souls of a hundred or more goblins dressed in black gowns had suddenly appeared along opposite sides of the walkway. Each goblin held a makeshift torch and took turns blowing their breath of pure funk in the faces of each passerby. To every goblin on hand, the walkway was sacred territory, and they were also subject to total annihilation if they dared to cross its plane.

"This angel preaches lies!" one of the goblins had yelled out. "Lies! Lies!"

"Just ignore them!" the Pope had pinched his nostrils together. As more time progressed, he began to gain more confidence in the walkway of light beneath his feet. It was like an invisible force field, one which he knew the goblins couldn't penetrate. "Their words can't harm you! Please, keep doing what you're doing!"

This was easier said than done. The goblins were both intimidating and freakish-looking with their acid-scarred faces. On average, they stood about six and a half feet tall. They were the kind of beings that no one in their right frame of mind would ever want to encounter. Depending on the level of gravity in a dimension, their strength could fluctuate between four to five times that of a human's. Labeled the Devil's grunts, they are most known for being vandals and sexually deviant. "What can this angel really do for you?"

"He'll tell you that there are many in Heaven like him when, in fact, only a handful of his breed still exists. The others were slain by the Trinity. Yet some managed to elude and seek refuge with Nero before their trials were scheduled to begin."

"Did he tell you this?" A goblin beamed with happiness. "Quick! Abandon the walkway and join our brotherhood!"

"And become like you, nothing but a bunch of wandering corpses?" Kelso turned and stuck his tongue out. "Thanks! But no thanks!"

"Then your fate will be sealed!" A goblin pointed his torch at Kelso's head. "This angel can't fight us all! Yes, hear this! Every one of you, flesh men, will suffer a mortifying death!" One of the goblins went so far as to lift his robe to reveal his genital area. "But not before I have my way with you! Not before I have my way with you!"

"No, let me fuck them!" A goblin with a deformed eye began to jump up and down. "Hurry! Come to me before it's too late! I can promise you amnesty! Wait! What does that word mean?" He and the other goblins began to laugh in sync.

Isaac found the goblins downright comical. He was sorely amazed how something so weird-looking and evil could possess a sense of humor. What tickled him the most was the notion that they were only getting under Kelso's skin. He was enjoying every minute of the skirmish, but never did he stop being cautious of them. He knew they weren't the kind of beings one could underestimate.

"I think you've done it, Kelso! I think you've done it!"

"Done what?" Kelso was uncertain what Zutermier was raving about. "I think you made the goblins vanish!"

"Hey, I think you're right." Kelso breathed a sigh of relief after checking the situation out for himself. "Now, maybe we'll have some quiet."

"Help! Help," cried a frail voice from the darkness. "Help me!"

"Know what? I think I spoke too soon," Kelso professed with a lifeless expression.

"Did you hear that?" The Pope had tapped Kelso on the back. "Don't turn, but didn't that sound like an old woman in distress?"

"Yes, it did," Kelso agreed. "But at the same time, the voice is probably fictitious."

"What if we're wrong?" The Pope wanted to weigh the possibilities. "What if she's a member of the housekeeping staff?"

"It's not likely," argued Kelso.

"I don't want to die!" The woman could be heard panicking. "You have to turn around! You must. They're going to torch the basilica! The evil ones are going to burn it down! You have to turn back and stop them! I can't hold them off much longer! Here t-t-they come!"

"No!" The Pope spun to his knees. "My word, what have you savages done? What have you done to this beloved shrine?"

He couldn't take it anymore. He couldn't stomach the sight of the basilica burning before his crying eyes. This was his worst nightmare come true. There wasn't anything he could do either. It was too late. A good sixty percent of the basilica was already up in smoke.

"How could they be so insensitive? How could they destroy a piece of history without their consciences eating them alive?" The Pope was referring to the goblins. "Wait a minute. If the basilica is really set ablaze, then why don't the windows give in to the heat, and why doesn't the fire alarm sound?"

Drying his tears and sitting on his buttocks, the Pope began to take a more detailed look at the spectacle.

"Why, it's not real at all!" he giggled, kicking his feet around in the air like a child. "The whole thing is nothing more than a hologram!"

The Pope was relieved. The turn of events couldn't have been any better. He speculated as he stood up while mending the small of his back. True, he was overwhelmed by the blazing sight. The special effect could have kept him occupied until night's end, but he knew it would be wise if he rejoined the company of the others. The last thing he wanted was for any of his cardinals to worry themselves sick over his departure, especially Kelso, with his bad heart.

"Hey, where have they gone?" he sputtered as his bottom lip trembled. He wasn't expecting anyone to be directly behind him, so to speak. However, he thought they would at least be within a bird's-eye view. "I can't believe they have departed the square that quickly. And to think, I only diverted my attention for a minute or two."

The Pope felt like he was frozen in time. He couldn't move or do anything. Rather awkwardly, he stood their limp, with a blank stare on his face. It was both cold and distant, but it was one he was familiar with. It was the same stare he had once known as a child when the German tanks had rolled into Poland during World War II and ravaged his homeland. He had lost almost every one of direct descent to the invasion. However, after several days of wandering the streets, he was taken in by an orphanage and raised. Kelso was the closest thing to a sibling he had growing up, and the thought of not seeing Kelso again had almost taken his breath away.

"I have to catch up with the others. I have to," he began to trot up the walkway.

He wasn't sure how long he would have to keep this up, but he knew it would be practical if he paced himself to go all the way to the palace if need be. Heaven knows he wasn't cut out for this. Yet it was something he felt he had to do. He had disobeyed specific instructions, and now he had to suffer the consequences of not knowing what dark encounters he would have to face on his own.

"I know the Lord and Darr are going to be upset with me. I just know it. I can feel it in my bones."

He was about to exit through the iron gate that protected St. Peter's Square from the general public when something caught his attention. It sounded like a stampeding cavalry, although he didn't see anything before him that might support this. Maybe his nerves were affecting him, he pondered for a second. On his behalf, he knew he would be physically safe from danger as long as he remained on the paved walkway set forth by his Heavenly Father. So, why was he so frigid? What did he think was supposedly out there to get him?

"I have to get a move on." The Pope had cautiously placed his hands on the iron bars. He was still undecided if he should open them or not. "Well, here goes nothing."

He couldn't believe it. Nothing had happened. Nothing evil had taken place as he stood just over the threshold. Gone were the prior sounds of charging horses; still, he knew he wasn't out of the woods.

The thought of explaining to Darr why he was so late returning to the palace was enough to make his stomach cringe. There wasn't anything worse, in his opinion than arriving somewhere tardy with a room full of press staring at you in the face. For most of his reign, he avoided scenarios like this by planning his public appearances weeks or months in advance. Nevertheless, the Lord's mission had required him to employ a technique he wasn't accustomed to. It had required him to act on the fly.

Beaten and beside himself, the Pope had slammed the stubborn gate shut. He was ready to catch up with the others when something stopped him in his tracks once again. It was the previous threat of stampeding horses. This time, it was for real. He knew his mind wasn't playing tricks on him as two headless knights on one horse appeared out of the blue. To keep from falling, he had placed the midsection of his back flush against the iron bars of the gate.

"I sure hope you three are on the side of righteousness?" The Pope crossed his fingers as the approaching horsemen unveiled their javelins. He wanted so badly to communicate with them, but they had no heads. "Oh, my! This doesn't look too promising!" he screeched while diving off to the side.

Those knights were no illusion, he had concluded while lying on his belly. They couldn't have been. They were too lifelike, and so were the javelins, which he could almost visualize piercing his body. It was unknown to him whether the horse was running in mid-flight or running amongst the walkway of light due to the medieval beast having too much speed on him. In his mind, he barely had enough time to avoid being the target of interest. But where had the knights gone? Did they simply vanish altogether, or were they waiting for the optimum time to reappear?

"This is horrible!" he had opened, then closed his eyes. "Horrible! Horrible! Why did I have to be so foolish? Why didn't I listen? Now I'm cursed! My life is over!" He had sobbed into his palms as he gingerly stood up.

The walkway of light was ancient history, along with the familiar landmarks to which he was accustomed during his scheduled trips to the basilica. He had somehow slipped into another dimension, one with two full moons and no stars. He was positive this ill fortune had occurred when he had dove away from the headless knights. By no means was he a happy camper. This new parallel universe was chilly, and the surface beneath his feet felt like dried-up mud. He hated this, and he also hated the realism of being trapped within the center of an endless maze of weeping willow trees. The branches were so lingering he had prayed none of them would become possessed and sweep him off his feet.

It was a wild thought, but the Pope figured if he stayed still long enough, the walkway would reappear before his eyes. He felt that Darr would see to it once it became evident he was no longer part of the group. After all, he felt it was essential to the Lord's mission for someone not to come back for him. Therefore, he stood and waited. This left him feeling hurt and alone as a cold pocket of air swept down against his spine, nudging him forward even though he had no desire to move in any direction. He feared that if he wandered from his initial point of entrance, he would never see the others or the light of day again. He couldn't stand this place, and he ridiculed himself mentally for ending up in this predicament.

Chapter 7

The Pope wasn't satisfied with his present situation. It just didn't feel right. He wasn't blissful with physical powers, but this didn't stop him from realizing he wasn't alone. There was something among him. Something he felt was either curious or interested in tasting his human anatomy. He could feel whatever it was searching him up and down. He wasn't certain of the predator's proximity, but the vibes were strongest behind him. What was it, though? What did he think it was as he bent to recover two weighted stones from the ground below?

From one hand to the other, he juggled the stones. He was contemplating that if he walked in a straight line, maybe he would stumble across a rip. A rip that would lead him out of this dimension. First, he felt a need to determine what was behind him. He didn't really want to. His out-of-control heart had told him this, but he didn't want to be ambushed either. He felt that if he was going to be eaten by whatever was out there, he would rather the attacker do so by looking it square in the eyes.

"My word! What bizarre creatures from the underworld are these?" the Pope asked, turning around as if someone had a gun pointed at his temple.

He was referring to the tree less than thirty yards behind him. In it were a host of silent creatures with eyes that were as overpowering as miniature flashlights. From what he could see, the creatures were fixed on his every movement, and not once did they ever blink an eyelid. This left him with mixed emotions because he didn't know what the creatures had in store for him. Better yet, he didn't even know what they looked like. Maybe the creatures weren't a threat at all; he kept this thought hidden deep within his conscience.

The Pope's situation didn't look encouraging. He was probably outnumbered fifty to one, and the arithmetic on him defeating the creatures with blunt force didn't appear rosy either. Knowing this to be factual, he thought it would be outlandish to throw the weighted stones in the direction of the tree. Much to his favor, the creatures weren't causing him the least bit of trouble, given they stayed where they were. With that in mind, he had turned around and had begun to sneak away in a fashion that wouldn't provoke them into a frenzy. Truly, this area wasn't safe any longer. It was hazardous—a hazardous place with visible and hidden peril.

Without question, his sense of direction was poor. It always had been. Even with a map, he still had difficulty finding his way around. Now was no different. He had no idea where the maze would lead him. He had just wanted to follow it in a straight line in hopes of stumbling into anything that might act as a portal and lead him back to the world he knew. He kept his fingers crossed that he would come across a find real soon, for his legs were beginning to cramp.

"That's it! That's enough! I need a break!" He had pulled up in his tracks. "I thought my luck would have changed by now, but I guess that's too much like right." He had crouched over while trying to regather himself.

The Pope was due for a pit stop. He had covered nearly a half-mile stretch of terrain, yet he knew it was nothing to brag about. He still hadn't turned the first corner of the maze. In his mind, he feared that he would be entrapped forever if he did. Several images of him being subjected to one dead end after another had deepened his phobia. Another image of him aging and dying like a hermit with a full-length beard had played a part as well. He wasn't too thrilled about making the sacrifice to venture off, but he remained optimistic that his completion of the maze would ultimately be key to his return to the Lord's walkway of light.

Sticking his head, not his body, around the first corner of the maze, he thought he had seen a twinkle of light. He had assumed his eyes were deceiving him until he had seen it again. This time, his veins were filled with a rush of adrenaline. Ironically, he thought the faint source of light was a lantern from Heaven, showing him the way out, the same way the burning bush had led Moses to the mountaintop. This had to be the case. There was no other explanation; he had begun to feel warm all over.

"Lord, please let this be a way out." He began to move forward. "Please, let it be." He crossed his heart.

The Pope's legs still didn't feel that great, but he was almost there. He was almost at the spot where he had seen the twinkle of light, yet where had it gone? He had no idea, but he did encounter something else that had piqued his interest within the confines of the maze. It was the boisterous cry of the wind. To his horror, it was blowing in every direction imaginable. As a result, some of the Weeping Willow trees had begun to sway back and forth while mimicking the rotten deck sound of a colonial slave ship and looking like giant monsters on the prowl.

"Come on! Show yourself to me!" He walked a few feet further before stopping. "I beg of you!"

He was referring to the twinkle of light. There were no signs of it, and he was doubtful if it would ever return again. One thing was for certain: he knew he had to keep pressing on. For the wind was literally beating him up like a boxer. Luckily for him, it wasn't a winter breeze. Still, he was undecided about which direction to travel. He didn't want to admit it, but he had become kind of dependent on the weak source of light to navigate him. Now, he was momentarily distracted. What else caused him anguish was the fact that he was becoming shorter and shorter. But this had to be a joke, right? It had to be! There was no way this could logically be taking place, and he debated before actually glancing down.

"Jumping fireworks, I've been in quicksand the whole time!" He dove forward. By doing this, the momentum of his body allowed his feet to pop free of their imprisonment.

The Pope didn't want to do anything too drastic. He knew he had to remain cautious because he didn't know the circumference of the quicksand. The last thing he wanted to happen was to stand upright and have the full weight of his body cause him to start sinking again. Thus, he crawled on his belly like a toddler until he reached a much sounder surface. From that point on, he came to his feet and began to scamper through the maze. He didn't have any leads or hints; he just ran on sheer gut instinct. He was too petrified to look back, and exactly as he had anticipated earlier, he came to one dead end after another.

"Wait a minute," he said, pulling up in his tracks. "Something isn't right. Something has to give."

The Pope sensed that he wasn't getting anywhere. He was more mentally drained than physically. He knew that at the ongoing rate, he would never make it out of the maze in time to be with Darr or the others. To help secure himself a chance, he felt he needed to implore a strategy. He thought he needed to map out his direction of travel. Since there were no real landmarks and the scenery around him never changed, he thought it would be most practical to mark the beginning and end of his trails with some broken twigs. This would ensure that he wasn't wandering in the same area more than once.

Even though the wind was still a tough obstacle to overcome, it didn't deter him from his main objectives. He had his mind pretty much made up about what he wanted to accomplish. He placed his hands into the pockets of his garment while proceeding to walk along a straight section of the maze. Despite the maze's often ghostly and hellish characteristics, he was baffled by why he hadn't been confronted by any evil villains. Not to say he was looking for any close encounters—he was just curious about what his surroundings had to offer. From his personal standpoint, nothing was far worse than not deliberating with one's inner feelings.

In his casual search for broken twigs, he saw none. He did see an opening up ahead on his left-hand side. Maybe his luck was about to change. Maybe this was a time portal. He was trying not to grin. He knew just as well as that opening being a lead way out, it could, in return, double as a trap.

The Pope wasn't crazy. He wasn't about to take any unnecessary risks. He was as sure as his name that he was going to use every precaution available to him. In doing so, he pulled the two weighted stones from his pocket and held them tightly against his outer thighs. These were the same stones he had gathered upon entering the maze. Peeking his head once, then twice, around the corner as if he were a member of a SWAT team, he saw that the coast was clear. He saw that there was no immediate danger, yet he kept the stones on display while he tiptoed inside the opening. If someone or something was there of a negative nature, he felt he would have no choice but to release the stones in self-defense.

"Hold the music! This isn't a way out. It can't be." He inched his way closer. "Why, it's nothing more than another dead end."

This was depressing. He was sick to death from these openings, which he felt led nowhere. He was so fed up he was starting to believe the entire maze was full of them. But there was something unique about this dead end. What was it, though? Unlike the other dead ends he had stumbled across, he felt that there was something at this spot worth exploring. He could sense it. The vibes were much different here. For one, there was no wind, and there was also an enormous tree in the center with spring-like leaves. It wasn't a Weeping Willow tree either. It was an oak tree, and he took a second longer to acknowledge it.

"Wait a second," he paused. "What do we have down here? Yes, what have we?" He walked and stood beside the tree.

He was still using precaution as he bent over to pick up a metal object. It was a gold coin. He smiled, holding it close to his face. Looking past this one, he could see thousands upon thousands more scattered all along the ground. There had to be about a million dollars worth of these shiny wonders, but where did they come from? Who could have left them there? He asked while placing the stones in opposite pockets.

Besides the coins being made of gold, he really couldn't see anything else. It was too dark out. He could only feel some faint insignias on both sides by touch alone. Was it a written language from this world or his? He didn't have a clue. As a matter of fact, he didn't even want to begin to flood his mind with any nonsense. He knew that without the aid of a proper light source, he would just be jumping from one silly conclusion after another.

Physically, he felt he had to do something. The situation was making him irate. What he wanted was to create a torch, not only for the sole purpose of viewing the coins but for his protection in the maze. To begin this vision, he had gathered seven branches of the same width from various locations on the ground, and he broke the ends off of each one until they were equal to the length of his arm. Then he had an idea. The idea was to unfasten the cloth belt from around his waist and wrap it several times around the tips of the branches.

"Now all I need is to get a fire going," the Pope grimaced as he reached into his right pocket, pulling out a matted-down pack of matches. "But that shouldn't be hard to do."

This was the same pack of matches he had often used to light the candles in his private library. To his discovery, though, only two stems remained. He couldn't believe it, not for one second. This was crude. He knew he had more matches than this. He didn't want to make a big deal out of it, yet he could count on one hand the few times he thought he had used this booklet. Now, he figured he had to make do with what he had, and still, he prayed he could light the belt on his first attempt.

Whatever the Pope did, he didn't want to fail. He didn't want to force the flame out. He knew he only had two attempts at this, so he held his breath and laid the torch parallel to the trunk of the oak tree. Still, something wasn't right. Something looked out of place. He shook his head in frustration while hiding the gold coin in his palm. What he didn't like was how the torch was situated. He was fearful it would kick out once he lit it. To prevent this from occurring, he rearranged the position of the torch. This time, he angled it on the tree and held the tip of his sandals flush against the bottom portion of the shaft. When he saw that everything was the way he wanted, he struck the first match along the coarse surface of the booklet and ignited the belt.

"Now, let's see what this coin says. It says that this is the legal tender of Julius Caesar. Julius Caesar? How historic!" he read, holding the coin close to the flame. "This is the treasury of the Roman Empire! This coin alone has to be worth a fortune!" He smiled while continuing to hold the tip of his sandal flush against the bottom portion of the torch's shaft.

This coin wasn't in the best condition, even if he could make out some of the wording. More than half of the letters were weathered, including the bust of Julius Caesar. Seeing that it was also difficult to wipe free some of the excess soil, he remained skeptical about what kind of shape the others were in. He hoped that maybe some of them would be unscathed after all these centuries.

With one hand, the Pope grabbed the torch and surrendered to his knees. There wasn't any doubt in his mind that these coins were from his world but from a generation long ago. In his aggressive search to find others, he came across a couple that were in better shape than the one he had initially held. He could see more and more details, yet he wasn't totally satisfied with them. He wanted one that was in mint condition. Having found it, he placed it in his pocket along with a dozen others he had collected. Nonetheless, he wanted more. He wanted some that were different in appearance and some that contained another ruler.

At the time, he was no longer interested in making it out of the maze. Nor did the Lord's mission or the torch-burning low matter, to say the least. They were both momentarily put on the back burner. His only concern was rambling through the coins. All he knew was that there was gold there and lots of it. If one coin didn't meet his specifications, he simply cast it aside and went on to the next. He believed that museums and archaeologists all across the globe would benefit from his findings. Rather inexplicably, for every coin he had put inside his pockets, a leaf fell to the ground. Blind to what was taking place above him, he continued to go about his search with no regrets.

"Hey, this one looks different." He stood up, holding the coin over the flame.

He was shocked. He knew he couldn't have hoped for anything better. Finally, he felt he had something worth raving about in his possession. Something extravagant. Something far different from the other coins he had collected. This one alone was nearly the size of his palm, but it had no center. Someone had stenciled it out. Someone had artistically created an eye over the top of a triangle, similar to the one found on an American dollar bill. Having not wiped the debris from it fully, he was still in awe of the workmanship.

The Pope had to stop and clear his head. He was a nervous wreck. There was something about this coin that made him uneasy, but he didn't know what it was. One thing he was quick to point out was how alive the coin felt within his palm. He could literally feel the energy within it penetrating his body. It was an illustrious experience. Upon further observation, he saw that the coin also contained some inscriptions—a written language that was vague to him, although he thought it resembled early Hebrew.

"If I didn't think my eyes were giving false readings, I would assume that these letters were changing before my eyes."

In an attempt to wipe free the remaining debris, he spat on the coin. Then he polished it to perfection with his opposite sleeve, but that's when the ground, of all things, began to tremor. However, the destructive force ended the moment he concealed the coin against his chest. It was too late, though. What he saw almost scared him out of his skin, and he remained motionless until he got the backbone to hold the coin out once more for viewing. Still, the letters continued to travel in a clockwise fashion but at a much quicker pace. His eyes couldn't keep up, and his head went around in tight spirals against his will.

The hypnotic field from the coin was so potent he could feel his eyeballs becoming relaxed. There was no question he was dizzy and out of touch with his surroundings. He was a walking mental factor, one who had found it arduous to maintain his balance. To reverse the effects, he thought it would be helpful if he encased his fingers around the coin.

It worked. "Why does everything bad always have to happen to me?" he asked, throwing the coin on the ground by his feet.

"Why is it so?" he clenched his fist.

The Pope had never taken his eyes away from the coin. He didn't want to lose it. This coin had a history, and he hoped that Darr could expose it to him. His only worry was apprehending it. He knew if he didn't die from massive heart failure, his fingers would probably fall off instead from the sheer drama. Yet, it was a risk he wanted to pursue. He had to have it. This coin was his and only his.

The consequences no longer mattered to the Pope. He wanted the coin to be displayed to Darr and the others. With it, he felt he could ease the tension his absence had probably created. Thus, he bent over and picked it up. Curious as to why the words were no longer moving, he gave the coin a good whack with his knuckles just to loosen up any implications, but nothing happened. The coin remained lifeless. In the back of his mind, he knew the coin was still a precious item, but he felt it was the rotating words that had made it remarkable. He had to see them again. He felt a weird addiction come over him, so he gave the coin two more whacks with his knuckles.

"Come on. What are you waiting for? Why don't you show me what I saw just a couple of seconds ago? How hard is that?" The Pope continued to work on the coin.

Upon the last thrust of impact, the coin did something malicious.

It had begun to bore its way into his palm like a hot branding iron. Both the pain and the smell of his own flesh were so overwhelming that he wobbled to his knees without bracing himself. He had no choice but to let the coin slide free from his grasp. He didn't want it anymore. He hated it. It was cursed with an evil spell, and he bewailed while rocking back and forth underneath the oak tree.

"Mother of God, my palm is killing me!" The Pope tightly gritted his teeth while fanning his hand through the air.

The feeling of pain was very intense. It was unlike anything he could recall to date. Even when he had been shot, he couldn't remember ever feeling this miserable. He couldn't block it out either. Nor did he have the will to inspect his palm. What if he saw something he didn't want to see? What if he needed medical attention? What if he fainted? This was too much to ask so soon; besides, he felt he would only benefit from it in the worst way. Despite his emotions, he knew he had to do something soon or risk going into shock. Accepting this as the truth, he blindly made a fist and placed it between the center of his thighs.

The Pope was gracious. He knew that his run-in with terror was minor compared to the other scenarios he had faced. He was hurt yet lucky to be alive. With this in mind, he came to his feet while placing his back flush against the tree. He was thinking. He thought it would be witty if he left this area of the maze before his torch burned out. The only thing was he wanted to see his palm. He was curious as to how bad it was, even though it didn't feel life-threatening. What seemed to cause him the most grief were these continuous drops of fine mist that fell from high above the treetops, hitting him in a designated spot at the back of his head.

"Precipitation? That's exactly what I need to make my situation even worse!" he stated, not wanting to look up at the source. He knew that a direct hit would probably obstruct his vision. "Unreal. I pick up a couple of loose coins, and all of this happens. Lord, what else can I expect to go wrong?"

The continuous drops were annoying as hell. They alone had a profound impact on him, turning out to be a psychological disadvantage. He knew he probably wouldn't have cared if the back of his head and the top of his shoulders weren't being targeted.

"I sure hope the end is in sight. I need to get out of here."

Every time the Pope felt a direct hit, his face would turn red, and his brows would flare up. He despised every second of this. It was like a form of torture—Chinese water torture, to be exact. He wanted to leave. He wanted to escape to the flat. Unfortunately, he became ill in the stomach when he thought about deserting the shelter of the tree. He was fearful he would get drenched or that the torch would burn out indefinitely. He already had a difficult time trying to harness the flame.

Chapter 8

The Pope was caught up in a bind, one which kept him on the sidelines looking in. One which had enabled him to do what he wanted to do, apprehensive that the torch would flicker out as a result. This, in return, gave him a lot of time to himself. Time is what he uses to study his present situation. He was content after about fifteen minutes that the drops were only falling in the area where he stood. He later confirmed this when he stuck the portion of his body that didn't contain the torch out beyond the trees.

"Would you look at that?" he cracked a smile.

He was relieved by the weather forecast but daunted when he tried to come up with a civilized explanation of what had taken place. Indeed, this wasn't normal. It was an unorthodox turn of events, foreign to him, to say the least. Nor did he expect anything in this dimension not to be. This gave him all the more reason to leave, to go back to his world, where reality was a common occurrence.

With his mouth open wide like a fish out of water, he took two steps backward. He was so preoccupied with collecting the gold coins he didn't recall any leaves falling. Yet, from one side to the other, he could see them. More than half of the ground was saturated, including his feet. He wasn't surprised by this either, given that the ground did tremor. If anything, he felt delirious that he didn't notice the incident while it was occurring.

The Pope couldn't take it anymore. The tension was building. He knew it was time for him to leave. He also felt it was time to inspect his injured palm. No doubt his nerves had gotten the better of him as he brought his fidgety fist toward his face. Pausing, he didn't know what to do next. He assumed he was at a loss for ideas until he, one by one, uncurled his fingers.

"Oh, my! What have I done? How could I have been so foolish in wanting to possess something so wicked? Now I'm hexed forever, doomed to my bitter death!"

What he saw had almost made him go insane. It was the symbol of the coin, which was fixed into his skin. To him, it was a big deal. It was worse than having an unwanted tattoo. Now, how could he go through life after knowing he had been permanently scarred by what he deemed a satanic object? Scared out of his wits, he had wanted to get rid of the evidence. Thus, in a series of violent attempts, he had tried to rub the markings away. However, it didn't work. Nothing he thought of seemed to work, for that matter.

"Heavenly Father, what have I done? What did I do to be marked for death?" At the time, he could think of a number of reasons for hiding his hand in his left pocket.

The Pope had felt feverish all over. Things definitely weren't going the way he wanted, and to make matters more bizarre, he had heard some ruckus behind him. The sound was so piercing that it made him twitch. From his initial perspective, something had crashed through the trees, breaking several branches. Strangely, whatever it was had never impacted the ground.

He was alleviated, still somewhat rattled when he heard the same sound about four more times. Unlike a minute ago, he had two versions of what he thought it might be. Grinning, he thought the Lord had answered his prayers by sending the angel Darr, who was to deliver him back to safety. He knew Darr had a thing for using trees as camouflage when spying, and he felt that this would validate the breaking of the branches he had heard. Even if he had wanted to believe this version, he couldn't. It was too good to be true. On a more serious note, he thought the tree behind him was about to give way.

Surely, he didn't want to be crushed. He didn't even want to be anywhere near the tree when it fell. Just for the sake of good measure, he figured it would be intelligent if he stepped a few feet off to his left before he turned around to see how much danger he was in. He had already declared in advance that if he didn't agree with what he saw, he would take off running. To make certain he had a chance, he pivoted his back foot in the opposite direction like a sprinter.

"Hold everything! What in the name of——"

The Pope didn't know what had hit him as a cold rush of air stormed up his nostrils, forcing him backward. It was presumably the stench, the sight of the naked tree, and what was in it that made his eyes the size of navel oranges. He was so wound up that he tried to speak, but nothing came out. What he wanted to protest were the six bodies hanging from six separate chains by their necks. Upon further analysis, he concluded that the bodies were the skeletal remains of Roman soldiers who still clung to their armor after all these centuries.

He felt that this would explain why the gold coins he found bore the name Caesar. They were the uncontested wages of the soldiers. Considering more of the evidence around him, he declared the coins had fallen from the soldiers' pouches after or while they were in the process of being hung. He knew it didn't take a real genius to come up with this information, but he felt it would take one to figure out who would commit such a grotesque act of homicide. What was their motive, especially since it wasn't robbery?

Just the sight of the bodies swinging through the air in togetherness like a wind chime made him want to puke, yet he felt compelled to stand there and watch. Up and down, his eyeballs went, searching for closure to the many questions still lingering in his head. With his palm already the way it was and the overall look of certain things around him, he wondered if his fate would be the same as the soldiers. Would he be the next to die?

Something he was quick to point out was that he wasn't about to make a target out of himself. He knew that his survival up to now was due to his trusting his better judgment. He didn't care how long ago the soldiers were murdered. There was no way in the world he was going to wait around and permit himself to be the next to get butchered. He had too much pride. He had too many goals in life that he wanted to accomplish. Gazing at his torch, he felt it was never intended for man to play prey for another host anyway. Thus, he turned his back and made a mad dash for the exit.

In the back of his mind, he was in a race. He was in a race against his surroundings. What he was trying to avoid was the sight of the bodies and the squeaky sound the heavy chains connected to them made. They were both beginning to have a dramatic effect on his psyche. Unfortunately, when he made his way towards the exit, something strange occurred. He noticed that he disappeared but reappeared behind the same oak tree that contained the bodies.

"No! No! This can't be!" he said in a lenient tone of voice as he leaned against the tree.

He barely had enough energy to stand, yet he wouldn't let this deter him. Something had to give, and he knew it wouldn't be him. Furious, he took off towards the exit. He was positive that the outcome would be much different this time, but exactly like before, he disappeared only to reappear behind the same oak tree.

"Stop. Stop." The Pope heard someone with a frail voice cry out from above his head. "If you enter the portal one more time, you will awaken the creature. It's the creature who resides here."

"Who said that? Are you an angel?" he whispered back. "Where are you? Please, make yourself known."

"It's too late for that, my friend." His voice was so faint the Pope could barely hear him. From the sound of things, it appeared his body had been inflicted with several wounds. "My fate is already sealed, but it's not too late for you. I have been watching. I didn't mean to startle you earlier with my drops of blood. I have been bleeding for centuries at the best."

"So that was you?" The Pope wiped the back of his neck. "I thought it was rain. Please, I don't belong here. How do I get out?"

"No one belongs here."

"I can't see you." The Pope hesitated to speak. "Where are you actually?"

"Just above the soldiers, but don't try to find me. I'm not a sight for the timid. You should only focus your attention on my words. Many have failed to do this."

"I will respect that."

"Good. Listen to me, for I can't bear to see another soul be tortured by the creature from beyond. Therefore, empty your pockets of all the treasure and leave. Go before it's too late. You see, the treasure is the creature's bait."

This was a hard pill to swallow, but it still made a lot of sense to the Pope. By pocketing the gold coins, he had prohibited himself from leaving at will. Like the others in the past, he had mistakenly taken something that didn't belong to him. Even he was surprised by his actions. He knew it wasn't in his character to let greed get the better of him, but he felt that the ancient gold could have done this to almost anyone. They were beautiful.

"When the treasure is no more, go. Leave this place of taboo and don't look back."

"But what about the markings on my palm?" The Pope grew worrisome. "Wouldn't it also trigger the creature?"

"If I knew everything, would I be in the predicament I'm in?"

"You have a valid point."

"I have seen the creature, and it's very unpredictable. You must leave before it's too late. For I fear you may have already awakened the creature from its hibernation."

"Wait. Is there anything I can do to repay you?"

"My days of requests are over. Just leave, my friend. Just leave."

"Thank you for your assistance and so long. I won't forget you."

"May you live long and prosper."

The Pope had felt a pinch in his chest the moment he spun around and jogged towards safety. This feeling of depression was brought on because he didn't want to abandon the stranger who was still in a compromising position. He wanted to do something. He wanted to turn back. He wanted to alleviate the pain the stranger was probably experiencing. Even though he was told to leave, he still wanted to do something in return. He knew he wasn't brought up like this. How could he not repay someone for their gratitude? After all, he knew it was the stranger's words that gave him a new lease on life in the first place.

"Hold it! I can't leave here like this!" He stopped dead on the spot.

Slowly, he turned his body once more to engage at the entrance to the oak tree. He was beginning to have second thoughts. They were creepy thoughts about setting the tree on fire. Clearly, he was out of danger and back in the thick of the maze, so the idea that he could be endangering his life never came into focus.

"The heck with this place!" He spoke in Polish. He was so ticked off that he bit a chunk of flesh from his bottom lip and didn't even grimace.

He didn't care anymore. He had only one objective in mind: to burn the tree to a cinder. Using a delayed count of three, he took off from where he was standing. There wasn't a hint of regret either the moment he swiftly entered over the threshold. He was praying he could dash in and dash back without any difficulty. He didn't see why not, for he had a clear path out in front of him. He was also jubilant to see that the leaves had automatically appointed themselves back to their original branches. Without a doubt, he knew this would heighten his chances for success.

"I had to do this."

Coming to a complete standstill, he held the torch above his head. He was too short to reach his main target of interest, the bodies. Thus, he stood on his tiptoes and ignited the first set of leaves he came in contact with.

"Again, I had to do this. The decision not to was tearing me apart," he said while running back to safety. His comment was directed to the stranger, who never responded. "I hope you won't be upset, my friend."

A wicked grin came across the Pope's face the moment he observed the tree go up in flames. He was tickled pink yet jolted at what he saw coming straight toward him by way of the fire and the parted sky above. It was the whining souls of the deceased, which resembled a mob of torn nightgowns. In a formation similar to a marching band, they hovered low to the ground until they began to form a giant hula-hoop around his body. His first impulse was to take off running, but he could see that he was halfway surrounded by their spectacle of yellow light.

Without question, he feared what he didn't understand. He knew if these souls meant him any harm, he was a goner. Surely, he was on their time as they continued to arrive from the fire and the parted sky above. On average, he figured that there had to be about a thousand before him. With this in mind, the idea of him going to the bathroom on himself almost became a reality.

"What do you want from me?" the Pope yelled, watching the last soul join the formation. "I was only trying to help." He staggered backward.

He had no clue what he was up against. Also, his phobia of coming into contact with the souls was starting to upset him. For one, he didn't like the fact that they were playing ring-around-the-rosy while using his body as the center of attraction. It was making him dizzy, among other things.

"Wait! You must stop! I beg of you! Stop!" he had pleaded while looking at his feet. "Can't you see that you're making me float off the ground?"

The Pope couldn't believe what he was experiencing. In less than three minutes flat, he had watched the souls elevate him more than sixty feet into the air. Being this high up, he knew he was almost certain to die if gravity ever decided to kick in. From his not-so-favorable vantage point, he could see the souls circling the ground below at a rapid pace. He could also hear the faint sounds of singing. It was the singing of the souls, which he believed had elevated him even higher at times.

By now, it was evident the souls weren't going to cause him any harm. It had taken a while for him to come to this conclusion, but he had eventually accepted what was occurring as the souls' natural way of showing their appreciation. And instead of him fighting, he had embraced the rite of passage by leaning his head back and throwing his hands freely into the air. He was allowing the souls the opportunity to continue with their celebration. After all, he knew he was in no position to disagree.

"Take me. Take me, I'm yours," the Pope had cried out in a subdued tone of voice.

Without delay, the souls had catapulted themselves into the air. One by one, they did this until each had a turn to pass through his body before rejoining the circle below. To his own amusement, he had experienced a little bit of ecstasy with every encounter—a high that had left him weak and susceptible to this enormous gorilla-like creature with dragon-shaped wings and a gold breastplate. A creature who was steadily sneaking its way toward him, using the dark sky as its camouflage. This creature was so hideous that it had produced a white foam from its mouth, similar to that of an animal infested with rabies.

On the one hand, the creature held a lengthy chain doubled up, while on the other, it was an ordinary African spear. This had heightened the Pope's fear of a midair confrontation. Besides the two weighted stones in his pocket from long ago, the torch was his only real line of self-defense. With it, he knew he could inflict his own mark of destruction if the creature didn't beat him to the punch with its spear. Taking two deep breaths, he elected to hide the torch behind his back, away from the direction in which the creature was traveling. This was all in an effort to deaden the target it had presented to the creature.

"Take me down! Take me down at once!" the Pope had pleaded to the souls below. He was frantic, yet he had still managed to keep one eye on the creature and its progress. "Please, the evil one is amongst us! You must release me! You must!" He was so high up that he was doubtful if his voice was even capable of reaching the souls.

The Pope was back to his old self. The feelings of ecstasy and liberation were gone, erased by the present danger that had lurked in the sky. Realizing the threat as well, the souls had lowered him to the ground quickly but carelessly.

"What is the meaning of this?" the creature had spoken in a possessed voice while spitting. At the time, it hovered over the Pope and the souls, its wings outspanning them both. "How dare ye defy me, human! How dare ye invade and destroy my macrocosm! Now, do ye think that I will let thee escape with thy life? Never! Ye will be made to suffer the price for this, and it is a high one to pay! No, everyone will suffer for this treason... this small uprising!"

"It won't be that easy!" the Pope had replied. "My Lord will stop you! We will stop you, for you receive pleasure at the discomfort of others!"

"I know not of thy Lord! There is no other but me! I am the uncontested deity of this parallel!" the creature had laughed. "Perhaps ye would like to feel the sting of my wraith? Oh, I think it's time! I really do!"

In a fit of rage, the creature swooped toward the ground. It was swinging its chain and jabbing its spear in four different directions, yet it came up empty. Wisely, the souls had divided themselves into two groups. The Pope, relying on his instincts, had followed the group nearest to him as the creature cursed and took to the sky. What was it plotting, he sought to know?

The Pope could sense the creature's frustration. It was evident in the creature's deafening growls. Not knowing what to make of this, he was contemplating if now was the perfect time to flee before the creature had a chance to return. Scratching his head, he didn't want the creature's second visit to the ground to be his demise. Right off the bat, he could see the creature didn't have many weaknesses he could exploit, but it had one. For starters, the creature was a poor flier with wings that didn't fit the contours of its muscular body.

"Listen to me! Do as I say!" the Pope insisted, talking to the group of souls nearest to him. "When the creature begins to make its break toward the earth, I want you, along with the others, to form a circle similar to the one I was in. But don't do anything until I give the approval. Now, communicate this to the others."

He was pleased that both groups of souls were moving, only they were moving too slowly for his taste. He didn't know how acute their hearing was. He just wanted to get phase one of his plan rolling. The only trouble was the creature had heard him as well, as its growls became louder and more ferocious.

"Creature, down here! There is no ruler greater than my Lord above, for He is the originator of Heaven and all things beyond! You are an idiot to believe otherwise!"

"Ye will suffer the most! I will see to it personally! In the end, thy soul will only know me and the sorrow I caused!"

The Pope's plan to enrage the creature even more was working like a charm. He knew that mentioning another being greater than itself would get its full attention. In just a short period of time, he had seen how conceited and arrogant the creature really was. He was also aware that the creature feared something about the souls. He wasn't certain if it was their multitude or if the creature was simply searching for a weakness. He only knew something was preventing the creature from striking at whim.

"Creature, you don't know the definition of power! You would crumble to thy knees in the presence of my Lord above! See, this is a living testament to His existence!" the Pope had screamed, flashing his silver crucifix. He had wanted to display confidence, but deep within, he was a nervous wreck.

"We will soon see who the master of master's is! How dare ye defy me, human!"

The creature had wasted no time preparing itself to carry out its threat. Unlike before, it had opted to use the spear as its premier weapon of choice. The creature had no need for the lengthy chain, which it had neatly doubled up and wrapped around its neck. This time, the creature had just one thing in its sights. Armed with the spear out in front of its body, it had dipped its head and had done a nosedive forward. In anticipation of this, the Pope had started blindly walking backward.

"It's time! It's time!" he had signaled to the souls while pointing at the sky. He continued to calculate the creature's descent. "Form the trap! Quickly! Quickly! Hurry, begin to rotate while the creature is at the halfway point!"

He was joyous to see that the souls had followed his strategic plan all the way through. Still, he didn't like what he saw from a distance. He didn't enjoy the fact that the creature was being elevated instead of being sent crashing downward. He knew if he didn't do something soon to change this, the creature would eventually escape the magnification range of the souls. In the long run, he knew this would be catastrophic for them all.

"What is the meaning of this? Ye can't defeat me! I am a proven survivor of the game!" The creature had broken out into laughter as it was steadily being elevated.

"Wait a minute!" The Pope rubbed his eyes. "I want you to rotate counterclockwise! Yes, keep going! Faster! Faster!"

The more the creature fought against the soul's magnification, the closer it was pulled towards the ground. Ironically, each soul, by nature, created its own spiral of wind. Thus, by joining together as one collective unit, they gave birth to a power that was on the same level as a mighty hurricane. The only difference was that this phenomenon pulled objects downward instead of slinging them across the sky.

The Pope was enlightened by this act of aggression. At one point, he didn't know whether to leap in the air or kiss the soil beneath his feet. The same feeling also applied when he saw one of the creature's wings snap and fall to the ground. Not far behind was the creature itself, which he heard make a thunderous boom upon impact.

"I think we've done it! I think we've done it!" The Pope ran over to the spot where the creature had plummeted to the ground. Cornering his eye over his right shoulder, he could see some of the souls beginning to migrate over the large crater as well.

From afar, there were no visible signs of the creature anywhere; still, the Pope wasn't buying this. A wee bit curious, he held his fading torch over the spot of impact and stuck his face in. However, he saw nothing. He saw nothing but ample darkness. By the looks of his facial expression, he didn't seem certain if the creature was alive or dead. For one, he couldn't see that far down. Nor did he hear any distinctive sounds that would suggest the creature no longer had a vital sign. On the rational side of things, he knew he had witnessed the creature fall some ninety feet.

"It's hard to believe, but I guess that's it," the Pope said as he slowly stood up. Now had to be the perfect time to escape. He had based this on the fact that a great majority of the souls had already started to leave the dead end in a chain-gang fashion. At times, he had often admired how they looked like cars passing by on the freeway at night. Other than the souls serving as his protection in the event of danger, he knew they were probably his best ticket out. He already felt the odds would be stacked against him if he decided to travel alone.

"Hey! Hey! Wait for me!" The Pope darted over, cutting into the middle of the formation. "Please, I need your help in getting out. Can you show me the way?"

For exactly ten minutes, he followed the soul's turn for turn through the maze. They were arranged in a low-to-high fashion, characteristic of a flock of geese. He knew that, with the lead souls having the advantage of a higher viewpoint, they could basically see things that the others or himself couldn't. To a degree, he was somewhat mesmerized by their intelligence. Suddenly, he felt that the pipe dream of him getting back would soon become a reality—one which he couldn't wait to experience.

"Stop! What are you doing?" The Pope began to panic. "Why are you moving so quickly?"

He couldn't figure out what was wrong. He didn't see any signs of danger, nor did he hear anything unusual. Without explanation, the souls were traveling at a much quicker pace than before. He couldn't keep up by walking; he had to run. He had to play catch-up because he was losing a substantial amount of distance by the second. No longer was he in the middle of the formation but at the back.

"Please, I want to get out of here just as badly as you do, but I can't keep up at this pace," he said, huffing and puffing. "There's no way I can do it."

The Pope had felt terrible all over. He was right; his body was in no condition to take too much more of this strenuous abuse. He was sucking up so much air in his effort to lessen the gap between the souls and himself, and his stomach felt like a rhino had just walked across it. He had assumed his respiratory system was about to fail him, along with his burning thighs and his aching knees.

Even though he had felt the way he did, he didn't want to end his pursuit. This was based on the fact he had felt his life was at stake. Unfortunately, the distance between the souls and himself was too farfetched. He knew if they made a sudden turn, he would lose them for sure. He only prayed the end was on the horizon, yet it didn't appear that way.

"So this is how you repay me? You call this leading me out? You lead me nowhere! Nowhere, I say!"

He was so fatigued he almost stumbled and fell several times to his knees. Miraculously, on each occasion, he had managed to regain his balance. There wasn't any objection in his mind that all of this physical activity was making him sick, too sick to even notice his torch was out. He wasn't blind by a long shot, but his vision became increasingly blurred. It was hampered to the point where everything had appeared to be elongated to him.

"I won't let you out of my sight." The Pope had babbled to himself. "I have to give it all I got."

The Pope was very devoted to keeping up with the souls. So much so that he wasn't observant of the terrain he was traveling over. He was acting downright irresponsible. As a result of this, he tripped and fell. He had plummeted into a pit of murky water which contained various animal bones and maggots. Even though he couldn't swim a lick, he still tried to doggy paddle as much as he could, but he found that difficult to do. The smell was too unbearable, along with the maggots that he could feel crawling into his ears and nose at random. This alone had created panic and had caused his body to start bobbing in the water.

Up and down he had gone, scrambling for air each time he resurfaced. He had noticed that the more he slapped the water in an effort to stay above it, the weaker he became. He knew if he didn't do something real soon, he would be spent on his remaining energy. The lower half of his body was already numb. He was almost certain his arms would be the next to follow.

"Is this how it will end for me, Lord?" he yelled before going under. "Is it? I want to know!" he babbled after coming back up. In horror, he would swallow some of the maggots; he didn't speak or breathe from his mouth until his head was clear above the water line.

The Pope had so many things working against him at once that he was contemplating giving in. He felt that even if he were fortunate enough to bypass the water, he would, in the long run, be hit with another one of the maze's many curveballs. This definitely wasn't something he was looking forward to, with no food and the souls no longer present. Nor did he want to continue with his palm still bearing the symbol of the coin. No, he felt it would be better if he saved himself from the aggravation by letting the curtain fall now.

The maggots were already trying to eat him alive. Crying, he felt that he had let the Lord down in more than one way. He knew that if he had taken heed of Darr's instructions, none of this would have ever happened.

"Heavenly Father, please relinquish me of my name. I'm no longer worthy to bear the honor," he wept towards the sky before straightening up his body and sinking downward.

Within seconds, he had seen his whole life flash before his eyes. Yet, had he really given up the ghost? Did he pass on to the other side? In a weird kind of way, he didn't think anything out of normalcy had occurred at all. To his surprise, he was still very much alive, but strangely, he was no longer sinking. Tapping his toes twice on the bottom of the muddy floor bed, he now knew why. He now knew he was so paranoid about being in a massive body of water other than a bathtub his mind had automatically gone into drowning mode when it shouldn't have. Clearly, this water was no higher than his armpits. He thumped himself on the forehead.

"Who knew, Lord? Who knew?"

The Pope was embarrassed. He felt like a total ass as he plowed through the contaminated water. He was headed for land when something entered his mind. It was a reality check. With tears proceeding to fall from his eyes, he couldn't believe what he had done. He couldn't believe he had almost tried to end his life by being so foolhardy. This was always a choice he had assumed he would never be faced with, yet he couldn't hide the realism that it had transpired.

There was no way the Pope was going to dwell on this mishap for any lengthy period. He was always a person who was quick to put something tragic behind him, similar to the time he was almost assassinated. It was in his nature to find forgiveness in the criminals back then, just like he knew he would do the same for himself if he ever hoped to get out of this world. He was a very rational man, though—one who didn't believe in fighting with himself.

"At last, I've done it," he said, gasping. "I made it out." He was exhilarated to be on solid land again, yet he knew this feeling would be short-lived. As a result of inhaling too much of the toxic fumes, he became woozy and collapsed sideways.

Chapter 9

Nonchalantly, the Pope opened his eyes to the sky, which no longer contained the two moons. The way his body felt, he wasn't certain if he was alive. Something was definitely out of place to him. He could sense it. For starters, he could no longer turn his neck. Gone was his capability to move a single muscle. Rather inscrutably, he could only look straight up into the air. To his own disbelief, though, he was moving. He was floating freely through the darkness as if he were some sort of insect.

It was this feeling alone that made him believe he was deceased. It was also this feeling that made him positive he was having an out-of-body experience. The last thing he could recall was falling unconscious by the pit of water; after that, he wasn't certain. Maybe he did lose his life? Maybe the gorilla-looking creature stalked and murdered him? At the time, this was a grim reality he couldn't rule out, even though he didn't want it to be true. He knew he still had a mission to complete.

"Lord, please say it isn't so! Please tell me that my life hasn't expired. If you could, Lord, just grant me the power to move. That's all I'm asking."

"Sorry, but your request has been denied!" An aggressive voice from out of nowhere shouted. "At last, your soul belongs to the brotherhood of sinfulness! We will control your destiny from this point on, fat boy!"

"Yes, no one can save you now!" a different voice pointed out to him while giggling like a lunatic. "Not even your Lord!

"This is your last stand! Soon, we will enjoy the pureness of your flesh."

"What? What is the meaning of this?" The Pope had a hard time saying.

He was a nervous mess, and his heart was beating at a dangerous pace. To make the situation even more complex, he was shocked to discover that those were the voices of goblins. Somehow, he had assumed the goblins had abducted him while he lay unconscious by the pit of water. He wouldn't swear to it, yet he knew it was a valid explanation of what had occurred. Worse yet, he knew escaping the goblins on foot would be difficult. If there were too many of them, he knew he would be easily caught. It was a tiresome thing to think about, but he knew he would have to come up with another strategy, one that wasn't based on running. First, he felt he needed to break free of whatever kind of confinement he was in.

"I want to be the one to ravish his body! Will you let me?" begged one of the goblins.

"No, it's for me to take!"

"You all can have his mortal flesh; I just want his soul to do what I desire!" a third goblin chuckled.

"Wait," a fourth goblin intervened. "We will take turns! We will share his mortal flesh and soul in one triumphant orgy!"

Laughter and celebration were quick to follow this response.

The Pope was speechless. He knew he was surrounded by ill company. He knew if he didn't attempt to do something soon, the goblins would have their way. He was already trying to move his hands, but they felt as if they were bound by a rope. He could feel the imprint of the fibers cutting into him. Even the skin on his neck and ankles were met with the same consequences. In his mind, he knew this would explain why he could only look up.

It didn't take a rocket scientist to figure out what the goblins were doing. They were carrying him to a predetermined destination, a place they had selected to close the chapter of his life. It was his belief in this that made him wish Darr or even the souls were present to save him and give him aid in his time of distress.

He didn't know how much time he had, but he knew it wasn't a lot. Not when he could see flashes of his own bloody execution, and definitely not when he could smell death in the air—his own death, to be exact. The signs were right before him. The only thing that had periodically taken his mind off dying was Kelso, and at the best of times, the two shared together. Yes, it was this apparent fear of not seeing Kelso that had triggered his second attempt to break free despite the pain of the rope cutting into his wrists like a razor blade.

"Come on, just a little bit more," the Pope had commented to himself. The goblins were quiet for some reason or another, and he didn't want to bring any attention to himself. He knew if he was fortunate, he could continue what he was doing without the risk of being caught. "There. I did it."

At last, he had the rope off his wrists. He knew this was a minor accomplishment, yet it made him feel blessed. It was the first time in a while, given his circumstances. Wasting not a moment more, he opted to bring his hands to his shoulders, where he hesitantly took the rope from around his neck. Much to his horror, the rope was in the form of a noose. A noose which he softly laid aside. However, he knew if he sat up to free his legs, the goblins would see what he was doing or what he had done prior. The goblins were goofy characters, but he knew he was in no predicament to underestimate them—not when his life hung by a thread.

"All right, Pius. Here goes nothing. Time to have a little peek," the Pope rambled to himself, turning his head sluggishly to the left and right. It was important to him to see where he was in the maze. It was also vital for him to learn how the goblins were arranged around him. But what if they were looking directly at him? What would he do? How would he react?

The Pope couldn't believe it. He couldn't come to terms with what he saw. He was almost certain that he would see four goblins on opposite sides of him. After all, who or what was holding him balanced in the air? He was correct in his count; however, the goblins who were carrying makeshift torches were several feet out in front of him. From what he could tell, no one had a hold of him. He was just gliding freely through the air as if he were on a magic carpet ride. He couldn't help but giggle. This was because the goblins were a lot shorter than the ones he had encountered at the basilica. Even he was a giant compared to them. It was a cocky thing to suppose, but he thought he could manhandle the midgets with ease if given the opportunity.

The time was almost right. He could sense it in his bones. These goblins had no idea what he was up to. They didn't have eyes in the back of their heads, nor did they ever turn around to check on him. They didn't have to. He was sitting upright, watching them the whole time. Seizing the moment, he had untangled the rope from around his waist and legs. Initially, he thought about ditching it to the ground, but he was wise enough to stuff it under his clothing. This way, he could use it as a weapon when it was convenient, along with the two weighted stones he still had in his pocket.

The Pope was no slouch, not when it came to fighting for his survival. He was very confident in his physical ability to neutralize the goblins, but he didn't want to go overboard with his arrogance. He knew he had come too far to rush into something without thinking it through. Besides, he didn't know what was holding him in the air. Was it the goblins? If so, then he wondered what else they were capable of. Always cautious since his childhood, he had created small periods in which he had used to sit up and lie back down. What he was trying to do was to map out his direction of travel. Much to his awareness, the goblins hadn't made a turn. They had just kept walking straight, and from his vantage point, there weren't going to be any sudden changes.

"There's something about this part of the maze that looks and feels familiar to me," the Pope had commented after lying back down. "Strange, but it appears to be the same route I first journeyed." He had based this on the fact that at no other point in the maze were the weeping willow trees horizontally spaced so far apart.

The Pope was hurt by this discovery. There was no simpler way to put it. He felt that, instead of moving forward in the right direction, he was now traveling backward and erasing all of his progress along the way. Just the visual thought of what was occurring had almost brought him to tears as he continued to lie on his back, looking up at the night sky like a stranger in a foreign land.

He wasn't about to give up, but he felt that there was no way he could escape and gain back what he had lost. There was no way unless he could knock out each one of the goblins; then, he deemed something such as this could be feasible. He knew that outrunning the goblins was definitely a waste of time, for he was too old to go the distance of the open field. He didn't understand much about the four goblins, yet he was almost certain they were using some type of telepathic power to keep him suspended. Bearing all of these facts in mind, he no longer felt that he could subdue them so easily.

"Fuck, I think we should turn back," the Pope had heard one of the goblins whisper. "I don't want to be eaten up like the others in the past."

This was the first time he had heard them speak in a while.

"No, we must press on. The gooey bats won't attack us unless we provoke them," the second goblin had insisted.

"Yeah! Just be quiet, you stupid son of a bitch!" the third goblin had lashed out.

"Oh, I wonder who is making all the noise now, ass wipe!" The first goblin was quick to fire back. "A circus monkey has more sense than you!"

The Pope could only shake his head. He was appalled by the goblins' vulgar language and cackling. He had only wished he had the ability to wash their mouths out with dish soap.

"You little shit, one of these days, I'm going to bite that middle finger clean off!" The third goblin had promised.

"Ladies and gentlemen, I think we have a fight! I think we have a fight!" The fourth goblin intervened, sounding like a sports announcer.

"Who's the lady, asshole?" The first goblin had chosen to mimic the dragged-out voice of Rocky Balboa.

The Pope had just licked his lips and smiled. He knew if he was fortunate, the goblins would spare him the trouble and kill one another. Based on their conversation, he knew it would only be a matter of minutes before they were to commit genocide.

"Stop! Stop this insanity!" The second goblin had pleaded. "Damn it! If we keep carrying on like this, then we will be eaten alive!"

"It's true," said the fourth goblin in a serious tone of voice. "We are within the gooey bats' striking distance. We are."

The Pope couldn't believe how silent everything was from that moment on. Just from eavesdropping, he could detect it was something out there more dominant than the goblins. He had proof. The same way he could smell his own fear circulating through the air earlier, he could now sense the same for the goblins. Suddenly, the tiny hell-raisers didn't appear to be so tough.

He now knew the goblins had a natural enemy, and he knew it was close by. Who or what it was, he didn't have a clue. He was positive this information wouldn't become available to him anyway unless he were to sit up and gaze off. He didn't want to, for the reason he was weary of whatever was out there himself. What if he was attacked instead? Just thinking about this was enough to make his arms break out with goosebumps. Nonetheless, he knew it was something he had to do if he wanted to get back on track.

"When the time is right, I will need to hurl one of these weighted stones at a goblin's head," he had said softly to himself. "If I'm able to connect, then this should break their telepathy."

Even though he was aware he would be endangering his life in the process, he didn't care. He wouldn't let the thought of dying indulge his mind, not even for a mere second. There was no way he was going to give in to the goblins without a struggle. Funny, he had felt it would be wiser if he had also included the opposition in his game plan. In the long run, he knew this would be better than tussling with the goblins alone. If everything had gone according to the way he had it worked out in his head, the two sides would cancel one another out, leaving him free to pick up a torch and wonder once again through the maze.

"Great, all I'm lacking now is the nerves to see what's really out there."

He said while holding the stones in opposite palms.

The anticipation was becoming too much for him to keep bottled up, especially with him lying on his back doing nothing. He had so many crazy thoughts popping in and out of his head at one time it was making him insane. What he had wanted to do was to stay focused on his initial strategy. This was the outline he had drawn out until he had sat upright for the first time in a while. It was then he had seen something that had almost made him black out. He couldn't believe it. He couldn't believe he was suddenly within full view of the creatures who didn't nictitate an eyelid. He didn't want to admit it, but the creatures were a welcoming sight. Although he didn't have a common bond with the creatures, they did share a common adversary in the goblins.

"I had a hunch the goblins were referring to you." The Pope had smiled. " I think they called you gooey bats."

The Pope wasn't afraid any longer. He had nothing but respect for the gooey bats. He didn't bother them, and they never missed him. Yet he knew the goblins were also trying to adopt this same approach. It was an approach he knew he would have to make some drastic changes to.

"This is far enough; release me at once!" He had stood up and demanded.

"Who said that?" asked one of the goblins.

"It wasn't me."

"Nor was it I."

"Shit! I thought I forbade anyone to speak! Isn't that what I said?"

"It was I!" The Pope had announced in flamboyant fashion. "Release me at once! This is far enough!"

Confused, the goblins had turned their attention towards one another.

They were still clueless as to where the voice came from. This was until they had turned in the direction of the Pope.

"Look! He's free!" one of the goblins had pointed out. "He's out of the ropes."

"Hey, what gives? One of the other goblins had yelled. "What do you think you're doing?"

The Pope didn't respond just yet. He had wanted to take a few seconds to clear his throat. With this borrowed time, he was shocked to discover he was no longer floating so freely through the air like a dog on an extended leash. This time, he was hovering in one spot, overlooking the goblins themselves. He didn't know what the goblins had in store, so he had prepared himself mentally for the worst.

"Now that you've seen what I've achieved with the grace of my Lord, you'll release me gently to the ground." He had felt it was key to mention this if he didn't want the goblins to just drop him. "Once you have complied with my first demand, then you will guide me back to my world without any funny business. There, we will go our separate ways. Do I make myself clear? Can you understand me?"

"Never!" one of the goblins had given the Pope the middle finger. "You'll die at our expense, in our world!"

"Now, did we make ourselves clear?" The second goblin had stomped his feet.

"Then you leave me no further choice!" The Pope grinned while revealing the two weighted stones.

The Pope was furious. He knew he wasn't getting the amount of respect he felt he deserved. He was only hoping to spook the goblins, not make them slouch over with laughter.

"Explain to us, weakling, what do you aim to do with those pebbles?" "Yeah, you can't even free yourself from the air!"

"Come on, child of God, show us something!"

"Show us a sign of your power! We want to see it!"

"Yes, convince us!"

The Pope's face was redder than a beet. He had never taken kindly to anyone who poked fun at the Trinity. This had also included the goblins, who he felt had faces only a mother could appreciate. He didn't want any trouble with them, though. He had kept his fingers crossed the whole time that everything would resolve itself without violence, but it didn't appear it would. In his own words, the goblins were just too bullheaded for anything reasonable.

"You say you want a sign?" He became furious. "Well, try this for measure! Here's your sign!"

In a fit of passion, the Pope reared back and faked as if he were going to throw one of the weighted stones in the direction of the goblins. Instead, he hurled it at the gooey bats, who responded by piercing the air with several loud squeals. Before he knew it, the gooey bats had vacated their posts and were spread out over the top of him. He could feel the heavy downspout of air that their wings had created, beating against his tired back over and over again. This time, he knew he had fooled the goblins with his intentions. He knew all along that the goblins were protected by a force field, the same one that had kept him confined to the air. He felt it was made obvious by the goblins' arrogant mouths, which he hated.

"Look at the size of those gooey bats!" he said with enthusiasm. "All twelve of them have to be over four feet tall, and their claws about ten inches long! At last, the little monsters are finally getting what they deserve! I do believe they are! Wait, don't bring them towards me! Take them elsewhere!" He had raised his voice.

He didn't enjoy the fact that the goblins were beginning to run underneath him.

"That's it! Let them follow you, demon!"

The Pope's blood was boiling. He was so excited by what he saw that he held his breath in anticipation of the moment the gooey bats descended from the air in unison like hawks after young hares. From his own position, however, he witnessed the goblins escape the gooey bats' razor claws by lying flat on their bellies. He didn't think this technique would work until he heard the gooey bats cry out in frustration. It wasn't long after this that he saw the gooey bats retreat to the sky. He hoped the gooey bats weren't about to give up on account of the goblins being too elusive for capture.

"What are you waiting for?" He was making reference to the gooey bats overhead. "Attack! Attack! Don't let the goblins get away! Launch one more assault!"

The gooey bats' lack of aggression was making him lightheaded. He knew the more the gooey bats stalled, the longer he would remain trapped and suspended within the goblins' invisible bubble. It was a confinement he wanted to see himself out of. For his life, he couldn't figure out why the gooey bats wouldn't finish what they had started when they clearly had the upper hand over the goblins. He knew if the roles were reversed, the goblins would have been so lenient towards the gooey bats. Still, he prayed the gooey bats were using the idle time to employ a new strategy—one which would tire the goblins out from hiding.

The Pope was no bonehead. He was certain his chances of successfully making it to safety would have to come from someone or something other than himself. He knew that without the assistance of an outside force, he would never be freed from the air. He knew the gooey bats were this force, even though he was aware they hadn't done anything worthwhile. However, just as he was ready to score a victory for the goblins, nine gooey bats dove towards the ground. In the process, all kinds of dust and debris were stirred up.

"Finally, another wave of action!" He clapped his hands together.

Somehow, through all this mayhem, the goblins found the tenacity to dodge the first of the eight gooey bats. Skillfully, the goblins managed to accomplish this by running crisscross. What the goblins didn't know, or suspect was that there were four more gooey bats right on their heels—the same four gooey bats who clawed and hoisted them into the night sky.

"Let us go! Let us go! We don't want to have our heads bitten off! We didn't do anything wrong!" The four goblins vociferated while kicking around in the air.

The way the gooey bats had their claws buried within the goblins' shoulder blades made the Pope feel remorseful. Like a bad dream, what was going on overhead had a strong influence on him. Being that he was a man of God and a man of forgiveness, he had never really wanted to cause the goblins any harm. Nor did he really want the gooey bats to do what they were doing—taking turns holding and eating chunks of flesh from the goblins' bodies. To say the least, he had only wanted to be released from the air and return to his world. A world he so much wanted to be an active member of.

"I don't know how much more abuse they can endure, but any minute, I should be freed from the air. My one concern is, I hope it's a gradual decline."

He had a right to worry. After all, he was more than sixty feet in the air. At his old age, he knew a drop from this height would kill him on the spot or break every fragment in his body. Yet, he couldn't help looking up at both the action overhead and the ground below. It was by design he had done this. One, he had wanted to be prepared for impact when the moment rose. Two, he didn't want the gooey bats to mistake him for a goblin. It was just how he was. He had never enjoyed being caught with his pants around his ankles, so to speak. Now was no different, with the level of danger involved.

"Oh, my! It's about to happen! It's about to happen!" The Pope had placed his fingernails in his mouth. He was making reference to one of the goblins, whose body was about to fall toward the ground as a result of having its head chewed off.

The Pope could no longer tolerate the violence. It was giving him chest pains. He knew, even as a youngster, he never had the stomach for watching anything gruesome. Thus, he had closed his eyes while turning away. Out of respect for the goblin, he had made a promise he wouldn't peek until he had at least heard the goblin's lifeless body smack the ground. Strangely, when it did, he felt himself descend about fifteen feet.

"That wasn't so bad," he thought, breathing heavily. Everything had happened so suddenly that he didn't even have time to yell. "I only pray the next three drops will be about the same."

Letting out a sigh of relief, the Pope once again turned his attention upward to the sky. What he saw were the gooey bats continuing with their dismemberment of the goblins. He didn't know how correct he was to think this, but he got the impression that it was something about the goblins' heads that the gooey bats found favorable. He felt this had to be the case for an animal to go through this much inconvenience. It wasn't natural—not even for this world, he further concluded. What else he thought wasn't natural was the neon yellow goo, which poured slowly from the heads of the goblins like soft taffy.

"So, that's how the bats got their name," the Pope pondered while massaging his chin in a downward fashion.

He was impressed by the goblins' biological makeup. It was like watching something straight out of a science fiction movie. He was also relieved that the gooey bats weren't doing what they were doing out of anger or pure nastiness but out of love for the neon-colored goo.

"Wait, what are you doing? What are you doing? Are you trying to kill me? You can't drop all three bodies at once! My word, they just dropped all three bodies at once."

Within minutes, the Pope felt his entire body grow frigid. He even experienced a minor setback in his ability to swallow. His worrying about his plunge didn't help his condition either. If anything, it made his situation more intricate as he held his breath in horror. He was trying to calculate in his mind the exact moment he thought the goblins' headless bodies would lose out to gravity. He was almost certain that he would be sent spiraling downward as a result, but what he got was another friendly jolt. Just as before, he had only dropped about fifteen feet when the second body landed below. Little did he suspect the other two bodies had fallen in separate locations. He couldn't see them, but he could hear them snapping branches as they fell among the weeping willow trees.

"I can't believe it, I'm free! I'm finally free! I knew you were watching over me the whole time, Lord!" The Pope kissed the soil beneath his feet. He knew if it wasn't for the weeping willow trees breaking the goblins' descent, he would have been a goner. "Please, Lord, don't make my journey back through the maze. I beg of thee. There must be another way out. There simply has to be."

Relieved that he had overcome his ordeal with the goblins, he crossed his heart and rose to his feet. But he was unsure where to go or what to do next, and the idea of going in the direction of the maze was absolutely out of the question. It was too risky. Not to mention, it would have been too much of a mental burden.

"A great plague in the sky; I think I better come up with something real soon!"

The Pope was alluding to the gooey bats overhead. What he saw had forced him to stagger backward. Like before, he had made a discovery. He had discovered that the gooey bats were lined up in a formation of attack. This wasn't too surprising to him. Not once did he suspect the gooey bats were on his side. He didn't even believe the gooey bats knew who he was, but he did believe they knew he was the one who had thrown the weighted stone at the tree.

Glancing downward, he made another startling revelation. It was one that made his jawbone drop out of place. He didn't know how, but the bottoms of his sandals were completely covered with goo. When an effort to remove the sticky stuff failed, he turned around and began to zigzag to his left. Aware that this would probably be the gooey bats' cue to unleash their claws on him, he sped up his pace. Never once did he blame the gooey bats for their misconduct. After all, he knew it wasn't their fault for thinking he was another meal.

"Wait a minute!" He stopped cold. He was pretty much dead on his feet. "I have an idea. I just hope it works." He couldn't see the gooey bats, but he could hear them in the distant background crying out.

The Pope was devious in his own way. He knew his only chance to get the gooey bats off his trail would be to get rid of whatever they were after. From his own personal observation, the gooey bats had poor vision. This meant the gooey bats would be susceptible to his trickery up to a degree. Feeding off this data, he unfastened the straps from his sandals and threw them in opposite directions as far as he could. He did this in an effort to divide the bats into two groups.

"It worked! It worked!" He began to jump up and down.

The Pope had wanted to stay and enjoy this moment. He even thought it would have been the perfect opportunity to catch up on some much-needed rest, yet he was timid that the gooey bats would return with a vengeance to repay him for his antics. Thus, he got scared and began to weave his way through the rows of weeping willow trees. Safety was his top priority—not to leave out his health, which was fading to the point where he was woozy and stumbling over his own two feet. He was all right, though, as long as he kept moving and stayed hidden within the cover of the trees' long limbs.

"The gooey bats would be fools if they came in this far after me. Fools who would knock themselves silly."

The Pope didn't care at the moment, but he was less than three feet from the spot where he first entered this world. This world of misfortune. On the bright side of things, he did notice how content the gooey bats had seemed to be with his sandals. He wasn't certain if it was the leather's jerky-like texture combined with the taste of the goo, which the gooey bats had found relishable. What had really mattered the most was that the gooey bats were no longer after him.

"Great, the sandals should allow me enough time to regain my strength," he confirmed while kneeling against the root of a weeping willow tree. "Now, I need to devise a plan to creep past the gooey bats. I hate to admit it, but still, it seems the maze is my only option out." He was about to weep openly into his palm until he remembered it was scorned by the gold coin. Thus, he used the sleeve of his garment instead.

The Pope knew he had no one to blame other than himself. It was he who had put himself in this predicament. In the end, he felt it would be up to him to direct himself out. No longer would he count on the Lord, Darr, or the souls to save him. It was his struggle now. He was about ready to get things underway when he felt something cold and hard creep around his neck. Being that he was in no position to see what it was, he tried to literally turn his body to one side. It didn't work. Whatever had him wasn't about to let go. If anything, he felt the pressure around his Adam's apple intensify.

"Stop. You're killing me," he uttered before becoming faint.

Chapter 10

The Pope knew he was a goner. He knew he didn't stand a chance against the force he couldn't see, but this was until he felt the pressure around his neck decrease. He couldn't explain why the opposition had relinquished their hold. At the time, it really didn't matter. What mattered most to him was that he was allowed to regain his composure. Oddly enough, it was from this point on that he realized something had changed. For one, he was suddenly back in his world. It was made obvious by the warmer climate, which in turn created a thick blanket of fog. It was also made relevant by the basilica and by the Lord's walkway of light.

The fog was so much of a problem that he had difficulty seeing past his own two feet on occasion. Yet that was only half of his troubles. Somewhere out beyond, he thought he saw the outline of a hideous figure. From what his brain was feeding him, the figure appeared to be stalking him while using the fog as a cloak. Was it Darr, or was it a monster of unknown origin?

"Maybe I'm hallucinating? Maybe there's no one out there at all? Maybe there's no one behind me even as I speak? If there was, I think they would have made their presence known by now." Still, the Pope wouldn't turn to confirm this. He was too preoccupied, staring off into the fog and chewing on his fingernails.

He wasn't certain how much time had elapsed while he was trapped within the maze, but in his heart, he had never expected to see the walkway of light again. He thought the Lord would have removed it. He thought this would have been gone the second he fell from grace. Now, all he had to do was walk out a couple of feet, yet that was easier said than done. Besides having a case of the jitters, he kept hearing this soft voice in his head telling him to turn around. When he finally did get the nerve to do it, he was greeted by a dark-skinned man dressed in ancient shepherd's clothing.

"So, it was you?" the Pope uttered while bowing. He was referring to the elderly-looking man who smelled like wild honey and whose beard and coarse gray dreadlocks could have used a thousand years' worth of salon care. "Wow! The angel Darr mentioned your existence! If it wasn't for you, I would still be trapped inside the maze! Thank you, thank you for everything! By the way, who informed you of my distress?"

The shepherd never smiled or said a word. Instead, he took his long staff, which was made of wood, and pointed it upwards at the sky. This was the same instrument he had used around the Pope's neck when he yanked the Pope back into his rightful dimension.

"Tell the Lord I am grateful," the Pope once again bowed towards the shepherd.

His Holiness had never felt happier. Besides feeling as though a ton of bricks had just been lifted off his body, he was also relieved by the shepherd's simple appearance. Unlike Darr, the shepherd looked to be created mostly from flesh and blood. The only visible hint of any supernatural existence was in the shepherd's eyes, which shined far and bright like two stars. Other than that, the shepherd, on the surface, appeared to be a normal man—a normal man with a distinct history of carrying out the Lord's testaments.

"Once more, words can't express how I feel. I will never erase from my mind what you have done for me. Because of this, I'm forever in your debt," he said while avoiding eye contact. "Oh, shepherd, none of this would have ever happened in the first place if I wasn't so zany. I'm sorry. Don't say it, but I know I must be a disgrace to Heaven."

He placed so much self-pity on himself that he was starting to feel embarrassed. No longer did he feel worthy of being in the shepherd's presence. If anything, the shepherd was beginning to remind him of how badly he had screwed up. To make up for this untimely error on his part, he wanted to get back with Darr and devote as much attention to the mission as he could, even if it meant he wouldn't be able to get much sleep. But before he could turn around and stride in the direction of the walkway, he was grabbed from behind by the elbow.

"Pardon me! I didn't mean to be rude. I just thought it was time I got back to the palace. You know, the others are probably worried sick about me," he tried to explain in a nervous voice.

The Pope was confused. He didn't know what to make of the shepherd's silence, nor did he know what the shepherd wanted from him. He wasn't a mind reader, although he could tell by the stern expression on the shepherd's face that the shepherd wanted to communicate something to him, something that was most likely important. As to what it involved, he had no leads.

"O great one of the Lord, is there something you would like to say to me?" If not, then he saw no reason why the two of them should continue to stare at one another. It was silly.

Again, the shepherd held true to form. He never spoke a single word. Instead, he took the Pope's hand, which contained the marking of the gold coin, and gripped it like he was giving a handshake. Not letting go of the hand, he positioned the handle of his wooden staff around the Pope's throat. Then he yanked it forward with his opposite hand until the two were cheek to cheek. It was at this time that he whispered something of Hebrew origin in the Pope's ear.

"Oh."

The Pope was taken aback by what had happened. It was the first time he had heard the shepherd speak. He didn't want to mention anything before, but he thought the shepherd was mute—someone with the inability to communicate verbally. Now, he didn't know how to take his present situation, especially when the shepherd spun around and shoved his face down into the dirt.

"Hey! What's the meaning of this? What did I do?" He had risen to his feet in a hurry. "Why did you... Why did you push me forward?" He knew this was a foolish question to ask if the shepherd was blessed with the same ability to read thoughts as Darr.

The expression on the Pope's face changed dramatically the second he lowered his eyes in the direction of the shepherd's torso area. No longer did he have a lingering attitude but a show of compassion, one which involved teardrops. These teardrops were for the shepherd, whom he could see had taken a pitchfork in the left breast, all to save his life in the name of the Lord's mission.

"You're injured! Will you let me be of some assistance?" he had asked while gently reaching for the pitchfork. He was attempting to help pull it out, but the shepherd had smacked his fidgety hand away before he could take hold of it.

The Pope didn't mean any harm. He had only wanted to do what was right. After all, he had felt accountable. He had felt guilty for what had happened to the shepherd, who seemed to be ticked off at him with good reason. He knew if he wasn't in the wrong place at the wrong time, none of this would have ever taken place. He couldn't stand it. He couldn't stand seeing how much grief he had caused. He knew if the Lord wasn't already upset with him, that was sure about to change, taking into consideration the new set of circumstances.

He was so enraged he was ready to go and do the unthinkable. He was ready to lay hands on the night assassin. He couldn't see the creature who had caused the shepherd bodily harm, but he could hear its cocky laughter. It was slicing through the blinding fog like sonar. If possible, he couldn't wait to see it with its throat cut. He wasn't a betting man, but he was convinced that this centaur from Hell was the same perpetrator who had come into contact with Peter.

"Child of innocence, standeth aside!" the shepherd had commanded as he snatched the pitchfork from his chest. Only for a brief spell did the Pope see the shepherd fall to one knee. Other than that, the shepherd showed no visible side effects, not even when he had motioned back and launched the pitchfork into the fog.

The Pope was left to ponder from that moment on. He didn't know whether the shepherd had struck the centaur or if the shepherd had only spooked it away. For one, he didn't hear any sounds of wincing, nor did he hear any more laughter. It was gone, and it was replaced by silence—a silence which he was wary to embrace. A silence which had, nonetheless, made him a little more cautious. This was because he didn't have the evidence to prove if the centaur was dead or playing possum.

"Did you get him? I can't see a thing, but I trust you can."

"Come." The shepherd signaled. By tapping his wooden staff three times on the ground, he caused the fog to briefly roll aside, the same way Moses had parted the Red Sea for the Jews. "The moment has arrived! Go back to thy world and do the will of the Lord!"

The Pope knew he wasn't the fastest person in the world; still, the shepherd couldn't match him step for step. He didn't know whether the problem was age or if it had anything to do with the shepherd taking a pitchfork to the chest. Something just didn't seem right, and his walking ahead of the shepherd didn't help to ease his mind. If anything, it made him feel disrespectful. He couldn't help it, though— not when he had knowingly tried on several occasions to cut his pace in half.

"Maybe we should rest for a minute?" the Pope paused to suggest.

While glancing down at the ground, he noticed that the shepherd had developed a bad limp. Nonetheless, he didn't want the shepherd to know this was his reason for stopping. He wanted it to seem as if it was more to benefit himself.

"Child, ye must journey the rest of the road alone."

"Your voice . . . It sounds so faint. Is everything all right? Maybe we should continue on together?"

"No. This is where we must part, for it is the way it has to be."

"But you're wounded," the Pope had tried to relay unto him.

"Indeed I am, child. Indeed I am."

The Pope could tell by the expression on the shepherd's face that he had never experienced pain of this magnitude before.

"Maybe if you escort me back to the palace, Darr can assist you."

"Ye have thy orders, child, so follow them!"

No longer did the shepherd have the meek voice of a dying man. It was instead replaced with hostility.

"Listen unto me; the angel Darr mustn't be distracted from the serious matters at hand! Nor shall he knoweth or be told of my involvement with thee!"

"But—"

"Don't intervene in affairs beyond thy control! Go! Do what I have instructed ye to do, for it is the will of thy Lord above!" The shepherd had nudged the Pope in the back with his staff. "Yet remember these words as ye depart: always serve thy Lord well! Serve him well. Serve him well, Pope Pius the Fourth."

"Bless you! It will be done! It will be done!" This was the shortest praise he could think of, on account he didn't want to use up any more valuable time. Not when the shepherd had the table set for his return.

The Pope had wanted to kiss the lighted walkway the second he had stepped foot on it. To his surprise, he was once again outside of the iron gate. This was the same iron gate that had served as a security barrier for anyone seeking admittance into St. Peter's Square. For the most part, he was very comfortable with his present position. One he knew he didn't have that far to travel; still, something was keeping him from pressing forward. Yet what could it be? Of all things, it was the shepherd's eyes. He couldn't understand for his life why they had suddenly become so dark and haunted. In a sense, this was beginning to irk him in a way that made him want to turn back around. Initially, he had told himself that he wasn't going to disobey any more orders.

He wasn't. He wasn't going to go through with it until he heard the reemergence of the centaur's laughter.

"Oh, my! I have to turn around! What if the shepherd's in danger?" The Pope had done so very hastily. "Look, I think he is!"

What had him in an uproar was the fact that the shepherd was helplessly on all fours as the silhouette of the centaur began to emerge from behind. To make matters worse, he had tried to yell, but nothing came out. He had even tried to use sign language, yet the shepherd never saw him. Thus, he could only grit his teeth and wish for the best. At the time, he didn't know whether the shepherd was praying or if the pain had worsened. He couldn't decide, not when the fog was beginning to dissipate his vision.

"Explain to me, Lord, how do I get myself into these sorts of binds? Why? Why does everything negative always have to center around me? What do I do to deserve this?" The Pope had begun to sob.

It was killing him mentally to watch this scene unfold. So much so that his body felt as if it were being tugged in two different directions. One was the palace, and the other was right there by the shepherd's side. Likewise, he wanted to go with the second option. However, every time he tried to step off the walkway, he could hear a familiar voice enter his conscience. It was the shepherd pleading with him to leave. Although he didn't want to believe it at first, it soon became a reality that the shepherd had the same telepathic capabilities as Darr.

"Get up! Please, get up!"

From what he could see, the shepherd was doomed. There was no nicer way to put it. He felt he had to intervene, even though he was aware he wouldn't be much of a physical threat to the centaur. Still, he figured he would at least be enough of a pest so the shepherd could escape to the safety of the lighted walkway. In his heart, he knew if he didn't act soon, it would be too late, for the fog was already in the process of swallowing the shepherd up. He knew that without the simple necessity of sight, he would be like a blind bird trying to guide its way across the sky. Yet when he had tried to step off the walkway, bolts of lightning had begun to fill every inch of the atmosphere. This fireworks spectacle, in essence, was followed by thunder, which was so violent it had caused the ground beneath him to tremble.

"This must be an omen!" he had cried out as the thunder and lightning were replaced by rain. By the time he could refocus on the shepherd's position, the fog had totally run its course.

The Pope had to press on. He couldn't stand the misery any longer. The raindrops were so cold that his entire body literally felt as though it were being doused with ice water. With this in mind, he had no choice but to jog up the walkway at a tempo he felt was comfortable. He knew this simple act was his only chance of bringing some much-needed warmth back to his legs, especially to his bare feet, which he could no longer feel.

The raindrops were no laughing matter to him, not when he was battling hypothermia. To keep from constantly being hit in the face, he had to tuck his chin into his chest. Thinking back, he could recall Darr saying that the lighted walkway was connected to the palace. He knew, despite the volume of the rain, it was a blessing in disguise. One, it had blocked out the evil beings he might have otherwise encountered. Two, it had helped wash away the filth he had acquired as a result of falling into that murky pit of water filled with animal bones and maggots.

"Lord, I'm almost there. I can see it. I can see the structure of the palace," he mumbled to himself.

Filled with newfound joy, he wasn't going to let anything stand in his way. He didn't care whether it was negative or positive. He was prepared to follow the walkway until he was at the door which led into the building. For some reason, he wasn't tired. Naturally, he knew it wasn't like him not to be. He figured it probably had something to do with the amount of self-pity he had placed on himself. After all, he had no idea whether the shepherd was alive or dead. He didn't even know how he was going to explain his lateness to Darr and his cardinals, for that matter.

"That's odd. It looks like every light imaginable is on inside the palace," he noticed as he made his way up a small flight of marble stairs.

The Pope was soaked from top to bottom when he approached two guards who were standing by the front entrance doors. Looking them up and down, he didn't recognize them. They weren't the usual pair of guards he had grown accustomed to, even though they were wearing the same traditional Swiss uniforms. No, these guards stood upright with too much honor. It was a trait he admired. What else he admired was the fact that the pair was tall and muscular. They were like giants in his eyes, giants who stood about eleven feet. Unlike the usual schoolboys who worked at the Vatican, this pair gave him the impression that they could inflict serious bodily harm upon anyone or anything. He knew this was a plus at the time, given the physical strength of the evil beings he had already encountered.

"Good gracious, even their wooden staffs are taller than I am." What else he had noticed were the exotic symbols depicted on them. "Indeed, Heaven must have sent them."

Earlier, when he had departed the palace, he had done so by way of the side entrance. Yet this time, he was going to make his decision based on security. Although he had fought long and hard with himself about changing his route, he kept it. He felt he wasn't going to let the guards intimidate or scare him away, not when he didn't know whether or not the lighted walkway had extended to the side of the building.

The best solution he could come up with was not to pay the two guards any mind. He didn't even want to glance up at their faces. Thus, he had put his head down and made a beeline directly for the doors. He was attempting to cut in between the pair when something had stopped him dead in his tracks. It was the guards. For some reason or another, they had obstructed his route with their staff by forming a perfect triangle.

"Wait, what's the meaning of this?" The Pope had become offended. "I have a right to be in there!"

Not knowing what to make of the guards' gestures, he thought it would be in his favor to take two steps backward. In conjunction with this, the guards had retrieved their staffs from the entranceway.

"Identify thyself?" Both of the guards had insisted in a tone that sounded more like a heavy growl.

Whenever the guards spoke, they were in alliance with one another. However, this alone had nearly made the Pope soil his underwear. One, he didn't know whether the guards were men or beasts who were portraying men.

"Greetings! I am Pope Pius the Fourth!"

"Human, by which way do ye seek to gain admittance?"

"I'm sorry, but I didn't understand your question. Can you please rephrase it for me without the allegory?"

The guards never spoke another word, nor did they once make visual contact with the Pope. In a sense, it was like he never existed. Still, why were they treating him like this? What did he do wrong unless they got wind of what had happened to the shepherd?

"Hello! Hello! I wonder why they're not responding to me?" he began to whine to himself.

The Pope was deeply hurt by his encounter with the guards. To him, it was like they had a personal vendetta against him. This alone made him feel as if he was a misfit or wasn't good enough. When in his heart, he knew the Lord would have never blackballed him from the mission. Fed up with the guards' silent treatment, he began to make his way towards the entrance. This time, he was prepared to scamper if necessary. Unfortunately, before he could do so, he was obstructed by the guards' same method of prevention.

"All right, I get the message loud and clear!" he said while taking two steps backward. "You do not want me to enter!"

Exactly like before, the guards had retrieved their staffs in conjunction with his movements.

"Human, by which way do ye seek to gain admittance?"

"By the same method in which Darr and the others entered!" he blasted off. The only reason he raised his voice was because he didn't believe he was getting the level of respect he felt he deserved. "I, too, serve the Lord! He has summoned me to do something special. He has summoned me to locate the sacred key!"

"Come! Enter the lost grip followed by the password!"

"Grip? Password? I don't know what you're talking about! Surely, you must be mistaking me for someone else! For I am the Pope of Rome! I belong inside of there!" he pointed.

"No one can enter inside without the correct requirements! No one! Not even thee!"

"Please! Please! There's no need to get so upset! Just let me retrieve the angel Darr, and we can put this whole thing—"

"Enough! Give us the response we demand, or we shall whisk thy soul from this world!"

Immediately, the guard standing on the left lowered his hand downward while tucking his staff underneath his armpits. "Ye may proceed!"

The Pope, for the umpteenth time, was in fear of dying. He, for one, had no idea what the guards were implying. This was until he saw something familiar on one of the guard's staff. It was a symbol; the same one the gold had left imprinted in his palm earlier. Relieved that his marking was now a religious one, he shifted his attention towards the guard's hand, which was suspended just above his forehead.

What he saw almost made his toes curl. It was the guard's hand, which, in reality, was nothing more than a giant lion's paw. Initially, he thought it was another illusion until he felt how sharp the claws were. Boy, was he fooled. All along, he had been thinking the guards standing before him were some form of superhuman created by the Lord. When, in actuality, they weren't. They were lions who only communicated and had the posture of men.

"So, I guess this would explain the heavy growls I heard," the Pope spoke in a low tone of voice.

"Come! It is time! Do what ye were instructed to do! Enter the lost grip! Enter it now!"

"Will you please give me a moment?" the Pope pleaded. "Talk about impatience." There was no hiding the fact that he had a phobia of lions. Even as a youngster, he had viewed them as savages. What had given him nightmares the most was the male species' mane.

The Pope was passive from the jump. He didn't quite know what to do until he remembered what the shepherd had briefly taught him. It was a grip, followed by a Hebrew word—a word he knew nothing about other than how to pronounce it. Though the guard's paw was much larger than his fingers, he felt it would be best if he administered the secret hold with two hands.

"Well, here goes nothing." He had taken a deep breath while biting the flesh from the inside of his cheeks. "I do hope I get this correct."

Once the Pope had administered the secret grip, the guard had never allowed him to retract his hands. Instead, the guard had begun to squeeze them.

"Please, my nerves can't take much of this. What did I do wrong? Will you tell me so I can fix it or try again!"

"Human, where is thy faith?"

"Hey, you're beginning to shrink! You're beginning to decline in size!" the Pope had exclaimed. He was so fearful of looking the guard in the face that he had tried on numerous occasions to turn or close his eyes. Yet he couldn't. He couldn't avert his attention long enough on account that he didn't know whether the guard meant him harm.

The Pope couldn't explain why he didn't collapse on sight at the guard's transformation. It was a modification period that had gone on for several seconds until both the guard and himself were the same height. But this didn't freak him out. What had made his spine tingle was the guard's paw, which had clung to his hands. Rather bizarrely, it had never changed. It had always remained the same—both enormous and deadly.

"The word. Have ye the word, human?"

"Oh, yes. How rude of me." The Pope had hesitated for a moment before whispering in the guard's ear. Much to his earlier prediction, the guard did have the face of a lion. A lion whose mane was well groomed, he noticed. "Is everything on the level?"

"The response thou hast entered was correct! Ye may now proceed onward!"

The guard had responded while releasing the Pope's hands.

Once the guard had returned to his original height, the palace doors were automatically opened from the inside rather than from the outside.

Chapter 11

"That odor! I can hardly breathe in here, let alone see without bending my eyes!" the Pope griped while covering both his nose and his mouth. His destination was the stairwell, which seemed like it was two hundred yards away instead of sixty.

Upon entering the lightly hazed palace, which reeked of ceremonial incense, he saw from the corners of his eyes a pair of guards standing on opposite sides of the doors. These guards, who had momentarily uncrossed their staffs so that he could walk by, were similar to the guards who were stationed outside. One of the two noticeable differences he saw was the gold medallions hanging around the necks of each of the guards. From what he could observe, the piece itself depicted a half-moon. He didn't know what this symbol meant. He guessed it was a mystery he would eventually have to solve with the help of Darr.

The Pope also saw a noticeable difference in the guards' height. Instead of being eleven feet tall, the guards inside measured in at a resounding seven and a quarter. Yet the guards still made a bold impression on him. What freaked him out the most, however, was how he could feel the hot air beating against the back of his neck whenever the guards exhaled. With this in mind, he never doubted that these smaller guards could perform the same duties as the much taller ones. Besides, he wasn't about to rule out the possibility of the guards being able to adjust their size either. He knew anything was possible whenever the Lord was involved.

What the Pope didn't know was that the lion-faced guards were actually called throne guards. They were the loyal protectors of the Trinity's inner chamber. It was this privilege that made many angels believe the throne guards held more rank than them. Rumor has it that the throne guards were created just before the revolt in Heaven. Rumor also has it that it only took a handful to cast the fallen angel Nero into Hell.

"I feel so weak; it's like I'm working against myself. It must be these damp clothes," he announced while leaning against the brass railing, which ran the entire length of the staircase. "What I need to do is rest here for a minute or two before I begin my long climb upward." At the time, he had one foot on the marble floor and one foot on the first step.

He knew from his position that he could determine how the first floor was set up. It was composed primarily of the throne guards he had passed by in the south and by two other sets of throne guards who had stood by corridors in both the east and west wings of the palace. Ironically, the corridor in the west had led to the same side door he had used to depart from earlier this morning. Yet the one in the east had led to a subdivided dining hall, which had also included a grand eating area for the Pope's cabinet and foreign dignitaries. The kitchen needed to service the dining halls, so seven gourmet chefs from various parts of the world were employed. They were expected to cook anything from Italian to French cuisine at a moment's notice.

The Pope was impressed with the level of protection he saw. It made him feel secure. It also made him feel as if he were staring at a live chessboard. He was even convinced that the Lord had throne guards strategically placed in other locations throughout the palace. To prove his theory correct, he had climbed the stairs to the second level, where he paused. There, he could see and hear three pairs of throne guards walking in rhythm like strict military soldiers. What impressed him the most about the throne guards were their high leg kicks.

"Oh, my! There's a pair coming straight toward me!" He dropped to his knees and crouched over in a fetal position.

The Pope's heart was ready to explode out of his chest. What had him so worked up wasn't the fact that the guards were coming straight at him. It was the fact that the guards held swords half the length of their bodies. In all reality, he thought the guards were going to seek some form of payback after what had happened with the shepherd, but they didn't. They had stopped and done an about-face within inches of his body.

"Lord, how can I ever repay thee?" He crossed his chest while springing to action.

Just as the relief was beginning to settle in, the Pope noticed something. It was a pattern. He observed that the guards would patrol a small, invisible border of space before turning back around. Over and over again, like clockwork, he watched the guards repeat this process.

"Wait a minute, how am I going to get by?" he debated with himself. "If I cross the guards' path, I wonder what would happen. I wonder if they would try to attack me. Then again, maybe they won't, but they look so serious—so deadly. I don't even want to assume that risk. However, I need to get by so I can climb the stairs to the third level. That's where Darr and the others are."

Never had the Pope seen intensity such as this, not even from Darr. It was indescribable the way the guards' movements reflected their willingness to serve and protect. In their pupils alone, he could see fifty or more guards standing before the throne of Heaven in a grand court session, each with their right hand over their heart. Unlike the present guards, the guards then seemed to be humble. They could often be seen dropping to one knee.

"Please, Lord, grant me a sign. For I don't want to be torn to pieces, even though I feel that I should."

Out of nowhere, the Pope heard a sound. It was a cough. It was the distinctive medical cough of Cardinal Kelso O'Connor, to be exact. For the last two years, it had become apparent to him that Kelso's health was starting to take a turn for the worse. He knew part of the problem was due to old age, and the other half was due to a heart attack, one which had almost put Kelso out of commission. He couldn't see Kelso or any of the others at the time, but he had a great idea where they were. If he were a betting man, he would have placed them just over his head, on the third level, where the sick bay ward was located.

"Hurry!"

"Who said that?" The Pope spun around in circles. "It sounded like a young woman."

"Hurry!"

The Pope didn't see anyone, nor did he recognize the voice. He had assumed it was just his imagination. Thus, he had gone about his business—the business of trying to locate a route past the guards, who never once acknowledged his presence. He was about to get the urge to do something rash until he saw the faint image of a beautiful woman standing before him in ancient attire. Strangely, the guards seemed to pass right through her perfumed spirit of innocence as if she wasn't even there.

"Hurry!" she pleaded. "You must join the others."

"Who are you? Where did you come from?"

Her colorless lips had never spoken another word as she stood there smiling.

"Tell me, who are you? I want to know."

"I am that I am," she replied in a distant voice.

"Are you the—"

"Shush," she told him. "Hurry, my child, you must rejoin the others. I will use my hands to alter the wheel that dominates time."

"I don't know what to say. I'm speechless, yet thank you. Thank you for all you have done for me."

The Pope felt like a new man—a new man who had been given a second lease on life. For the love of God, he couldn't figure out why a stranger was always being sent to encourage him to get back up when he had fallen on hard times. It was a mystery, but it was becoming a thing of regularity. He had also concluded in shame.

"Go, my child, for the way has been set. Run. Join in formation with the others and live up to thy title. Make it right, but remember."

"Remember what?" the Pope asked softly.

"Remember to always serve the Lord well."

"It will be done. You have my word on it."

The Pope had tears in his eyes, and his voice was starting to crack. He had felt all alone on a deserted island as he stood there and inhaled the fading aroma of perfume. Gone was the beautiful woman from his sight. She had left, not before opting to fulfill her promise to him—a promise which had frozen the throne guards where they stood.

With this opportunity, he maneuvered his way past two pairs of guards who were blocking his path to the stairs leading upward to the third level. He was cautious not to rub or bump into any of them, for he had a terrible vision of what would happen if they were somehow awakened. Since his chamber door was located to the right of the stairs, he was positive he could dash in and dash back out with a fresh change of clothing in minutes. He felt he had to do this for cosmetic reasons, as he was still drenched from the rain. Nor did he want to give the others the impression that anything unusual had taken place. He had figured that what they didn't know wouldn't hurt them.

"I can't believe it! There they are!" He pointed out while climbing the last couple of stairs. He was cheerfully referring to Darr and the others, who were only an arm's length away from entering the sick bay ward. "Wow! They, too, are in the same motionless state as the throne guards!"

Other than what the Pope had seen to his left, he had also spotted something else on this level—something that was absent on both the first and second floors. Something which had forced him to stop in his tracks. It was about twenty or so lion-faced archers who were positioned along the width of the top floor banister-like statues. Did they once have him in their sights? He wasn't certain, but he felt they had enough arrows in their quivers to fight for days. He was confident that, at their given angles, they could pick off an imposing enemy with ease. Yes, these were the Lord's sharpshooters, and he was aware that they were driven by the same intensity as the rest of the throne guards who had patrolled with swords.

"What's this?" he had asked while walking dumbfounded towards his chamber door. "Are my eyes misleading me?"

He couldn't believe it. He couldn't believe someone had found all of the pieces to his chamber door, nor could he believe it was once again sitting upright on its hinges. He knew if he wasn't the one who had destroyed it, then he would never have suspected that anything traumatic had taken place. Even when he had gotten as close as he was able, he couldn't find any evidence of the door or the framing ever being distressed.

"Great. I'm impressed, but let's see if that awful squeak was repaired in the press." He was more than prompted that it wasn't.

Gently, the Pope had placed his nervous hand over the knob. It was cold and hard to twist at first, so he gave it a little more oomph. The result was instant success, as his wrists had automatically locked into position. Without question, he was ready to open the door, but something had held him back. Something was preventing him from moving another muscle. What it was, he was starting to second-guess if there would be a supernatural life form waiting to greet him. At the time, he didn't care if that someone was good or evil. It didn't matter, not when he knew he had wronged both sides. What mattered was that he knew he was starting to waste a lot of time. He felt that he was going to brave the darkness and enter his chamber, or he wasn't going to. The choice was his to make alone; unfortunately, he knew he didn't have a lot of time to decide.

"Heck! I made it this far!" he said, kicking the door wide open. "To turn back would be a slap in the face. Then I would have to explain to the others how I got wet or how I lost my sandals."

This gave him all the more reason to enter despite the haunted atmosphere and the fact that he couldn't see a thing. Mentally, he wasn't really worried about either of the two. He knew these conditions were just temporary setbacks, ones that could be corrected with a flip of a switch—a light switch that was located somewhere along the left-hand side of the door frame.

"Come on, where are you? Where are you?" he had repeated, running his fingers nonstop down the course of the wall. He had always enjoyed talking to himself, especially when he was in a crisis. "At last, I found it! Now to turn it on!"

What the Pope saw had almost made him choke on his own tongue. It was his room. For some unexplainable reason, it was no longer in shambles. Someone had gone to the expense of straightening it up. Someone, but whom? From what he could observe so far, everything was back in its original state. Everything, even down to the page, he had marked off in the Holy Bible.

"It was you, Heavenly Father, wasn't it? You were behind this. You had to be, for this looks like the work of the greatest carpenter of all time."

The Pope was so moved by what he saw that he had fallen to his knees and crossed his heart three times by the foot of his bed. What had captivated him the most was how the Lord had paid attention to detail and had left nothing undone. Not even something as petty as the squeal of his hinges was ignored. Instead, it was fixed. It was fixed better than he could ever recall.

"Lord, please continue to stand by me. I know sometimes it may seem as though I give up easily. I don't. Well, sometimes I do get a bit discouraged, but I'm old. I'm not the man I used to be, yet I'm honest. Look at my body. It's wrinkled with time, yet I still make do and press on." He had stood up while stripping off his wet clothing. "Really, Lord, I'm a fighter! A fighter with one purpose in life: to see that your teachings live on forever in the conscience of mankind! And until the day I give up the ghost, I will continue to fulfill this legacy! Always! This I owe to thee!"

In a mad dash, the Pope had run stalk naked over to his wardrobe and froze. He didn't know how much time he had until the others were reawakened, so he swung the doors open and grabbed from the hangers another article of clothing exactly like the one he had taken off. However, it wouldn't fit. It was too tight around his hips. Thus, he dried his hair and body with it before tossing it aside. Embarrassed, he had reached in and selected another, one which matched the contours of his body. From what he could recall, this was one of his newer garments.

"Ah! That's more like it." He grinned as he leaned over and picked up a pair of brown leather sandals from the bottom of his wardrobe. After putting the sandals on, he closed the door and walked over to his dresser. There, he had taken out a pair of folded underwear.

The Pope was aware that it would have probably been easier to take his sandals off first before putting his underwear on, yet he didn't care. He had already completed the job. To bend down now and undo the straps, he felt, would have been a great misuse of time. Besides, he had something else on his agenda. Something which involved rummaging through his bottom dresser drawer. This was the same drawer where he usually kept news clippings and his religious journals.

"Where is it?" he had asked, fumbling around wildly in his drawer. "Where did I put it? I know I'm not losing my mind! I can't be, or am I?"

What he was searching for was a German-made pistol. One he had found in the gutters of Poland during World War II. A pistol that had brought him a lot of mental comfort after an attempt was made on his life. Since his recovery, though, he had hidden the pistol away. Only Kelso knew he had the weapon, but he never told Kelso where he actually kept it. He was too fearful Kelso would hold true to his beliefs and dispose of the device.

"There you are!" A weird glow had come across his face the second he had held the weapon against his chest. It was forged from heavy steel and was designed with an unconventional long barrel for shooting at further distances. Although he had never fired the weapon, he felt much more in control, knowing he had placed it in his left pocket. "I wonder why the Lord didn't take this away from me? I wonder why I was allowed to keep it?" He had thought for a moment as he slipped his bottom drawer shut with the tip of his sandal.

With the way society was, he knew he should have set an example and gotten rid of the pistol eons ago. He didn't. He had decided that he didn't want to be hurt anymore, especially by the hands of man. Nor did he want to give up his third form of protection. His other two forms were the Lord and the Vatican guards. True, he didn't think it was a sin to possess a pistol as long as he felt the owner acted with good intent. Still, he knew from being shot in the side how destructive a pistol could actually be if it ever fell into the wrong hands. However, five out of ten times, he felt it did.

Since Darr's disclosure of the mission, he had made it his top concern not to lag behind. Yet he felt he was doing just that. Maybe he was trying too hard? Maybe he was overanalyzing things? All wasn't totally lost, though. From what he had experienced in and out of the maze, he knew the Lord was making a conscious effort to work around his mistakes. This had given him the boost of confidence he felt he needed as he closed the door on his way out. Prior to that, he had flicked off the lights.

The Pope was in stride to finally join the others who were unfrozen when he discovered something. It was his face. It was dripping wet with tiny beads of perspiration. Nonetheless, he wasn't too stressed about this. He knew this symptom was most likely caused by having a loaded pistol in his pocket. A weapon that he wasn't about to surrender, only if Darr found out and insisted he do so. Other than that, he was going to keep it. He knew if he ever got the chance, he was going to set a lot of things straight with it, even if it meant he would have to fire off a couple of rounds.

"Kelso, speak to me!" The Pope had snuck up and hugged the senior cardinal from behind. "How are you?"

"Am I missing something?" Kelso shrugged away. "Damn it! Why were you annoying me the whole way here, and why are you perspiring so heavily?" He turned and rolled his eyes.

"Why, I had a little business to take care of. Don't take it so personally. Besides, I was enjoying the scenery."

The Pope winked at Kelso. He knew this simple gesture would loosen the tension between them, just as it had done in the past.

"Truth be told, I was also taken in by what I saw," Kelso said, raising his eyebrows before chuckling. "Zutermier was just commenting on how he could see and feel the presence of the Lord surrounding us like a giant blanket."

"Yes, I couldn't have said it any better myself," the Pope acknowledged. "The Lord's walkway and the new palace guards do tend to make a bold impression on one, don't they?"

"They sure do." Kelso turned to stare at the Pope. "What's wrong? Why are you looking at me in that manner?"

"Your face, Pius."

"What about it?"

"Why, you're sweating as if you were a lamb about to be slaughtered."

"Is it really that bad?" The Pope asked as he wiped his forehead with the sleeve of his garment. In order to do this, he had to turn his back. "It must be the heat."

He was worried. He knew if Kelso could detect something unusual about his persona, then he felt Darr would be able to do the same. Only he felt Darr wouldn't have to ask about a thousand questions. Instead, he could count on Darr to invade his mind with telepathy.

"You have it, don't you?"

"Have what?" The Pope snapped at Kelso. "Stop it, Kelso, for crying out loud! Don't try to put your hands in my pockets; that's very rude!"

"Shush! We're about to enter," said Zutermier.

Chapter 12

There was immediate silence as Darr and the others had begun to file one by one into a room. This was the sick bay ward, the last room at the end of the hallway on the third floor. Although rarely used for treating the terminally ill anymore, this room had since been used by past guests of the Vatican, who didn't want to give up the hospitality of the palace to stay elsewhere. To keep it simple, this was a large room divided into two equal halves. There was the left side, which consisted of two rows of four horizontal medical beds. Then, there was the right side, which was a mirror reflection of the left. The only difference between the two was that the right side had an entranceway to a bathroom.

In all, there were twelve beds total, and each one was constructed from thin pewter. Usually, there were no elaborate furnishings on any of the beds, just plain white sheets, which some said felt like cardboard against their skin. However, five of the beds on the left side appeared to be dressed with silk sheets and pillowcases. Where did they come from? Who could have put them there?

Two years ago, architects came in and stripped the walls bare of any decorative paper or religious paintings. This was done so the painters could paint the entire room white. The only problem was the priceless items were never returned. In fact, within four days, the architects had enlarged the only window in the bathroom. They had also installed new ceramic tiles, dual sinks, two new toilets, and a shower. Yes, they had made all of these modifications to a bathroom, which originally used to be home to a single sink and one noisy toilet.

"Think Darr needs a hand with Peter?" asked Kelso.

"No." The Pope had conveyed as he watched Darr gently lay Peter down on the first bed on the left. "He's fine."

"Is that food I smell?" Isaac had sniffed the air before laying Peter's unconscious body on the nearest bed to his left. "It has to be!"

"I do believe it is," the Pope had proclaimed.

"Still, ye are to remain here until I investigate the situation thoroughly," Darr had warned.

"Be our guest. We don't have a problem with it. Do we, Isaac?" The Pope had playfully elbowed him in the stomach.

"No, we don't, Darr." Isaac had rubbed his belly in anticipation of the feast.

"Good. Now, would ye please seal the door, Zutermier?" Darr had commanded. At the time, he was headed toward an enormous marble serving table at the back end of the room.

On the table itself was some baked rockfish, which was stuffed with Maryland crab meat. Not far from this dish was a large bowl of salad, some steamed vegetables, various pasta dishes, two loaves of bread, and some mixed fruits. Also on the table was a red serving cloth, some dining ware, five silver chalices, and two vases. One contained water, and the other a dark wine.

"What do you suppose Darr's looking for?" whispered Kelso.

"I don't know." The Pope had hunched his shoulders. "Your perception is probably better than mine," he had concluded as he continued to watch Darr stalk the table area.

"Wait a minute," said Zutermier. "Something's—"

"Darr appears to be reaching for—"

"What is it?" asked the Pope. "I can't see a thing. Darr can't eat food, can he?"

"No, Isaac. I don't believe Darr can or really need to," Kelso grabbed his forehead out of disgust. He had no interest in answering any more of Isaac's foolish questions. He was sorry he had let this one slip through.

"Buzzard," Isaac had gripped. "I don't know why you always have to act this way." He had directed his comments toward Kelso, who had turned red in the face.

"Let it end, you two. Let it end." The Pope had verbally intervened. "I won't allow you to cut up in front of Darr. Are you insane?"

"Look," pointed Zutermier. "I don't believe it."

"What is it, Zutermier? Tell me, what do you see?" The Pope had become impatient.

"Yes, I saw it myself," Kelso had grinned.

"Saw what?" Isaac had inquired while moving fast from behind Kelso.

"Will someone please inform Isaac and me what they saw? Because the only thing I see at the moment is Darr with his back turned towards us," The Pope had lashed out under his breath.

"What Darr has in his hand is a scroll," Zutermier had gleaned. "Need I say more?"

"No. No. It's probably just a detailed message from the Lord," The Pope had responded while looking down at his scarred palm, which he went to great lengths to keep hidden from the others.

The Pope was literally sweating bullets. He was concerned. He was worried if the scroll Darr was reading contained any information about himself. Judging by how long it was taking Darr to finish skimming over the words, he was convinced that it did.

"What was that?"

"Excuse me, Zutermier, but I think it was my stomach growling for food," Isaac had apologized.

"Food?" Zutermier had begun to chuckle. "How could your stomach possibly be growling for food when it sounded like you had just digested several of the throne guards?"

"Well, I am hungry enough to devour that whole table of food," Isaac had said.

"I bet we all could." The Pope had acknowledged the fact. "It sure smells scrumptious," Kelso had added his two cents.

"Worthy ones of the Lord, wait no longer. Please, come and rejoice at the cloth!" Darr had instructed them with open arms.

"In other words, it's time to eat."

"Since you put it that way, Isaac, I guess it is time." The Pope smiled as his cardinals started to walk side by side toward the back of the room. He was elated to see that Darr was in a pleasant mood.

"Wait a minute!" Kelso had caused everyone to freeze in their tracks. "What about Peter?"

"Pope Pius, do you want me to leave or carry him with us?" Isaac had walked over to Peter's bedside. "You know, he hasn't said a word the whole way here."

"That's a good question." The Pope had thought it over. "Isaac, leave Peter where he resides. He can be seated at the Lord's table later. Right now, his rest is more important to me."

Not saying a word, Isaac had done as he was told. He had left Peter behind while glancing across the room at the table—a table which he thought resembled the one depicted in the scene from the Last Supper. Like that scene, he had observed that everyone had sat in the same row. Since Darr held the highest rank and was the leader of the mission, he wasn't surprised when the angel had elected to be seated in the center with the Pope and Kelso off to the left.

"Well, Isaac. Are you going to join us at the table, or are you going to continue to stand there?" The Pope had raised his eyebrows. "Come on, come on. Grab a seat to the right of Zutermier." He had motioned with his hands.

"Oh, I'm sorry. I didn't mean to keep everyone waiting." Isaac had glanced up and frowned. Unfortunately, he wasn't expecting to be the main attraction. He had simply forgotten where he was.

Embarrassed, Isaac rushed over to the table and took his seat to Darr's right. Looking down in the opposite direction, he could see that no one was really lingering on what had occurred except for Kelso, who had his hands smothered over his face. Yet he wasn't shocked by this. After all, he knew from firsthand experience that this was Kelso's normal way of reacting, especially whenever Kelso thought he was behaving like an imbecile. He wasn't upset, yet he didn't take too kindly to Kelso showing him up in front of Darr. To him, it appeared as though Kelso was trying to force his impressions upon Darr, who was glancing straight ahead at the moment.

"Please, if I can have everyone's undivided attention," Darr had stood up and announced. "The Lord has made this possible. He has united us here, as one at this table, one which He has anointed with His prayers. Bless this food which ye are about to eat. Bless this bread which ye are about to break, and bless this drink which thy mouths are about to savor. Many have received their spiritual calling in life, but few have ever been called to serve the Lord in a manner such as this. Today, this great honor has been bestowed upon each of thee. It is through the grace of the Lord that the impossible is made possible. Salute, for He is the Son and the center of His Father's universe. Need I say more?"

"Amen." The Pope and his cardinals had spoken in unison.

"Behold, ye may now begin to fill thy bodies with whatever is desired," Darr had informed them upon being seated.

"Darr, I take it that you won't be joining us?" The Pope thought he would ask before the others and himself had scattered about the table in an effort to fill their plates.

"Perhaps not, but I will sip some wine from Peter's chalice," Darr had informed him upon reaching and doing so with his long arms.

Zutermier and Isaac each had a little bit of everything piled on their plates as they sat back down and began to chow away. The same, nevertheless, couldn't have been said for the Pope and Kelso. Although they both were placed on strict diets by their personal physicians for medical reasons, they each had a plate full of salad without dressing and a baked piece of striped bass. For drink, the two had selected water.

"Isaac, since you're in motion, will you do me the honor and pour me another glass of wine? That is when you have taken care of yourself."

"Sure, Zutermier. I have no problem with that. Better yet, I will pour yours first."

"Remember the Lord's mission!" the Pope had reminded them as he watched Isaac fill Zutermier's chalice. "I don't want either of you to consume too much of that stuff! We may need to act sooner than we think!"

The loaded pistol in the Pope's pocket was a reminder of this—a reminder that he had some unfinished business to settle with the centaur near the maze, the one who had wounded both the Lord's shepherd and Peter.

"Calm thyself, O noble one! Let them enjoy all that has been put forth," Darr had said rather convincingly. "For no one knows the strict urgency of this mission better than the Lord. Do you disagree?"

"No," the Pope had answered.

"Then, in knowing the ways of the Lord, why would ye suspect him of placing intoxicating wine before this table?"

"I guess you have a point there," the Pope grinned at Darr before turning his attention back toward his plate of half-eaten food. "Although on this planet, we Catholics often associate wine drinking with drunkenness—a social act that distorts one's judgment," he had concluded while placing a crunchy piece of lettuce in his mouth.

The Pope wasn't trying to be a comedian. He didn't even believe what he said was that humorous. Still, the Cardinals couldn't help themselves. They couldn't stop giggling when he had hit his cue.

"I can assure thee, Pope Pius, that this grape is a nonthreatening one. Worry thyself not," Darr had told him. A hint of joy could also be detected in the angel's voice.

"Darr's right. Why is the wine we serve at communion stronger than this?" Zutermier made light of the situation.

"It's not the wine I'm worried about. Trust me." It was the Lord's shepherd and Peter whom the Pope had concerns for. From where he was seated, he had a great view of the fallen cardinal's body.

"Darr, this food was scrumptious! Who prepared it?" Zutermier had wanted to change the subject.

"I have to admit. It did taste unlike anything from this world. And believe me, I have sampled many different styles of cooking in my lifetime," Isaac had gone out on a limb to announce. "For once, I'm full, but my body feels light. It almost felt as if what I had eaten didn't contain any calories. Why? Why is that so?"

"Usually, I don't necessarily agree with what Isaac says or does. Perhaps this time, he's correct. Darr, who did prepare this healthy feast in our honor?" Kelso had wiped his lips.

Everyone was finished with their plates except for the Pope, who was a gobble away from doing so himself.

"Chosen ones, who would ye have me say prepared it?"

"Someone from Heaven, of course," Kelso had rubbed his belly.

"Well, cometh again!" Darr had told him.

"It has to be. It's the only logical explanation."

"If it wasn't someone from Heaven, then it had to be the throne guards outside. Yeah, that's it!" Isaac had replied.

"No. That isn't correct, either. However—"

"Wait a minute, Darr. Can I have a stab at it?" Zutermier had asked politely.

"Then respond," Darr had folded his arms.

"Don't mind if I do." Zutermier had stood up. "I know one thing is for certain, and that is the food, the china ware, and the silverware were all native products from inside this palace – not to mention the silk bed fashions. However, the chalices, the table, and the matching bench had to have come from outside the storage room. You know, the one Peter had mentioned."

"But how can you tell?" Isaac had wanted to be enlightened.

"Look closely." Zutermier had demonstrated as he lifted his silver chalice to reveal a signature on the bottom. "This person is from the early Renaissance period, would you agree?"

"It's true, Isaac. This marble table, along with the matching bench, is some of the lost work of Michelangelo himself." The Pope had cared to brief him.

There was no way Isaac could deny this was true. Not when he had seen the evidence with his own eyes. It was a signature carving of Michelangelo himself, along with two other well-known artists from that time period. One artist's name was on the bottom of the silver chalices, and the other's name was on the flip side of the red serving cloth, which was made of velvet.

"Behold, the Pope and Zutermier are correct with their responses!" Darr had stood up and applauded before being seated.

"Sure they are." Kelso couldn't deny this. "I knew this much for myself. Still, the question remains: who prepared the feast?"

"Please allow me, Darr," Zutermier had turned and elected. "Why, Kelso, our own staff prepared it."

"That's blasphemy!" Kelso had lost control while covering his ears. "Pure blasphemy!" He didn't want to hear anything else. He couldn't believe it. He couldn't believe that Zutermier had let such a remark come out of his mouth. Of all people, he would have never suspected Zutermier to say something so ridiculous, especially with Darr still present.

"Kelso, that's rude! Take your hands down! What has gotten into you?" The Pope had looked him square in the face without batting an eye.

"There's no way you can tell me that our own staff prepared this meal! You can't! It's too perfect!" Kelso had shaken his head repeatedly. "No! No! No human on the face of this Earth could cook this well! This is the healthiest meal I have ever eaten! Even my own doctor couldn't have prescribed a more suitable diet! Darr, tell them! Convince them that what I speak is true!"

"It's true." Darr had spoken to Kelso in a calm manner. "Thy own staff did prepare this meal."

"But how?" Kelso had implored while taking a sip of water. For a moment, he thought that Darr was concurring with him. "How were they able to accomplish this?"

"The Lord is working through them. The same way He used the Babylonians to destroy the temple."

"In other words, nothing out of the ordinary has really changed then?"

"For some, this is correct." Darr had seemed to hesitate for a second. "Yet for the rest, the Lord has put them under a deep sleep. As ye may have noticed upon entrance to the palace, it is heavily guarded. It is for their souls as well as yours. Only the Trinity, or possibly the evil angel Nero, can unlock their chambers."

"That's why we must aid you in recovering the sacred key!" The Pope had jumped up and pleaded his case. "It's the only way to put an end to Nero's plans for total world destruction!"

"I don't understand," said Isaac. "Why would Nero want to destroy the whole entire planet? How would the dark one seek to capitalize on this?"

"Gain?" The Pope chuckled after being seated again. "You want to know how Nero would gain from this? Do you really?"

"Yes, besides supremacy over the Earth," Isaac was quick to point out. Isaac knew this much for a fact. He wasn't a lame brain, nor did he want Darr to have second guesses about that. What he wanted was for someone to elaborate further on the powers of the sacred key and how it basically tied into this world of his.

"Let me clear one thing up. I wasn't trying to be sarcastic, Isaac. The truth of the matter is that it's probably too difficult to put into words what Nero has in store for this generation of ours and the one to come. Yet, I'm certain, given Nero's reputation, we can expect dark times ahead. Maybe some of the darkness in the history of mankind. Still, like I said, it's really too hard to say, so we'll just have to use our imaginations," explained the Pope. He had a nervous look about him. "Isaac, I take that back. Expect all hell to break loose! Expect life as you know it to be flipped upside down!"

"Nothing is over yet!" Kelso grunted. "So I say to the two of you, this conversation of yours never took place! Forget about it. Wipe it out of your minds! That's a must!"

"This may seem a bit crude coming from myself, yet in many instances, the fallen angel Nero is like our Father. They both love to be admired and feared in the same sentence. Unlike our Father, Nero is incapable of compassion and is incapable of creating any intelligent forms of life of his own. Up until the time of Natas Christopher's escape from Heaven, Nero's only purpose in this world was primarily to cause torment. Now, that could change. If Nero is capable of decoding the sacred key, that would, in turn, unlock the genetic chemistry of all things in life, including the makeup of myself."

"Then not only would that spell doom for Earth, but doom for the kingdom of Heaven as well!" Zutermier had come to this fully drawn conclusion.

"Oh my! This doesn't sound too promising!" Kelso had become sick to his stomach as he pressed his belly together with both hands to relieve the natural urge to vomit. "I almost hate to mention it, but this could give Nero the distinct advantage of the angel-making department!"

"I won't lie to thee, yet ye may have a point. However—"

"However?" asked the Pope. "Please continue, Darr. We want to be informed."

"As ye may," Darr had signaled with a slight nod. "In order to create beings similar to myself, Nero would have to give of himself in a way that would reduce his powers. It's like thou stated, one would have to go with the odds when ye take into consideration the history of Nero."

"And what are the odds?" Zutermier had wanted Darr to spill the beans.

"They are three to one in favor of Nero not subjecting himself to this risk. For I was once told by Gabriel that Nero was always too conceited and envious for his own good."

"Darr, if you don't mind my asking—"

"Please, feel free to ask me whatever."

"Thank you," Isaac had responded. "What I would like to know is how often God creates angels of your magnitude?"

The room had grown silent as Isaac's body had begun to tremble. He prayed that he wasn't inquiring about anything top secret. He wasn't trying to be nosy; he had just wanted answers.

"Angels are created on a periodical basis, but why do ye seek to know the answer to this?"

"For I was only curious," Isaac had replied while taking a deep breath. "That's all."

"Curious about what?" Darr had sought to find out.

"Curious to know if the Lord also weakens whenever He creates many angels like yourself?"

"Thou hast shocked me! This is a unique question!" Darr had told Isaac. "Yet, unlike Hell where there is one, in Heaven ye have the Trinity. Yea, it is through all three that angels are created. This also applies to the throne guards who surround this palace."

"Thank you for sharing this with me," Isaac had graciously said.

"Darr, I would like to ask you something as well, if you don't mind?" "Feel free to ask it, Kelso."

"Darr, the others, and I couldn't help but notice that you were reading something when you first made your way towards the serving table. And if what you stated is true about the Vatican staff who prepared this meal, then did one of them also leave behind the golden scroll? If not, then who did?"

"Kelso has a point there. Who did, in fact, leave behind the golden scroll, and what did its contents allude to?" The Pope could only scratch his head. "I know for certain that the scroll which I received during the early part of the day was written by the Lord but delivered by an unknown source."

"When did this happen?" Kelso had whispered in the Pope's ear. "You never told us about any of this."

"Can you explain this, Darr?" Zutermier had held his breath as he sat anxiously on the edge of his seat. What Zutermier had really wanted was a supernatural explanation of what had transpired. Something far-fetched. Besides Darr's physical features and the palace guards, he was starting to become accustomed to the scenery, which he thought to be normal at times. What he thought could change his view was for him to witness a miracle or at least hear of one.

"Listen to me, the scroll was a written message from the Lord, addressed to myself. I know. I know I'm getting to it, Kelso. I can read thy thoughts; just be patient." Darr had cut Kelso off before Kelso could form a mouth to utter anything.

"Stop it, Kelso! Contain yourself!" The Pope had turned and snapped. "Sorry, I apologize. Do continue, Darr."

"Unlike the Pope's scroll, this scroll in particular was left behind by the archangel Gabriel. This was done well after thy staff had placed the food in this room. Do ye want to know something else?"

"Sure!" The Pope had elected to speak for the others.

"The vase of wine, which none of ye thought to pinpoint its origin, was also left behind by Gabriel. It was a dinner gift to thee. A dinner gift to congratulate everyone on thy commitment to serving the Lord in this time of need. Once again, I, too, thank you." Darr had stood up and applauded before being seated in his rightful place.

"Holy cow! You mean to tell us that the mighty Gabriel was within these very walls?"

"This is correct." Darr had said unto Isaac, who looked as if he was going to faint backward onto his head.

"So, where did the wine which Isaac and I drank come from?" Zutermier had wanted the details. "Was it conceived in Heaven or on Earth?"

Zutermier couldn't wait for Darr's reply. Neither could anyone else.

"Actually, as the story was told unto me, it was once water. Water which was gathered from a well in the region of the world known today as the Middle East."

"Water?" Zutermier had lightly contested.

"Yes, water!" Darr had confirmed, pointing to the object of discussion.

"Do you doubt this?"

"No!" The others had spoken in unison. They had no reason not to.

"But how did this transformation occur?" Isaac had become intrigued.

"It occurred when Jesus was asked by his mother, Mary, to turn several vases, like the one before thee, into wine. Need I say more?"

"No. No, you have said an earful," the Pope responded while pouring his chalice of warm water over his head.

Even though the Pope's stunt had brought on an onslaught of laughter, he felt he needed to do this. He felt he needed to momentarily wake himself up.

"Darr, correct me if I'm wrong, but that story, which was a great biblical one, would date that wine to be over a thousand years old."

"This is true," Darr nodded. "At the time, whatever wasn't consumed at the wedding celebration was brought to Heaven by angels. You see, this was Jesus's first recorded miracle."

"Then, before I lose my humanity, will someone please pass down that container of wine?" Kelso insisted while imploring the accent of a southern gentleman. "Come on, my palate lingers for it."

"You old buzzard, not until my stomach bursts!" Isaac laughed as he jumped up from the table. There wasn't any doubt; he wanted the wine all for himself. This became evident when he continued to drink from the vase like some half-crazed drunk.

"Cut it out! Look what you're doing! You're spilling more down your face and neck than you are down your own bloody throat! Give it to me!" Kelso confronted Isaac. "You heard me. Share some with the rest of us! Come on, where's the decency? Don't ignore me!"

Kelso became so enraged by Isaac's foolishness that he wrestled the wine away. In doing so, he also slung Isaac's chest first onto the floor.

"Child of the Lord, spare me that scene! Don't retaliate against thy fellow brother! Please, be seated!" Darr had stood up and communicated.

"I do apologize. No hard feelings were ever intended," Isaac smiled as he made his way back to his seat. "I don't know what came over me."

With both hands surrounding the vase, Kelso firmly placed his lips onto the vase and began to allow the contents to pour down his throat. It was as cold as it was refreshing to him. A light wine, which was more suited to be in the flavored water category, he had deemed. Yet he felt it was an honor to have it in his possession, and when he had his fill, he had passed the vase unto the Pope, who had taken two sips before lying it back on the table.

"That sure did hit the spot," Kelso had loudly sighed.

"That it did," the Pope couldn't disagree as he turned to glance at Darr and Zutermier, who were both in the process of consoling Isaac.

Other than a case of the chills, the Pope had felt the same. The wine he observed had done nothing out of the norm to alter his body's chemistry. From what he could tell, none of his cardinals had changed. Thus, he had assumed the real threat was a physiological one—one which he thought was based on the knowledge of knowing that Mary, Gabriel, and Christ himself had once touched this very vase.

"Darr, there's one last question which remains on my mind," the Pope had sounded somewhat disturbed. "What was written on the scroll? I take it there wasn't anything on there about me, was there?" He knew this was a lame thing to ask, especially when the loaded pistol at his side was a constant reminder of what had taken place near the maze.

"No," Darr had paused. "What the scroll had contained was an up-to-date status report, which brings me to what I'm about to say next. I will be leaving thee shortly to address some important matters in person."

"Wait a minute! You can't abandon us!" Kelso had become livid. "For we don't know what direction to go in without you!"

"Exactly. Who will guide us in your absence?" Zutermier had also felt a need to be concerned.

"Yeah, who will we get to protect us from the clutches of evil?" Isaac had become both curious and nervous if there ever was such a thing.

"Oh, I feared this would happen! I kept telling myself! I kept telling myself!" Kelso had repeated twice as he hid his face beneath his fingertips.

"Kept telling yourself what?" The Pope had snatched Kelso's hands away. "I kept telling myself that if Darr left, we would be hung out to dry."

"Silence! What has gotten into thee? Aren't ye aware that the mighty Father will always be there to guide and comfort thou, even if death were to reveal its face? I was told that the Pope of Rome and his cardinal would know of this which I speak! Do I stand to be corrected?"

"No." The Pope had shouted. He had found it a little difficult to speak on behalf of his cardinals on account of a bulge in his throat.

"Then what's the problem?" Darr had stood up from the table, drawing everyone's undivided attention. "Ye have to have faith! Behold, this is the problem with this world! Mankind has no real credence in the Trinity! Since the dawn of his creation, it has been this way!"

"I don't understand what you're implying, Darr. There's nothing wrong with our faith. Why, all of us here believe in the Trinity."

Kelso didn't like the fact that Darr, of all people, was questioning this. Nor did he enjoy the fact that Darr was raising his voice.

"If thee had faith, then how could ye even entertain the thought of being abandoned? How could thee, when the Lord has provided thee the very guards which surroundeth His throne?" Darr hollered as he slammed his fists into the center of the table, creating multiple cracks throughout it.

"You didn't have to go there!" Kelso had sprung up and confronted Darr from a distance. "All we ever asked... All man has ever asked was to be pointed in the right direction!"

"Control yourself!" The Pope had turned pale as he reached out and pulled Kelso back into his seat by way of his elbows. "Are you aware of whom you're arguing with? Are you? The Lord will strike you down for this! Down! Down into the ground!"

"I'm sorry, Darr." Kelso had wasted no time in apologizing while wheezing for air. "I didn't mean to lose my sanity, but put yourself in our places. Then you'll see that, unlike yourself, we never had any prior training on how to conduct a search for a supernatural artifact."

"And let the truth be told, we know nothing about this Natas Christopher character either. Heck, I've never heard his name until you arrived," Isaac had stated while staring into Darr's face. It was a bold move, but he was trying to determine whether Darr had calmed down or if Darr was still ruffled around the collar. "I always thought a reptilian was a myth created by the internet, but now we're talking about a hybrid reptilian."

"What the others are really wanting to say is that we only know what you tell us. That's why none of us want you to leave, even though we see you must. You're our guide, Darr. We feed and react to your information, but please don't take this human emotion as a sign of frailness. For each of us will gladly give our souls in the name of the Trinity." Zutermier was so sincere that he walked around the table and succumbed to one knee. "When you return, will you show us? Will you show us, Darr, how to recapture the lost item?"

"Arise, Zutermier. Arise and return to thy seat." Darr had stood and bowed. "Will ye all find it in thy hearts to forgive me for my aggressiveness? Yes, Kelso was correct. We are two different types of beings who live two different kinds of lives. Mine is in Heaven, and thine is here on Earth. While I have a physical bond with the Trinity, ye have a spiritual one. However, our love for the great ones is equal."

"When will you be returning?" The Pope didn't want to keep Darr any longer than necessary.

"Sometime tonight. Perhaps when ye are fast asleep," Darr responded.

"Still, that depends on my investigation."

"I can live with that," Kelso nodded in approval.

"Good. And to add to thy comfort, two throne guards will be assigned to thy inner quarters. They are right outside this door as I speak. Yet let me be the first to warn everyone: ye are not permitted to harass the guards in any way. Nor will the guards allow ye to exit this room without the proper grip or password, which none of ye have. Each section has its own. Are we up to date on this?"

"Sure, Darr," the Pope and his cardinals spoke in unison.

"That pleases me, for it is the will of the Lord that this be communicated unto thee."

"I take it this was written on the scroll as well?" Zutermier could only imagine.

"Indeed," Darr answered while walking towards the front of the room. "You aren't about to leave us now, are you? For we still need to get a few personal items from our rooms." Kelso became worried. Besides clean underwear, his heart medication was another item on his long list.

Darr said nothing. He didn't even turn to acknowledge Kelso. Instead, he paused by the entrance door and gave it three distinct raps with his right fist. A second passed, and three return raps were administered from the opposite side. Taking heed of this signal, Darr then opened the door and told two guards with pointed metal staffs to enter in Hebrew. One guard had stood to the left of the door, which Darr had closed, and the other to the right.

"Remember everything which I have told thee," Darr had pointed out as he began to turn his back towards the Pope and his cardinals. "These guards and every guard who is in or around this palace with a face like theirs are acting under the strict commands of the Lord. Although their intent is not to harm thee, please do not test their patience. It could prove to be to thy disadvantage."

"I hate to be rude, Darr, yet I don't think I will be able to get much sleep with the guards breathing in and out like that. It's even worse than Kelso's snoring," the Pope had commented with a smirk.

"Thanks. Thanks for throwing me under the bus," Kelso had rolled his eyes. "Still, I will say one thing in my defense, Darr. I will have you know that there's no odor keener than the smell of the Pope's sweaty toes."

Everyone had fallen out with laughter, including Darr, who had laughed with his head aimed toward the ceiling.

"I do see thy concerns. The guards are kind of noisy. So, to add to thy comfort, the guards will not enter this room unless someone requests them or when the Pope himself falls asleep. Those are the only options which I can give unto thee," Darr had made this perfectly clear.

"Then we will take this option." the Pope had responded before his cardinals could have a chance to voice their opinions.

To be perfectly honest, the Pope had seen no need for the two throne guards. He didn't even want them to enter when he had fallen asleep. Was he being foolish? He just didn't see a need for them to keep such a watchful eye over the others and himself. He guessed this was partially due to his fear that they would spoil his plans to rescue the Lord's shepherd once Darr had left.

"Do they talk?"

"Does who talk? Whom are you referring to?" Zutermier had wanted Isaac to be more specific.

"I'm referring to the two guards by the door. You know, the lion-faced ones right there." Isaac had made it known as he walked towards them.

"I'm afraid not," Darr had responded. "The Trinity didn't create these two with that function."

"Come on, Zutermier, have a look with me. I have never seen a lion before, not in person, anyway. I want this to be a memorable experience," Isaac had proclaimed, stopping ten feet in front of the guards. Zutermier was soon to follow.

"So, what do ye think?" Darr was referring to Isaac.

"T-T-The guards are much larger than I had earlier anticipated! J-J-Just look at the muscle definition in their arms and legs alone!" Isaac had stuttered. "Why, not even Earth's greatest bodybuilder could achieve this!"

"It's the truth! Even their heads are about double the size of a natural lion's!" Zutermier had exclaimed.

"I don't know. The guards just look and sound so fierce. Maybe it's just my nerves have gone bad, but I really do think Zutermier and Isaac are treading on thin ice being that close. Maybe you should say something to them," Kelso had forewarned.

"Maybe you're right," the Pope had thought it over. "Maybe they should show the guards some respect."

"Except for the Trinity, no one else really knows the true boundaries of the guards. They are shrouded in mystery. Believe me, it has remained this way before I was ever created. However, I have heard about one in particular who attempted to test their power, but he was cast out of Heaven along with his followers like stones thrown into a lake."

"Ahhh! I have a good idea in mind, which is to whom Darr is referring:" Kelso had arched his eyebrows while pointing downward with his thumbs. He was making reference to Nero, the ruler of Hell.

"So, the throne guards are the enforcers? But you are also both an enforcer and an ambassador of goodwill as well?" The Pope has slightly turned his head towards Darr.

"This is true, yet the throne guards are probably the most loyal of all God's creations. Yet, at times, they can be both savage or unpredictable to anyone other than the Trinity. Not to mention that, like myself, they have never been in the presence of man before. To make a long story short, Zutermier and Isaac should rejoin us at once! Ye can summon them, or I will!"

"No. No, I will do it." The Pope had frowned his face away from Darr. "You must be leaving us shortly."

He knew the longer Darr stayed, the more complicated things would become. The more the loaded pistol would burn at his side. He also knew the chances of finding the Lord's shepherd alive would decrease. Those were odds he couldn't live with.

"All right, you two, that's far enough!" The Pope had communicated in a deep voice. "Leave the guards alone! Come on back! The show is over!"

"Look! Isaac didn't hear a word you just said!" Kelso had become livid. "He's starting to move closer! See what I mean!"

"Isaac, did you hear what I said?" The Pope had tried to gain his attention by clapping. "Stop being so bullheaded! You are to come back at once! Return! Return! Return! Darn it, I think he's totally ignoring me."

"Do you want me to grab him?" Zutermier had stopped and asked. He was about halfway back. "Because it wouldn't be a problem."

"No, just come on back." Kelso had motioned with his hands. "There's no need for both of you to be in harm's way."

Zutermier had done as he was told and returned, but Isaac didn't. He had begun to shuffle his way even closer. He did this despite the Pope calling him from afar, which he could hear. Still, he knew this cadence alone wasn't enough to break his forward progress. He was in awe of the guard's gold medallions, which he had every intention of touching. He didn't understand why at the time. He guessed his mind was just magnetized by the throne depicted on each piece. What he didn't know was the closer he got, the louder the guards' growls had become. To the others, it had looked as if he was fighting his way through a severe windstorm, one which he was about to lose.

"Darr, you must do something! You have to stop him! You have to stop, Isaac!" The Pope had pleaded on his knees while grabbing a hold of Darr's garment. "The guards have their staffs drawn and pointed towards him."

"Guards, this human knows not what he does! He is not to be harmed! It is the will of our Lord! Put down thy arms! I command thee!"

"Look, the guards are doing it! They have lowered their staffs!" Zutermier had observed as he helped assist the Pope to his feet.

"Listen unto me, Isaac. Ye art in a light trance! Ye art to put thy head down at once and slowly walk backward! Can ye follow these instructions without glancing into the eyes of the guards?"

"I don't know," Isaac had stuttered. "But I'll try." What he was attempting to focus on were the throne guards' feet as he backed away.

"Ye must render an effort, or the guards will take thy current attitude as an act of aggression! Do I make myself clear?"

"Yes," Isaac had begun to shiver.

"That's it. Just a little more, son," the Pope had instructed. He had felt somewhat responsible for being Isaac's eyes. "You're doing fine."

It was a tedious process—one that was difficult to watch, but Isaac was doing remarkably well. He was following Darr and the Pope's orders to a tee until the guards let out two back-to-back roars. The continuous blasts were so violent they forced him, butt first, onto the floor. From the floor, he got up and started to slip and slide his way towards the group.

"What were you thinking?" Kelso wanted to know. "You nearly scared the life out of us."

"I don't know what happened!" Isaac complained, bent over and out of breath. "One minute, I was standing there fine, then the next, I was being drawn by the guards' medallions of all things. It was so strange."

"What was strange?" Darr walked towards him.

"A voice that was whispering to me from one of the gold pieces."

"Whose voice was it?" Zutermier also moved closer.

"I don't know. I just don't know."

"Well, what did the voice say?" Zutermier further questioned him.

"It said, 'Come. Come closer, my child. Come.'" Isaac tried his best to mimic the voice.

Everyone broke out in laughter except for Isaac, who had a lost expression on his face.

"The good news, Isaac, is that you're out of danger and back with us." The Pope hugged him from behind. He and the others were laughing about how Isaac had been running like someone drowning in alligator-infested water.

What Darr didn't know was that Isaac had a long history of coming up with tales like this, especially whenever he got caught doing something he wasn't supposed to be doing. Now was no different.

"On a more serious note, let this be a reminder that no one is permitted to leave this room unless accompanied by me."

"Now we know firsthand, Darr, and there won't be any more episodes like this one. Trust me," the Pope went out on a limb to announce, hiding his hand—which bore the scar—deep within his pocket.

"Good. For in the next room, ye will find a gift along with a few items needed for your personal hygiene, including any prescribed medications," Darr revealed, pointing the scroll toward the bathroom door. "Ye may enter."

"Come on, let's see for ourselves!" Kelso was the first one to jet in. "Come on!"

Chapter 13

It was inconceivable what the Pope and his cardinals felt the moment they stepped into the bathroom. It was a cold rush of air that had penetrated their bodies, briefly sweeping them backward. From the initial contact, they deemed this phenomenon to be the wraith of the Lord—an accusation primarily brought on by five lambskin robes with hoods. At the time, the five robes were suspended in a perfect horizontal line just above the only window. Was this the gift Darr was telling them about? Other than the monk-styled robes, the others found the bathroom area itself to be somewhat of an emotional letdown. In their minds, they were expecting a royal setup. Yet, all they got in return were plain bath necessities, their underclothing, and a few personal items like medications, neatly spread out in groups along the countertop.

"Wow, this place sure does smell like ammonia," Isaac complained, holding his breath.

"Yeah, I wonder how much disinfectant they used?"

"Probably the whole bottle," Kelso responded to Zutermier's question as he turned to observe the robes.

The Pope was also observing the robes, but he did so from a respectable distance, almost as if they were a rare museum exhibit. Still, he wouldn't give in to the temptation of touching them. One, he was too afraid he would get electrocuted.

"They are a beauty, aren't they?"

"That they are, Zutermier," the Pope answered, taking his eyes away from the subject. He could barely find the right words to express himself.

"No, you two have it all wrong! The robes are more than exquisite!" Kelso said with conviction. "They are a gift from our Lord!"

"Then why don't we try them on?" Isaac had grabbed him and gotten down to business. "Hey, you should feel how soft and smooth they are!"

"Isaac's right!" The Pope had fallen to his knees after caressing a robe for himself. "They are soft."

"And lightweight, too," Zutermier had added while putting on his. "You know, I think I would float if I wasn't wearing my old clothing underneath."

"I find that hard to believe," Kelso had become supercritical. "If those garments were made of pure lamb, then they would have to weigh at least eight pounds apiece if not more."

"If you don't believe us, then why don't you put yours on and see for yourself?" Zutermier had challenged him. At the time, Kelso's and Peter's robes were the only two left.

Kelso was in awe. Like a helium-filled balloon on a string, his robe had descended toward him with just the slightest tug. What had impressed him the most about the garment was how lightweight it actually felt. The others were definitely telling the truth; a weird grin had come across his face. He had also noticed that whenever he ran his hands along the course of the sleeves, his fingers would vanish in the plushness.

"R-R-Remarkable," Kelso had stuttered. "I, too, feel as though I could drift away."

"Now, do you see what we mean?"

"Exactly, Zutermier," Kelso had winked. "I see firsthand what you were implying."

"There's only one thing that makes me suspicious about these robes."

"And what would that be, Isaac?" the Pope had wanted to find out. "How could one possibly find fault in such craftsmanship?"

"I understand that a lamb is supposed to be a symbol of purity, but why are these robes black? This almost makes me wonder if these robes are really a gift from Heaven or a curse from Hell."

"Nonsense, child!" the Pope playfully swatted his hand at Isaac. "Why, these robes are only dyed this way as a form of camouflage! That's all!"

"Obviously, Isaac, it would be easy to detect someone if he wore white. Wouldn't you think?"

"I guess you have a point there, Zutermier. I guess I never thought of it from a military standpoint."

"Do you know what I think? I think we should wash up first before we parade around in these garments," Kelso expressed his opinion by pulling off his robe. "It's like my dear mother always said: cleanliness is next to godliness."

"Likewise," Zutermier concurred while taking off his robe in the process.

Isaac was the next to do the same.

"Don't anyone get too comfortable!" the Pope scowled upon watching the three robes sail up into the air. "I can see exactly where this is headed!"

"You can see where what is headed? What are you babbling about now?" Kelso tried to determine this.

"Later!" the Pope cut the conversation short as he blew past Kelso and made his way toward the door, where he paused. Placing his ear on the center of its cold surface, he observed that he could no longer hear the heavy breathing of the throne guards.

"Fine! It's okay with me if you don't want to communicate properly with the rest of us!" Kelso threw his hands up in disgust. "Don't even say a word, you two. I have no idea what he's up to!"

There was a sudden change in the energy. The Pope could feel it. He could detect it through the doorknob as he stood there in silence, mentally blocking out the distractions of the cardinals behind him. He was also contemplating several things. One was how to escape from the palace, and the other was where Darr would be positioned the moment he opened the door. He hated surprises. It was nothing new, but he was taken aback when Darr didn't enter the bathroom behind them. He knew it wasn't like Darr to withhold information and details. Thus, this had him thinking: did Darr go back to Heaven, or was Darr hovering in midair, eavesdropping on their conversation? With Darr's acute hearing, he knew this was always a possibility. A possibility that he would have to solve himself physically.

"What have we here?" the Pope mumbled while cracking the door and sticking his head out. Like a substance fiend, his eyeballs were searching high and low. Still, he could find no signs of Darr or the two throne guards. Not that he was wishing to see any of them. "Yes, everything seems to be going as I hoped." He pumped his fist upon shutting the door.

"Would you care to tell us what that little episode was all about?" Zutermier asked as he and the others slowly moved toward the door, encasing the Pope in.

"Not now! It's too lengthy, but I'll explain on the way," he said, pushing them aside. "Trust me, we have some very important business to take care of outside this palace."

"But Darr's orders were for us to remain inside this room!" Kelso frowned. "Not even you can disobey these orders!"

"I heard what Darr's orders were. Only one thing: Darr's not here to stop us," the Pope pointed out. He was still going to great lengths to keep his hand, which contained the marking of the gold coin, hidden, along with the loaded pistol in his pocket. "Listen to me. What Darr doesn't know won't hurt him. You have to believe me in order to make what I have in mind work. Peter's life, and maybe another life, may be at stake."

"All that might be true in a sense," said Zutermier. "Yet, how do you suppose we get past the small army that is stationed around the palace?"

"You saw what those throne guards nearly did to me!" Isaac hated to rehash the situation. "They almost tore me to pieces! Who's going to be here to stop them this time? Who?"

"I saw it! We all saw it!" The Pope grabbed Isaac by the cheek.

"Only this time, things are going to be different." He released him.

"In what way?" Zutermier inquired.

Without Darr present, he was thinking more about the level of things that were actually taking a dive for the worse.

"You'll see. We'll have some help along the way. There are others here besides Darr," the Pope assured them with a smirk. He was daydreaming about the beautiful women who had frozen the guards where they stood, allowing him a chance to catch up with the others.

"I don't know," Kelso yawned. "This whole matter still sounds kind of risky to me. I think we should get some sleep."

"I'll agree," said Zutermier. "I think what we witnessed about an hour ago with those goblins was only a prelude to the kind of evil we may be up against."

"Yeah! We'll sure get slaughtered," Isaac complained, holding his forehead. His temple area suddenly felt congested. It was almost as if a severe migraine was coming on. "But where did you have in mind to go?"

"Back to the gates of the basilica!" The Pope's nostrils flared.

"Why there, of all places?" Zutermier wanted to know.

"Because I have a score to settle and a debt to pay to a friend. A friend who saved my life and put me back on the right path."

"I'm confused," Kelso chuckled. "When did all of this take place?"

"Yeah. Were we anywhere in the picture?" Zutermier confronted him.

"Come on, I'll do the explaining in there," the Pope motioned with his hands. "That way, we can also check on Peter's condition."

"This I have to hear," said Kelso.

"Good. I'll lead the way."

The cardinals were on the Pope's trail as he walked out of the bathroom and made his way over to Peter's bedside. Once there, his emotions got the better of him. The feelings were so strong that tears rushed from his eyes like raindrops. He had to turn his head. He didn't want the others to see him acting this way, for he feared it would dampen the recovery mission. Thus, he crossed his heart and collapsed to his knees in deep prayer. He was going to say one out loud, but he knew his voice would crack. Keep one thing in mind: he wasn't used to seeing Peter this helpless and pale. Neither were the others, judging by their silence. To him, Peter's face was sunken in, and it literally looked as if the fingertips of death were squeezing his cheekbones.

"How are his wounds?" the Pope wanted to know, arriving gingerly to his feet.

The room was so quiet; it reminded him of a funeral parlor, especially how everyone was draped around Peter's bedside as if he were laid out in a coffin.

"Like before, Peter's wounds are healed. The three of us couldn't detect any new evidence of bleeding," Zutermier turned and said with optimism.

"Good. That pleases me." The Pope wiped his face. He saw this as a plus.

"May I also ask a question?"

"Sure, Isaac. Go right ahead. Ask it." The Pope had given his approval. "I don't know if it's me, but does Peter appear different in any way? I mean, look at him. R-R-Really," Isaac stuttered.

"He does seem a bit weathered," Zutermier checked. "In fact, if I didn't know any better, I would have sworn that someone switched his body."

"I don't know what hit him, but whatever it was, it's killing him! It's slowly sucking the life from him internally! I can't continue to stand here and watch it any longer! I can't! I can't! Peter's my friend! I love him like the son I never had!" Kelso became outraged.

He was so displeased by what he saw that he jogged off and stood on the threshold of the bathroom. It was there that he turned his back toward everyone and began to pound his head lightly against the molding of the door. He knew, if only for a minute, that he needed to be alone. He needed to be able to breathe air that was not inhabited by anyone else. This was all in an effort, he felt, to gather himself back together.

"Kelso, everything will be all right. You'll see," Zutermier rushed over to console him. "Please, stay with us. We need you to remain mentally strong."

"That's it, Kelso. Let those tears flow," the Pope walked over and embraced him. "Let them flow until they're all gone because if you don't, you'll make yourself sick. You'll make your heart weak."

"I'm all right now. Please. Please," Kelso pleaded while holding the two at bay with his outstretched hands. A limber smile could be seen across his face.

"Isaac!" the Pope called out, grabbing his attention. "It's no use, son. There's nothing you can do for Peter. I saw the object that did this to him, and believe me, his condition is a lot better than what I suspected. A whole lot better."

"Oh, would you care to explain then?"

"Certainly, Isaac," the Pope responded. "But why don't you come over here with us?"

Isaac was quick to do just that, leaving Peter's bedside behind in a flash. Except for maybe supper time, the Pope couldn't ever recall seeing him move so fast.

"It all began when we were exiting the basilica with Darr," the Pope went into detail. He had made it almost a habit to look each one of them in the eyes as he talked.

"Then what happened?" Zutermier wanted him to continue. "Don't stop now."

"Well, do you recall when Darr first gave us the dos and don'ts about the Lord's sacred walkway of light?"

"I do recall what he said," Zutermier admitted. "Darr said if we stayed up on the walkway, no harm would come unto us. Yet he also said if we ventured off the path, he wouldn't be able to help us. As a matter of fact, he said he wouldn't even glance back until he was inside the palace."

"So, what does this have to do with anything?" Kelso was tired of the Pope's beating around the bush. It was driving him insane. He wanted answers, and he wanted them now. He felt if the Pope had something that needed to be said, it should be made public without giving everyone the runaround.

"To make a long story short, Kelso, I did what we were instructed not to do. I stumbled off the path."

"But you were behind me the whole time! Weren't you?" Kelso sounded uncertain.

"No, no. I didn't join up with you until you were about to enter this room."

"By God, how did this ever happen? Isaac had comically stirred up towards the ceiling for answers. "How?"

"Let me guess." Zutermier paused. "It was those bloody goblins, wasn't it?"

"Yeah, they did have terrible breath, didn't they?" Isaac giggled. When he saw that no one was doing the same, he quickly changed his attitude back to one of seriousness.

"Actually, I made it past the goblins. I was doing just fine until, out of nowhere, I heard this distressing cadence of a poor woman. She sounded about ninety. She said that someone was after her. She said that we needed to turn back. Unfortunately, that's not what did me in."

"What did, then?"

"It was when I heard her scream. The basilica was on fire, Zutermier. And when I turned, it was. It was on fire. However, when I finally realized that I was bamboozled and the whole scene was nothing more than a cheap hologram, you three had already passed through the entrance gate. Yet, as I was about to exit through the gate, I was approached by headless knights on horseback. They were coming straight towards me with their javelins aimed at my heart!"

"Don't even say it." Kelso covered his ears. "Don't even say it."

"Yes, that's when I jumped and entered another dimension. A dimension parallel to our own world. A dimension made up of mazes and unusual creatures."

The Pope was elated. He knew he had his cardinals' undivided attention. He could sense he was feeding on their desire for fantasy. Even though they weren't giving him the third degree like he thought they would, their negative body language said a mouthful. Their enlarging eyeballs also informed him that they wanted to hear more of the specifics.

"Once trapped in this world with two moons and no stars, I stood dumbfounded in one spot for about ten minutes. I thought that Darr, or maybe one of you, would detect that I was no longer with the group and send help. Nothing ever happened. No one ever came, so I was faced with reality. I was faced with the notion that I needed to find my own way out. Truth be told, that's when I looked up in the direction of a tree several yards away and discovered I was being watched. Yes, I was being sized up by some creatures called gooey bats."

"So, how big were they?"

"They were about the size of a full-grown Italian Greyhound, Zutermier, with eyes that stood out like miniature flashlights."

"Wow! That's big!" Isaac exclaimed. "Tell us, what did you do next?"

"First, I got some protection. It was a rock or two that I had placed in my pocket. From there, I tiptoed off without exciting the bats, and I began my journey through the maze, which was made up of, of all things, weeping willow trees."

"Yikes! I bet that was kind of creepy?"

"It was, Kelso. Still, it wasn't as creepy as the constant thoughts of failing everyone and being stuck in this world with no way out."

"So, how did you spend your time?" Zutermier felt obligated to ask.

"For what seemed like hours, I roamed from one dead end of the maze to another. My body was spent, and I was thinking about giving in until I laid eyes on something that caught my attention. It was a series of sparkles of light, yet it was also in the direction of what would be another dead end," the Pope told them with an irritable expression on his face. He wanted to show them just how fed up he had become with the one-way entrances.

"Go on! Go on! Don't stop now!" Isaac was compelled. "Please, continue with the rest of your story."

"Well, upon my investigation of the light, I came across this lone oak tree. And underneath that tree were the damnedest things: gold coins. Yes, it was the gold coins that gave off the reflections of light I saw from afar!"

"Gold coins?" Kelso had to catch his breath.

"That's right, gold coins. Don't hold me to it, but I believe they were minted when Julius Caesar was emperor," the Pope said rather nonchalantly. He was acting as if the coins meant nothing to him.

"Were these coins real?" That's basically what Zutermier wanted to know.

"Sure," the Pope massaged his throat. "They were real, to the best of my knowledge."

"Tell us, what did you do after finding these coins?" Kelso changed his position. He and the others were now standing with their backs towards the bedside of Peter.

Kelso, with his new positioning, was trying desperately to win the Pope's attention by doing an awful lot of cheesing. This was almost out of character for him, as he was normally so reserved and combative. He was doing this just in case the Pope had obtained some of the gold coins. Since they had remained close friends for what seemed like the dawn of time, he saw no particular reason why the Pope wouldn't give him maybe one or two.

"Cut it out, Kelso! I know what you're up to." The Pope had caught on. He knew Kelso like a book, and he wasn't about to play along with his childish antics. "At some point in time, everyone, I constructed a torch. With it, I began to pocket as many gold coins as I could. Some were in a lot better condition than others. What I kept; I was going to have analyzed. But as I was about to leave, I came across this rare find. It was a coin much larger and different than the rest. In fact, it even came to life in my palm. See!"

"Did it hurt?"

"Sure it did, Isaac." The Pope had placed his hand back in his pocket.

"Wait a minute!" Zutermier had grabbed the Pope by the elbow. "Let me see that again." He began to examine the markings up close.

"Explain to us. What do you think it is?" Isaac waited patiently for Zutermier's response.

At the time, Zutermier was repeatedly retracing the image with his fingertips.

"It's a symbol of some kind," Zutermier concluded while releasing the Pope's hand. "Other than that, your guess is as good as mine."

"Zutermier's correct. It is a symbol. A heavenly one at that. Only now, the image seems to be becoming fainter by the minute." The Pope took a second look himself.

"Enough small talk about that," said Kelso. "I want to hear more about the coins."

"Give me time, and I was just getting around to it!" The Pope raised his tone of voice. He didn't like Kelso rushing him. He wanted to tell his story at his own pace. "Twice, I tried to exit the dead end which contained the coins. However, every time I entered, an invisible portal kept throwing me behind the oak tree. At this point, you have to understand I was becoming furious. I was becoming paranoid until I heard a man's voice from high above the tree."

"What did he say?"

"He said, Isaac, that it would be wise if I emptied my pockets of the gold coins if I wanted to leave. If not, he warned that I would awaken the guardian of this world with my third attempt."

"So, what did you do?"

"I emptied my pockets, of course, Kelso! I didn't want to be enslaved in that world forever!"

"Let me get this straight. Have you emptied your pockets for everything?" Kelso repeated with a disgruntled look. He couldn't believe the Pope would totally trust someone he didn't know or couldn't see. "So, you didn't even keep one?"

"Believe me, it was the only way, Kelso." The Pope didn't know why he was defending his actions. "The coins were nothing more than fool's gold—a trap, if you prefer, or bait."

"And it was a wise decision at that." Zutermier gave his approval by applauding. "The person must have sounded sincere?"

"He did," the Pope recalled painfully. "That's why, when I was freed from the dead end, I returned there once more. I guess I just wanted to repay the Roman soldier who helped me. Besides, I didn't want the trouble I could have gotten myself into to happen to someone else. Anyway, that's why I torched the tree. But once I had done this, about a thousand souls of yellow light emerged from the flames. Little did I know, the guardian of this world had also appeared. It was a huge gorilla-like creature with wings about double the size of Darr's."

"I bet you were scared out of your wits?" Zutermier added with a smile. He wanted to ease some of the tension in the Pope's mind.

"I was beyond afraid," proclaimed the Pope. "To make a long story short, the souls I freed helped me break one of the creature's wings, sending it downward to its death. From that point on, I followed the souls on foot until I fell into a shallow pit of animal bones and knocked myself unconscious. I think the souls were going to lead me out, yet I guess I will never know for certain."

"Good heavens!" Kelso exclaimed. "That was some adventure, but what happened once you came to your senses?"

"I was hog-tied and held captive in midair by four-foot goblins, who were taking me back to where I had initially entered this dimension." The Pope could only chuckle. "My guess is the tiny devils were using some type of telepathy on me."

"You had to be frightened?" Isaac could only imagine. "I know I would have been!"

"Sure, I was terrified. They had numbers over me."

"Wait. You have to be kidding, right? Do you really expect us to believe this—"

"This what?" The Pope's mouth had sprung open. "Go ahead and say it, Kelso!"

"Well, this part of your story!" Kelso had replied sarcastically. "It's a little over the top, don't you think?"

"Of course, it's the truth!" The Pope was shocked he was defending his integrity. "I have no time for games! This is not science fiction! It's the real deal!" He had made this clear when he revealed the scar on his palm for the second time.

"Relax." Zutermier had patted the Pope on the back. He had wanted to relieve some of the stress before the situation escalated out of control. "All of us can attest that you never bore that marking until today. So how did you do it? How did you manage to escape the clutches of the goblins?"

"Simple." The Pope had beamed with pride while turning his attention toward Zutermier. "I managed to get one of my hands-free, which allowed me to undo the rest of my body. Then, once the timing was right, I cast a stone in the direction of the tree that was home to the gooey bats. You know, the creatures I mentioned earlier."

"So, what happened after that?" Zutermier pressed the Pope further for details. "What was the gooey bats' response to your actions?"

"Yeah, out with it." Isaac had put it bluntly.

"Once I had done what I had done, the bats became hostile and began to attack the goblins in an all-out aerial pursuit, which was difficult for me to watch. I mean, the bats would, one by one, swoop a goblin into the air with their razor-sharp claws, then they would take turns feeding and sucking the neon yellow slime from the goblins' heads.

"I guess this yellow goo was the goblins' blood and ultimately how the bats got their name," Zutermier began to piece the facts together.

"The bats continued to feed like this until a goblin's head would disengage from its body and fall towards the ground. But as harsh as this may have sounded, it did the trick. It somehow weakened the goblins' mental stronghold over me just enough so I could take flight into the weeping willow trees. That's when it happened."

"That's when what happened? What are you talking about, and why are you wearing that weird smirk across your face?" Kelso could see no reason for it, especially with the horrific story that was told only moments ago.

"Tell me, Kelso, why shouldn't I have a smile on my face? Can't you see that something wondrous happened to me?"

"Where and when?" Isaac calmly asked while rubbing his hands together.

"For starters, I was guided back to my rightful place of being by the Lord's shepherd!"

"You were what?" Kelso almost swallowed his tongue.

"I said that I was guided back to my rightful dimension by the wooden staff of the Lord's shepherd," the Pope went on to repeat.

At the time, there was no way for him to tell if Kelso was playing dumb or if Kelso hadn't, in fact, heard what was spoken.

"So, what did the shepherd look like?" Zutermier felt compelled to ask.

"He was about Isaac's complexion and dressed in traditional biblical attire," stated the Pope. "Other than that, the shepherd appeared to be an ordinary-looking elderly man with wild, wool-like hair and a beard to match. Wait! There was something magical about his eyes, come to think of it."

"Was the shepherd mad or upset with you in any way?"

"My sentiments exactly, Isaac. What did the shepherd say to you?" Kelso earnestly wished to find out.

The Pope didn't know what to do. He was at a loss for words. For some apparent reason, he felt himself becoming too emotional. This was because he really didn't want to rehash what had happened to the shepherd. It was too painful. All he could think of was to turn his head and try to hold back the tears that were beginning to spill from his closed eyelids.

"Are you all right?" Zutermier tried to comfort him. "Please, take all the time you need to gather yourself."

"I'm okay." The Pope dried his eyes. "Unfortunately, the shepherd was injured in the process by the half-man with the body of a horse."

"You mean the centaur?" Zutermier wanted to clarify. "That's what they're called."

"Yes. The shepherd was injured or maybe even killed by this creature, and it's all my fault. If I hadn't been so bullheaded, none of this would have taken place. Oh, what am I to do? I feel so damn awful!" The Pope wept openly into his palms.

"You said the shepherd was injured. Perhaps you got a glimpse of what kind of weapon was used?" Zutermier thought this would be very useful information if the Pope could remember.

"Yes," the Pope had responded while collecting himself. "It was a pitchfork that the shepherd had pulled from his breast—not before giving me a secret handgrip and a secret password, which I used to reenter the palace. This is how I was able to catch up with the group."

"I take it this was the same instrument used to do Peter in. The same bloody thing," Kelso had repeated while biting his bottom lip. His voice was low and eerie.

Kelso was mad as hell. Nothing but pure plots of revenge were stampeding through his mind. The others could sense it as his hands had begun to tremble like a drunk's. His forehead, in particular, was so hot one could fry an egg on it—or attempt to. In moments such as these, everyone knew it was best to leave him be until he had snapped back into reality.

"Now, do you see why it's important we go back to the entrance gate?" The Pope made it a point to look into the eyes of his cardinals. He was hoping the shepherd and Peter's ordeal with the centaur would be reason enough. "Now, do you see why?"

"Sure," Isaac was the first to respond. "But what do you want to do?"

"Kill it! Kill it! Kill the creature dead, then remove its head, which is probably the main source of its power!" Kelso had come back to life. His eyeballs were almost bulging from their sockets in anticipation of committing this act.

"I agree," said the Pope. "It's a cruel act, but it must be done. If not, the centaur could come back to life and seek our heads. You see, something happened once the shepherd was injured."

"Like what?" Zutermier hoped he could be specific.

"The shepherd had become deformed with madness. In and out, I stood there with my heart in my mouth as his body went into these swing stages of light and darkness. There was nothing I could do. It was almost as if the shepherd was transforming into a monster right before my very eyes. Still, I'm amazed the same hasn't occurred with Peter."

"Then we'll do whatever it takes in the name of our Lord to see that the proper punishment is administered!" Zutermier confessed, poking his chest out.

"You can count me in as well!" Isaac banged his fist into his palm.

"So be it," Kelso stood tall. "Now, all we need to do is devise a plan to exit the palace without the throne guards seeing us."

"This is elementary," the Pope informed with a smile.

He signaled for his cardinals to join him in the bathroom while repeatedly tapping his earlobes. He knew from trial and error how acute Darr's hearing was, yet he was somewhat optimistic about the throne guards' range. In fear of the unknown, he wanted to use every prudence available. This meant he didn't want to give Darr or the two throne guards any reason to storm in after them. A lot was at stake. He only hoped his cardinals deemed this to be true once they had disobeyed Darr's orders with their intentions for revenge.

"Listen up," the Pope whispered. "To ensure that our second journey to the basilica is a safe one, only three of us will make the trip. The other party member will stay behind to tend to Peter and distract the throne guards if need be. Also, he is to inform Darr where we have gone and what we have done if we have not returned at a desirable time. Is this agreeable?"

"Yes. It sounds like a wonderful plan."

"Good, because Kelso, you're the one who will do this. Please, don't argue with me. The reason I have come to this decision is primarily due to Zutermier and Isaac being the strongest. Needless to say, I have chosen myself for the simple fact that I have some knowledge of the whereabouts of this centaur."

"I can live with that. I know my health is a concern here." Kelso accepted his role, not wanting to deprive anyone else of their responsibilities. Besides, it also made a lot of sense for him to stay behind with someone he loved, like a blood relative. Still, he was dying for a piece of the action and would have traded places at the drop of a hat.

"Once we find this centaur, how will we fight it?" Isaac whispered. "What strategy will we employ?" He brought all of his concerns to the forefront.

"My thoughts exactly." Zutermier had begun to worry if the Pope was being realistic.

"Kelso and I weren't kidding; we have to focus all efforts on this creature's head. It's probably the only logical tactic we can use to lift the curse from the shepherd and Peter. I saw the gooey bats do it to the goblins, and we will do it to this centaur."

"With what?" Isaac asked, out of tune. "Surely, you don't expect us to take down a creature such as this with our bare hands?"

"Shush. Lower your voice," the Pope ordered Isaac while yanking one of his ears downward. "It's simple. We will each carry one of those carving knives from the table. However, once the centaur is enraged,

I will use this to bring it to the ground." He pulled the loaded pistol from his pocket.

"I knew it! I knew you had it!" Kelso began to jump up and down. "I could tell. So that's why you were sweating earlier from the face like some greasy hog?"

"Lower your voice, Kelso. Take it down a notch." The Pope's eyebrows flared up. "Yes, I still have it. See."

"But I was under the impression you got rid of it." Kelso grabbed his heart.

"Then again, I'm glad he kept it." Zutermier congratulated the Pope with a pat on the back. "This weapon could come in very handy. It could be the great equalizer, even if we were confronted by Natas Christopher."

"Would you look at that," said Isaac. He could only imagine what kind of stories the media would run if they knew what the highest-ranking official of the Catholic Church had tucked away. "Is it loaded?"

"Sure, it's loaded." The Pope had double-checked. "It has never been fired."

"Please, Pius. Put that bloody killing machine away until the time and purpose arrive for it."

Kelso was becoming jittery. He didn't like the Pope's behavior, nor did he like how the Pope kept his finger so tightly on the trigger mechanism. He knew accidents were prone to happen, especially whenever you mixed the presence of evil forces and an inexperienced gun handler together.

"Now that everything is out in the open, how will we get past the throne guards?" Isaac wanted to know. "Leaving the way you entered has to be out of the question, Pope Pius, for we will most likely get stopped. Neither Zutermier nor I have the secret grip or password."

"True. You would be stopped," replied the Pope. "I guess I never took this into consideration." He was thinking long and hard.

"I know a way," Zutermier's voice squeaked. "Several years ago, the builders of this room installed a fire ladder as a safety feature. Don't get me wrong, it's only heavy-duty rope, but it'll drop to the ground nonetheless. Better yet, it will also make it easier to reenter the palace as if we never left."

"Good idea," Isaac announced. "I was beginning to wonder what that little device under the window ledge was used for."

"Then it's a go!" exclaimed the Pope. "We will wear the new robes over top of our old garments, then exit the palace by way of the bathroom window."

Chapter 14

With it already planted in the mindset of Kelso that he wouldn't be making the journey back to the basilica with the others, he had done something uncommon for his ego. He lingered behind and gathered four knives from the table. He took one for himself, even though he felt he wouldn't need it with the palace being so heavily fortified. Still, he grabbed it anyway before reentering the bathroom. There, he saw the others dressing themselves hurriedly in the sacred robes. No one was saying much of anything, he observed. He guessed they were either too nervous or rethinking their steps. Whatever the case was, they didn't appear their normal selves to him. They were acting more like CIA agents than men of the cloth—CIA agents who knew they had to kill or be killed to accomplish their objective. Knowing the others were most likely upset that they would probably have to perform such an act, he didn't interfere or try to change their mood. Instead, he set the knives on the sink as he bent down to retrieve a lantern from the cabinet underneath.

"Kelso, I take it there's enough fuel in there to complete our mission?" The Pope was looking for the truth.

"Sure," Kelso responded while holding the lantern close to his face. "There's plenty," he said, shaking it side to side. He was trying to show the others for their own observations.

"Perfect! That just might be enough," Zutermier breathed a sigh of relief.

"It is, but hopefully, we can leave and return without having to worry about any of that," the Pope assured them with a wink.

"Maybe it will, or maybe it won't," Isaac pondered as he placed his hand underneath his chin.

He didn't agree with or share the Pope's point of view at all. To him personally, he thought things would be a lot more complex than described. He had also felt the others would be more oriented toward battle, knowing their journey for the centaur would be no walk in the park.

"Pope Pius, tell me something."

"What is it, Zutermier?"

"About how long do you estimate our journey should really take?"

"Zutermier has something there, Pius." Kelso had laid the lantern beside the knives. His hands were now free. "I also need to know. You see, I need to know when to start worrying that the others and yourself might be in some sort of bind. At least this way, I have an idea of when to send help."

"Truthfully, it depends. I'm being honest. Neither of us has ever killed anything of this magnitude before. This goes far beyond bug-squashing." The Pope had relayed this information to anyone who was facing him. "If the creature is where it was when I last saw it, our journey shouldn't take long at all. Yet, if we have to go elsewhere in search of it, then we might be a while. Give and take two hours at the most. If our quest doesn't turn up any leads by that time, then we'll return."

"That sounds reasonable enough." Zutermier had shaken his head in agreement.

"Yeah. But note this so we're on the same page: I will call for help immediately after the two hours have passed. Any objections to this?"

"No. We can live with a decision like that from you, Kelso." The Pope had embraced him. "Even though you physically won't make the journey with us, you still play a very active and supportive role here. It will be up to you to make a decision like this. It could very well save our lives. Besides, you might be the one who has to do all the explaining to Darr if anything were to happen to us." He chuckled as he walked away.

"Thanks for the warning." Kelso had playfully rolled his eyes. "Now set your watch with mine or I'll set mine with yours."

"I would, only I'm not wearing one." The Pope had told him. "Neither I'm I." Zutermier had held up his wrist.

"Oh, wait." The Pope had paused. "I do believe Isaac is wearing his."

"I'm wearing it all right, but hold that thought." Isaac had maneuvered away.

"What's wrong, child? What do you see out there?" The Pope's heart began to race. "Tell me!"

"I don't know." Isaac had responded, as he walked and stood in between the door frame. He had his attention focused mostly on the bedside of Peter. "For a moment there, I thought I saw something from the corners of my eyes. However, it appears to be nothing." He had turned back around.

"Your eyes will be doing a lot of that, son, once you 're out in the darkness. Everything will look like someone or something." Kelso had relayed this information onto Isaac, while the two had synchronized their watches.

"It's the truth," said the Pope.

"So we'll just have to keep our composure."

"Holy mother of pearl!"

"No! Not you also, Zutermier?" The Pope had clutched his forehead in grief.

He didn't know what to think or believe, the moment he had seen Zutermier dart past him and repeat the same steps as Isaac. He only hoped it wasn't Darr returning. He knew time was running out, and he had wanted to behead the creature without any interruptions.

"What is it? What do you see?"

"I don't know, Kelso," Zutermier hesitated to answer. "Maybe I'm seeing things too, but for a glimmer, I could have sworn I saw the body of Cardinal Peter Nicholas drift up into the air."

"Hey! That's exactly what I thought I saw!" Isaac rushed back over for another peek.

"I don't believe what I'm hearing." Kelso became woozy. "I don't believe it!" His legs were too numb to even move an inch.

"Out of the way! It's all a bunch of nonsense, I tell you!" The Pope pushed both Zutermier and Isaac aside. "Why, the body of Peter is right—"

"Right, where?" Zutermier asked him, standing over his shoulder.

"Hey! Look up there!" Isaac pointed towards the ceiling.

"It's Peter!" Zutermier focused in.

"Damn it, don't just stand there with your asses over your faces! Help me get him down! This applies to you too, Kelso! Come on! Come on! Get the led out!" The Pope elaborated with his hands.

"Is he conscious?" Kelso wanted to know as he jogged past the Pope into the other room.

"I don't think so," replied Zutermier. "Peter still appears to be in a deep sleep."

"A coma is more like it," Isaac put it bluntly.

"This is awful," Kelso complained, while straining his neck. "I wonder what made his body do this."

"Do what?" asked Zutermier.

"Float up to the ceiling," replied Kelso.

"Come on! Don't just stand there with your hands in your pockets, debating about how Peter got up there!" The Pope was becoming upset with his cardinals' lack of urgency. "Help me get him down before he further injures himself!"

"But what do you want us to do?" Isaac threw his hands up. "We don't have wings. I know, maybe we should summon one of the throne guards to assist us?"

"Nonsense!" The Pope prevented Isaac from moving by squeezing Isaac's cheeks together. "I will never condone you doing this! We'll do it ourselves," he made it clear while releasing Isaac's face.

"Okay, I agree. We'll do it ourselves, Pius. Unfortunately, we'll need a ladder and a long pole with a hook on the end to get the job done." Kelso gave his opinion, but to no avail. The Pope just hunched his shoulders as he turned away.

"That sounds promising, Kelso. Nevertheless, it won't be necessary."

"Sure, it won't be necessary, Zutermier," the Pope stopped in his tracks. "Because it's damn near impossible."

"What is?" Kelso became defensive.

"Your suggestion!" The Pope began to pace back and forth. He felt no need to elaborate any further.

"So, what do you suggest?" Kelso asked rather sarcastically. "Come on, let's hear it."

"Stop! Stop!" Zutermier raised his tone of voice. "You two are missing the point I'm trying to drive at!"

Unlike the others, Zutermier wasn't fazed by what he saw at all. He was only disturbed for a second or two at best. This was due to the fact that when Peter's body drifted into the air, the bed sheets went along for the ride. Thus, this made Peter appear to be a Hollywood ghost. Still, this hoax wasn't enough to prevent him from viewing the situation at hand with a scientific approach.

"You were saying, Zutermier?" The Pope had turned his attention toward him. "Go ahead, we're listening."

"Thank you." Zutermier bowed before taking the floor. "Roughly about four minutes had passed between the time when Isaac thought he saw what I saw only moments ago."

"And your point is?"

"Well, given my theory of elapsed timing, Pope Pius, my point is this: in a matter of seconds, I think Peter's body should be descending from the air."

"Look! He's speaking the truth!" Isaac showed them, while tracing the downward spiral of Peter's body with his index finger. "Do you see it?"

"Amazing, isn't it?" Kelso had never taken his eyes away.

"Sure." The Pope couldn't disagree. "Who would have ever imagined that it would have been as simple as this?"

"Only Zutermier." Kelso smiled.

"Believe me, it was nothing," Zutermier tried to play down the attention. "It would have happened without me saying anything. Honest."

The room became silent the moment Peter's body returned to its natural state. His descent was so gentle the only sound that could be heard was the one-time squeak of the mattress. Like before, his medical condition hadn't improved at all. If anything, it had worsened. It had worsened to the point where the Pope and his cardinals couldn't recognize him anymore. It was like someone, or something had cast a spell to make him appear decrepit.

"Stand back, everyone! Part the way!" Zutermier gestured with his hands as he ran forward and dove in midair. When he finally landed, he did a belly flop across Peter's chest. He hoped his 204 pounds would be enough to prevent Peter from taking flight again.

"Great call," the Pope commended Zutermier, patting him on the back. "Listen up, you two. I want you to assist me in gathering some sheets from the other beds."

"What for?" Isaac wanted to know.

"So we can restrain Peter's limbs," Kelso hastily instructed.

"Oh, okay," Isaac responded, going about the deed.

"Hurry!" the Pope pleaded. "I need the two of you to move a little faster!"

A silhouette of doubtfulness could be seen on Zutermier's face the moment he watched the others maneuver around the beds, pulling off the sheets. He was literally sweating bullets—a nervous reaction caused by the illusion in his head that he was lying across a volcano. He could feel the active mound vibrating his entire body, including his teeth. It was building force—the same unknown power that had catapulted Peter into the air. Would his added weight be enough to prevent this? He generally wasn't afraid of heights, yet he knew this set of circumstances was different. He felt he would no longer have the option to come down when he became woozy.

"Listen up. I'll tie Peter's arms, and you two tie his legs," the Pope communicated while getting into position behind the bed frame.

"Like this?" Isaac displayed his knot technique.

"Yes, that's fine," the Pope glanced upward. "Yours should do as well, Kelso."

"Say, is it okay if I remove myself?" Zutermier had thought he asked before doing so.

"No, not yet." The Pope had grimaced. He was still trying to secure his knots. "I'll give you the cue when to vacate."

"Hurry, Pius," Kelso had warned. "I don't think he can hold on much longer."

"There."

"Finally!" Zutermier had breathed a sigh of relief as he rolled off to the side of Peter. His body was still feeling the effects of what he thought was jet lag.

"Holy moly!" Kelso had grabbed everyone's attention with his comment. "Although Peter's body is tied down, it still tries to take flight!"

"How bizarre." Isaac had tried to understand the situation for himself. "It almost appears as if Peter's having a major convulsion."

"You know, I think we're doing Peter more actual harm than good," Zutermier had suggested to the Pope.

"What do you mean?" The Pope knew he could always trust Zutermier's opinion. It was usually full of wisdom.

"I know this may sound silly, but Peter's body seems to be throwing a temper tantrum from being subdued."

"What?" The Pope's jaws had locked. "You're out of your mind!"

"But he has something there, Pius." Kelso had taken to Zutermier's defense. "See this? Peter's lower torso area is under a lot of strain from all that kicking back and forth."

"I know this much is true." The Pope had closed his eyes. "However, we just can't keep letting him drift back and forth. It's not human!"

"Nothing makes sense anymore! Nothing! But maybe I can shake Peter back to his senses." Kelso had wanted to set the record straight as he crawled his way onto Peter's bed. "Damn, I feel like I'm riding a real bucking horse."

"Should Isaac and I assist him?" Zutermier had tapped the Pope on his shoulder. He knew exactly how Kelso felt.

"Yes. Why don't the two of you try to contain the movement of Peter's legs? Yet, be careful not to get kicked. We still have a mission to complete."

"You heard the Pope. Let's do this." Zutermier had clapped his hands together to signal Isaac.

"Listen. I'll grab Peter's left ankle while you take the other."

"That's fine by me." Zutermier could be seen stretching his arms before he took on his responsibilities.

The Pope's optimism was low. The way he saw it, Peter was already deceased. He couldn't even see signs of the cardinal breathing. Were the others aware of this? He did not know, but he knew he couldn't break the spirit of Kelso, who he could see working like a bee to shake Peter back to awareness. Nor did he feel he could do the same to Zutermier and Isaac, whom he could see using one or maybe two hands at a time to hold Peter's ankles down.

"How is he?" The Pope had walked up to where Kelso was.

"It's frustrating. I'm not getting anywhere." Kelso had paused to wipe the perspiration from his face and neck. "Peter won't respond to anything I do, and to make matters worse, his eyes are completely blood shot."

"Blood red?"

"Yes, blood red," Kelso repeated for the Pope. "Here, have a peek for yourself. I know Peter's face doesn't look like what we're accustomed to, but come closer. You have to see this. Really."

"Hold that thought," the Pope shunned him away. "Zutermier and Isaac."

"What is it, Pope Pius?" They both raised their heads.

"You two take a break for a while." The Pope was concerned. He was worried they would become worn out before they even made their journey back to the basilica. He knew it was bad enough; they would probably have to go without a good night's rest. "Kelso, I'm ordering you to do the same. Please, take a break."

Kelso didn't disagree with the Pope's suggestion at all. In fact, he did as he was told. He climbed off the mattress and took his spot on the floor next to Zutermier and Isaac, who were both kneeling in prayer at the foot of Peter's bed. What he had just seen appalled him to the core of his soul. He had seen dying people and unmasked graves before, but Peter looked and smelled of a different type of death to him—one which he couldn't place a finger on. Besides concealing his tears within his palms, he knew there wasn't much more he could do for Peter when most of his attempts had already failed.

"This is insane. There has to be an answer to this madness." The Pope leaned over Peter. "There has to be."

The Pope's breathing was slow, and his eyes never blinked once. He had the precision of a master surgeon as he used his steady hand to guide open Peter's eyelids, one at a time.

"Oh, my!" The Pope jumped backward.

"What is it?" Zutermier rushed over. "What's wrong?"

"Kelso was r-r-right!" The Pope could hardly get the words out. "Peter's eyes are the color of cherries."

"Cranky!"

"What's wrong, Isaac?" Kelso stood stone-faced.

"It's Peter's stomach. I think it's starting to bleed once again."

"Impossible!" the Pope barked. This was the last thing he wanted to hear. "We watched Darr heal Peter's wounds ourselves."

"True. But now I see tiny specks of blood." Isaac was too disturbed to examine the situation thoroughly.

"Move!" the Pope had ordered Isaac to one side. "Let me have a look at his midsection!"

At first glance, the Pope could see for himself that Isaac had hit the nail on the head. Peter was bleeding. This was evident from the saturation of the sheets. Yet why? He couldn't understand what could have triggered the wound area to reopen unless Peter's seizure-like activity had caused it. Searching for a definitive explanation, he snatched the sheets aside and peeled Peter's clothing back. What he and the others, whom he could feel breathing against his neck, saw were four pin-sized holes with fluid oozing out.

"It's just what I feared." The Pope had bitten at his fingertips. "Peter's wounds have resurfaced. Do you see these marks? They were made from the tines of the centaur's pitchfork."

"Is there anything we can do to stop his bleeding?" Zutermier had pushed his face into Isaac's ribcage for a closer view.

"I don't know." Curious, the Pope had taken four of his fingers and had positioned them over the holes.

"Great," said Kelso. "The pressure seems to have done the trick."

"Yes. I think we can duplicate what the Pope has done with some bandages," Zutermier had gone on to suggest.

"Well, it's sure worth a try." The Pope had stalled.

He wasn't buying into this claim just yet. It was too good to be true. He knew something else was up—something sinister. For one, he could feel another life form within Peter's chest. It was this presence, he believed, that was causing Peter to float toward the ceiling. The moment he removed his finger, Peter confirmed what he had only speculated. Peter broke out of his arm restraints and sat upright like a mummy, forcing him to stagger backward over the others. He noticed Peter was no longer kicking his legs back and forth. Instead, Peter was as motionless as a chameleon with its eyes shut.

"Peter!" Kelso had called out.

"I think he hears us!" Isaac had watched Peter point his ears in the direction of their voices, much like an android would.

"Don't anyone move another muscle! Stay where you are! I don't like the vibes I'm getting!" The Pope had held everyone at bay with his outstretched arms. "With the uncharted strength, I fear Peter possesses, I know he could easily rip one of our limbs off!"

"Hey! What happened to the lights?" Isaac had yelled. "I can't see a thing!"

"There must be a line down somewhere," Zutermier had speculated for the better.

"Should I retrieve the lantern?"

"No, Kelso! I forbid you to!" The Pope had become irate in the darkness. "Stay where you are! This goes for everyone! Don't worry. The backup generator should kick in within a couple of seconds! There! Even evil takes a back seat to technology."

"Great news. Peter's still with us," Zutermier had beamed.

"But he won't open his eyes or say anything," Isaac had observed. "He only snorts as if he were Darth Vader." He couldn't understand how someone could snap back with that much authority after lying ill for so long. It just didn't seem possible to him.

"Peter! Peter!" Kelso had again tried to communicate with him.

"That's not the Peter we know!" The Pope had pulled his loaded pistol from his pocket. "It's a hideous monster with a hellish-like attitude!"

"I agree!" Isaac had pumped his fist. "It's not him'!"

"Tell us, what have you done to our friend? Tell us! Tell us!" The Pope had cocked and aimed his pistol in the vicinity of Peter's forehead. "In the name of the Trinity, respond or else!"

The Cardinals couldn't believe it. They thought the Pope had gone postal, but they knew he was bluffing. They knew he only wanted answers because he had winked at them. No matter how bad the circumstances had become, they knew he would never resort to premeditated violence against Peter. They believed it would make him ill to even think about such an act. However, this was until Peter had launched this soot-like vomit in the direction of their feet. The substance was so potent that it sizzled and gave off smoke.

"Not again! This is pure madness!" Isaac fussed about the lights being off for the second time in a row.

"My sentiments exactly," Zutermier concurred. "Talk about bad timing."

"What I need everyone to do is take three steps backward," the Pope ordered. He wanted them to do this as a precautionary measure.

"Gee! What is that smell?" Kelso could be heard talking through his nostrils.

"It's that black stuff," Zutermier explained to him in the darkness. "I believe it's some type of toxic acid."

"Shush," the Pope whispered. "Kelso, just keep your hands over your face and try not to inhale any of the fumes!"

The Pope wanted the room as quiet as possible. His ears were his eyes, and he used them to create an inferred layout of the entire room. What he was anticipating was anything out of the ordinary—anything that might suggest it was time to be defensive. There wasn't any doubt about it. His technique primarily revolved around his photographic memory of where he thought things were. With this being the case, he never once took his finger off the trigger. He kept the loaded pistol aimed in the direction of Peter.

"Save yourselves." A voice echoed throughout the darkness. It was faint and weak. "Please, save yourselves."

"What was that?" Isaac had waited for answers.

"It was the voice of someone or something." The Pope was ready to let out a hail of bullets. He didn't know why, but he felt he needed a little more convincing before doing so.

"You know, it kind of sounded like Peter." Kelso had played the message over and over again in his head.

"I could go along with that," said Zutermier. "Only what was meant by his words?"

"Who knows!" the Pope had replied bitterly. "Besides, we aren't really sure if that was Peter or just a voice-over. I won't be tricked again by evil."

The Pope had numerous things on his mind. One was why the generator wasn't working. The other was a concern about why the throne guards standing outside didn't storm in after the first incident with the power. Out of the two, this had bothered him the most, for he didn't understand the guards' strategy unless the lights going off was an isolated ordeal meant for his cardinals and himself.

"Great," proclaimed Isaac. "The electricity is finally back on!"

"But I believe Peter has suffered the worst fate yet," exclaimed the Pope while putting the pistol. "Look for yourselves!"

"What are you implying?" Kelso was trying to figure this out. "True, Peter is lying down again, but I can see his chest pumping clear from this spot. He's alive."

"Kelso, one can never be too certain." Zutermier didn't want him to be so narrow-minded. "However, I insist we all move in closer. That was a really violent sequence of events which we watched Peter go through."

"I feel the same way, for I have never seen a human regurgitate a substance like that before, except in the movies," Isaac had mentioned.

"Is this really what everyone wants?" The Pope had looked at each one of them for approval. "Well, let's go back over for another visual."

"Wait just a second," Isaac had pleaded with his hands. "First, let me redo Peter's restraints. I'll signal for you when I'm done. If anyone gets injured, I'd rather it be myself."

"Hold it. I'll go along with you." Zutermier had followed behind Isaac. They were both approaching the bed as if they were walking on egg cartons.

"One of you take Peter's arm, while the other takes his leg!" Kelso had hollered these instructions from across the room.

"That's it. Tie it real tight." The Pope had supervised. He had gotten kind of emotional, knowing they were risking their lives.

"Okay," Isaac had motioned. "Everything is set."

"Perfect, because here we come." The Pope had licked his lips.

"What kind of condition is Peter in?" Kelso couldn't wait. He had wanted to know before he got there.

"He's alive." Isaac could be seen checking Peter's temples and neck for a pulse. "I didn't think he would be after what we saw him do. That's about all I can say. Everything else still remains a mystery."

"Everything?" The Pope had almost choked. "Then the bleeding persists?"

"No. Actually, it has stopped, but three of the four holes are enlarged on Peter's chest." Zutermier had confirmed his findings.

"It would appear that something—only God knows what—had made its way out." Isaac had thought twice about sticking his fingers in the holes. "See."

"I would have to agree. For once, I no longer feel as if I'm about to be shot into the air like a cannonball. Nevertheless, Peter will probably need to undergo extensive plastic surgery to hide these scars." Zutermier had weighed the pros and cons.

"Not necessary. Darr should be able to handle this task once he returns," the Pope had sounded certain of himself. "This is only a minor deed for him."

"Just like he had healed the wound suffered to my finger." Isaac had held it up for everyone to observe again.

"That's right," the Pope had acknowledged by clapping his hands. "This miracle was so long ago; I had almost forgotten."

"I didn't," Zutermier had taken an extended breath. "Nor did I forget that Darr had healed Peter's stomach before. What I'm getting at is—"

"I don't mean to intervene," said Kelso, "but does anyone else hear that sound, or is it just me?"

"What sound?" The Pope had spun around.

"That sound," Kelso had told him.

"My ears hear nothing," confessed the Pope. "Nothing at all."

"Mine neither." Zutermier had stood motionless. He thought the stress was becoming too much for Kelso to endure. He thought it was causing Kelso to assume things he normally wouldn't.

"Shush. Listen closely," Kelso had bid them. "Now, do you hear that hissing sound?"

"I hear it!" Isaac had come forth.

"Me too, now that you've mentioned what it was." Zutermier had gotten a sudden case of chills.

"Yet what is it, and where is it centered?" The Pope was looking at his cardinals for suggestions.

"The sound appears to be coming from underneath Peter's bed." Isaac had begun to trace it. "That's where it seems to be strongest, Pope Pius."

Isaac, wanting to get to the bottom of this, took to one knee. He was trying to catch a glimpse of what was making the noise. Although his attempt had turned up nothing but darkness, he wouldn't give up. He began to move his head closer until it was flush against the cold pewter of the bed frame. That's when he stuck his lead arm out and started to poke it around in a blind fashion.

"I would advise you not to keep doing that, Isaac." Zutermier tapped him politely on the back. "Believe me, you may be asking for trouble." He watched Isaac ignore him.

"Listen to him, damn it!" Kelso became furious. "What you're doing is only making whatever this is louder! Cut it out! Stop it!"

"So, what do you suggest we do?" Isaac yanked his head away while sitting upright. His face was frowned upon, and his breathing was heavy.

Besides, he didn't enjoy the fact that Kelso had raised his voice at him. He wasn't a kid, and he didn't enjoy being treated like one. Hurt by this, he believed Kelso could have used a much calmer tone of voice, along with a better choice of words, to achieve the same results, but he knew this wasn't Kelso's persona. Kelso's persona was to ridicule you in front of others, he had deemed. This brought him back to the first time he had met Kelso. He couldn't help but recall how they would oftentimes go round for round, word for word, when debating world issues and how to solve them. For years, this had always made him feel as if Kelso had some kind of personal vendetta towards him until he later found out Kelso was this feisty with half of the staff at the Vatican, including the Pope.

"Isaac, please get up from there." The Pope had visions of something awful happening. "I guess we'll just have to put our collective minds together and come up with another solution to this problem—one which is a lot safer," he added while helping Isaac to stand.

"I got it." Zutermier snapped his fingers together. "Why don't we slide the bed back a couple of feet?"

"You mean like this?" Isaac put his head down and began to drive the bed forward, using his muscular thighs.

"Yes, but you're doing too much on your own. I fear you're going to burn yourself out." The Pope wanted to change Isaac's outlook. "You have to learn to let us assist you!"

Whatever the noise was, it was drowned out by the screeching sound of Isaac pushing the bed's metal legs across the floor.

"It's no use." Kelso shook his head. "He is as strong as a bull, but his head is harder than a rock."

Isaac could hear them. He knew this was supposed to be a team effort. Yet, with Peter out of commission, he was aware that he was now ranked the lowest out of the supporting cast. He felt it was almost his sworn duty to sacrifice his body in this time of need, even if it meant he would have to do the bulk of the mule work alone. It didn't matter to him as long as the others stayed in good enough condition to finish the Lord's mission.

"Isaac, stop! Stop this very second and glance at your feet!" The Pope insisted. "Heed me, son! Heed me!"

Isaac didn't hesitate. He could tell by the Pope's facial expression and by the way the others were pointing that something was wrong. Thus, he took his eyes off where he was pushing the bed and glanced downward. To his horror, what he encountered were three king cobras. They were all black in color with massive hoods about the size of an infant's head. Not to mention, they had nine-inch fangs. He also noticed that the two to the left and right of him were coiled in a traditional posture, but the one in the center was en route. It was headed straight toward him. Its movements were so rapid all he could do was freeze. It was too late to run. This was conclusive, and he cringed as the cobra started to weave its way up his body.

"S-S-Shoot it! S-S-Shoot it!" Isaac had stuttered without moving his lips. He was so paranoid that he couldn't even blink or swallow. "What are you waiting for? If you don't do as I want, then the viper is going to crush and eat me whole!"

"Just remain calm," the Pope had explained to him in a soothing voice. "And try not to do anything drastic." He knew this was a lot easier said than done.

The cobra's additional weight was enough to make Isaac scream out. On more than one occasion, he could literally hear his lower vertebrae cracking. However, he knew he had to stand tall despite the cobra's long, reciprocating tongue, which he could repeatedly feel slapping against the bridge of his nose. This feeling was so degrading he had to close his eyes. He also had to close his mouth on account of the ongoing slime that was dripping from the snake's lower jaw. He didn't know if it was a wise tale or not, but he remembered hearing as a child that this species of reptile had hypnotic powers if you stared at it for too long.

"Did those snakes spawn from out of Peter's body?"

"My guess is that they did, Kelso. Only, I think they were a lot smaller at the time—maybe about the size of an actual worm," Zutermier had commented.

"You're kidding, right?"

"No, Kelso, I'm not." Zutermier had shielded his mouth. He had wanted to lower his voice in order to prevent the vipers from going into an all-out attack mode. "See the cobra, which is wrapped around Isaac? It's a lot larger than the two on the left and right. My guess is they haven't grown into an aggressive state yet."

"Give them time." The Pope had wiped a bead of sweat from his brow. "Give them time."

"Then we need to do something fast," boasted Kelso.

"What do you have in mind?"

"Oh, no. That's a decision for him to make, Zutermier." Kelso had pointed towards the Pope. "He is the one with the dreaded weapon."

"Okay, listen up." The Pope had brought the two cardinals closer. He wasn't taking any chances. He wasn't certain if the cobras were intelligent enough to understand what he was about to say. "This is my plan. I will attempt to shoot the snake in the center, but I will need time. I will need one of you to divert the attention of the others so I can have time to aim and fire on them afterward."

"Brilliant. I can do this. I can do this." Zutermier had assured the Pope while walking backward. On the down low, he was making his way into the bathroom to regain the knives that Kelso had left on the sink.

"This is mad! What if you miss it? What if you hit Isaac instead?" Kelso had given the Pope the third degree.

He was skeptical if the Pope had ever fired a gun before. He wasn't even confident if it worked after all these decades of being hidden in a drawer. In his mind, the gunpowder was probably all stale and gunky.

"Please, be careful if you're still going through with this," Kelso wanted to warn him again.

"I know I might miss. You know I might miss." The Pope was feeling the pressure. "Yet what else is there to do? What? Isaac doesn't have that much time with the hood of that cobra raised just above his head, ready to strike."

"I guess we're damned if we do and damned if we don't. Just don't miss, and be prepared for a misfire," Kelso had given him these final instructions.

"I don't plan to miss with the help of the Lord."

"Here! Take one of these!" Zutermier had shouted as he returned with three knives.

He had given one of the knives to Kelso. The other two knives he had kept for himself. The second one was for Isaac, and it was about whether the viper had ever permitted him a chance to obtain it.

"Isaac, are you still with us?" The Pope was questioning his mental stability.

"Y-Y-Yes."

"Good. On my count to three, I want you to fall straight back."

"Son, are you ready?" Kelso had waited for the events to unfold. He did get a kick out of watching Isaac's legs tremble.

"Y-Y-Yes. What's taking you s-s-so long? Do something." Isaac had become impatient. He was tired of looking away from the cobra's face and dodging its dripping slime. It was making his neck stiff.

Zutermier was nervous. He knew there was no stopping a bullet once it was fired. This was a proven fact unless you were Superman. For Isaac's sake, he had kept his fingers crossed that Isaac wouldn't get second thoughts about what the Pope had wanted him to do.

"A little advice. Make sure you shoot the cobra square between the eyes." Kelso knew this placement of the shot would stop the cobra dead in its tracks.

"I'm also ready whenever you are, Pope Pius." Zutermier had it already figured out. He would attempt to stab the cobra on the right once the firearm was discharged.

"Please, b-b-begin the count."

Isaac's demands were reason enough for the Pope. With this being the case, he cocked and aimed his pistol. Yet he noticed something bizarre when he had done this. He noticed that the cobra had switched its focus from Isaac to himself while hissing more aggressively. He didn't believe it to be true at first, but he thought the cobra had maybe taken offense to him pointing his pistol at it.

"Don't pay any attention to it. It's only trying to play mind games," Kelso had said, referring to the cobra's hostile gestures. "Just take a nice breath and calmly squeeze the trigger."

"I will, only my vision is doubled," the Pope had complained while blinking his eyes repeatedly.

"Come on. You can do it," Kelso had tried to encourage him. "I have faith in you."

"Well, here goes nothing. One! Two! Three!"

Isaac did as he was ordered. He fell straight back, hitting his head flush against the floor. This was because he was unable to free his arms, which had remained pinned to his sides. However, as the Pope was about to pull the trigger, the cobra did something magical. The cobra had uncoiled its body with a supernatural display of speed.

"I can't believe it," said the Pope. "Except for TV, that act was unlike anything I had ever seen in person."

He was so dazzled by what he saw that he momentarily let his guard down. In fact, before he could snap back to his senses, the cobra had already launched itself vertically into the air like a cat. He thought all eighteen feet of the reptile was trying to escape over him until its head whipped down and made a beeline for his midsection. As a direct result of this, he had the wind knocked out of him once he fell sideways into the wall.

"This is where it must end," Zutermier informed the cobra on the right before he lunged at it.

The cobra was too quick. Twice, Zutermier missed his mark with the knife. He couldn't believe it. He was almost certain he had poked it. Nevertheless, before he could rear up for his third attempt, the cobra unleashed itself on his chest. The collision was so violent that it sent him backpedaling to the floor.

"Oh, no! This is horrific! Everything seems to be going to hell in a handbasket!" Kelso had timidly displayed his knife. There wasn't any dispute in his mind that the others were deceased. He kept telling himself this while retreating from the last cobra, which had singled him out. "Get back! Get back, you slithery filth!"

"Kelso." The Pope had called out. "Kelso, can you hear me?" His voice was so faint it sounded as if his ribs were broken.

"Your Holiness, you're alive!" Even though Kelso was elated, he never took his eyes off his aggressor. He figured he would keep pacing backward until the cobra had him cornered or it decided to go elsewhere.

"What do you mean? Of course, I'm alive. So are the others. They're only unconscious for the time. It was the power of the sacred robes that saved both Zutermier and me. The snakes vanished the moment they came in contact with the fibers. Unfortunately, you're not wearing one." The Pope didn't want to alarm Kelso but thought he would pass this information along.

"Thanks for delivering the good news."

"Well, it's not like you weren't instructed to put yours on."

"I just wanted to shower first. Is that a crime?"

"Listen. I can see you." The Pope could be heard moving about. "Just keep doing what you're doing. Lead that last cobra into the bathroom. That's where I'll send it to its grave."

"Likewise," Kelso had motioned with his free hand.

At the time, everything seemed to be going as planned. The last cobra was falling for the bait. Unaware that there was a scheme in place, Isaac was beginning to recover. He was beginning to come to his wits when he observed that the tip of the cobra's tail had just slid past him. There was no way he was going to let this go uncontested. He knew he had to do something. He knew he had to acquire at least one of Zutermier's knives, who was still out cold from his earlier ordeal.

"Die, you bloody serpent!" Isaac yelled while pricking the cobra multiple times in the body. "Go back from whence you came!"

"Isaac, get down!" Kelso warned.

It was too late. Isaac didn't have time to duck. All he could do was take both hands and extend them past his face. He did this as a natural reaction. Yet, when the cobra snapped its head in his direction, his limbs were the first thing its open mouth engulfed. Luckily for him, the cobra disintegrated upon contact. He, in return, escaped with a minor thump to the floor.

"Is everyone all right?" The Pope limped out of the bathroom.

"Yes," Isaac stood up. "I'm all right."

"Thank heavens, the cobras are gone!" Kelso ran up to hug Isaac. "I thought you were a goner."

"You and me both," Isaac couldn't stop embracing Kelso.

"What happened? Why is everyone standing over me?" Zutermier awoke while repeatedly rubbing the back of his head.

"We survived our ordeal; that's what happened," Kelso helped Zutermier to his feet.

"It was the robes." Isaac patted him on the back. "The evil serpents didn't stand a chance against them."

"You saved the day once again, Lord." The Pope crossed his heart while glancing up at the ceiling. "Speaking of robes, Kelso, I think it would be in your best interest if you went and put yours on. You saw for yourself what they could do."

"Good idea." Kelso strolled off.

"While you're doing that, the others and I will fasten Peter back to the bed." After they had done this, the Pope saw no reason why they couldn't leave for the basilica.

Chapter 15

It was about to happen. The event the Pope was longing for was finally about to unfold. Even though he felt it had taken what seemed like hours of continuous prayer and planning to get everyone mentally on the same page, nevertheless, they have done it. Now, he and his cardinals were each armed and ready to make their way back to the basilica by way of the bathroom window. They were also prepared to die in the name of the Trinity. This included Kelso, who was chosen to stay behind with Peter, whose health and skin coloration were making a dramatic improvement.

"There. The final piece. Everything is now in place for the journey." Kelso made the others aware of this as he dropped the ladder made of rope toward the ground.

"Isaac, would you please hand me the lantern on the sink?" Zutermier stuck his hand out.

"Here. It's already lit, so be careful."

"Thanks." Zutermier turned the flame up. "If it's okay with everyone, I'll move out first to scour beneath for any signs of throne guards."

"Yes, Zutermier. That sounds like an excellent idea." The Pope respected his bravery. "Just don't wander too far, for I don't want to be held up any longer than necessary."

"I'll keep my search short and to the point."

"Perfect." The Pope gave his approval with a nod. "See you shortly."

In one motion, Zutermier turned his back and made his way onto the window ledge, where he set the lantern. He wasn't afraid of being up this high, yet he had his disputes about the ladder he would be using. It was the material. He wasn't comfortable with how it felt. He was also wary if it was strong enough to support his weight. At some point in time, he even noticed that the ladder stopped about five feet short of the ground.

"Is there something wrong?" The Pope had stared at Zutermier with a blank expression. "Tell me, what do you see?"

"Nothing," Zutermier had answered. "I'm just doing some assessing."

He didn't want to trouble the others with his accusations, so he stepped onto the ladder and began to climb down. He took one step at a time, often switching the hand in which he carried the lantern. He was hesitant at first, but eventually, he gave in and started to trust himself. By the midpoint, he even grew bold and turned around to face the right way. Unfortunately, the bottom of the ladder proved to be a bit of an obstacle for him. He knew if he were to wing it and just jump, he would run the risk of dropping the lantern or burning himself. So he had come up with a solution—a solution that involved him wrapping his legs through the ladder and arching his head straight back until he was upside down like a bat. Once this was done, he had then carefully lowered the lantern, followed by himself.

Once on the ground, Zutermier had paid no attention to the lantern. He had left it where it was. He felt either it would give him away or prevent him from running fast. The key was to stay low and limber, he deemed, as he jogged around to the right side of the palace. It was there he had come to a halt.

"I can't believe it. It's still there. The Lord's walkway made of light is right where we last saw it."

Zutermier had estimated that it was maybe six hundred yards away.

"I have to get back and inform the others of this. This is wonderful news."

On his way back, Zutermier didn't see any signs of other life forms. Yet, he did hear the ruffling of leaves in the woods behind him. By the sound of it, someone or something had taken two steps and stopped. Who or what it was, he didn't have a clue. Needless to say, he knew the others, and he himself would be fair game to negative hostility while they were out of the palace and off the walkway of light.

"WHO'S THERE." Zutermier froze. "In the name of the Lord, please make yourself known," he called out again. This time, he stuck to his objective. He kept traveling in the direction of the ladder.

Zutermier never received a reply. Not that he was looking for one. He just didn't like the feeling he felt. It was one of not knowing who or what was watching him. There was one thing he had learned from life, and that was to always trust your first suspicion, which told him something was out there. Something had a fix on his current location. He was nervous, but he wasn't intimidated to the point of cowardice. Deep within, he knew he would have no problems confronting whatever was out there if he felt threatened. This was another thing he had learned from life: if it doesn't bother you, then you don't bother it.

"Come on. The coast is clear," he called up to the window in a light voice.

"Fine work, Zutermier."

"Thank you, Pope Pius."

The next thing Zutermier saw was Isaac climbing down the ladder. He knew Isaac was terrified of heights and probably had his eyes closed the whole time.

"Don't stop, Isaac. Just keep going." Zutermier was trying his best to guide him. "You're doing fine. I'll inform you when you're at the end."

"No! No! I won't jump! You can't make me do anything!" Isaac could be seen holding onto the ladder with one hand and grabbing at his ears as if he were trying to rip them off.

"What's wrong with him? Why is he doing that?" Kelso appeared confused.

"He hears voices in his head," the Pope stood there helpless. "Evil ones."

"We have to do something! If not, he'll fall and break his neck."

"We can't do anything!" The Pope went off on Kelso. "For one, it's too risky! He'll have to fight his demons alone! I'm sorry to have to say this!"

"Then may the Lord guide his soul." Kelso crossed his heart before bowing his head in silence.

It was tough love, but Zutermier knew what the Pope was saying was true. Even if he manually attempted to bring Isaac to safety, he was positive the ladder would give in. He had already concluded it was barely sturdy enough to support his weight. It was sad to see, but he knew Isaac was in a real life-and-death situation, one which he felt could only be solved by Isaac's strong determination and everyone's prayers.

"No, I won't take my own life! The Lord is my savior, and through him, I shall not fear anything! Not even you!"

"That's it, Isaac, keep battling!" Zutermier continued to shout encouragement. He didn't care if the throne guards heard him or not. He was only concerned with saving Isaac's life. He was aware that Isaac had lost both parents to suicide several years back. He was also aware that the voices in Isaac's head were most likely feeding on this information.

"This is insane! I can't stand here and watch this go on another second! I have to intervene!"

"Kelso, wait! Where are you going?" The Pope lunged at him but failed.

At first, he was petrified that Kelso was going to rat out their mission. This was until he heard the sound of running water behind him. Although he had never turned to check, it appeared to him that Kelso was filling up some sort of container. When he did turn to see, it was too late. Kelso had already thrown the glass of water over his head in the direction of Isaac.

"Thanks, Kelso!" Isaac could be seen drying his face with the sleeve of his robe. "I needed that!"

"You did it, Kelso! You saved him!" The Pope embraced with a gentle hug.

"Now it's your turn. The others are calling for you, but remember, I'm only giving you one hour to conduct your search."

"One hour is all I'll need to find that creature." The Pope winked his eye while making his way onto the window ledge.

Kelso knew this expression all too well. It meant he couldn't trust a word the Pope was saying.

"Remember, Pius. One hour means one hour, not a minute more." He thought he would clear this up.

The Pope never made eye contact again. He was too preoccupied with his descent. He felt that in order to keep the voices out of his head, he would, in fact, have to lower himself from the ladder as quickly as his aging body would let him. This meant he would have to overcome his feeling of queasiness. He didn't know what it was with heights, but he felt that evil was always associated. Even in the *New Testament,* he felt this was the case when Christ himself was tempted on the mountaintop to do all kinds of unspeakable acts.

"That's it, Pope Pius. Let yourself down nice and easy. Don't worry, Isaac and I have got a hold of you."

"Okay! Okay! You can let me fend for myself!" The Pope tossed and turned. In their effort to lower him, the pair unknowingly began to compress his kidneys. "Thanks. It feels so good to be back on solid ground."

"Gentlemen, I'm starting my countdown," Kelso whispered while pointing toward his watch. "Did you hear what I said?"

"We read you loud and clear," Zutermier gave Kelso the cue to retrieve the ladder.

"You had us worried, Isaac," the Pope informed him as he started to walk away. "I thought we had lost you for a second. What had gotten into you up there?"

"I don't know," replied Isaac. "Something sinister just came over me, I guess. It's really hard to put into words."

The Pope figured he wouldn't press Isaac any further about this. He could see for himself that Isaac was still shaken from the ordeal. Physically, he knew Isaac was as strong as a bull, but emotionally, he recognized Isaac had some vulnerabilities. One was his difficulty in expressing his true feelings, and the other was the death of his parents—a loss Isaac was still working through with counseling. From what Isaac had told him, his parents had left behind a final letter explaining that they had both been diagnosed with severe memory loss. Isaac also shared that his parents had made a pact to end their lives with sleeping pills once one was unable to care for the other.

"Don't let it get you down, Isaac. It was only a dumb ploy, a cheap shot below the belt," Zutermier assured him with a smile.

"It's true, Isaac. Remember my story at the basilica. I, too, was deceived by voices."

"Believe me, I'm okay. I just want to concentrate on the mission at hand. I don't want to fail the Lord."

Isaac wished the others would leave him be. He was tired of them, along with everyone else, feeling sorry for him. His parents were dead, and there wasn't anything anyone could do to change this. He knew it was a decision they had both made together and he never once condemned them for their actions.

He'll be the first to admit that there are days when he gets depressed, but he felt it was nothing out of the ordinary or nothing too taboo. After all, he wasn't a robot. He knew it was natural for a human to grieve when someone dear had departed. Would his parents be in heaven? He didn't see why, not because their love for the Lord and each other was strong. He felt they only did what they did when it had become imminent that they were about to be stripped of these very values and become walking corpses. He could sense they were in a better place the moment he arrived back home to arrange their funeral. This is why he had never taken the liberty to question Darr, whether it was true or not. In his mind, he had already had his answer.

"STOP! STOP! EVERYONE STOP! I THINK I HEAR SOMETHING COMING THROUGH THE BRUSH!" The Pope had wasted no time in pulling out his pistol. He was longing for it to be the centaur so he could blast it away.

Isaac stopped, but Zutermier didn't. He had kept walking while holding the lantern out in front. He was hoping that the others would catch on and begin to pursue him, but they didn't. To his surprise, they had stayed where they were. The more he had watched them focus their attention on the sound from afar, the guiltier he had become. For this was the same exact spot where he had also heard movement. Now, he felt like a complete imbecile because he didn't investigate it further. In his prior judgment call, he never anticipated that whatever was out there was probably waiting to ambush the Pope.

"Pope Pius, I have to stress that we're sitting ducks. Anything can happen to us here. It's not safe. Please, we have to make it to the Lord's walkway of light."

"He's right." Isaac had begun to backpaddle his way towards Zutermier. "Come on, let's get a move on."

"Relax, you two. Calm down." The Pope had insisted they do so. He had even gone to great lengths to show them that there was nothing to fear by putting his pistol away. At the time, he didn't know if what he was saying was really true or not. He had just figured out the noise in the brush was too light in weight to be anything dangerous.

"Pope Pius, do we have to do this?" Zutermier had questioned him rather rudely. "We're almost there! We can make it in time! There's no need for this!"

"No need for what?" the Pope had chuckled as the trampling of the foliage became louder.

Zutermier couldn't respond. He was too choked up. He thought either the Pope was going insane or his mind was infested by demons. Whatever the case was, both Isaac and he had drawn their knives out. This was before they had formed a human shield around the Pope, who they both felt had let his guard down totally.

"This is not wise. There's no need for a confrontation, Pope Pius."Isaac had blindly yanked on the Pope's robe from behind. He was trying forcefully to get the Pope to come along with Zutermier and himself.

"What are you two so in fear of? Tell me. Are you maybe in fear of that?" The Pope had parted his cardinals while pointing towards the ground.

"It's a cat!" Zutermier had erupted with laughter. "A bloody cat!"

"I don't believe it!" Isaac smiled while breathing a sigh of relief.

"Yes, it's a cat, but not just any cat. This one is my personal pet. We share a common bond. I call him Koal."

It had only taken a whistle from the Pope to make the black cat with shiny fur emerge completely from the lower vegetation. It was running and meowing the whole time. This cat was one of several strays that had hung around Vatican City. The cats were only tolerated by the locals on account that they had helped reduce the rodent population—a public nuisance that was blamed on the heavy migration of pilgrims to the area during the early eighties.

"Come here, Koal," the Pope had called out, snapping his fingers together.

"Come here, boy."

"Wait a minute." Zutermier did a double take. "I think I recall this guy. Don't tell me this is the same black cat you've been feeding since it was a kitten?"

"That's the one."

"He's huge."

"Yeah. Tell me about it, Zutermier. Either Koal has been eating a lot of vermin, or the Pope here has been feeding him well. I wonder which of the two is the correct answer?"

The Pope never gave a verbal response. He only shrugged his shoulders. He was too preoccupied watching the others rub the cat's head. It was somewhat of a mystery to him why the cat would walk off a few feet, then turn and come back.

"Does he always behave like this, Pope Pius?"

"Sure, Isaac. Koal has always been this affectionate. It's in his nature to be, I guess."

"Sorry, but I think you misunderstood me," Isaac cleared his throat. "I mean, does he always meow this loudly? He hasn't stopped once."

"No." The Pope began to think to himself. "This is a first. It appears that something is wrong. It appears that Koal is trying to get us to do something."

"My hands!"

"What about them?" The Pope twitched. Zutermier nearly spooked him out of his skin with his tone of voice. "What's wrong with your hands?"

"They're red! I have red stuff all over them!"

"I do also!" Isaac had rushed over to where Zutermier was examining his palms with the lantern.

"Any clue as to what's on them?" The Pope stood motionless, biting at his fingernails.

"Well, it's definitely not barbecue sauce." Isaac put a small portion of the substance near his nose.

"Then what is it?" The Pope walked over. "Do you know?"

"I think it's blood," Zutermier blurted out. He, too, took a whiff of the substance.

"Blood?" The Pope had suddenly become lightheaded. "Did you say blood?"

"Yes, blood. But it's not the cat's." Zutermier made sure to check the feline over. "It's probably humans."

"But whose?" The Pope mumbled to himself. He wasn't certain if the others had heard him or not. "I have to get to the bottom of this."

The Pope had a grim look on his face as his stomach began to feel upset. In a weird way, he could almost hear his inner organs tossing and turning like a washing machine. He had so much on his plate earlier that he had forgotten that he had sent both Senior Cardinal Vincent and Julias on a wild goose hunt for the priest who had bitten Isaac's finger. To make the situation even more catastrophic, he hadn't seen or heard from them since. Was this, in fact, their blood? He wouldn't swear to it, and he knew he wouldn't feel at ease until he saw where it originated from.

"Hey! Did you just see that?" Isaac observed the cat standing up on its hind legs and tapping him twice on the thigh. "I believe the Pope's right! I think this cat wants us to follow it."

"I guess we'll just have to do it," Zutermier had led first. "Maybe it will turn up something."

"Hopefully, it won't." The Pope had kept his fingers crossed. The last thing he had wanted to stumble across was the mutilated remains of Vincent and Julias.

For added security measures, the Pope and his cardinals had armed themselves to the teeth. They weren't taking any chances. They had their knives drawn while they forcefully navigated their way through this heavily wooded area. Ironically, they were looking for anything unexplainable.

"Wait just a second." The Pope had stopped cold in his tracks. "This is nonsense. This is far enough. We could be walking for days. See for yourselves, Koal has already wandered away."

"HOLY MOTHER OF PEARLS! This is true, but focus your attention on the tree stump over there!" Zutermier had pointed while jumping up and down. "Do you see it?"

"My word! What is it, Zutermier? I can't quite make it out."

"It kind of looks like human remains." Isaac had tried to fix his eyes on where Zutermier was shining the lantern.

"You could be right." Zutermier's heart had begun to race. "However, we won't know for sure unless we investigate."

"Well, what are we waiting for?" The Pope had tapped Isaac on the back.

"Zutermier, turn up the flame."

Isaac wouldn't go near the scene entirely. He thought it would be best if he just glanced from afar. It was too bloody, and he didn't want to fill his head with too many negative images. The only reason he had come as far as he did was to please the Pope. He thought it was weird, though, how the moonlight had reflected off the male Caucasian bodies, which were both naked and inches apart from one another. He had also thought it was unusual how both victims had their left foot and right arm chopped off. In a way, it almost felt as if the violence was part of some sort of twisted ritual.

"What do you suppose happened to them?"

"It's hard to say, Zutermier." The Pope was ready to puke. "But I do know they're missing limbs, and both of their testicles have been removed. Not to mention, their throats have been cut to the extent that their heads appear as though they're about to roll off. That's what probably did them in."

"This is what I also came up with." Zutermier had kept his pitch down to a murmur. "Look at this. Now, I know these are bite marks, but how do you suppose these long welts got on this person's back?"

"They're whip marks, I guess."

"Whip marks?" Zutermier had carefully thought it over. He was kind of drained by what he had seen. He didn't know how someone could perform such a brutal act on another living being. "So, who do you think they are, Pope Pius?"

"Again, it's hard to say. Their faces are both disfigured. Nevertheless, if I had to make a choice, I would say that they were cardinals or members of the Vatican's staff."

"No way. Everyone from the Vatican was accounted for."

"Are you certain of this, Zutermier? How do you know?"

"While Darr was leading the others and me back to the palace, I tried on numerous occasions to open some room doors at random. They wouldn't budge. Not even the handles would turn for me. It was like the Lord himself was on the opposite end, preventing me from gaining admittance." Zutermier had gone into detail. "Not to be discouraged, I did manage to get Kelso's door and my own open."

"But you two weren't in there." The Pope began to ponder. "Yet neither was I when I went to acquire some dry clothing."

"My point exactly."

The Pope was elated by Zutermier's accusations, yet it was only temporary. One, he was discouraged by the two mutilated bodies in front of him. He was also worried if the killer or killers were still in the area. Even though it was now clear to him that the victims were too muscular in build to be Vincent and Julius, he remained livid. This was because he had compassion for all walks of intelligent life, not just Catholic clergymen.

"OVER HERE, YOU TWO! TAKE A PEEK AT WHAT I FOUND!"

"What is it, Isaac?" Zutermier came over in a flash, followed by the Pope.

"It's some photos from a broken camera. I found it, along with two female purses. However, both of the purses are empty of any contents."

"Judging from the pictures, these people were dressed like tourists." Zutermier thumbed through the stills as he handed the lantern over to Isaac. "You can see that their lens was never focused. The camera must have started snapping these images when it impacted the ground."

"So, where are the women?" Isaac began to turn his head in every cardinal direction. "There are only two bodies here. Do you think they escaped?"

"I can't answer that truthfully," said Zutermier. "But I think they were abducted by goblins."

"Poor souls." The Pope tearfully crossed his heart. "They never stood a chance." He walked and knelt in prayer over the two male victims.

"I'll say they didn't stand a chance. Look at the horror in this one's face. They captured their own deaths." Isaac dropped the two purses to the ground.

"This last image, I can't quite make it out." Zutermier held the photo out for Isaac. He was hoping that Isaac could maybe shine some light on the situation. "So, what do you see?"

"Nothing but the ass of a horse." Isaac had put his hand over his mouth. He didn't mean to put it this rudely.

"What did you just say?" The Pope had sprung up. "Never mind." He had snatched the camera away. His breathing had become so intense that he was beginning to cast a light film over the laminated screen.

"Well. Do you agree with Isaac?"

"Yes, that's the creature! That's the centaur we're in search of! Come on, we have to get to the basilica!"

"Hold it." Zutermier had whistled for the Pope and Isaac to halt where they were. "There's something I must do." He had begun to strip off his clothing.

Zutermier didn't want to leave the bodies in their present state. He had wanted to give them a formal burial, but he knew he didn't have enough time to dig a hole. He knew the others were in a hurry. He knew they were eager to face off against the centaur. Thus, he had begun to contemplate leaving the robe, which was given to him, over the two bodies, but he had never gone through with it. He deemed it would be wise if he kept the Lord's gift for himself after remembering how its powers had out-favored the evil cobras. Still, he did manage to tear the cassock he was wearing underneath into two long shreds before placing them over the victims' faces and torsos.

"I think a prayer is needed for the two victims," Isaac calmly insisted.

In a show of solidarity, they had formed a tight circular around the victims' bodies before saying a silent prayer.

"That was a mighty kind gesture of you." The Pope had commemorated Zutermier with a pat on the back as he watched him get dressed. "I mean it."

"It was nothing," Zutermier had responded in a somber voice. "But finding this centaur and putting an end to its circle of bloodshed will be a big deal."

"Then let's take the fight to it." Isaac had turned up the lantern's flame. "It's about time we became the aggressors." He had led the charge through the woods.

Chapter 16

One could tell by Isaac's body language as he bobbed and weaved through the branches in his way that he didn't want to reside with the two bodies any longer than what was required. It was giving him the creeps. In fact, the pace he had set forth from the wooded area was so concentrated that it had landed everyone back at the iron gates of the basilica in less than eight minutes flat. From there, the search had begun. Up and down the square, they went, looking for clues. Since they were aware that no harm would come to them as long as they remained on the lighted walkway, they didn't feel a need to arm themselves. Yet they had agreed if the opportunity arose, the Pope would indeed take a pop shot at the centaur. This was all in an effort to try to eliminate the creature from a safe distance rather than trying to stab it to death at close range.

"It's no use." The Pope had bent over near the steps of the basilica. "Let's take a break," he said, gasping for air.

"I think we're just wasting time," said Isaac. "I don't think the centaur or the Lord's shepherd are still here."

"Maybe you're right!" The Pope had sat down. "We searched everywhere! We even formed a human chain so I could look inside the maze!"

"That we did." Zutermier took a seat beside the Pope. " What's next? Do you want to turn back?" He was hoping the Pope would say no or just ignore what he had mentioned.

"Not yet." The Pope picked his nostrils. "I know we still have some time left, but about how much?"

"Exactly fifty-eight minutes." Isaac glanced at his watch.

 "Great. That leaves us enough time to search one more key area."

"Do you mean the area in which Peter's altercation took place?"

"You took the words right out of my mouth, Zutermier." The Pope had gotten up from where he was camped. "Come on!"

Upon the Pope's request, the others immediately followed him up the stairs to the centermost door of the basilica.

"Would you like us to remain here until you've had a chance to check things over?"

"Don't be silly, Isaac. We're in this together." The Pope placed his hands over the door handle.

He was ready to enter. He didn't care if someone was in there or not. Although, he anticipated he would feel a little funny in the presence of the Christ replica. After all, he knew the others, and himself were disobeying direct orders. To deal with his dilemma, he felt he would avoid visual contact with the replica. In fact, he would act like it wasn't even there.

"Hey! Take a look at those shooting stars across the southern sky!" Zutermier shouted. "Do you see them?"

"Yes. There are literally thousands of them." Isaac tried to keep count.

"They're magnificent, but there has to be a great explanation for this occurrence. A person in one lifetime is lucky if he or she ever gets to witness two. No, this has to be the doing of the—"

The Pope cut his sentence short. He didn't want to alarm or create widespread pandemonium; thus, he kept his opinions all bottled up. However, he didn't believe what the others were seeing were falling stars. No, he believed they were angels. Angels who were sent forth by the Lord to wage some type of military campaign on Earth. Judging from where the angels were landing, it appeared to him as if the battle was going to take place in the valley.

"Just like that, it's over! The stars have stopped falling!" Isaac sounded saddened by this. "Zutermier, you're into astrology. What do you think caused these events?"

"Your guess is as good as mine." Zutermier was still searching the night sky for answers.

"I'm just elated; the entire universe didn't collapse down on us."

"Be careful of what you wish for." The Pope had turned his back before entering the basilica. "What? Don't look at me like that. It was meant to be a joke."

"A funny one at that, I might add." Zutermier had briefly smiled.

"Isaac." The Pope had called out as he twisted his body to look past Zutermier, who was directly behind him. "Isaac."

"Yes. I hear you."

"You can reduce the flame some and set the lantern on the floor by the door we just passed through. We can require it once we return."

"Are you certain of this?"

"Sure. We won't be long." The Pope had assured him with a wink.

Isaac did as he was instructed. He retracted the wick of the lantern just enough so the flame wouldn't go out entirely, and then he placed it on the floor by the centermost door. He had done all of this before he trailed Zutermier down the main aisle. It was from this point on, nevertheless, that he detected something unusual. He detected that it was a few degrees hotter inside than earlier. He felt this was odd, as the temperature wasn't this warm when it was daylight. To him personally, it appeared as if the basilica was once occupied by an eminent force—a force that gave off heat like a blast furnace.

"Is it just me, or does it feel strange in here?" The Pope began to wipe the sweat from his forehead.

"Trust me, it's not you." Isaac had begun to mimic the Pope.

"I see why it feels so strange in here!" Zutermier had dropped to his knees. "Look, the Christ replica is missing!"

"This had to be the work of the goblins! They are the only ones who could have broken inside and done this!" Isaac had run to the replica's last location. "Buzzards! Buzzards! Those evil bastards! Awe, what have they gone and done?" He had fallen to his knees while pounding his fists on the floor.

"Why would they do such a thing? Why would they decimate a representation of our Lord like this?" Zutermier had turned and questioned the Pope. "I thought they weren't able to cross holy ground?"

"To be honest, I don't think the goblins had anything to do with this."

"You don't." Zutermier had scowled his face. "Then you don't suppose the replica had up and left by itself?"

"No, of course not." The Pope had almost swallowed his own tongue. It was a scary thought. Yet, it was also a good case in point. However, he had seen no real evidence supporting this. "Come on, I'll explain myself better on the way." He had led Zutermier to where Isaac was standing motionless and confused.

The closer the Pope had gotten towards the front, the clearer everything had become. From what he could detect, he knew whoever had abducted the replica had done so in a respectable manner. There were no visible signs of damage to any of the objects in the basilica, something he knew the goblins were too reckless to avoid. He didn't know why, but he thought Darr had apprehended the replica for some unexplainable purpose. He felt this was most likely done when Darr had departed after dinner.

"Can you two see what I see?"

"You mean the metal clamp rings?" Zutermier had followed the Pope's finger.

"Yes," the Pope had replied. "I'm referring to the metal clamp rings."

"What about them?" asked Isaac. "There are four altogether, which serve the purpose of fastening the replica to the wall."

"I know that much." The Pope had walked and stood directly underneath.

"He means, look how someone had the decency to unfasten and reassemble the nuts to the threads—not to mention the washers. If I were evil-minded, even I wouldn't have been this delicate."

"That's exactly what I'm implying, Zutermier. It's too perfect to be a crime. If you ask me, it appears more like an inside job."

Unlike the others, the Pope knew from a past encounter that the replica had the ability to communicate and come to life when Darr was present. It was a defining moment; he could recall it so vividly. Unfortunately, there was no way he was going to spill the beans and inform his cardinals of this. He knew they would never stop asking him questions. Still, at the same time, he didn't want to continue to lie to them either. It was making him uncomfortable. All he had ever wanted was for them to stop insisting the goblins had any part in the mischief. He was worried it would make them too flustered to do battle if they were to embark upon the centaur.

"Great. Another mystery." Isaac had withdrawn his attention from the wall as he walked up a small flight of stairs that led to the brass canopy.

He was headed toward the single door—the same door Peter had used to gain admittance to the narrow hallway, the same narrow hallway that was intersected by both the bathroom and storage room.

"So, we know the goblins didn't take the replica! Well, does anyone have an idea who did?" Isaac had wanted to get this off his chest.

"That I can't tell you, son." The Pope had joined Isaac by the door. He was also accompanied by Zutermier.

"Isaac, maybe this was done by the Lord's throne guards to prevent the goblins from destroying it."

"You know, Zutermier, you might be onto something." Isaac nodded. "Yeah, can live with that."

"Anything is possible, but enough discussion on this topic. We have to move on. Besides, we only have a small window of time left to conduct our last investigation before Kelso sounds the alarm. Heaven only knows what will happen then."

"The Pope's right." Isaac began to hastily twist the knob.

He was one who didn't need to be reminded of the throne guards' wrath. It made him too weak to think straight, just knowing how they had almost done him in. He didn't understand why at the time, except that he believed they had no tolerance for anyone other than the Trinity.

"Is there a problem?" The Pope watched Isaac struggle with the knob.

"It's this door!" Isaac began to grit his teeth as he pulled back with all of his strength. "It won't budge! It appears as if something is holding it shut!"

"Stand aside. Let me have a turn at it." Zutermier eagerly swapped places.

"So?"

"Isaac's right, Pope Pius. I can't get it to budge, either. If you don't believe us, then you may try it for yourself."

"That I will. You may move, Zutermier!" The Pope bull-guarded his way into position. He was unsatisfied with his cardinal's efforts. Now he was going to show them how it should be done. Now he was going to show them that this old man still had gas in his tank. "Come on, door! Why do you have to be so stubborn?"

"We could be here all night," Isaac had whispered behind the Pope's back.

"Well?" Zutermier had raised his eyebrows after about sixty seconds.

"But this can't be!" The Pope had turned red. He had to stop. All of that yanking back and forth was making him dizzy. "Look, this door doesn't even have a mechanical lock."

"Maybe the creature is behind it. How big did you say it was again?"

"Don't make light of the situation, Isaac. Now is not the place." The Pope's voice had hardened. "This goes for you also, Zutermier. I hear your cackling."

The Pope was at a stalemate. His cardinals and his failure to open the door had left him feeling depleted. What was he to do, though? He knew if the others and he were to leave and try to gain entrance through the basilica's back door, they would run out of time. Worse yet, he knew they would no longer be on the Lord's sacred walkway. Biting his bottom lip until the taste of blood had swelled his mouth, he had unconsciously taken his fist and banged it three times against the newly painted surface. He was miserable. He was miserable that he would never get the chance to remove the centaur's head and undo the curse that was placed on Peter and probably the Lord's shepherd.

"Tell me, what am I to do? What am I to do?" He had placed his head on the door and one hand on the knob.

Rejected, the Pope was ready to leave. He was ready to make the journey back to the palace when the door swayed open from the other side. Naturally, he was caught off balance by this and was sent flying into the dark hallway on his knees, where he felt a hand. A much larger hand gripped the knuckles he had never removed from the knob.

"You!" the Pope had heard an authoritative voice yell out.

He had never seen a body to match the voice, which had smelled of rotten flesh. He did, however, see an arm extend out and grab the others by their throats. Before he knew it, they were upside down and shivering next to him along the wall. At one point in time, he could feel their hearts beating against his kidneys. This was before he had watched the same large hand slam the door shut.

"Get up! Get up!" The voice had threatened the Pope and his cardinals with the sound of a whip. Neither one of them could see the whip, but they could feel the wind it had generated as it struck the floor twice.

The Pope and his cardinals had immediately complied, fearing they would get hit if they didn't. Despite the blackout conditions, they had managed to stay together. They had also managed to stutter-step their way forward while pawing their hands back and forth in the air. This was a natural reaction they had each come up with, to give them a heads-up if they were about to bump into a wall or one another.

"Move until I tell ye to stop!" The unknown voice had spoken. "Move, I said!"

"Who is this, Pope Pius?" Zutermier had whispered. "Do you know?"

"I'm afraid I don't." The Pope was being honest. "Just do what he says, and don't do anything dramatic like pulling out your knives."

"Whoever it is, his breath sure stinks." Isaac had squeezed his nostrils together. "He's definitely not an angel. An angel's mouth wouldn't smell this foul."

"How would we even know?" The Pope had mumbled.

"Keep moving! Do what I say!"

"Do any of you hear what I hear?"

"No, Zutermier. What's that?" The Pope was waiting to be told the answer. He had kept his voice so low; he wasn't certain if he had even been heard.

"Listen closely. Listen real closely."

"What? Are you referring to that clucking sound behind us?" The Pope had turned to where he thought Zutermier was.

"Yes. That's the sound."

"What do you suppose it is?" Isaac's teeth had begun to clatter together.

"Hooves," Zutermier had said discreetly. "Rather large hooves."

"You know, I think you're right." The Pope had cleared the wax from his ears.

"So, what does all of this imply?" Isaac had put his hand over his mouth. He had wanted to conceal his voice as much as possible, even though he had felt the hooves echoing throughout the hallway were doing a good job at that. "You don't suppose the blank is behind us?"

"Yes." Zutermier's voice had started to crack. "I do think the blank is behind us."

"This is appalling." The Pope's lips could barely form the words. "Appalling."

"Tell me about it." Zutermier could see his whole life flash before his eyes.

"Where do you think the centaur is taking us?"

"Who knows, Isaac." The Pope had placed his hand in his pocket. He was letting his fingertips, one by one, caress the cold steel of the pistol. "But if we don't do something soon, we're going to be sacrificial lambs. This I do know."

The Pope wasn't about to get played for a buffoon. He was ready to react. He was ready to eliminate the centaur. He was ready to take out his aggression for what it had done to the Lord's shepherd and

Peter. His only concern was, he might shoot the others in the process. True, his target could see him, but he couldn't see it. Still, he had remained optimistic that he could turn and illuminate the hallway with a round of shots, if he could somehow get the others off to one side.

"Have we passed the bathroom yet?" The Pope was curious if any of his cardinals had noticed.

"I'm not sure," Zutermier was the first to reply.

"Why do you ask this?" Isaac was a little curious. "Are you thinking what I'm thinking?"

"Just sing out before you hit the floor." The Pope's lips had formed a sinister grin in the darkness.

What he had in mind was to have his cardinals duck into the bathroom the second they passed it. This was so he could twirl around and start blasting without regression.

"Halt! Halt! I command you goblins to obey!" The centaur had shoved everyone to the floor.

"Hey. Did you just hear what it called us?" Zutermier was beside himself.

"Yes, I heard." Isaac had a hard time believing it also. For a second there, he thought they were all goners. Now he knew there was a slim chance they might survive their ordeal.

"Listen up, you two." The Pope spoke under his breath. "We need to work this situation to our advantage. This means keep your heads down, your hoods on, and don't say nothing. Play the part is what I'm asking you until help arrives in one form or another. If we're fortunate, then maybe we'll get taken to Natas Christopher." He kept his fingers crossed.

"Feeble fools! Don't just lie there! Get up! Stand at attention before ye feel the thrash of my whip! Ye goblins will learneth to obey, or else!"

"I don't know how much more of this abuse I can withstand," Zutermier felt like a cornered rat. "But I think we better do as it says." He fought back the urge to pull out his knife.

"Trust me. I know how you feel." The Pope had struggled to get up. Before he could erect himself entirely, he had felt a hand, a much larger hand, grip his knuckles similarly to the way they were squeezed when he had first entered the hallway. It didn't hurt, and it was over before he knew it. Still, why was the centaur doing this to him? He didn't have any indication, and he remained uncertain if he was to administer the same grip back. Not that he believed he could duplicate the hold.

"Form a line!" The centaur had forcefully aligned the Pope and his cardinals into position. "A straight line!"

"Look down," said the Pope. "We must be near the storage room." He was making reference to a thin stream of light at the bottom of the door.

Other than sticking out like a sore thumb, the light was too hampered by the door itself to light up the hallway entirely. The Pope was still unable to see past his own two feet. Yet, he was certain this would soon change once his cardinals and he were inside. With this soon to be the case, he wondered if they could continue to pass for goblins. This was very crucial to him, on account that he knew he would have to change the game plan if he suspected they couldn't.

"Kelso should be singing right about now." Isaac had calculated that a whole hour had gone by. "Yep, he should be belting like a canary."

"How certain are you?" the Pope had questioned him.

"About a hundred percent." Isaac had thought about pushing the indigo button on his watch to confirm this, but didn't for safety purposes.

"Silence, I say! Now, kneel and bow thy heads!" the centaur had instructed, just before it reared back and threw its pitchfork into the mist of the door. The Pope and his cardinals couldn't see the weapon, but they could hear it as it spiraled through the air.

A minute had gone by, and nothing new had happened. The door had still remained a mystery with the centaur's pitchfork stuck amongst it. At first, the Pope had assumed this was another random act of violence. However, as more time had elapsed, he saw that it was, in fact, part of a ritual—a ritual which he had believed was taking place on the other side by another party. But by whom? What had drawn him to this conclusion was the centaur's mood change. It was obvious to him the centaur was too patient for something not to be developing. The centaur had also reminded him not to try anything risky, just by dragging its whip across his lower back.

"Don't any of you goblins think about rising up!" the centaur had growled. "Continue to kneel until I command ye to cease!"

Three more minutes had gone by when the storage room door had finally drifted open. It was the first time in about twenty minutes that the Pope and his cardinals had seen any light. So much so, their eyes had to make a hard and painful adjustment. From within the room, they could hear strange laughter spilling out. They could also see a ten-foot bull standing upright like a human. This creature, who was dressed in gold breast plating and wore gold shin guards around his ankles, was called the Gate Guardian. To their dismay, the Gate Guardian had a face that could hamper one's soul into submission, and when he exhaled, a mist of skunk-like musk had saturated the air. In one hand, the Gate Guardian held a circular shield. It was made from solid oak but decorated with gold tin, and depicted on the shield itself was an image of a Billy Goat centered inside of a pentagram. For a weapon of choice, the Gate Guardian wore two swords similar to the make of Darr around his waist.

Zutermier knew the Gate Guardian was nothing to toy with. He could see that the Gate Guardian's broken horn and battered shield told a story. It told the story of the immense struggles the Gate Guardian had endured. The Gate Guardian was a survivor; there wasn't any doubt in his mind about this. He could also see that the Gate Guardian was the poster child for evil, with its strength and loyalty being the axes or the foundation on which the hell was driven on.

"Centaur, what is thy calling?" the Gate Guardian asked as he snatched the embedded pitchfork from the door. "Answer me!"

"Sir, I have three more who wish to serve."

"Only three!" The Gate Guardian seemed unimpressed as he examined and felt the tines of the centaur's pitchfork.

"Yes. Only three, sir."

"Hmmm!" The Gate Guardian rolled his eyes. He became so irate in that short period of time, he began to stomp his feet back and forth like a rodeo bull ready to plow its horns into someone or something.

"Art ye not pleased, sir?"

The Gate Guardian didn't respond. Instead, he turned his back and violently slammed the door, generating a pocket of air strong enough to almost lift the Pope and his cardinals.

"Sir, is there something wrong?" the centaur asked the second the Gate Guardian reopened the door.

"There is plenty wrong!" the Gate Guardian replied while breathing heavily. "For one, ye art out of thy jurisdiction! Ye should have never abandoned thy post at the square! Never! Ye know the creed, centaur! It hasn't changed! Already, five gates which grant passage into this world have been sealed off, and many of our brethren lost! That's why if ye weren't so highly ranked as a warrior, I would have long implanted this pitchfork into thy chest!"

"I am gracious." The centaur had taken to one knee. "That I am, sir."

Zutermier was impressed. He couldn't believe how the Gate Guardian could determine the centaur's military status and assignment just by staring at its weapon unless the information he felt was somehow inscribed on one of the tines.

"What is the hold-up here?" Another centaur, dressed in a black decorative breastplate, had appeared from behind the Gate Guardian. This centaur had the body of a beautiful Morgan and the face of a blue-eyed prince with blond dreadlocks. Unlike the other centaur, this one had also worn stunning diamond rings and smelled of perfume.

"This warrior has three more who wish to serve, Dramaticus, only he has broken the creed!" The Gate Guardian had stepped aside, allowing the ruler of the centaurs visual access to the hallway.

"Then put the guilty to death!" Dramaticus had turned his back while rearranging the rings on his fingers. "Put them all to death, for that matter!"

Isaac had to do a double take. He couldn't possibly perceive that there was more than one of these creatures roaming about.

"Unfortunately, Dramaticus, this cannot be done! He is an elite soldier! Besides, it would be too time-consuming to replace someone of his stature!"

"Then return his working tool and erect those who wish to render their services!"

"Centaur! Consider thyself fortunate!" The Gate Guardian had drawn his attention by tossing his weapon through the air. "Now, assemble the workers!"

"Goblins, stand!" The centaur in the hallway had communicated while striking the floor twice with his whip. "Abide and prepare thyselves for labor!"

"Excellent." Dramaticus had nodded. "I am pleased that they are obedient. You know, good help is always hard to come by."

Out of the blue, about a dozen more goblins had appeared, marching their way up the narrow slope of the corridor. Accompanying them at the time were two barbarian-looking centaurs who were armed with pitchforks and whips. They weren't a sight for the squeamish, with their long, matted hair and long, matted beards. Nevertheless, they both had upper bodies that would make a professional wrestler envious. One was stationed at the front of the goblins, and the other was stationed at the rear. The pair had also taken turns wastefully drinking brew out of a large ram's horn. Even though the goblins were still some distance away, the sheer vibration of their footsteps could be felt the entire time. The goblins had sounded like a small platoon approaching. A small platoon that was each armed with a miner's tool called a poll pick, which was a combination of a hammer and a chisel.

"What of this smaller goblin? What should we do with him?" The Gate Guardian had turned towards Dramaticus. "Should we eat him or maybe molest him?"

"Neither!" Dramaticus had blindly responded. At the time, he was still positioned inside the storage room in the direction facing the army of foot soldiers.

"Tell me, where does thy answer leave us?" The Gate Guardian had become hostile.

"Just permit the smaller goblin to travel inside with me!" Dramaticus had suggested. "I will tend to him myself! The other two can fall in behind this garrison!"

"Advance this dwarf forward? But he will be of no use to us in combat!"

"Perhaps in time, he will. I can justify my actions."

"This better hold some weight!" the Gate Guardian had grunted.

Zutermier and Isaac had both breathed a sigh of relief, but it was only momentary as they watched the Pope get tossed inside like a rag doll by the centaur in the hallway. They both knew that within a matter of minutes, he would be ostracized from them. It was a harsh reality they weren't prepared to accept. This was due to the fact that they weren't certain if they would ever see him alive again. Yet what could they physically do when they were aware they couldn't even save themselves?

"Would ye care to express thyself now?"

"Most certainly," said Dramaticus. "What I have learned over the course of time, Gate Guardian, is that this dwarf breed of goblin has powers all their own. I have seen them clear large objects away just by using telepathy."

"Impressive."

"But this service ye see isn't worth a fuck unless they art in numbers! So, where are the others?" Dramaticus had stuck his pitchfork underneath the Pope's chin. "There were supposed to be more! Where are they?"

The Pope was speechless. His jaw literally felt as though it were made of rubber bands. He knew what had happened to the others. He had seen them get eaten in the maze by the gooey bats. Still, Dramaticus, he felt, was preventing him vocally from making this known, on account of one of the tines being positioned directly over his Adam's apple. Besides, he really didn't want to say anything anyway. He was too fearful he would give the others and himself away. Thus, he had shrugged his shoulders in an attempt to get Dramaticus to come to reason and remove the weapon.

"COMING THROUGH! COMING THROUGH!" the lead centaur marching up the corridor had shouted.

The ram's horn of brew was no longer visible. One of them had apparently ditched it off to the side in an effort to conceal their drunkenness from the Gate Guardian and their ruler, Dramaticus.

"Halt, I say! Hold thy position!" the Gate Guardian had ordered while drawing one of his swords. "What is the destination of this mission?"

"Sir, Operation Bring Back!" the lead centaur had snickered. The centaur in the rear could also be heard doing the same.

"I never heard of it!" the Gate Guardian had placed the tip of his sword in the midsection of the lead centaur. "I said it's not familiar to me!"

"Guard, must I remind ye that thou art in the presence of royalty and a senior officer!" Dramaticus was quick to point this out. "So, if I were thee, I would answer properly! Now, what is thy objective?"

"Operation Bring Back, Your Majesty!" the lead centaur had snickered again.

"Just say the words, Dramaticus!" the Gate Guardian had tightened the grip on his sword's handle. "Please, just say them!"

"Wait, I-I-I can explain!"

"Then do so!" Dramaticus's eyes had become enlarged. "Believe me, you don't want to press thy luck!"

"But, Your Majesty, the angel Pendelkon's entourage requests assistance," the lead centaur had pleaded with a look of earnestness. "You see, their——"

"Well!" Dramaticus leaned forward. "Out with it!"

"The angel Pendelkon's entourage is lost, Your Majesty!" the lead centaur had paused to swallow after communicating this. He had seemed confused that his remark had caused both the Gate Guardian and Dramaticus to erupt with laughter.

"Wait! Ye mean to tell us that the great angel Pendelkon is bemused?" The Gate Guardian had put away his sword. He could no longer control his emotions. "Is this really a case in point?"

"Yes." The lead centaur seemed reluctant to agree. "It appears they can't navigate their way through the seventh gate."

"Impossible!" Dramaticus's smile had turned to a frown. "How can the successor to the infamous Nero be lost?"

"Tell me, my friend, who gave ye these instructions?" The Gate Guardian drew his sword once more. This time, he held it at the lead centaur's throat. "Speak!"

"It was Christopher." The lead centaur had difficulty getting the words out. "Natas Christopher gave us these instructions, sir."

"Then carry them out, but do so cautiously! For once the angel Pendelkon breaks the threshold of this world, his atomic mass will alert the Trinity. This is if he hasn't done so already. Since its construction, the seventh gate, which is under this basilica, has gone unnoticed. Not even the Trinity knew it existed, yet I feel this will soon change. Yes, be prepared to fight the battle of thy lives, my warrior friends." The Gate Guardian withdrew his sword, allowing the small, coherent army room to pass.

"And you!" Dramaticus turned and pointed out into the hallway. "Remember to report back to thy post in the square until further notice!"

"Yes." The centaur in the hallway bowed. "Thy orders will be obeyed, Your Majesty."

"Excellent! That pleases me!" Dramaticus twiddled his fingers in the air just before the Gate Guardian slammed the door shut.

Chapter 17

The Pope had felt vertiginous and lifeless the instant the storage room door was closed. He couldn't believe this was happening to him. He couldn't believe he was all alone with two hideous monsters who were literally shoving him in the back down the narrow slope of the corridor. The air within was so tainted the further he traveled; at times, it felt as if someone was suffocating him with a cheesecloth. He wasn't an environmentalist, but he was positive the airborne toxins were a direct result of the sulfuric gases that had ripped loudly from the villains' asses.

With great reason to be, the Pope was so frightened of being found out or sexually assaulted that he could barely feel his legs move. In all his years at the Vatican, he could only remember traveling this route three times in thirty years. Other than those instances, he had never seen a need to be in here. The corridor was always too confined for his taste, despite the fact he was aware it would widen out into a colossal-sized ballroom. Still, he didn't like the poor lighting or the cobwebs that had infested the ceiling throughout. Personally, he had always believed the storage unit had the feel of a medieval wine cellar rather than a bomb shelter. A bomb shelter, which he had the architects convert after the renovation project to the basilica in order to house some priceless artifacts and relics.

"What do ye think of Natas Christopher's exile?"

"I think his confinement in Heaven has made him foolish, Gate Guardian!" Dramaticus, the king of the centaurs, had replied bitterly. "He is an imbecile if he believes he can pass through Hell's seventh gate in his present spiritual state. No flesh-breathing humanoid has ever entered the underworld. It's impossible, I proclaim. The extreme pressure of the dimension will do him in long before the climate ever has the chance to make his blood boil."

"This I can't deny."

"Then why do we wait to be slaughtered?"

"We have our orders."

"Orders?" Dramaticus had chuckled.

"Yes. Despite the fact *we are alert that Natas Christopher remains ignorant to some important issues, he has other warriors deployed on this Earth, and the creatures camped in the valley believe in something far different.* He has them sold; he has more attributes of an archangel rather than a reptilian. For this, they will turn on and lay to rest anyone who opposes. Trust me, the best are here from both sides."

"Archangel, he is not! This I can prove!" Dramaticus had frowned while nudging the Pope forward.

"Lower thy voice."

"I swear to thee, Natas Christopher is only a reptilian. He looks like one, and he thinks like one. Worse yet, I can still detect the odor of his humanoid body as if he were walking before us now."

"Bite thy tongue, for he has done a marvelous job convincing our Lord Nero otherwise. I think he may be much more myself."

"Really? I didn't know this, Gate Guardian."

"Yes. Even I am baffled when it comes to Natas Christopher's genetic makeup," the Gate Guardian had proclaimed. "Since his birth in Heaven, the recipe to his creation has been guarded as a secret by the Trinity. Only they, and a select few, ever knew the realness of the matter. However, I think our Lord Nero may be one of them."

"In time, the truth will be exposed to both of us. I will see to it personally!"

"And what do ye seek to do?" The Gate Guardian had stopped in his tracks.

"Make him earn his rank!"

"Be mindful of the words which ye speak, for they may be interpreted as treason by some."

"I can assure thee, my loyalty to the fallen angel is pure! You needeth not remind me of this!"

"Then thou must be aware that our Lord Nero loves Natas Christopher like a son and is eager to guide him through the seventh gate at any cost of life. This includes in Hell and in Heaven." The Gate Guardian had made this perfectly clear as Dramaticus, and he had continued to walk forward.

The Pope had never stopped.

"Right, ye are. For the angel Pendelkon's arrival to this world will signify just that."

"Signify?"

"Death. And lots of it."

"Yes, hopefully not ours." The Gate Guardian had become depressed. "For we have done battle a long time together, that's why I'm pleading to thee to play things by feel. I can remember when ye were a runt. Now you're king of thy kind."

"Say no more, Gate Guardian. Say no more."

The Pope was alert, and he was comprehending as much as he could. He was filtering the valuable data in through his ears and storing it in his memory banks for later usage, much like a computer would. There were two things he had picked up on right away from the tyrants' conversation. One was envy, and the other was deceit. He was hoping he could use either one to his advantage, the same way he had turned the gooey bats against the goblins in the maze. Would his loaded pistol be enough to stop any of them? He didn't think so. Nor did he believe he would see the others alive again. For some reason, he had pictured them burning in Hell. After all, it was no mystery to him; he knew they were traveling there to escort the angel Pendelkon's entourage back to this world.

The Pope could feel the stress mounting the more he thought about things to come. He could feel it taking its toll on his nervous system. This was it, so to speak. He knew he was in way over his head to turn back, even if he could. He was also at the end of the corridor. This had become evident when he had encountered a pair of mythical beasts. To his amazement, the beasts had the head, torso, and wings of a bald eagle but the body of a lion. Initially, he thought the beasts were a studio illusion or someone dressed up in an expensive monster costume. This was until he had glanced into their reckless eyes and saw their chests moving inward and outward with life. On average, the beasts, who were called griffins, stood eight feet tall like exotic statues with their pointed metal staffs drawn across the double doors.

"DON'T HESITATE! PROCEED ONWARD!" The Gate Guardian had shouted these instructions up ahead to the Pope. A hint of amusement could be heard in his voice.

The Pope knew the two villains, who were some footsteps away, were playing him for a fool. He knew they wanted to see violence. He knew they wanted to be entertained at his expense, but he wasn't having it. He knew the griffins would put him to death the second he broke the threshold of the door. From what he had observed, no one had respect for the goblins. They were like bottom feeders or slaves, who he felt performed much of the grueling tasks. Going on this assumption, he froze where he was and did an about-face with his head down in order to conceal the paleness of his face. Then he took his forearms and formed the letter X. He had his mind made up; he wouldn't travel anymore until the griffins retracted their staffs.

"YOU LOSE, GATE GUARDIAN!" Dramaticus' laughter became erratic. "SEE, HE'S NOT AS PIG-HEADED AS YE THOUGHT!"

"ENOUGH OF THIS ZANINESS! GUARDS, ADMIT THE VERMIN! LET HIM PASS!"

With his head still bowed, the Pope slowly dropped his hands from the air. He took it that the Gate Guardian's disdainful comments were meant for him. Thus, he wobbled around and proceeded to stroll toward the open door with caution. He had his eyes on both griffins. There was no way he was letting them out of his sight so easily. He still didn't trust them, even though they had retrieved their weapons.

"Keep going!" Dramaticus had yelled while striking the floor with his whip.

The Pope should have been a psychic, for it was just as he anticipated: there was another pair of griffins poised at the corners of the inner door. They were even more ferocious looking than the others. His heart had begun to do somersaults. He knew it would be almost impossible to draw his attention away from the prolific beasts, but he felt he had to as he began his descent down the center of the smoke-filled room—a room that looked as if it were being lit by a single forty-watt red light bulb. However, there was something about the griffins that made him feel they once had a prestigious origin, one which he believed had them patrolling the outer rims of the Holy City long before they had defected to Hell. What had most likely sold him on this vision was, ironically, the griffins' staffs. He couldn't block out how identical they were to the Lord's own throne guards, except for the demonic symbolism.

"Oh my, what have they done?" The Pope had lip-synced these words upon realizing that the room was gutted of all its religious contents. There was nothing left—a move he knew was done for space rather than personal profit.

It was no Chinese puzzle to him who had carried out this horrific act of vandalism. He placed the blame chiefly on the goblins, who were arranged in a straight military line on both the left and right of him. He wasn't sure, glancing out of the corners of his eyes, but he believed he had counted the unsightly faces of about twenty per side. To his displeasure, all of the goblins towered over him like pro basketball players, and they were armed to the teeth with an array of weapons, from swords to poleaxes—not to mention torches, which they held in their left hands.

The Pope knew right away that the poor ventilation in the room was due to the torches. He wouldn't mentally admit it, but the goblins' fire sticks of light were literally affecting him to the point where he saw stars. It was worse than inhaling cigarettes; he fought the urge not to cough. Somewhere amongst the heavy smoke, he had lost track of both the Gate Guardian and the king of the centaurs. Were they still behind him? He couldn't say. Still, he had the presence of mind to know it would be frowned upon and considered a sign of weakness if he turned to check. The goblins were already giving him what he thought were dirty vibes. Could they really detect that he wasn't one of them?

To make his situation more intriguing, he had spotted six or seven more barbarian-looking centaurs lurking near the front of the room. It was a no-brainer to him why they were using the revolving smoke as their cloak. He felt they had to be protecting someone of great importance, someone such as Natas Christopher. It was also apparent to him that they had their pitchforks cocked and pointed in his direction. This alone made him feel as if he was being singled out or made a target—a marked target whose insides he knew would be made to resemble Swiss cheese if he got any gutsy ideas like storming ahead. Something he wanted to do in the name of the Lord but felt he couldn't risk just yet, even though he was aware his potential objective was no more than forty yards away.

"What is this before me? I can't quite make it out," the Pope mumbled to himself while trying to adjust his eyes. "And why is it giving off so much heat?"

He was hesitant about what to do next. One thing was for sure: he had to stop. He had to pull up in his tracks or risk getting burnt to a crisp by a large, flaming representation of a pentagram—a symbol used in the dark science to represent the devil. A symbol which he could distinctly see had divided the room in half. He wouldn't give it too much thought, but he believed the symbol didn't ignite until he came within three feet of it. Was this an alarm to Hell's cast of characters that he was an imposter? He didn't think so. He felt the symbol's only purpose was as a landmark—a landmark that forbade anyone to travel any further without the proper authorization. Something he didn't have.

Due to the abundant flow of carbon dioxide around him, he had dropped to his knees, not out of respect for the symbol, but for survival purposes only. From where he was positioned, he felt the air quality was much better. His eyes were no longer watering. He had a hunch this would work, since it was proven that smoke, in most cases, would journey upwards.

"Gate Guardian, I want thee to remain by the outer door until the angel Pendelkon arrives!" A dominant voice had given these instructions from up ahead. The sound waves from the voice were so extraordinary, they had parted the smoke in two while eventually eliminating it altogether. With this being the case, it had allowed the Pope a chance to see who had given these orders. His heart had skipped a beat when he discovered that it was none other than Natas Christopher. The misbehaving priest of Arabic descent with a goatee, whom he had briefly encountered under the maple trees. The same one who had bitten Isaac's finger. The same one who had alluded punishment in Heaven. Now he had visual contact with the villain, who was sitting stark naked and oily upon a makeshift throne, which was elevated into the air by way of a steep platform. At the base of the platform were two griffins, and stretched out in front of them were seven barbarian-looking centaurs. The same centaurs whom he had noticed through the smoke only moments ago.

The Pope had to clear his mind. He had to put the new set of circumstances in front of him into perspective while he was still able. Suddenly, he knew getting his hands on Natas Christopher was not going to be a cakewalk. He could see that it was going to take patience. Even if he had fired off a hail of shots in desperation, he knew the bullets would be gobbled up in the flesh of Natas Christopher's armed entourage like secondhand candy. No, he knew the only chance he had of taking Natas Christopher out was if he got him to come down from the platform. Then he felt he could put a wave of rounds in the tyrant's skull. Would this work? He didn't know, but he felt his chances of succeeding were a lot better than him trying to overpower Natas Christopher, which he deemed was futile.

Natas Christopher, when standing, stood about eight feet tall. He had the physique of a hairless bodybuilder and was tattooed from head to toe with pagan scripture which concealed his pale, snake scales. Some of these same obscene images were depicted along the staffs of the griffins. Although he had many qualities that were humanoid, he had several that weren't. Take, for instance, his eyes, which were reptilian, and his nails, which were four inches long and the color of onyx. He also had long, pointed ears like a Doberman Pinscher and K-9 teeth that extended to the bottom of his chin. These extraterrestrial features alone gave him the appearance of a demented savage—one who would spit on the legacy of Christianity and one who would put his middle finger up while in the presence of God.

"Horsemen, dispatch! Report back to thy posts at once!" One of the griffins at the base of the platform came forward and proudly shouted these instructions before retreating.

The griffin was making reference to the seven barbarian-looking centaurs, the same ones who could be seen taking refuge on the far outskirts of the room, in plain sight behind the goblins.

"Your Highness, the marksman's call at the door has been answered."

"Well done, Dramaticus, king of the centaurs. Ye may approach the front! Come forward in proper form and taketh thy place within the star! Please, enlighten me with the information thee have gathered! Ye may do so now!" Natas Christopher spoke while holding a chalice made of gold and rubies. He appeared to be bored.

"If this is thy wish, then so be it!"

"So be it!" Natas Christopher replied, taking his attention away from the chalice.

Was it safe to get up? The Pope wasn't taking any chances. He was still cautiously down on all fours. He felt he would remain this way until his presence was at least acknowledged in the room. However, it was while in this posture that he experienced a brief spat of air which brushed over his back. It was the king of the centaurs making his way towards the star, which was no longer lit, he later observed from the corner of his eye. His oversized hood had allowed him to accomplish this without raising any suspicion that he was an impostor or a phony.

"Is he drunk? What is he doing? What is he doing?" The Pope had asked himself this over and over. "Why is he shuffling his hooves back and forth like that?"

The Pope couldn't answer this at first, then it dawned on him. It dawned on him that Dramaticus was doing something ritualistic with his feet as well as his hands. He only prayed the king wouldn't get clumsy and step on any of his fingers, which he had balled up in a knot just in case. Deriving from the information he had previously collected out in the corridor; it was apparent the king had low regard for Natas Christopher. He wouldn't abide by it, but he believed the king hated his guts more than he did. In the long run, he was interested in how this dilemma would pan out and how he could work it to best suit his mission.

"Your highness, there were three goblins about the door who wished to serve." Dramaticus bowed his head. "I was informed they checked out, thus I sent two of them to assist with the arrival of the angel Pendelkon."

"EXCELLENT. BUT WHY HAVE YE BROUGHT THIS ONE MISERABLE SERVANT BEFORE ME? WHY? WHAT IS HIS SIGNIFICANCE?"

"Your Highness, if ye art referring to this dwarf breed of goblin, he has a unique quality which I deem will be most useful to thee. I personally requested seven others like himself but only received one in return. In thy name, I promise I will behead the Lord of their parallel myself!"

"Useful? Useful to me?" Natas Christopher chuckled. "Do ye not know who I am? I have no need for witchcraft or wizardry! Fool, direct thy attention to the left!"

There was no way the Pope could pass up the urge to peek. It would have eaten him alive if he didn't. He was curious as to what Natas Christopher was pointing at. What he saw, despite the small pockets of steam—which were present nowhere else but at the front of the room—was an enormous black metal pot. The pot itself smelled like a brewery, and it was massive enough to fit a cow in, he concluded. He also concluded that the pot resembled something a fictitious witch would use to cast spells. To his horror, in the boiling pot, he saw an unknown figure emerge upside down, with their melting boots facing east to west.

"There! That is the fate of thy witless bitch!" Natas Christopher roused up as he continued to laugh.

"Your Highness, this is the third sorceress ye have condemned! The other two ye brutally fucked to death inside of the sacred star!"

"Yes! For they were of no service to me! Each one was unable to use her viper productively! They failed me!" Natas Christopher sat back down. "They failed to do what I desired!"

Out of nowhere, a noisy raven appeared. It seemed to be headed toward the pot of brew, where it began to rest its mouth. Nevertheless, once it had its fill, it was taken back to the air. This time, it circled the room twice before perching itself upon the armrest of Natas Christopher's throne.

"Behold, my faithful set of eyes has finally returned!" Natas Christopher gently stroked the crown of the creature.

"Your highness, the acts ye have committed are an outrage!" Dramaticus had professed. "Their deaths were unjustified, even if the sorceress were unsuccessful in *their* attempts to gain information or possess the souls of the other clergymen!"

"Their punishment was sanctioned by me! It was meant as a deterrent, king of the centaurs, for those who *may* wish to linger in their footsteps of failure! Do ye have a problem with this? I think I acted justly!"

"There is a problem, your highness. These sorceresses were all rich in ceremonial exercise. Their knowledge would have coincided very well with the arrival of the angel Pendelkon."

"They were useless! Bloody useless, I say unto thee! Besides, they knoweth no more than I do! It was I who served in Heaven with both Nero and Pendelkon, not them!"

"This is true. But as it stands, your highness, we are already shorthanded of workers. The odds, I feel, are ever increasing against us. Twice the angel Gabriel has been sighted in or around the palace, not to mention that pesky angel Darr. I fear the Trinity has also unleashed a presence, which has never been felt on this Earth before."

"Thy point?"

"We will be butchered!"

"Have faith!"

"Have faith? Have faith? Is that all ye can say, your highness?"

Dramaticus had pulled out his pitchfork. "Ye have been away a long time. I was counting on thou to have more expression than that!" He had become so bitter that he had trampled out of the star while hoisting his weapon towards the ceiling. This act must have been seen as an act of aggression by the griffins on account that *they* could be heard shifting into a defensive mode.

"Stand down, king of the centaurs! Stand down! I will tell ye no more!" Natas Christopher snarled.

"Forgive me, Your Highness," Dramaticus bowed while making his backward reentry into the star. "Forgive me, but the majority of my warriors are in no condition to fight, especially against an elite army made up of archangels! For ye have poisoned their minds with brew! It's all they think about! It's all they crave!"

"I have done nothing but given them pleasure!"

"What ye have done, Your Highness, is ye have made scores of my troops their own dictators! Ye have turned them against me, their commander-in-chief! The forces of the angel Darr will have their dizzy heads with ease—I already foresee this!"

"Darr, I'm not worried about it! His presence on this Earth doesn't excite me! He is as noble a warrior as only he is led to believe! The humans he has been sent to aid will sloweth him down miserably! In the end, the creatures in the valley, whose ancestors Nero had a hand in creating, will see to their eternal destruction. This is why I have allowed Darr to exist!"

"Indeed, this was a clever decision on thy part. Still, what about the angel Gabriel? How do ye intend to deal with him, Your Highness?"

"Gabriel, on the other hand, is ancient. I do believe he has knowledge of the seventh gate. However, my faithful set of eyes has told me that there is some uncertainty of its exact location." Natas Christopher paused to sip from his chalice. "No matter, in time, Gabriel's legacy will also cometh to an end. The angel Pendelkon will see to it personally." He began to laugh out of control, along with the goblins and the other barbarian-looking centaurs.

"Thine eyes are drunk with insanity, so are theirs!" Dramaticus frowned as he pointed his weapon around the room.

"That will be all, Dramaticus!" Natas Christopher yawned. "Ye may be dismissed!"

"Enough of this madness! Hand over the key which belongs to the fallen angel Nero! Hand it over, I say, before all is lost!" Dramaticus had trampled forward out of the star.

Once again, his actions must have been seen as an act of aggression by the griffins on account that they could be heard shifting their weapons and moving straight ahead.

"Guards, leave him to me!" Natas Christopher had stood up, while hurling his partially filled chalice at the king of the centaur's hooves.

"Dear boy, ye knoweth nothing! Do ye knoweth not who I am? I was spawned long before thee! I am the key! I am the chosen one! The living life force whose blood alone will tip the scales and lead Hell to victory over Heaven! Do ye knoweth this? Do ye knoweth, dear boy, that I was drafted by Nero himself as a gift to the Heavenly Father? But it was the Son of God who had made Nero's presentation a reality, and the Holy Spirit who then later gave me the qualities of an archangel. Needless to say, it was these same two who had condemned me to chains! They put me, Nero's creation, on the back burner for two inbred mortals called Adam and Eve! They never presented me! They never gave me my chance!"

"Thy origin is not appealing to me. It is purely one of make-believe. Although, it does have some merit. It does explain why Nero has such a desire to conquer the souls of mankind, but archangel ye art not!"

"Ye have it all wrong, for I am the key! With me, Nero can do away with unfaithful subjects like thyself and construct a new army of loyal clones! Ones who will abide by his every command, and ones who will enslave the native occupants of this world! Only then, will the earth becometh his throne! Yes, the genetic blueprint to that process is here! It's here within the blood that flows through my veins!" Natas Christopher was applauded by the goblins and the other barbarian-looking centaurs.

"Prove it!" Dramaticus spat on the floor. "Prove to me that ye possess the traits of an archangel and not those predominantly of a reptilian! Talk no more! It's time to earn thy rank!" He came forward with authority.

"So be it!" Natas Christopher replied as he did a frontward flip off the platform. "Guards, do not interfere! This is a direct order!" he commanded, while shoving the Pope aside with one hand.

As the Pope lay on his back, he finally saw the opportunity he had been longing for. He, without a doubt, had Natas Christopher in perfect range. Personally, he felt he couldn't have dreamt it any better. With the amount of distance that separated the two, he knew it was nothing for him to spring up to his feet and put six rounds into Natas

Christopher's skull, yet he was skeptical. He was curious if Natas Christopher possessed the powers of an archangel. If the villain did, then he didn't see any foul in wanting to observe him in action. This way, he felt he could look for signs of weakness before he attempted to do anything drastic on his own. Besides, he didn't think Natas Christopher would survive the battle with the ruler of the centaurs anyway.

"Arm thyself!" Dramaticus yelled at the approaching Natas Christopher.

"Arm thyself!" he insisted, jabbing his pitchfork in the direction of Natas Christopher's midsection.

"There will be no need, for my hands art my weapons!" Natas Christopher demonstrated his strength by bending three of the four tines on Dramaticus's pitchfork. "Yes, boy, it was these hands which sprung me from Heaven. Just like it will be these same hands, boy, that will squeeze the life from thy disheartening body!"

"Those art bold words for a bastard!" Dramaticus grunted, just before he tossed his weapon aside. Tainted, it was no longer any use to him. "Now, we will see who is superior! And remember, bastard, my ears will be ignorant to thy cries of helplessness!"

Chapter 18

The Pope was a spectator, and he was loving every minute of it. There was so much drama taking place within the center of the room, no one had protested his change of position. No one had cared that he had slipped towards the back of the room, but he didn't dare press his luck. The thought of trying to escape had never entered his mind. One, he felt he was obligated to the Lord to finish Natas Christopher off if anything had gone wrong. He also didn't want to test the alertness of the two griffins, who were no more than twenty yards away.

"See how they cheer for thee?" Dramaticus had made mention, as both Natas Christopher and himself had danced around in half circles like two street gangsters. "Ye don't want to disappoint them! Now strike at me! Show them something!"

Natas Christopher was turning into a rabid dog. His system had built up so much adrenaline in that short period that it had literally begun to seep from the corners of his mouth. Wasting no time, he was the first to initiate contact. This had come about when he had Jack slapped Dramaticus's face four times, which had spun around like a wet mop. The idea of hand-to-hand combat had seemed to entice him so much so that he had become offensive-minded once more. This time, he had launched himself into the air in what appeared to be an attempt to put a stranglehold around Dramaticus' neck. Instead, he was shaken loose and body-slammed sideways to the floor.

Once on the floor, Dramaticus had tried on numerous occasions to end Natas Christopher's life. He was rearing back on his hind legs and thrusting the sheer weight of his body forward. This was in an effort to cave in the skull of Natas Christopher, yet each time he had missed. Each time he had come within inches. Nevertheless, on his eighth attempt, Natas Christopher had caught his front hooves in mid-flight. If this didn't surprise him, it did when Natas Christopher had taken the heels of his own feet and had monkey-flipped him forward.

"This fool's blood will look like a drop compared to what I have in store for the rest of mankind." Natas Christopher had played to the delight of the crowd. He was the first to get up. In doing so, he had managed to successfully maneuver a sleeper hold around the neck of Dramaticus, who was lying helplessly on the floor. "Don't fight it; death will come to thee shortly! I promise!" The veins had bulged from his forehead as he struggled to apply more pressure.

All at once, the boisterous cheers in the room ceased to exist. Instead, they were replaced by an unknown silence. Yet what was the reason for this?

"Out of my way, half-pint!" The Gate Guardian had recklessly emerged through the entranceway, shoving the Pope to his stomach. A minute had gone by, then he was proceeded by one barbarian-looking centaur and eight goblins, who were traveling in pairs.

The Pope never saw what hit him. It was almost as if a runaway truck had slammed into his back. Curious as to what caused this sensation, he flopped to one side facing the door. It was from this position that he first encountered the six Egyptian high priests, who were dressed like the ancient god Anubis. From what he had observed, each one of the jackal-headed guardians stood about eight feet tall, and they were walking in pairs of three, with the lead two patriotically waving red war banners of a flaming image of a goat's head.

Nevertheless, what made his blood turn to ice water was the fact that the priests were guiding a gargantuan-sized gold sarcophagus of a dragon by way of telepathy—the same method the miniature goblins had used to transport him through the maze. By the look of things, he figured they were headed towards the pentagram until they were held up by the Gate Guardian.

"I don't believe it," the Pope mumbled at the sight of eight more goblins and another barbarian-looking centaur who had entered the room.

This had him thinking. He wondered if Zutermier and Isaac were amongst this new parade of characters. He wondered if their mortal bodies had been held together in Hell's extreme climate.

"Enough! What is going on here, Natas Christopher? Cease this activity at once! I beg thee!" The Gate Guardian made his way toward the ongoing feud. He seemed somewhat repelled by what he saw, yet he never intervened. "This inner fighting among ourselves is so out of tune! It has no purpose! We are all brethren! Brethren of darkness with one common goal: to serve in Nero's holy war! Now, make way for the fire demon! Clear this sacred star for the angel Pendelkon; I command thee!"

"His words. They have meaning, Dramaticus, ruler of the centaurs. Thus consider thyself fortunate. Consider fate to be on thy side, at my call." Natas Christopher released his grip while sticking his tongue out. Escorted by the Gate Guardian about halfway, he could be seen making his way toward his makeshift throne.

"SOLDIERS OF THE STRUGGLE, SALUTE THY PRINCE NATAS CHRISTOPHER!" Dramaticus spoke with some difficulty as he eased to his feet while massaging his throat. "I SAID, SALUTE THY PRINCE! FOR HE HAS PROVEN HIMSELF IN BATTLE! HE HAS EARNED HIS RANK!" His voice became much clearer.

Within a matter of seconds, the somber mood of the room turned back to one of pure celebration, but not everyone was rejoicing. Take, for instance, the griffins, who didn't seem fazed by the events. The same could also be said for the Gate Guardian and the six Egyptian high priests, who stood stone-faced and motionless.

"Pope Pius, is that you?"

"Zutermier?" The Pope had to do a double take. He thought he had recognized the voice coming from the back, but he wasn't a hundred percent sure with all of the chaos taking place.

"Yes, it's me."

"But you're alive?" The Pope continued to whisper. He felt warm all over, but there was no way he was letting his guard down, especially since there was another armed, barbarian-looking centaur standing at the back of the formation.

"Sure, I'm alive." Zutermier extended his hand outward to help the Pope up. He knew the two could communicate much better if they were standing at the same level.

"Thank you." The Pope grimaced. "So, where's Isaac? Did you lose him? Were you two separated along the way?" he asked while favoring his lower spine.

"No. He's right beside me."

"Excellent." The Pope watched Isaac nod his head without turning.

"Don't mind him, Pope Pius. The two of us have been to the gates of hell and back. You know, these robes saved our lives. They allowed us to accomplish the unimaginable." Zutermier's eyes widened.

"The Lord is great."

"All the time."

Other than feeling a little tanned and drenched, Zutermier felt fine. He felt like he was in perfect condition. Yet, he couldn't say the same for Isaac. From what he detected; Isaac hadn't spoken a word to him since their departure to the underworld.

"Is that him? Is that Natas Christopher?"

"Yes, the oily one sitting upon the throne," the Pope elaborated for Zutermier.

"He doesn't appear so tough. I think we can take him."

"That's what I thought, until I saw what he did to Dramaticus."

The Pope didn't want to come across as weak or timid. He just didn't want Zutermier and Isaac to do anything simple minded. He didn't want them to feel as though they had run into a brick wall the instant they got a taste of Natas Christopher's power.

"Believe me, Zutermier, looks are deceiving. Natas Christopher is more than a humanoid like you and me. He could be half-reptilian. He might even be on the same level as Darr. So don't do anything foolhardy unless I give the go-ahead. This goes for you also, Isaac." The Pope had made eye contact with him. He had wanted to be certain that there weren't going to be any mishaps.

"Don't look back, but we're not alone."

"I can see that, Zutermier. There's an armed centaur behind us."

"No, there isn't." Zutermier shook his head from side to side in disagreement. "Remember, looks are deceiving. Those were your own words."

"I know those are my own words, but how can one not mistake that creature for a centaur? Maybe your journey to Hell has disrupted your eyesight?"

"Not hardly." Zutermier smiled. "Come closer. What you see isn't a centaur. It's the Lord's shepherd. When we first met him, he was in the form of an unknown priest. You know, the one who bit Isaac's finger on the hillside. Not to mention, he has been with us ever since we entered the hallway. You would have known this right off the bat if you had recognized the secret grip he administered unto you."

"But——"

"The shepherd was alive the whole time. He only faked being wounded to lure the centaur near the square so he could take its form and gain entrance inside the basilica. I have seen him in action. He has this ability."

"I don't dare doubt this. Not even for one second."

"Good, because if all goes well, Natas Christopher will be the shepherd's call. We just have to stay alive and out of the way."

"I don't like this. Where is Kelso with the backup when you need him?"

The Pope was convinced the shepherd was capable of awesome feats, but battling all of these supernatural villains at once was out of the question. At best, he figured the shepherd could eliminate some goblins and maybe a griffin. The situation didn't look promising to him, and the more he thought about it, the bleaker things became. He knew the only reasonable way the shepherd could accomplish his objective was if the others and he were to contribute by taking up arms. It didn't even matter to him if they lost their lives in the process. The way he saw it, the shepherd could do the world more good alive than the others and himself combined.

"Your highness, the time must be now!" The Gate Guardian stood in the center of the room and saluted Natas Christopher. "These Egyptian high priests are strong, but they cannot withstand the sheer mass of the angel Pendelkon for prolonged periods of time! They must set him down! They must do so within the sacred star which the fallen angel Nero has provided us, or the curse of the Trinity will be upon us all!"

"We wouldn't want to allow this. Would we, Gate Guardian?" Natas Christopher glanced up with a spiteful expression. Just the mention of Trinity made steam blow through his ear.

"No. We wouldn't, Your Highness."

"Then have them proceed, Gate Guardian, but in non-ancient form. I know they must be exhausted from their journey. Thus, I wouldn't want to further hinder them."

"O' Egyptian high priests from the fifth dynasty, ye may approach the legendary mark!" The Gate Guardian turned and communicated this. "Ye may do so while traveling in regular form!"

Moving with a sense of urgency, the six Egyptian high priests made their way towards the pentagram. It was at this spot, however, that they gently lowered the sarcophagus. Ironically, they did so without ever laying a hand on it. It was done by telepathy as they turned in unison to face the front of the room.

The angel Pendelkon's sarcophagus of a dragon was constructed from pure gold, and it had two rubies fashioned for eyeballs. On average, the eyeballs were about the size of dinner plates. This feature alone gave the angel the illusion that he had visual contact with the entire room. If the fact that the angel had his mouth open in a roaring position to display countless rows of jagged teeth wasn't intimidating enough, he held a massive sword fit for a ruler. To the Pope and his cardinals' dismay, along the length of the diamond blade were the inscriptions of eleven plagues. Legend has it the ruthless angel could inflict any or several of them upon the world just by stabbing it into the Earth. Last but not least, the angel possessed two human-like penises that were fully erect. Oddly, the penises were cast out of gold as well.

"Zutermier, there are muffled breathing sounds coming from that sarcophagus. Do you hear them also?" The Pope became curious as he watched from afar. "Don't tell me that beast is alive?"

"Ah. Yes and no." Zutermier stalled.

"Yes, and no? Just what is that supposed to mean?"

"Well, the angel Pendelkon, or the beast as you have called him, is alive, but he's in a semiconscious sleep mode, thanks in part to his specialized sarcophagus."

"Let me figure this one out. This was an effort to conceal his genuine structural mass from the Trinity and Darr."

"Right," Zutermier continued to speak in a lowered voice. "Yet what you don't know is that the angel Pendelkon is about a hundred times the size of his sarcophagus. In other words, he's nothing more than a large, angry genie waiting to be unleashed."

"Oh my. How are we ever going to contend with something like that?" The Pope scratched his chin. "So, did Isaac and yourself witness this firsthand?"

"Witness what?"

"The angel Pendelkon's true size."

"No." Isaac was quick to respond. It was the first time he had spoken in a while. Other than feeling dehydrated, he was fine. "We just heard about it from the Gate Guardian, who proceeded to brag to the entire garrison. I thought he would never shut up."

"I hate to say it, son, but I guess someone in his position would know a thing or two." The Pope briefly stared at Isaac. Words couldn't begin to describe how merry he was to learn that Isaac hadn't been emotionally scarred from his journey to the seventh gate. This was a good thing, as he felt the Lord's shepherd could benefit from Isaac's brute strength.

"Maybe you're right," Isaac confessed. "Still, one thing's for certain: his breath sure smells like toilet water. In the end, I want to be the one who flushes him."

"Your Highness, everything is in place." Dramaticus knelt. His position was still in the midst of the room, just a few feet off to the left of the pentagram.

"Excellent!" Natas Christopher nodded. "Excellent!"

"Your Highness, may I advance? May I send for the special sacrifices needed?"

"By all means, Dramaticus. Please do, I insist!"

"Guards, prepare the subjects for transport!" Dramaticus spoke into a blue sphere of light, which suddenly appeared from within the center of his right palm.

The Gate Guardian and other high-ranking commanders were also known to have this same diamond-shaped insert. It was called a dimensional transmitter.

"Sir, shall I bring the candidates in myself?" a voice had replied from the sphere.

"Negative! Hold thy position, centaurian! I'm on my way!" Dramaticus had folded up his palm.

"Yes. Soon, all the pieces will be in place." The Gate Guardian had ensured Natas Christopher.

"You torchless goblins in the rear, clear the opening or lose thy heads! Move to one side or another!" Dramaticus had turned and pointed. He could be seen gallantly making his way towards the exit, followed by two-armed, barbarian-looking centaurs from the front.

Quickly, the Pope and his cardinals had done as they were told. They had moved to the left-hand side of the room. Yet, as they watched the Lord's shepherd join in and follow the evil trio, a revengeful joy had come over each of them. They were silently praying that at some point in time, the shepherd would take them out one by one.

"Ye may not be aware of this, Natas Christopher, but the Egyptian priests are capable of performing this delicate ceremony with perfection." The Gate Guardian had stood front and center. He had one eye on the vanishing party and one eye on Natas Christopher. "Believe me, ye have nothing to worry about."

"Why would I? The odds were made favorable just with the arrival of Pendelkon! When he awakes, he will allow me a safe passage to be with my creator, Nero!" Natas Christopher had broken out in laughter.

"But if all else should fail, Your Highness, ye may yet have a fifty-fifty chance of survival if we place ye inside the angel Pendelkon's sarcophagus. His unique molecular makeup, I believe, should preserve thy reptilian characteristics. Nero's ultimate goal, ye see, is to have thee reign on Earth, not in Hell."

"That's what I like about thee. Ye are always looking out for my best interest." Natas Christopher had shown his appreciation by toasting his chalice in the Gate Guardian's direction.

The Pope and his cardinals weren't stupid. They knew from the beginning that Hell's cast of villains needed someone without sin to be the sacrificial centerpiece of their ceremony. In all regards, they were bracing themselves to see a local priest shoved through the door. Instead, they saw an attractive, totally nude Caucasian woman with red hair being led in, followed by Dramaticus and the other three Centaurs, one of whom they knew was the Lord's shepherd in disguise. At best, the young woman, who was blindfolded and gagged, appeared to be no older than twenty or twenty-five years old.

"My God, what do you suppose these bastards are going to do to her?" The Pope could barely stand to watch. He recognized the girl. Her face was on the camera, which Isaac had found on the ground near the murder scene in the woods. "Can't they see she's terrified?"

"The girl's fate is obvious." Zutermier lowered his head. "They are going to deflower her."

"But why?" Isaac became confused as he watched the three barbarian-looking Centaurs make their way toward the front. "Why didn't Darr or anyone intervene, and why is all of this taking place within the back door of our holy shrine?"

"Are you mad? Lower your voice. You have to pull yourself together." Zutermier turned and put his elbow in Isaac's midsection. "Don't you know? Don't you know that evil runs parallel with good? Without one, the other wouldn't exist. This is the way it has always been."

Due to the identical similarity in facial and structural features of all the barbarian-looking Centaurs in the room, neither the Pope nor his cardinals could tell which one was the Lord's shepherd. With this being the case, they knew they would have to be wise. They knew they would have to put their aggressive intentions on standby until they got some sort of sign. However, they each had an idea of what the shepherd was trying to achieve by moving within range of Natas Christopher.

"Dramaticus, I thought you said there were two? Where is the other?"

"There was one more, Your Highness, but her womb was impure. I had the wench put down."

"Very well," Natas Christopher had yawned. "On with the proceedings." He didn't seem that bothered by what Dramaticus had done.

The young woman was so traumatized as she was escorted to the foot of Pendelkon's sarcophagus, where she was left; her teeth could literally be heard clattering. In fact, she had become so unstable she had to be held up by the Egyptian high priests, who had each taken turns slapping her on her pale ass. From that point on, they had begun to lubricate her body with some kind of clear-like gel, which they were mainly retrieving off the tip of their long canine tongues. Once she was covered from head to toe with the substance, she was then hoisted into the air by way of telepathy, where she was made to mount the two erected penises of the Pendelkon. One was inserted into her vagina and one in her rectum. Still unable to see her surroundings, she cried out in agony as she was forced by black magic to hump the two shafts. This defloration went on until she burst into flames and disintegrated into a fine, powdery ash.

"Just like that, her life has ended. How can it be, though?" The Pope had babbled to himself. "How can it be that she was cremated before our very eyes? Bones and all. Bones and all."

"The smell is so awful. I think I'm going to be sick. I think I'm going to puke."

"No, Isaac," the Pope had cringed. "Please, fight it. We know it reeks, but a lot is at stake, child."

"Look. You two have to see this. There is a glowing swarm of fireflies coming from the angel Pendelkon's mouth. There are literally thousands upon thousands of them. Can you hear them buzzing around like baby bees?"

"Yes, I see them." The Pope had adjusted his eyes. "There is also a harsh breeze blowing about as a result of the pests who keep emerging."

"Harsh is not the word. Look. The high winds are forcing the goblins' torches out, one by one, like dominoes."

Zutermier was in awe. He couldn't believe how cheerful the goblins had become. So much so that he had watched many of them drop to their knees. To him, they seemed to be paying their respects in a profane manner, with their flickered-out torches held high above their heads, singing demonic songs.

"Everyone, quickly do as they do." The Pope got into position to mimic the goblins.

"If you still have that urge, Isaac, now is the time to do something about it." Zutermier had encouraged him to take advantage of the chaos in the room.

"You can stop worrying about me; I'm much better," Isaac had assured him.

"Just perfect. If it weren't for the fireflies, the room would be totally blackened," Zutermier had observed.

He wasn't totally oppressed by the new set of circumstances. In a sense, he felt it was a blessing in disguise. He only prayed it would give the Lord's shepherd the camouflage needed to assassinate Natas Christopher or some of his supporting cast without suspicion. The last thing he wanted to take part in was an all-out confrontation, especially if the villains in the room had night vision.

"That's it. That's the last of the fireflies," Isaac had whispered, even though there was still widespread excitement amongst the goblins.

"Hey. Turn your faces upward at the ceiling." The Pope had thought about pointing but reneged. "If I didn't know any better, I would say that the fireflies were trying to form the outline of a dragon."

"I think you're right," Zutermier had acknowledged. "The speckles of yellow light must be the angel Pendelkon's soul."

"Well, so much for keeping this mighty beast under wraps," the Pope had wished this wasn't the case. "For the sake of the human race, let's just hope the Lord's shepherd can accomplish his goal or Darr can magically appear with backup."

"SILENCE! SILENCE! THERE MUST BE UTTER SILENCE!" The Gate Guardian could be heard moving about while striking the tips of his blades against the floor, creating sparks.

Chapter 19

The Gate Guardian had gotten what he demanded. Within minutes, the room had become nonexistent of sound. This was just as the last of the fireflies had begun to join the millions of others to form the body and the wings of the angel Pendelkon, which was really a dot matrix image of a dragon. However, once the image was complete, the fireflies took off at blinding speed around the room. Eighteen times, the fireflies rotated, creating torrential winds and engulfing both the ceiling and the floor in an inferno of flames. In the process, many of the goblins could be seen and heard as they were sucked into the inner furnace of the fireflies like a vacuum cleaner going over lint balls.

"NO! NO! THIS IS ALL WRONG! THE CEREMONY WASN'T SUPPOSED TO BE THIS VIOLENT!" The Gate Guardian could be heard expressing his disapproval in the darkness.

"Pendelkon is furious, but why?" Dramaticus sounded clueless. "Where did we go wrong?"

"I fear the answer is beyond me!" The Gate Guardian replied as he watched more goblins be swept up into the air.

The Pope and his cardinals were no different. They were also affected by the winds. Even when they tried to cling to one another for support, they could still feel themselves being tossed aside like bales of hay.

"ARE YE INSANE? MAKE THIS STOP, GATE GUARDIAN! PUT THE LID BACK ON THE ANGEL PENDELKON'S WRATH, I COMMAND THEE! DO IT AT ONCE BEFORE WE END UP WITH ILL FATE AS WELL!" Natas Christopher had become hysterical. It was the first time a hint of dismay could be detected in his voice.

"But how, Your Highness?"

"Order a retreat! It is the only reasonable solution, Gate Guardian!" Natas Christopher had screamed. "Request it at once!"

Isaac couldn't speak for any of the others at the time, but he had felt strange. He had felt almost as if something was grabbing at his head. Was it the wind doing this to him? He didn't think so. He had believed it was an unknown phantom trying to unveil his identity. At the time, he didn't have enough evidence to mention this to the others. Yet every time he went to put his hood back on, he could feel it being snatched off again as if it was some kind of game of hide and seek.

"O' mighty six, heed me! I beckon thee to use thy age-old wisdom and cometh up with a spell! A spell which will bringeth forth new light, and one which will returneth the wraith of Pendelkon back to his prior occupancy! I request all of this if it's feasible!" The Gate Guardian had spoken with some difficulty through the wind, which didn't seem to bother the griffins.

The Egyptian priests were very obedient. It was this trait alone which had allowed them to endure for thousands of centuries under Nero's rule. With this being the case, they silently undid the mark of the angel Pendelkon. This meant the flames from both the walls and the floor were sent in reverse fashion back into the open mouth of the sarcophagus, along with the swarm of fireflies that had infested the ceiling. Not even one was spared. In the process, the goblins who remained had their torches relit, and the electricity to the room was restored.

"Pamper me! Pamper me with information!" The Gate Guardian had requested while pacing back and forth in front of the Egyptian priests. "Explain to me why so much aggression was used. Now, more than half of the goblin warriors on the right-hand side of the room are gone! Why is this? What significance does it have?"

"Have them stand! Goblins, stand! Do so in silence, or I will finish thee myself!" Dramaticus had threatened with a pitchfork he had snatched. "Here! Take back thy weapon and give me a live count!" he had instructed a barbarian-looking centaur standing off to the side of him.

Using sign language, one of the Egyptian high priests from the front had come forth with an explanation.

"What does he mean she was only a virgin in appearance?" Natas Christopher had uncorked. "Gate Guardian, have him cometh closer!" He had stood up and motioned before sitting.

"Fool, what are ye insinuating? Who switched her soul?" The Gate Guardian had croaked loudly for air. "And with what?"

"With one of my men? But this is impossible! I inspected both human winches myself upon arrival!" Dramaticus had turned and pleaded his case as if there was some question of his loyalty. "She had a soul! My word is my bond! They both did!"

Using sign language, another Egyptian high priest from the front had come forth while the other one to his left had stepped back into formation around the sarcophagus of the angel Pendelkon.

"Gate Guardian, yield either way," Natas Christopher had swayed. *"I'm curious. I want to see this one's elaboration."*

"He said that both women had given up the ghost long ago to a much higher presence."

"Ask him when Gate Guardian? Ask him when?"

"He said while they were in our presence, your highness."

"Tell me, who was this so-called higher presence?" Natas Christopher had frowned upon standing. "Reveal their name unto me! Their trespassing will be worthy of eternal death!"

"He doesn't know," the Gate Guardian was quick to relay this information. "Nevertheless, he says the angel Pendelkon has detected several questionable links within the realm. Many of whom were terminated, yet he says a great many more may still stand to combat thee in thy hour of glory."

"Is this so? Then let them cometh, and I promise thee I will slay them from their roots like the weeds they are!" Natas Christopher chuckled while being seated. "That will be all." He signaled the Egyptian high priest back into formation.

"Your Highness, I always said the goblins were unreliable subjects. Now let me eliminate them for good. With the angel Pendelkon here, their services will no longer be required!"

This remark by Dramaticus seemed to anger the goblins. So much so, many of them could be seen displaying their poll picks in an aggressive manner. Still, the Pope and his cardinals did nothing but continued to look on. The comment didn't seem to have any effect on them whatsoever. As a whole, they could have cared less, as the goblins were still vicious foes in their sight.

"Silence! Let there be silence!" the griffins by the platform ordered. Whenever they spoke, they received what they demanded.

"Ruler of the centaurs, ye will commit no such act before me!" Natas Christopher made this clear. "Be it that it may, I find the goblins to be on the level. They have done no harm but only what I asked. Yet ye wish to persecute them for this. No. There is only one I know of qualified to carry out this kind of treachery."

"Your Highness, I'm confused. Not even archangels have the capability to switch souls!" Dramaticus argued. "It is a known fact that even Nero himself can only possess a soul or steal it outright by temptation."

"This is true." Natas Christopher didn't beg to differ. "No archangel committed this act. It was done by the Lord's shepherd."

"The Lord's shepherd, but no one has ever seen his face." The Gate Guardian threw his hands into the air. "He may be more myth than reality, I feel."

"Don't be too sure of thyself, my trusted friend," Natas Christopher replied with a gleam of rage in his eyes. "He is as real as the clouds in Heaven and the raging flames in our Nero's Hell. Still, he is no match for the army at hand. He's just deceitful in his ability to change into any shape or form."

"Granted if he steals one's soul."

"Yes. Granted if this were to be done, Gate Guardian."

"Then he may be amongst us as we speak!" Dramaticus became alarmed. "We must conduct an intensive search of this room and take him hostage at once!"

"Never! For he is too cowardly to face me without numbers." Natas Christopher closed his eyes while putting his hand on his temples. "What is it, my notorious father? Speak to me. Speak to me in riddles only I can comprehend. Let thy twisted tongue unlock everything which is holy. Reveal my new agenda unto me. Cut forth thy blood."

"Can you feel that?" Zutermier began to tremble. "Can you feel that hot breeze blowing about the room?"

"Yes, I can feel it." The Pope disguised his voice. "Just keep it down. I think Natas Christopher may be onto the shepherd and possibly us also. We may have to act sooner than we think." He fiddled with the loaded pistol in his pocket.

"So, where do you suppose this breeze is coming from?"

"Possibly Hell," Zutermier answered Isaac. "It could be the very breath of the Devil himself. Sort of like an electronic frequency traveling by sound waves."

"Nonsense. Hush your mouth." The Pope clenched his fists. "Look, here comes the guard."

Isaac had stood in a silhouette of fright as the barbarian-looking centaur taking count passed by. The fact that he was a human, perpetrating as a monster, had always lurked in the back of his mind. Yet he had remained optimistic about his chances of deceiving and defeating his foe. It was Nero with whom he had a problem. Like a paring knife to an apple, he had always believed Nero would slowly peel away at the layers of one's soul. Then, once the core was within reach, he felt Nero would bite down like a serpent and inflict the poisons needed to entrap the prey in his parallel of darkness. He felt that such was the case when both Zutermier and he made their journey to the seventh gate. He felt that his core was exposed.

"Guard, how many?" Dramaticus had watched his warrior complete his rounds. "How many goblins stand before us?"

"Sir, there are thirty-two-foot soldiers out of forty left," the barbarian-looking centaur had saluted before replying.

"Excellent." Natas Christopher had acknowledged while reopening his eyes.

"Your highness, it's time! It's time for ye to make thy awaited journey!" The Gate Guardian had struck the floor with the tip of his sword. "Ye and the angel Pendelkon must embrace and become as one!"

"He speaks the truth!" Dramaticus had bowed. "For the security here has been breached! We all may be in grave danger!"

"Wait! Not just yet, there is something my father wants me to see!" Natas Christopher had stood up. The warm breeze was no longer present. Its winds had gone astray. "Guard, now hear my commands through. I want thee to turn and bring forth that miniature goblin in the rear!"

"As you wish, your highness." The barbarian-looking centaur had moved swiftly into action.

"Look," Zutermier had whispered. "Here he comes again."

knew there was still a little time left to devise a plan. "What do you want us to do?"

"Nothing." The Pope had felt a headache coming on. "Don't do anything. I don't want to put the shepherd in a compromising position."

"But we can't just let the guard take you either." Zutermier had begun to sweat. "I couldn't live with myself, knowing I had allowed something to happen to you."

"I can't believe I'm saying this myself. However, it's the only reasonable solution. I don't want to see a lot of killing. Please, don't do anything." The Pope had pleaded once again. "I can fend for myself if things become grim. Besides, this guard may be the shepherd himself."

Zutermier knew exactly what the Pope was insinuating. He just hoped the Pope wouldn't be too nervous to aim his pistol straight.

"YOU! COMETH WITH ME!"

"I'm sorry, Pope Pius, but I'm the weak link. I have to disobey your orders, anyway. His breath reeks of brew," Isaac had responded while hitting the barbarian-looking centaur flush on the jawbone.

"No, child!" This was the only thing the Pope could shout as the barbarian-looking centaur had crumbled to his back. "I think you knocked him out cold!"

"Well, so much for plan A." Zutermier had grinned while taking out his knife.

Isaac had already done the same.

"Listen," said the Pope. "We'll fight with our backs towards one another until there's no scum standing. So, ready yourselves for plan B."

"Plan B?" Zutermier had frowned. He couldn't recall ever hearing such. "What is this plan B?"

"Bust heads." Isaac had gladly elaborated for him.

"Oh, I see." Zutermier grimaced just as he watched the goblins form a tight circle around the others and himself.

He found it nearly impossible to concentrate as the angry mob moved in with their torches. Clearly, he could see that they had the advantage in numbers and a better arsenal of weapons to fight with. What he longed to do was trade up his knife for at least a poleaxe. Still, he knew the only way he could do this was if he confiscated it from one of the fallen.

"We just have to outsmart them," the Pope responded to Zutermier's negative body language.

From every angle imaginable, the goblins rushed in. Some were using their torches as weapons, and many were swinging their pickaxes as if they were baseball bats. Nonetheless, Zutermier and Isaac managed to hold them at bay by kicking and punching them. When that wasn't enough, they stabbed several of them until green goo poured from their exit wounds. Not to be outmatched, the Pope pulled out his pistol and fired a single shot, which flew through the skulls of two goblins. Impressed by the results, the Pope let off a couple more rounds in opposite directions.

"That's it, Pope Pius! Keep aiming for the clusters!" Zutermier cheered him on. He couldn't believe how easily the goblins were dropping. "That's it!"

"Clumsy fools! If they had half a brain between them, they would realize they are mortally wounding one another with their wild swinging!" Isaac revealed, taking one of the goblins hostage. It was his idea from the start to use his victim as a living shield.

"On my count to three, I want everyone to lower their heads!" The Pope put away his pistol for a pickaxe. He wasn't certain, but he believed he only had one or two bullets left in the chamber. "Get ready! One! Two! Three!" He swung the weapon with all his might, landing the sharp edge in a goblin's eye socket.

"Seize them!" Dramaticus gestured with a throat-slash sign. "Take them at once!"

"But alive!" Natas Christopher reiterated. "Alive!"

On cue, the Gate Guardian and Dramaticus each put away their weapons. Not once did the pair ever turn to acknowledge Natas Christopher's instructions. Instead, the two continued to stalk the room with the confidence of two experienced game hunters—two experienced hunters who were trying to force their targets into making a judgmental error. With this being the case, it became obvious that the two were going to keep relying on their stealth-like tactics in order to remain anonymous behind the goblins.

"Look!" Zutermier dropped his hands to his knees. "The goblins are backing away!" He was almost out of breath.

"I can see that," replied the Pope. "Just keep fighting anyway!"

He was also winded. Yet at any minute, he was expecting the Lord's shepherd to join in. Instead, he felt a large hand wrap around his throat. Unable to speak or warn the others, he watched the same hand grasp Isaac's neck from the rear.

"Drop them! Drop thy weapons or pay dearly!" Dramaticus had threatened while lifting the Pope and Isaac off their feet.

"The same also applies to thee!" The Gate Guardian had palmed Zutermier by the back of the head before switching his hand to Zutermier's throat.

"Well done!" Natas Christopher applauded the knives, and the poll pick hitting the floor. "Now, bring them towards the star!"

It was a wrap. The Pope and his cardinals knew there was no escaping. They knew the wicked duo literally had the upper hand, as their limp bodies were carried through the air like rag dolls. To their surprise, not once did their feet ever graze the floor. Yet they weren't really concerned about this. They were more worried about their eyeballs popping out or not being able to swallow their own saliva.

"Order," shouted the griffins by the platform. "There must be order!"

"Guard, pick thyself up and assemble the goblins back into their proper formations! Don't keep me waiting!" Dramaticus had yelled without turning. It was almost as if he had eyes in the back of his head. "And whence this is complete, ye can take another head count of those who remain!"

"Sir, what about the fallen?" The barbarian-looking centaur had stood up gingerly. This was the same one whom Isaac had struck. "What shall I do with them?"

"Fuck them! Fuck them all!" Dramaticus had turned his nose up in the air like a French aristocrat while continuing to walk forward with the Pope's and Isaac's body. "There will be no compassion for the deceased! Not today!"

His remark had caused everyone to spill out with laughter, except for the griffins and the goblins.

"Guard, ye can dispose of their bodies in one pile." Natas Christopher had tried to conceal his smirk. "After all, they *art* our brethren."

"Dramaticus, is this far enough?" The Gate Guardian had paused.

"No!" Natas Christopher had replied. "I said I wanted them all released, just in front of the star!"

"So be it!" The Gate Guardian had become bitter as he walked a few paces more, before finally choke-slamming Zutermier to the floor. "There!"

The Pope and Isaac's outcome wasn't any better. They were also abandoned from the air in the same reckless manner, only they weren't knocked unconscious. One side of their body had just felt numb. Yet despite their physical setbacks, they had both managed to crawl on their hands and knees to console Zutermier, who was face down in a small pool of blood. At least, this was until the Gate Guardian had stood between them.

"Is he?"

"No." The Pope had shaken his head. He knew exactly what Isaac was insinuating. "Zutermier is still with us."

"Move, I say! Separate at once!" The Gate Guardian's voice had become defiant. "Do it now!" He had faked as if he was going to cave either the Pope or Isaac's ribcage in with his foot.

Fearing the Gate Guardian's bluff, the Pope and Isaac did as they were told. They had both rolled continuously until they were about three feet apart from one another, then they had taken to their bellies and hid their faces beneath their jittery fingertips. In their minds, they were anticipating the worst was yet to come.

"Nero, my father, why has my vision been blurred? Tell me, what irony lies with these three before my mercy?" Natas Christopher had closed his eyes while going into deep meditation.

"Your highness! Your highness!"

"What is it, Gate Guardian?" Natas Christopher had snapped back to his senses. "Speak."

"Shall we unveil them?"

"By all means, Gate Guardian. Please do, I insist. Enough time has been wasted already."

Isaac was beginning to panic. He had a weird feeling the entire room would erupt into mayhem the second it became obvious that they were of the human race. Thus, he wasn't shocked when it did, but he couldn't believe how much spit and vulgar language could fill the air at one time. Nor was he surprised that the abuse was coming primarily from the goblins. He could sense they resented the fact that three mortals had done so many of them in. With this being the case, he couldn't understand why the Lord's shepherd hadn't come to their aide. Truly, he didn't want to die at the hands of these monsters. He had wanted to live and die of natural causes.

"Order! Order!" The griffins at the base of the platform had struck their metal staffs multiple times against the floor. "There must be order!"

"Do as you're told, goblins, for ye have introduced an unpleasant taste to my mouth!" Natas Christopher had stood up in disbelief. "For how can ye let three men dictate the outcome of battle when thou art supposed to be five times stronger? Tell me, mortals, have ye come to summon me my fate as well, or has the shepherd offered to do it for ye?"

"We'll tell you nothing, you circus monkey!" Zutermier had slowly started to regain his wits.

"Oh! Ye will tell me all that needs to be told, or even thy soul will perish, child!" Natas Christopher had warned, pointing his index finger. "Don't tempt me! I'm not that forgiving! Trust me, I'm nothing like thy Lord!"

"Go to Hell!" Zutermier had exclaimed, as he started to taste his busted lip for the first time. He was also feeling the spit wads, which were matted throughout his hair. "And when you get there, tell them I sent you!"

"How thoughtful of thee!" Natas Christopher had chuckled while being seated. "Strong are ye! But in the end, I will take pleasure in breaking thy spirit! The others also!" His smile had turned to a frown.

"Your Highness, these aren't just any humans before thee," Dramaticus had revealed. "Why, this one on the left is the Pope of Rome. He is the head of an organization known as the Catholic Church, a religion based on the teachings of Jesus Christ."

"Don't ever mention that name before me again!" Natas Christopher had flung his chalice through the air. "Fool, I knew who Christ was! He is nothing compared to me! He is just another who lets a man dictate his final outcome!"

"Wait! It all has to be a misconception, I proclaim!" The Gate Guardian had become disoriented, stomping his feet like a child. "For how can these three be mortals when these two on the right have been to the seventh gate and back! Truth be told, not even I detected them!"

"That's absurd!" Natas Christopher had protested. "If I can't accomplish this, then certainly not they!"

"Unless the Trinity has ordained them with some unique powers!" The Gate Guardian had balled up his fists.

"If this is true, then it would explain why Nero has allowed them to go unnoticed for so long," Dramaticus had tried his best to evaluate the situation. "Maybe Nero was putting them through trial and error."

"Still, what has been given unto them?" Natas Christopher had jealously looked the Pope and his cardinals up and down. "They appear so plain."

"Answer him!" The Gate Guardian had yanked the Pope up to his feet by way of his ears.

"This is my secret, you hideous beast!" The Pope had blindly pulled out his pistol. To his own disbelief, he was out of bullets. "No! This can't be!"

"You ass!" The Gate Guardian had slapped the Pope to his knees. In the process, the pistol was knocked aside. "Do ye dare to contest me with man-made devices? Try it again, and ye will perish!" He had yanked the Pope up by his ears again.

"Let's try this again! Tell me, what has been given to the others and thyself?" Natas Christopher had said with emphasis. "The next time I ask, it will be by great force! Do ye want this? Then tell me what I crave!"

"I don't know what you're talking about! The Lord has given us nothing, so stop asking me!" The Pope knew his cardinals and himself would be put to death the second Natas Christopher found out about the robes. That's why he had wanted to prolong the situation as much as he could until help arrived.

"He lies!" Dramaticus had exclaimed. "The holy man lies! The others and himself have been spotted numerous times with the angel Darr!"

"Fine! Have it thy way! Now I will seek what I acquire by my own methods! Go, my faithful set of eyes! Go!" Natas Christopher had launched the raven, which was perched on his throne. "Seek out the dark one, and wait for my commands!"

Once airborne, the noisy raven had made a characteristic pit stop for the enormous pot of brew. This was before it took up residence on Isaac's forehead. At any minute, he was expecting the bird to start pecking and eating his eyes out, but it didn't. He knew that despite the bird's fragile appearance, he wouldn't be able to deter it from such an act. This was because the bird's claws had somehow suppressed the nerves in his brain, making him feel partially paralyzed.

"YE WILL STILL DIE AT MY HANDS, CHILD. YET UNLIKE THE OTHERS, I WILL GRANT THY SOUL AMNESTY. SHIT. I MIGHT EVEN LET THEE RESIDE IN HEAVEN AND VACATION IN HELL, IF YE TELL ME WHAT POWERS THE TRINITY HAS BESTOWED UNTO THEE!"

"You're wasting your time! Like the Pope, I, too, will tell you nothing!"

Isaac had noticed the more he talked, the further the raven dug its claws into his flesh. "I despise everything you stand for, Natas Christopher! You'll have to murder me first before I allow you to rule the Earth!"

"Yes, child! Yes! That's what I seek to do after I finish physically fucking ye and the others over!" When Natas Christopher spoke this, the whole room erupted into laughter, including the normally emotionless griffins. "Let me end thy suffering!"

"Over my dead body." Isaac struggled to get the words out. He could now feel the blood pouring down his neck. "Get this creature off of me."

"In the end, Natas, you will also suffer!" The Pope scowled. "So will the others that cowardly follow you! None of them are a match for the Trinity! Not even this hideous creature with bad sinuses, which ye have summoned from the deep depths of Hell!" Twice, he thought about slapping the bird across the room. Yet each time, he knew his actions would only cause the bird to become more belligerent towards Isaac.

"Gate Guardian, silence this fool! Silence him before I rip his soul from this world!" Natas Christopher's pupils had become enlarged. He seemed to get a kick out of hearing the Pope gasp for air. "That's enough! Now, for the last time, speak the words I want to hear! Say them!"

"Never! Don't tell him anything, Isaac!" A weird grin came across the Pope's face. "The Lord has our back!" He tried to cross his heart before the Gate Guardian could grab him by the throat a second time.

"The hour has arrived, my faithful pet; bring forth the information I desire from the pathetic human!" Natas Christopher drew the raven's undivided attention. "Ransack his memory banks from beginning to end, as only thou knowest how!"

It all happened, so suddenly, Isaac didn't know what hit him. He was at a loss for adjectives the second the raven magically entered his skull in the form of a dark spirit. At first, he thought it was going to be a painful experience, so he squinched his eyes together to combat his phobia. However, as more time elapsed, the out-of-this-world invasion became quite a sensation to him. It didn't hurt at all, to say the least. In fact, he thought it felt like someone was sticking a pair of wet Q-tips down his eardrums.

"Let him go, you heathens!" Zutermier adverted his face. He couldn't bear to watch any longer. He couldn't believe how the whites of Isaac's eyes would turn solid black whenever the spirit of the raven changed its direction.

"He'll tell you nothing!" The Pope screamed at the top of his lungs. "None of us will!" He, too, could only imagine the damage the bird was inflicting internally. "I won't beg you any longer! Not for my life or for my cardinals! Do what it is you have to do, Natas! But do it with quickness!"

"Lord, please give Isaac the strength to endure," Zutermier prayed silently. "Please, Lord! Hear me, I don't believe he can hold out much longer."

Using sign language, one of the Egyptian high priests from the front came forth. At the same time, the raven magically reappeared from Isaac's skull. It had done so first in the form of a spirit, before changing back into a bird. Once in flight, however, the bird made another dash for the pot of brew. It took two swallows before it finally perched itself upon Natas Christopher's throne.

"Have ye lost thy mind?" The Gate Guardian spun around and quickly withdrew one of his swords. "Back into formation!"

The Egyptian priest wasn't a fool. He immediately bowed and complied. Yet, he never turned his back in doing so, fearing being beheaded.

"Tell me, Gate Guardian, what did the priest have to say? Find out if it was of any importance. For my faithful pet could come up with nothing! It has informed me that the human's brain was too twisted with negative thoughts to render any knowledge worth using!"

Isaac found this amusing. He couldn't stop laughing, as the blood from his head started to seep into the corners of his mouth like a vampire.

"Silence or die!" Dramaticus placed his hooves on Isaac's backside.

"So, in other words, this cardinal is lame or thy pet is intoxicated? I wonder which is which?"

"Ruler of the centaurs, why do ye continue to test my tolerance?" Natas Christopher asked, as the fire raged in his eyes. "Step out of place again, and ye will have thy head impaled on Hell's seventh gate just like these humans before thee!"

"Forgive me, your highness." Dramaticus made a gesture of goodwill with his hands while still using his front hooves to inflict discomfort. "I can assure thee, no malice was intended."

"Well, Gate Guardian, what have thee found out?" Natas Christopher turned and looked past Dramaticus, as if he wasn't even there. "What news do ye have to relay unto me? Please, come forth with it."

"Your highness, ye won't believe this." The Gate Guardian spoke in an excited tone of voice. "The Egyptian priest has just communicated unto me that the humans speak the truth. He says that their Lord has given them no unique powers, only the robes on their backs. The Egyptian priest believes, given thy genetic makeup, even ye can journey through the gates of the underworld if ye were to acquire one."

"Excellent! Then what art thou waiting for?" Natas Christopher leaped up from his makeshift throne. "Seize them from their fragile bodies! Strip them off, at once! Dramaticus, I want ye to aid in assisting him! This is a direct order!"

Chapter 20

The Pope and his cardinals could literally feel death staring them in the face, their own to be exact. They had just prayed that their one-time experience would be both painless and swift, for they each knew within a matter of seconds, they would have their limbs brutally ripped apart from their bodies like a farmer shucking corn for a harvest. Nevertheless, before any of Hell's villains could lay a finger on the robes, a cool but forceful breeze swept through the room. With it also came a cloud—a gray, mysterious, but odorless cloud.

"Gate Guardian, where art thou? What's happening, and what is the meaning of this untimely spectacle?" Natas Christopher sounded confused. "Answer me! I can't make out anything at all!"

"Neither can I, your highness!" the Gate Guardian replied while clanking his swords together. "I think the cloud has engulfed us!"

"That cloud has brought nothing but mayhem, especially amongst our goblin warriors!" Natas Christopher objected. "Listen to them! Why, they sound as if they are being slaughtered! Silence! Silence, I say! Hold thy positions, for this may either be a sign from Nero or one of Heaven's immaculate deceptions!"

"I don't know which one holds the most weight, your highness, but I believe I can vaguely see the goblins' torches flickering out one by one!" Dramaticus took notice.

"Shush. I think I hear roaring. It's a sound I haven't heard in eons," the Gate Guardian's voice crackled. "Can ye hear it also?"

"Yes. Yes, I can hear it!" Natas Christopher hesitated to respond. "If I didn't know any better, I would say that we're in the presence of throne guards—several of them, to be exact! But would the Trinity really make such a bold play? Could they be this extreme in their efforts to persecute me or save these mortal men's lives?"

"It's an answer we can't afford to find out!" The griffins by the platform had shouted in unison. "Retreat! Retreat, towards the sacred star at once! There we can find refuge!" This time, they had sounded as if they were airborne.

The Pope was totally beside himself. He had so much swimming through his mind, he could feel himself drowning. One, he couldn't figure out why his cardinals and he weren't put to the blade. Nor did he understand why Hell's villains had fled, leaving the valuable robes, which the Lord had given them, intact on their backs. Could it be that they were contemplating back? All he knew, he wasn't getting up until he was a hundred percent sure the coast was clear. The last thing he wanted was to have his head mistakenly chopped off by an overaggressive throne guard the second he made himself visible.

"Darr, I don't see them at all. Do you think they were taken hostage?"

"Did the two of you just hear that?" the Pope had whispered through the clouds. "Well?"

"Yeah. It sounded like the voice of a man," Zutermier had pointed out. "Kelso, to be exact."

"But what if it's a trap?" the Pope had wanted to convey this message. "Listen. Don't anyone do anything rash; continue to stay down."

"I don't think you have to worry yourself about that," Zutermier had verbally enlightened him.

"I think I can see the angel Darr with Kelso," Isaac had tried to strain his eyes. "Wait, it is him."

"That old buzzard," the Pope had beamed while lying on his side. "He got here just in the nick of time."

"Worthy ones of the Lord, arise!" Darr had insisted. "Arise upright into the light, for no harm shall cometh unto thee. This I can assure you."

"Look, Darr!" Kelso had run towards the front of the room. "I can see them! I can see them emerging! They're alive! They're alive!" He had hugged and kissed them endlessly.

"Calm down." Zutermier had playfully resisted Kelso's embrace.

"You don't know how worried I'd become." Kelso could feel his blood pressure decreasing. "I thought you were goners. I thought I would never see the three of you alive again until I saw you lift out of that smog, which was only calf level at the time."

"I thought I would never say these words, but it's good to see you also."

Isaac had shed a tear as he embraced Kelso once more. He had wanted to greet Darr with the same compassion, but they were some distance apart. He felt this was one instance where Kelso's strict discipline in doing things by the book had paid off. He knew never again would he criticize Kelso about his procedures.

"For a moment there, Kelso, we were beginning to worry if you'd come or not." The Pope had briefly turned his attention away.

His demeanor had changed from one of excitement to one of discomfort just that quickly. What did him in was the smorgasbord of goblin body parts and the green goo, which was smeared from the walls to the floor. Not even the ceiling was spared, he had later observed.

"They never saw what hit them." Kelso had made reference to the deceased goblins. "Darr and the throne guards had come through here like a whirlwind and had wiped them all out. Even those big beasts with wings slouched over there by the door." He showed them with his index finger.

"That I can see," said the Pope.

"It's called a griffin," Zutermier thought he would enlighten Kelso. "That's what those big beasts are called."

"A what?" Kelso had twisted up his face. "Well, whatever they're called, they're a smoldering mess now." He laughed as he passively swayed his hand through the air.

When Zutermier was asked to come to his feet, he assumed he would be standing in a room full of red lights like before. Instead, he was greeted by bright lights—man-made lights, to be exact. He figured somewhere between the arrival of the clouds or the departure of Natas Christopher's evil entourage, the main generator had kicked in. He also didn't think that the room would be overrun by so many throne guards. He knew he had counted two standing motionless by the entranceway and maybe another twelve. To his curiosity, the twelve were concentrated in the exact area where the pentagram was once positioned.

"What's wrong with Darr?" The Pope had turned to Kelso. He had the impression that the angel was avoiding him.

"Besides Natas Christopher, nothing that I know of," Kelso was being truthful in the matter. "Why do you ask?"

"I don't know." The Pope shook his head. For starters, he knew he had directly disobeyed orders to stay put at the palace. "Darr just doesn't seem pleased to see us. Maybe I should have a word with him and explain our involvement here." A sense of guilt came over him.

"Don't," Zutermier prevented the Pope from moving. "I believe he's meditating."

"Yes, he's probably receiving information from the Lord," Isaac could only speculate.

"Why certainly," Kelso got the same impression.

"Zutermier, do you think they're gone?" The Pope was curious to get another opinion.

"Are you referring to Natas Christopher and his band of tyrants?"

"Exactly." The Pope had waited for Zutermier's honest opinion. "Well?"

"I just can't say."

"What kind of answer is that?"

"Just look at how those twelve throne guards keep poking their staffs down at the floor." Zutermier had paused for a moment to allow the Pope to follow him. "Why do you suppose they're doing this? Think about it. By the grace of Heaven, we have been rescued. Yet why do they not escort us back to the palace?"

"Maybe they can see something we can't."

"I think you're right, Isaac." Zutermier saw no reason to be objective. "But between us, let's just pray you're wrong. We saw what kind of destruction the angel Pendelkon can cause."

"Please, don't ever remind me."

Isaac didn't want to hear any more. He was still spent from his earlier confrontation with the goblins. Besides, he already knew there was much more work that needed to be done to rid the Earth of nuisances like Natas Christopher and Pendelkon, who he felt only had hate for mankind. He only hoped the loose ends would be capped off within the next hour or so. He was sleepy, and his body was longing for the comfort only his bed could offer.

"Tell us, Kelso, was it difficult explaining to Darr where we had gone? How did he take the news?" The Pope had pressured him for details. This was very crucial to him.

"I kind of ran into him by accident."

"Do explain?" The Pope had come closer.

"It was Peter."

"Peter?" Zutermier flinched. He could tell by Kelso's facial expression that what he had to report wasn't going to be good. "Yes, Peter." Kelso took a deep breath.

"How is he?" The Pope wanted it straight. "Well?"

"Terrible. Peter's doing terrible." Kelso hid his face beneath his sweaty palms. "Oh, how can I say this?" He sobbed openly.

"Come on, Kelso, out with it." Isaac grew impatient while pulling Kelso's arms apart. He hated long stories, especially cliffhangers.

"Okay. Okay." Kelso shoved Isaac away. "Moments after all of you left, Peter became possessed by another spirit. A spirit that demanded I undo Peter's makeshift restraints. It was also seeking information."

"Information? Like what?" Zutermier wanted him to be more elaborate.

"Like what higher presence was inside the palace, and why it was so heavily fortified."

"And what did you tell it? I'm talking about this evil spirit." The Pope found Kelso's account to be fascinating.

"I told it nothing, but it kept interrogating me over and over again like a broken record. It wouldn't leave me alone, not even for one second," Kelso confessed. "And the more verses I recited from the Holy Scripture, the stronger its demonic influence over Peter became. The next thing I knew, Peter had broken free, and his hands were around my throat, choking me." He demonstrated on the Pope. "Just like this."

"Obviously, you're alive." The Pope broke free from Kelso's grasp. "So how did you do it?"

"After a few attempts, I did manage to escape. However, Peter's body had begun to drift upward and downward like before. Kelso had paused to wipe his nose with his hand. 'My weight alone wasn't enough to prevent this from occurring, so I quickly summoned the two throne guards outside the door, fearing the evil spirit would transform into one of those dreaded cobras.'

"And what did the guards do?" Zutermier was eager to find out.

"They tore him to pieces, meaning our beloved Peter." The tears had rolled down Kelso's face. He couldn't hold himself together any longer. "They murdered him in cold blood. That's when I fled the palace and ran into Darr on the steps of the basilica. However, the same guards, and many more, were giving chase after me."

"Did you witness this event with your own eyes?" The Pope had remained kind of skeptical. "Be honest."

"My words exactly," mumbled Zutermier. Even if it was somehow true, he knew the throne guards probably used just cause to do what they had done.

"No," Kelso whimpered. "I just assumed the worst. For the guards roars was enough proof for me. I had to get out of there."

Zutermier could sense that Kelso was stretching the truth just a bit. Even though he was aware the throne guards had a low tolerance level for anyone other than the Trinity, it was still a struggle for him to believe they would take an innocent life, especially one whom the Lord had sent them to protect. Indeed, he felt Kelso had made his premature assumption not based on any visual or solid evidence but based on his emotions, which had gotten the better of him this time.

"Look!" Isaac pointed. "Darr is conscious again!"

"And he is making his way towards us," Zutermier could feel his heart racing. He had almost forgotten how captivating and mysterious Darr was up close.

"PRAISE BE UNTO THEE, WORTHY ONES OF THE LORD."

"Darr, I-I-I can explain everything," the Pope stuttered. He had almost felt obligated to do so."

"There will be no need for this, Pope Pius of Rome. For ye and the others have done what ye did not out of discontent for the Lord, but out of love and admiration. Ye have exposed the hostile truth. Ye have risked thy very souls, and all in Heaven adorn ye for this." Darr had bowed. "Yet at this time, I must ask thou and the others to leave, for there is a great danger which still lurks within this room. Ye will find safety in the basilica. There, no harm shall come unto thee. Yea, it is the safest holy ground on this planet. Go there, I say unto thee. Go, and may the Lord be with thee!"

These words were soothing to the Pope to hear. They had assured him that Darr held no mixed feelings toward his cardinals or himself.

"Darr, there is a seventh gate." Zutermier had wanted to share this information with him. "Both Isaac and I have traveled there."

"We could also see a buildup of front-line forces," added Isaac. "They were made up of forty fallen angels and eighty centaurians."

"Worry thyself not, for this matter is being addressed as we speak by the archangel Gabriel and his coalition," Darr had assured them. "Kelso told us of the hole out back, which Peter last spoke of."

"Then this is a good thing." The Pope had nodded in approval. "Yes, I do believe so." He had glanced in Kelso's direction.

"Still, I'm baffled, Zutermier and Isaac. I'm at a loss for words. No human has ever accomplished what ye said thou did," Darr had informed them. "It was a test probably sanctioned by Nero himself. He probably wanted to observe the durability of the robes which the Lord has given unto thee. With this being said, I must warn again that ye flee this room before the hourglass runs out. For his breathing is becoming louder as we speak. It's the robes that they want."

"Who's breathing?" Kelso had turned wildly. "I don't hear anything at all. The room is silent."

"I do believe Darr's referring to the fallen angel Pendelkon." Zutermier had put his hand on Kelso's shoulder in order to calm him.

"This is correct." Darr had placed his hand over his temples. He seemed to be upset that the others weren't heeding his warning. "I sayeth, the sound which I hear can only be heard with the eternal ear. For Pendelkon is cleverly jumping in between dimensions, but such won't be for long. Guards, position thyself for a four-directional assault! Widen thy circle! Giveth them enough distance to emerge from the star while displaying their format, then act accordingly! Remember, this is a defensive stand only!" He had withdrawn his sword while walking stone-faced toward the front. At the time, he was also accompanied by the two throne guards who were once standing by the entranceway.

This was it. As the throne guards moved swiftly into position, the Pope and his cardinal put their heads down and began to make their way toward the exit, which felt like it was some twenty miles away. They each took the liberty to leave, even though their hearts forbade them. They weren't heroic fools either. They knew, given their combat agility, they would have been of no use. They figured they would have been more of a distraction than anything. They also knew the longer they hung around, the more they would be forcing the Lord's supernatural army to fight a soft battle. Yet their departure just didn't seem right. It felt too easy for there not to be any repercussions of any kind.

"Hey! What was that?" Isaac had grabbed his ears the second the others and he stepped out into the narrow corridor.

"I don't know." Zutermier seemed surprised. "I think it was an explosion."

"But it felt more like an earthquake." The Pope took a glance back.

"It doesn't matter what it was!" Kelso hollered. "Just keep walking! We have to make it to the basilica without any interruptions! We're halfway there!"

"Wait a minute!" The Pope grasped his forehead. "I have to see if Darr's alright. He and the throne guards might be injured."

"No, Pius! You can't! They can take care of themselves!"

"I have to, Kelso! I must! I wasn't raised in a barn!" the Pope exclaimed as he turned and ran back down the corridor.

"Lord, forgive him. You know yourself that his head is as hard." Kelso spoke these words while gazing up at the ceiling. "Come on! Let's go after him!" He signaled to the others.

Isaac noticed the closer he got toward the entrance of the room; the louder the throne guards' roars became. He felt it was almost potent enough to make the hairs within his ears fall out. Although he knew the throne guards were on Earth with all the right intentions, he was still kind of leery about seeing them in battle. What if the throne guards became offended by this? He thought twice about turning away.

"Look," shouted the Pope! "The floor is beginning to open up inside of Darr and the throne guards' circle! It's the return of evil and the return of the fireflies!"

"I see them!" Zutermier crossed his heart. "They seem to be pouring in by the thousands from the tiny cracks beneath the floor! God, have mercy on us all!"

"Whatever you do, Pope Pius, don't break that threshold, or you'll be sucked up into the air as were the goblins!" Isaac had a terrible vision of this happening to someone. "Like Darr stated, it's the robes that Natas Christopher wants! What we have to do is prevent him from acquiring them!"

"If I didn't know any better, I would say that the flaming image of a satanic pentagram was about to appear within Darr and the throne guards' circle!" Kelso held his breath for a second. "Damn, it is true!"

Unlike the others, Kelso was a virgin. He had never seen the flaming pentagram or many of Hell's cast of characters before. This also included the fireflies, which he saw take flight and form what were about forty individual tornadoes of yellow light. The tornadoes were only seven feet tall, but they were arranged in rows of eight, and they gave off a substantial amount of heat.

"What you see, Kelso, is the wraith of the fire demon!" Zutermier pointed out to him. "He's the one whom we were referring to earlier as Pendelkon. He's a fallen angel with the body of a dragon. He has the ability to wage either fires or plagues upon our planet."

"Good grief!" Kelso grabbed his chest. He was beginning to experience some complications, but he didn't think it was severe enough to be another heart attack. "Is this Pendelkon the same beast from Revelations?"

"I myself have found many similarities." Zutermier counted about seven of them on his fingers.

"Tell me, what do they wait for?" the Pope asked in vain. He was referring to the tornadoes of light, which he watched hover motionless in midair like flying saucers from a '60s science fiction film.

"I'm afraid not even the Lord may hold the answer to this."

"Unfortunately, you may be onto something," Zutermier concurred with Isaac.

"Hey! Everyone direct your attention back toward the star!" The Pope became excited, jumping up and down. "The barbarian-looking centaurs are starting to leap from the raging flames with their pitchforks drawn!"

"Yes, but they're quickly being beheaded as they emerge!" Zutermier cheerfully rooted for the side of righteousness. "They're no match!"

It was true. The barbarian-looking centaurs were easily killed with little effort by Darr and the throne guards. Yet their deaths brought about one thing: it had broken the Lord's supernatural army's circle. It had also allowed the Gate Guardian and the two griffins standing on opposite sides of him distance to appear, even though they hadn't left the center of the burning flames. Despite these changes of events, there still were no signs of Natas Christopher or the other villains of darkness. Where were they, and why weren't they visible?

"No! Leave the Gate Guardian to me!" Darr had instructed the throne guards not to intervene. "However, the griffins ye may dispose of at thy own accord when the time permits!"

"Gee whiz!" Kelso had to do a double take. "Is that what I think it is standing upright?"

"I'm afraid so." The Pope had watched Kelso slump unconscious to the floor. The others and he didn't bother to pick him up, as they didn't want to miss any of the action.

"Damn, can you believe that?" Kelso had expressed his disbelief while lying on his side. "A walking bull."

He was at a loss for words. Before, he could never accept that there were actual beings from Hell like the ones he was seeing at the present. For a good portion of his life, he had always believed man had conjured up his own evil spirits by spreading greed, lust, and hate around the world as if it were the common cold. Now he knew otherwise. Now he knew there was a third-wing political source, which had fed their ungodly views and propaganda through mankind's veins like it were second nature.

"So we meet at last!" The Gate Guardian had exhaled large quantities of smoke from his mouth as he appeared from the flames along with the two griffins.

"Yet it will probably be the last!" Darr had withdrawn his sword.

Likewise, the Gate Guardian had also displayed one of his two swords for combat, along with his wooden shield.

"Hum! The Son of Man has gone to unusual measures!" The Gate Guardian had made reference to the throne guards he saw. "This leads me to suspect that he must be somewhere on this Earth. Only where? Answer me not, for I shall conduct my search after I taketh thy head!"

"Ye should know the answer! Ye once guarded the gates of Heaven, along with those griffins!"

"Don't remind us of our past, ye fake, noble bitch!" the Gate Guardian grunted. "We pledge our allegiance to only Nero! Nothing has changed, nor can we be persuaded to think otherwise! Try thy mind trickery elsewhere, perhaps on mankind!" He laughed, along with the griffins.

"I see thy attitude hasn't changed. If anything, it has only hardened, but so was thy fall from grace! Well, listen to thy choices!" Darr tapped the tip of his blade several times on the floor. "Either ye and the others can live to fight another day, or ye can have thy judgment now! All thou hast to do is surrender Natas Christopher over to me and unwind the wraith of the angel Pendelkon!"

"Never!" The Gate Guardian spat at Darr's feet. "Never will we surrender! If today is our day to fall, then so be it! Woe, but let it be recorded that we gave our very lives in order to preserve the future! Fireflies, descend and surround these holy whores!"

"Will you have a go at that," mumbled Zutermier. "The tornadoes of light are starting to touch down around the outer portion of Darr and the throne guards."

"I see, but what are the tornadoes transforming themselves into? That's what I'm most concerned with!"

"It appears to be an army of fire demons," Zutermier took a wild guess as he sought to answer the Pope's question. "I swear, just glancing at them has the same effects as staring into the sun." He complained about the black and yellow blotches that hindered his vision.

"I agree!" Isaac had shielded his eyes with his hands. "Hey, the demons are also armed with weapons!"

"Move back! Move back!" Kelso had crawled his way up from the floor. "That one seems to know we're watching it!" He had almost stumbled over the Pope, who was also trying to get out of the way.

The fire demons, who had bat-shaped wings and monkey-like tails, were very intimidating. As a collective troop, they had stood about seven feet tall, and they had resembled warthogs in their face. If this wasn't frightening enough, they would exhale lightning-fast fireballs from their nostrils on average every two seconds. They were also militant minded in the way they had twirled their swords which were each cut from a single diamond, while walking forward in unison like zombies. It was no doubt that their weapons had resembled the fallen angel Pendelkon's, but just on a much smaller scale.

"Ye leave me no other choice, Gate Guardian, but to close thy eyes with eternal darkness! No longer will thou and the others be permitted to serve out thy sentence in the realm of Hell with the devil Nero! For each of thee have broken a great commandment when thou first stepped foot upon the threshold of my master's world! Now that thy judgment has been rendered, ye must be eliminated forevermore! You two, giveth me distance and prepare to engage the griffins with the same fury!" Darr had instructed the two throne guards standing on opposite sides of him.

"Fool, speak to me no more!" The Gate Guardian had pointed one of his swords at Darr's head. "No number of words has ever won a battle, nor will they today! Yea, for the only sound I want to hear is the clings from our mighty weapons!"

The duel between Darr and the Gate Guardian had started off as a strategic one. This meant that both combatants had gone through a series of stages, where they were trying to feel one another out and jostle for positioning. Even though they both had a difference in moral objectives, it was evident from the opening that they had mutual respect for one another's ability to inflict a fatal blow. Despite this, when the two did participate in swordplay, it was a sight to behold. The friction they had generated together was so intense, sparks from their blades had touched off several brief fires.

"I see ye have progressed!" The Gate Guardian had congratulated Darr. He had interrupted their confrontation by backpedaling about fifteen paces. "Yet thy skills are only partial! They aren't enough to defeat me!" he had boasted as he flicked his wrist, sending his wooden shield sailing through the air like a Frisbee towards Darr.

"Oh, I don't know how much more of this I can watch!" The Pope had thought about closing his eyes. "Darr has dropped his weapon!" His heart had filled with concern the second he had watched the Gate Guardian unveil his other sword. Now he had two.

"I think Darr's hand was hit," Isaac couldn't believe what he had seen. "I think it was t-taken off," he had stuttered to get the words out.

"I can't see to be certain," said Zutermier. "Darr's back is towards us, although he is hobbled over as if something is wrong. He may be doomed. I know, maybe I should go and distract the Gate Guardian."

"Stop!" The Pope held Zutermier back. "You wouldn't get there in time! Besides, you would only be putting your robe in the Gate Guardian's evil grasp, along with your life! Think back, Natas Christopher only needs one robe in order to pass through the seventh gate! One robe!"

With victory in his eyes, the Gate Guardian had rushed in for the kill. Just like a world-class sprinter, he was pumping his arms really fast through the air while clenching tightly onto his two swords. He had assumed Darr was down and on the ropes. He was also basking in the glory that Darr's head was turned opposite of his travel. What he didn't know was Darr had caught his shield in mid-flight while doing a three-sixty twist.

"How can it be?" The Gate Guardian's jaw had dropped the instant he had seen Darr uncoil and return his shield through the air.

"Help me, Nero! I can't stop myself in time!" he hollered as his legs were taken out from underneath him by his own device. In the process, he pierced his neck with one of his swords during his impact on the floor.

"Remember, Gate Guardian, ye called thy hand! Thus I must deal thee thy final card! The death card!" Darr picked up his noble sword and held it high above his head. "There will be no mercy for ye! Thou will get what ye deserve!" He was escorted forward by the two throne guards who were behind him.

"What are ye waiting for?" The Gate Guardian grimaced as he gingerly pulled the blade from the side of his neck. "Defend me! Attack them at once! Fight until there's no one left standing to oppose thee!" He coached the griffins and the fire demons into battle.

It appeared to be painful and almost difficult at times for the Gate Guardian to communicate. Yet he managed to do so by placing his hand over the large gash, which was oozing some sort of foul, jelly-like substance. It appeared to be rustic orange in color.

"Don't let them get airborne! Go for the griffins' wings, then their heads! Watch!" Darr demonstrated in two moves how it was to be done. "This technique also applies to the fire demons!" He watched the headless griffin curl to the floor, where it exploded.

"Those fire demons are putting up a good fight, not to mention that other griffin," Isaac noticed. "Yet once the fire demons are beheaded, watch how they disperse back into their original form of fireflies."

"Yes, they seem to be retreating back towards the cracks in the floor."

Zutermier couldn't help but observe this.

"Speaking of retreating, has anyone seen where the Gate Guardian has gone?" The Pope had become worried. He knew the Gate Guardian still had enough strength left to impose his will upon the others and himself with ease if given the opportunity.

"The last I saw, he was trying to crawl his way back into the open flames of the star," Kelso had gone into detail. "Yet I don't know if he ever succeeded. There was too much going on at the time."

"That's an understatement. Look who has just arrived within the pentagram." The Pope felt sick to his stomach.

"I see them," Zutermier had observed. "It's the return of Natas Christopher and the Egyptian high priests. Wait, I also see Dramaticus. I think our situation has worsened!"

"Keep your voice down, Isaac. Do you want them to hear us?" The Pope had pushed everyone to the back of him. "Bastards. They have the Gate Guardian's body draped over Pendelkon's sarcophagus. I prayed he would be expired by now."

"So that's where those fireflies are going." Isaac had peeked through the gap between the Pope's legs. "They are headed back into the open mouth of the sarcophagus." He had also noticed that the raging flames from the pentagram had transformed back into a smoldering outline.

"Let's get out of here! I think they spotted us! Come on!" Kelso had hurried everyone up the narrow corridor. "Darr and the throne guards' hands are tied. They may be unable to cut the tyrants off in time!" He had snatched the door open, which led out into the hallway.

Nothing had changed. The hallway was still darkened, despite the fact he could see some visible traces from the tiny window on the back door that it was early dawn.

Chapter 21

The Pope was the last one to exit. He was so anxious to catch up with his cardinals, who were already out in front of him by a surmountable distance, that he didn't even bother to shut the door. He didn't feel a need to. He had figured it would do little, if anything, to deter the evil beings he had left behind. Even though he knew Darr and the throne guards didn't have it easy, he was confident they would win the confrontation.

"Wait a minute. Wait a minute," repeated Isaac. "I think I see someone!"

"Don't be silly! What are you all stopping for?" the Pope had shouted from afar. "Go ahead and open the door to the basilica!"

"We can't," Kelso had informed him, out of breath. "I don't think it's going to be that simple."

"Yeah," Zutermier had confirmed what Kelso was insinuating. "I think we have a big problem."

"What do you mean? All you have to do is turn and pull!" the Pope had continued to express his displeasure. "Don't tell me the door is stuck again?" He had eased up into a light stride, thinking it would be best to conserve some energy.

To his surprise, no one had answered him.

"Does the cat have your tongues? Out of my way!" The Pope had reached forward in the darkness, in the direction where he had anticipated the knob to be. "I'll open it myself!" He had persisted until he had felt a much larger hand grasp his own. He knew right from the initial engagement that the hand squeezing his didn't belong to any of his cardinals. It was too rough and coarse for one, not to mention hairy. At times, he thought it had smelled and felt like it was affixed to some sort of mutant creature. One who was out for retaliation and blood first, then the robes.

The Pope was highly upset with himself. He knew he could have run back and gotten the help needed if he had taken his cardinals' silence into consideration and realized they were in danger. He couldn't see any of them at the time, but he knew they weren't dead yet either. He had envisioned they had some sort of crude device pointed at them, keeping them hostage against their will.

"Forgive me." The Pope lowered his head in agony. "Now I see what you all were insinuating."

"Behold! There they are!" Natas Christopher laughed in the darkness. "What a welcoming surprise!"

"Centaurian, halt! Don't let those humans enter through that door! Keep thy whip around their windpipes!" Dramaticus ordered as he and Natas Christopher approached.

It was apparent they could see what the Pope and his cardinals couldn't.

"I guess this is it," the Pope muddled. "If we weren't so hardheaded, we would already be inside the basilica." A tear ran along the side of his cheek.

"Kneel, I say! Kneel at once!" the centaur commanded, moving his hand towards the Pope's knuckles. "Do as I say!"

"So it was you all along?" The Pope administered the same grip back. "I remembered how to do it," he whispered to the Lord's shepherd, who was still disguised as a barbarian-looking centaur.

The Pope didn't want to inform his cardinals of the joyous news just yet. He didn't want to give the shepherd's plans away. It was a scheme, which he felt consisted of getting the two villains within striking range of his pitchfork.

"Guard, excellent work! Now relinquish the humans over to me, then fall out in front! Our destination is the seventh gate!" Dramaticus bullied his way forward.

He was so close that the Pope and his cardinals could feel the heat from his wicked eyes scorching their flesh.

"Guard, did ye not hear what I just said? Ye art to relinquish, then fall out!" Dramaticus had raised his tone of voice. He didn't seem too thrilled to be repeating himself to someone of a lesser rank.

"Inform him that he's also out of his jurisdiction!" Natas Christopher could be heard backing up while pulling a diamond dagger from a metal sheath.

"Guard, I will sayeth this only once! Let me read the tines on thy weapon, or I will spilleth every drop of thy blood!"

"But of course, my majesty!" The shepherd could be heard jabbing his pitchfork through the midsection of Dramaticus. "I wouldn't have it any other way! Trust me on this!"

"Christopher . . . Christopher, don't let me perish in vain." Dramaticus had moaned in the darkness. It sounded like the more he had struggled to communicate, the deeper the shepherd had driven the tines into his flesh. "Keep up the fight. Pursue the humans and get their robes. Fulfill Nero's wishes, for ye art the one. Ye art the Antichrist."

"Come on! Let's make a run for it!" The Pope had screamed while frantically twisting the knob of the door until it had opened. "Hurry up! What are you waiting for? That centaur is really the Lord's

Shepherd!" He had stood at the threshold. He had the door cracked just enough so his cardinals could guide their way toward the light.

"We're right behind you!" Zutermier had crawled his way inside.

He was followed by Kelso, who had also crossed over the threshold on his knees.

"Isaac, please seal that door!" The Pope had instructed. "We don't want to let Natas Christopher in!" He wasn't worried about Dramaticus, on account of the Lord's shepherd having him military pressed up to the ceiling with the tines of the pitchfork emerging out of his spine.

"I'm trying to close it, Pope Pius, but something is preventing me from doing so!"

Isaac knew that something was Natas Christopher. He could feel the villain pushing back from the opposite side, as if he were ten men rolled up into one. It was a tug-of-war that was zapping him of all his strength. Not to mention, it was making the muscles in his arms and legs cramp in pain.

"He'll never do it alone." The Pope had rushed over to aid Isaac. He knew Isaac was too proud to personally ask for any kind of assistance.

"Keep pushing!" Zutermier had begged the others. "We almost have it shut!"

"Damn, what is he made of?"

"I have no idea, Kelso. And I don't want to find out the hard way either." The Pope had gritted his teeth.

"Neither do I." Kelso had closed his eyes in order to zone out the pain in his lower back. "Neither do I."

"Then may I suggest we keep doing what we're doing."

Zutermier didn't know how the others felt, but he was more than oppressed by what he saw when he had entered the basilica. In his mind, he guessed he was expecting to see something extravagant. He guessed he had expected the basilica to be heavily fortified from top to bottom with archangels and more throne guards, yet it wasn't. It was a hard pill to swallow, but he knew he had to put his emotions on standby if he wanted to contribute at his best. Besides, he knew they only had two options at the most. He felt either they could try to force the door shut on their own, or they could keep Natas Christopher stalled until the Lord's shepherd could deal with him.

"I thought the basilica was supposed to be the safest holy ground on the planet?" Zutermier had asked while taking his focus—not his hands—off the door. "Isn't that what Darr told us?"

"Yes." The Pope had answered through his teeth. "Yes, that's what Darr said." He was so exhausted; he hardly had enough energy to keep himself upright.

"But it's empty!" Zutermier had shook his head. "There's no one here, only the four of us!"

"He's here!" The Pope had turned and dipped his head in the direction of the Christ replica.

Even though the basilica had appeared vacant and vulnerable to evil, he had thought otherwise. He had felt it had a mysterious aura about it. A divine one, which he suspected was invisible to the eyes of mortal men such as himself. Was this why they had difficulty keeping the door shut?

"There's nothing wrong with my faith in the Lord, but that's just art on the wall." Zutermier had looked at the Pope strangely. "Natas Christopher is a living being with a mind for killing! Anyway, how did the replica get back up there?"

"No, son. It's a little more than art." The Pope had smiled to himself. He was still keeping his secret—a secret that he had once observed the Christ replica come to life when the wraith of the Lord had occupied it.

"Foolish ingrates! Give it up! Thou are no match physically for someone of my breed!" Natas Christopher had boasted as he watched the Pope and his cardinals fall flush to their backsides the instant he had given the door a good thrust. "Let me hear ye crave to be in my presence!" He grinned while slamming the door. Still on his shoulders was his pet raven, which had been called out twice before it took up residence on the Christ replica's head.

"Get out of here! Get out!" Kelso had hissed. He was so beside himself that the finger which he was pointing was starting to tremble to the point where it looked as though it was about to fall off. "Don't you know that this is the house of the Lord? Have you no respect, heathen?"

"I don't think thy Lord's home! In fact, he hasn't made his presence felt in this world since men like thyself had him persecuted! Tell me, human, can you or others find written text anywhere to denounce my claim? Can ye? If it wasn't for my escape, not even his army would be amongst thee!"

"It was his destiny!" Zutermier had become offended by Natas Christopher's accusations. "Not the will of man!"

"You don't have to explain anything to this animal!" The Pope had stood up. "For his tongue is as slippery and foul as a serpent's! Anything you say, he will only try to contradict it! You see, this is his gift!"

"Blasphemy is all he speaks, damn it! And I want to put a stop to it! He has no right to be here!" Kelso had jumped up and ran towards Natas Christopher with his fists balled up.

"No! Stop! You're making a mistake! Vengeance is mine, says the Lord!"

The Pope had tried to grab hold of Kelso's robe, but it had slid through his fingers like fine silk. He knew Kelso was about to embark on more than his ancient body could withstand. He was also fearful that Kelso's ignorance of Natas Christopher's supernatural strength would get him disfigured or killed. The last thing he wanted to envision was Kelso without his head and organs. Instead, he watched Natas Christopher slam Kelso to the floor, where he had been motionless for five seconds before finally snaking his way back towards the group.

"Are you injured, Kelso?" The Pope had wanted to thoroughly check on his condition but didn't. He just didn't think it would be too sensible to take his eyes off of Natas Christopher, who he knew was as cunning as a fox.

"Trust me, I've felt better." Kelso had squinted while gingerly standing. "I've felt better."

"You shouldn't have done that, fiend!" Zutermier had come forward while massaging his knuckles. He had every intention of striking Natas Christopher.

"Yeah, wrong move!" Isaac had also come forward. "You had your chance to flee! Now we're going to throw you out!"

"Unfortunately, ye won't succeed!" Natas Christopher had taunted them with his laughter. "Thou will never conquer me, for ye art just men! Thus, I suggest ye surrender the robes, and I will have pity on thy souls."

"Watch it, you two! Don't forget Natas Christopher possesses a dagger!" The Pope was being mindful.

"We have our sights on him, Pope Pius. You and Kelso can continue to keep your distance. At best, he can only stab one of us." Zutermier had his mind made up; he didn't care whether he lived or died. He just wanted to get his hands around Natas Christopher's neck and prevent him from spreading his bloodline throughout the world.

"I don't need a weapon to inflict my destruction on mankind, only my intellect!" Natas Christopher had slid his dagger towards Zutermier and Isaac. "Take it! Defeating thee will be easier than pulling a newborn from its mother's womb!"

"Don't any of you touch it!" Kelso had run up and kicked the dagger aside. "It may be laced with voodoo! So help us, Father, when we lay our hands on you, you'll see how screwed up man can really be!"

"Zutermier, you go for one leg, and I'll go for the other," Isaac had called out his recipe for success. "Let's put this rat on his back!"

"Sounds like a plan." Zutermier had joggled his head around in order to work the kinks out of his neck.

He had no moral or religious conflicts with killing Natas Christopher. The thought that he might be committing a sin had never entered his mind. Yet, he did believe he would be doing the Trinity a noble service if he were to accomplish this. In his eyes, Natas Christopher wasn't human. He viewed Natas Christopher as a foreign being, one who was never conceived from a natural birth and one who stood to jeopardize his eternal resting place in Heaven.

"I'm ready whenever you are."

"Go for it!" Isaac motioned to Zutermier.

The Pope was standing on pins and needles as he watched Zutermier and Isaac swoop towards the floor as if they were two gliding hawks. From the moment they went on the offensive, he prayed that the two could hold Natas Christopher down. But he knew this wouldn't be the case the second he watched the two miss their objective, colliding forehead-first into the door. He didn't know how, but he figured they were probably caught off guard by the forward flip Natas Christopher did before the two could grasp his ankles.

"He has the agility of an acrobat!" Kelso stood dumbfounded. "How can we compete against that? How will we get our hands on him?"

"Snap out of it, Kelso! Keep your composure! It's up to us to lead the way; Zutermier and Isaac are both out cold!" The Pope watched Natas Christopher reach back without turning and grasp the two by their throats.

"See how simple it was?" Natas Christopher held the bodies of the cardinals in the air.

"Let them be," yelled the Pope. "It's me you want! I am more powerful than my loyal subjects!"

He wasn't worried, not in the least. He knew he had time, but not a lot. He knew Natas Christopher would never make a play for the robes as long as Kelso and he were still standing to oppose him. What he wanted to do was to use Kelso as a decoy or vice versa. From what he observed, Natas Christopher wasn't making any attempts to pursue them. They had brought all of the physical contact to him. Now, he wanted this to change. Now, he wanted Natas Christopher to be the aggressor so either Kelso or he could double back and reopen the door.

"Leave, Natas Christopher! Leave! Release my brethren and go back out that door to confront your fate!" Kelso was referring to a showdown with the Lord's shepherd. "None of us are afraid of you! If it's the robes that you want, then you'll have to pry them off our deceased bodies! We'll give you nothing without a fight! Nothing, I say!"

The Pope had seen his game plan go down the drain the minute Kelso had scampered forward while landing a series of unorthodox haymakers. Even though he knew Kelso's timing was off, he knew he had to react. He knew he had to swing for the fences. He knew he had to seize the moment and punish Natas Christopher as much as possible while his hands were still full. The only thing was he didn't want to injure Zutermier and Isaac in the process. Thus, he had tried to trip Natas Christopher to the floor, but with no success. In a sense, he felt it would have been easier to move an elephant instead.

"This contest has concluded itself! The real victor has been declared!" Natas Christopher had licked his tongue out before he hurled the unconscious bodies of Zutermier and Isaac through the air. His aim was so precise the Pope and Kelso were both simultaneously knocked to the floor like bowling pins.

"Kelso. Zutermier. Isaac. Can any of you hear me?" The Pope had called out lightly. He had grown worrisome as he saw Natas Christopher approaching. "Just say anything if you can acknowledge the sound of my voice."

The Pope had felt all alone. None of his cardinals were answering him. He wasn't injured; he just knew he would be indisposed for a couple of seconds. This was due to having the wind knocked out of him when Zutermier landed on top of him. He felt this was most likely the case when Isaac fell on Kelso. Was this how the curtain was going to fall? He had prayed silently that it wouldn't. He had prayed silently that the Lord would give him one last breath to stand. However, he had seen nothing to make him believe this was going to occur until he heard Darr's voice enter his consciousness, giving him key instructions. If Darr hadn't used this same method to communicate with him earlier in the day, then he probably would have thought it was a form of trickery employed by Natas Christopher.

"No longer will I continue to waste precious time! Now I will plunder what gifts thy Lord has professed! Starting with thee!" Natas Christopher had grabbed the Pope by his collar.

"Okay, Natas Christopher. You win. I-I-I surrender. Here. Take my robe!" The Pope had quickly taken it off upon being released. Not once did he think twice about what he was doing. "Do with me what you want, but I won't let you take the lives of my cardinals!" He had thrown the robe underneath the Christ replica.

"A wise decision! I see ye do have some sense after all!" Natas Christopher had applauded as he started to strangle the Pope. "Hurrah, for ye may have bought thyself the honor to die elsewhere! Tell me, did ye ever foresee thyself burning to death on the threshold of the seventh gate? In the end, thy soul will make a very nice welcoming gift for Nero!" He had laughed in triumph as he shoved the Pope to the floor.

Everything had seemed to be going as suspected; the Pope felt a tingle of relief come over him. Natas Christopher was so obsessed with attaining the robe he was left just footsteps away from the door. To his presumption, on the other side, had awaited Darr and the rest of Heaven's army. He knew he had to just get to them; still, he was confused as to why they didn't just tear the door down themselves.

"That's it, fool," the Pope had whispered. "Keep doing what you're doing."

When Natas Christopher had turned completely away, he knew it was time to make his move. He couldn't wait either to slither backward and turn the knob, yet that was until Natas Christopher had spun in his direction. He knew the villain didn't have eyes in the back of his head. No, he was fully aware that Natas Christopher was tipped off by the noisy raven, the one which was still perched on the head of the Christ replica, the one whose eyes and feathers he had also wanted to pluck out.

"Don't test my authority, or I shall rewrite thy fate. Like man, I am also unpredictable!" Natas Christopher had dragged the Pope over towards the others, where he had taken their robes one by one. "We will exit when Nero sends his mark. In life, death is just the beginning as the soul travels onward. But in thy case, it will signal the end of existence."

The Pope was powerless. His will to endure evil had felt like it had just evaporated. In the rear of his mind, he knew the wicked pentagram was nothing more than a time portal. He felt if Darr's grand scheme didn't transpire before this occurrence, then he truly believed there would be no deterring Natas Christopher from reuniting with the fallen angel Nero in Hell.

"Who is this tortured soul suspended from above?" Natas Christopher had asked while fashioning himself with the Pope's robe. He had appeared to be both fascinated and somewhat jealous of the figurine. "Is he thy Messiah?"

"You should know the answer to this." The Pope had wasted no time firing back. He could hear and feel his cardinals starting to move about. "Do with me what you want, but I won't be your entertainment. Not even in death."

"We shall see!" Natas Christopher had tried to rip the Pope's tongue out before turning his attention back towards the Christ replica.

"May the hands of the Lord have mercy on you!" The Pope quickly wiped his mouth.

"So this is what became of thee. Can thou speak? Is this really how ye appeared on that monumental day? How tragic it must have been to violently be dismissed by the same hypocrites ye had come to deliver. And still, thou adorn them. Why?" Natas Christopher had chuckled in disgust. "O how ye maketh me sick." He had reared back and spit into the air.

The black raven had also shown disrespect towards the Christ replica. For instance, it would yank out strands of hair, and it would peck repeatedly at the forehead area. At times, it would even squawk in a tone that made it appear as if it were having the gala of its life.

"Did ye hear me? Thy Father should have sent me! I wouldn't have failed! Never would I have allowed man to taunt and persecute me! No, I wouldn't have died for man's sins! Man would have died for mine! That is what divides the two kingdoms, and that's why I have always despised thee! Thou art a failure, and so art thy offspring!"

"He's a born lunatic," whispered Zutermier, who was leaning just over the Pope's shoulder, along with Kelso and Isaac. "Who does he think he's talking to?"

"My guess is the Lord." The Pope turned and acknowledged everyone. Even though he felt the mood was too serious to smile, he was still gleeful to see that none of his cardinals were permanently injured.

"Where's that dagger?" Kelso began to stumble around frantically on his knees. "I'll run it through his spine." He was tired of Natas Christopher speaking blasphemy. He didn't want to be a hero, but he wanted it to cease. "Where is it? Tell me!"

"Damn it, Kelso. You'll do nothing but lower your voice." The Pope motioned for Isaac to restrain him.

"Why should I?" Isaac openly complained but did as he was told. He had never disobeyed the Pope before, but he was suddenly contemplating doing so. The image of Natas Christopher parading around in the sacred robe with his back turned, telling tall lies about the Lord, was too much to let go uncontested.

"Kelso has a point. I would rather die than live knowing I could have done something to prevent that monster from existing in our world. We already have enough murder and madness."

"This is true, yet the mission is over for us," the Pope had explained with his hands. He had wanted to remain calm so his cardinals would put their trust in him. "We did our part. We led that twisted moron here, didn't we? It's out of our hands now. Please, let a higher presence bestow judgment on Natas Christopher. This is the will of Darr. Don't interfere with that. All you have to do is believe, and a better outcome will arise."

"But he has your robe on and ours by his feet," Kelso had tried to worm his way free. "We have to stop him. We have to seize the moment while it's still before us."

"I did my part." The Pope had given Kelso a tongue-lashing in his ear. "I did as I was instructed. Get in touch with yourself before you jeopardize everything."

Zutermier himself could rationalize some of the things the Pope had said. Still, there were a couple of circumstances that had remained a mystery to him. One, he couldn't figure out who or what was making the basilica's many doors inaccessible to Darr and the others. Nor could he interpret what this strange voice was saying to him while he had lay unconscious by the door. He thought the voice had sounded like it belonged to a man. A man who spoke with a lot of bass. A man who had also appeared to be far away, yet traveling toward him. The heavy footsteps were obvious, he felt, along with the constant crashing of thunder and wind. Was this man from heaven? Reality had told him no, but his heart had said yes.

"ONCE AGAIN, SON OF GOD, I HAVE OUTWITTED THEE! I HAVE PROVEN MYSELF SUPERIOR! I HAVE BEATEN THEE AT THY OWN GAME! SOON LEGIONS CREATED FROM MY BLOODLINE WILL RISE FROM HELL TO DETHRONE THEE IN THE NAME OF NERO!"

"I don't believe it!" The Pope had stood up. "There's a white light coming from the Christ replica's eyes!"

He had also noticed that the replica was trembling and making an unbearable noise from within—a sound of raw energy. A sound that reminded him of a jet's turbine engine before liftoff. As a result of this, he felt he had no other choice but to drop to his knees and push his fingertips in his ears for comfort. Glancing over, he could see that his cardinals had already done the same themselves.

"The Savior has returned! He has come back to settle the score!" Kelso had fainted backward.

"I see! I see!" Isaac had traced the flight and fall of the raven as it was instantly encased in a block of ice. This was done when the Christ replica had blown upon it.

"Those two beams are very brilliant!" Zutermier could be seen squinting. "Whatever you do, don't stare at it for a long period of time! You could become blind!" Although he knew the beams were meant to defuse the enemy, he still felt it was better to be cautious than sorry later.

"Look! The beams are starting to lift Natas Christopher up to the height of the replica!" The Pope had continued to cover his ears. "I think they're going to be face-to-face!"

"THOU ART HERE, BUT HOW CAN IT BE?" Natas Christopher had sounded surprised. "WHAT DO YE MEAN, YE HAVE COME TO JUDGE ME? WAIT, I CAN EXPLAIN MYSELF! I ONLY WANTED TO EXIST! I ONLY WANTED TO BE LOVED, BUT THOU WOULDN'T ALLOW ME! YE STOLE MY GLORY THE SECOND TIME! YE SENT THYSELF INSTEAD!"

Without making so much as a sound, the basilica's centermost door had methodically swung open, and standing in the midst of the frame was Darr himself in all his holy grandeur. He wasn't alone either. He was accompanied by three throne guards, one of whom had taken his staff and had speared it through the block of ice that had fossilized the raven. Twice, the guard performed this procedure before finally retrieving his staff for inspection. Unlike the other guards who wore medallions depicting the moon, these guards wore medallions depicting the sun.

"Creatures from the valley, I beckon thee! I beckon thee to attack!" The veins were bulging from Natas Christopher's neck. It was almost as if the Christ replica had an invisible chokehold on him. "Fulfill my wishes! Unleash thy destruction! Ravage the cities of mankind!"

"It's over, Natas Christopher!" Darr had come forth. Before, his presence had gone unnoticed by the Pope and his cardinals. "The Lord has made peace with the creatures in the valley. He has soothed their wounds. He has turned them back to their rightful places, and he has also destroyed those who opposed his treaty with a spectacle of burning lights."

"No! It can't be!" Natas Christopher had dipped his head back in Darr's direction. "It's a lie! Nero would never allow this!"

"Guards, hold back thy instruments!" Darr had physically prevented the pair from advancing towards Natas Christopher. "Ye will spill no blood in this sacred temple!"

"Release me! Release me at once or suffer the ill consequences! Nero is on his way for me! I can hear him?"

"Sayeth no more, infidel!" Darr had pointed. "For thy judgment has been rendered! No longer will the mighty Trinity allow ye to exist! Thy reign of terror is over!"

When Darr had spoken this, something had occurred. Something magnificent. Something spectacular. For the second time, the arctic air from the Christ replica's mouth had entombed evil. This time, the evil was none other than Natas Christopher, who was sent to the bottom of the floor in the form of an ice block about the total length of his body.

"Just like that, it's over." The Pope was heartfelt as he watched the arctic air, which had once occupied the Christ replica, dance its way up the main aisle. "Praise be unto you, mighty one." He and his cardinals had crossed their chests while standing in unison.

"Zutermier, what's your assessment?" Isaac had turned towards him joyously. He had felt about ten pounds lighter now that he knew Natas Christopher was subdued. "Did you see how fast he was frozen? I would have never pictured an ending like this."

"Indeed. But I felt the punishment was cogent. It was a fitting exclamation by the Lord," Zutermier had replied as he and the others had walked over for in-depth observation of the giant ice cube.

"Is he alive?" Kelso had become skeptical. "I thought I saw his fingers move."

"I don't think so." The Pope had smiled. "I think it was just your imagination."

"How remarkable." Kelso had begun to pace the block of ice. "From a distance, I would have never anticipated how much craftsmanship was involved in creating this sculpture. Not that I'm underestimating the ability of the Lord. I mean, everything had just happened so rapidly."

"I know exactly what you're deriving at. Believe me." Zutermier was on his hands and knees, examining every detail. "Extraordinary. Why, the entire block looks as though it was created from a million pieces of hail. Each about the size of a tiny gumball."

"Worthy ones, ye can admire the work of the Lord, but I forbid thee to touch," Darr had warned them while approaching the group with his hands extended outwards. "Trust me, it would be ill-advised."

At the time, Darr was being escorted by two throne guards who were walking in perfect rhythm with their high-leg action. However, the guard who had impaled the raven on his staff had never moved. He had continued to stand motionless at the top of the aisle.

"Who knew, Darr? Who really knew the Lord was here all along?" Kelso couldn't stop beaming. "I think even Natas Christopher was caught off guard."

"What ye have witnessed was only the wraith of our Lord," Darr had clarified as he gave way to one side while signaling for the two throne guards.

The Pope and his cardinals had mimicked Darr's movements. They had departed to one side. This was done more out of fear than it was to allow the throne guards room to maneuver into position. Despite the spacing, which they felt was surmountable, the guards still made them feel uncomfortable up close. They didn't know whether it was the fact that the guards had resembled lions in the face or the enigma of what had supposedly occurred with Peter. One thing they were all quick to agree on was how seriously the guards had gone about their work. This was none more evident, they felt, as the guards had reared back and had driven their exotic staffs into opposite ends of the ice block just before hoisting it over their shoulders.

"Guards, remove this spoiled fruit! Cast him and his beast from this righteous temple of worship! Launch them off the highest cliff to the bottom of Hell's deepest river of fire, then seal off the main artery!"

On cue, the throne guard who had impaled the raven on his staff had fallen swiftly into the front of the formation. He was the one who had opened and closed the single door, which had led into the narrow hallway.

"No! This could be a grave mistake, Darr!" The Pope had cupped his cheeks together. "What if Natas Christopher is somehow still alive?"

"He's right! You have to summon the throne guards back while there is still time. Natas Christopher still has the sacred robe on." Kelso had wanted to remind Darr if the angel wasn't already aware of this.

"Thou who is always full of doubt, Natas Christopher has nothing. The power of the robe will work just the opposite on him. It will denounce his supernatural qualities, which the Son and the Holy Ghost had given unto him." Darr briefly chuckled. "When the ice thaws, the robe will act as linen on his flesh. Thus, his body will burn to a fine, powdery ash before his beloved Nero's throne."

"Fascinating," Isaac proclaimed. This news made him feel warm all over. "In other words, Natas Christopher never needed the robes to enter the seventh gate?"

"Ironically, his demise came to be when he believed he did," Zutermier concluded. "Talk about greed and jealousy."

"Yes," agreed the Pope. "Both are a sin for man but a curse for a reptilian."

"You're number one, Lord," Kelso blew a kiss toward the Christ replica.

"Come, I have much more to share." Darr motioned for the Pope and his cardinals to follow him up the main aisle.

"We're right behind you," Zutermier acknowledged. "It should be about dawn." He gave way to the Pope, Kelso, and Isaac.

"So, Darr, whatever became of Pendelkon and the others?" The Pope was curious to find out. "Were they destroyed as well?"

"No. The effects would have been too significant for this world to endure," Darr replied, as he led the Pope and his cardinals through the basilica's centermost door. He didn't turn around until he was outside on the top of the stairs. "This I sayeth unto ye: when the Egyptian priests surrendered and undone their dark spell, they were then whisked away by the wraith of Nero before the throne guards could oust them. Not to worry, the seventh gate will be forever sealed when Natas Christopher makes his journey downward."

"I am very relieved to hear this," the Pope glowed from within.

"All life which was lost, the Lord has granted them His gift of amnesty. He has resurrected the pure at heart, but they won't have any recollection of what took place. They will go on as they did prior to their deaths." Darr had enlightened the Pope and his cardinals while individually caressing each one of their hands. "With this being said, ye art free to talk amongst thyselves. Yet thou art prohibited from documenting anything in writing. This is the Lord's covenant, and may it be fulfilled."

"You have our word, Darr," the Pope had spoken on behalf of his cardinals, who nodded in compliance.

"Yes, we will never break this vow," Kelso had elected to say something for himself.

"This we promise to Heaven." Isaac had bowed in Darr's direction.

"Speaking of the pure of heart, I think I see Peter!"

"Where?" Kelso had wanted Zutermier to show him.

"Right there!" Zutermier had pointed once more. "I believe that's him entering the square! You know, I can detect that walk of his a mile away!"

"I don't believe it!" Kelso had looked like he had just seen a ghost. "It is Peter! He's alive!"

"Come on, let's go greet him." Zutermier was the first to do so.

"Are you coming with us, Pope Pius?" Isaac had turned to ask. He had to do a double take. He couldn't believe how transparent the sunlight had made Darr appear to be.

"No, but you three go right ahead." The Pope had insisted by waving Isaac onward. "This is sure turning out to be a lovely morning, Darr."

The Pope was grinning from ear to ear. He was relieved Peter was alive and strong enough to move about, but he was equally pleased to see some pilgrims doing the same. For some reason, he believed these were the people who had fallen victim to Nero's army. They were popping up from everywhere; he had once tried to keep count. Unlike the usual pilgrims who would flock to the square in order to take pictures or sell their religious paraphernalia, this crowd, in particular, seemed to be traveling as if they were under a spell—a spell ordering them to return to their sanctuaries.

"They can't see us or the Cardinals, can they?"

"Nay." Darr had turned towards the Pope.

"Wow. Their numbers are great."

"Pope Pius, this is for thee."

"What is it, Darr?"

"It is another golden scroll."

"But what does it contain, too?" The Pope had never turned his body. "Tell me, Darr, what does it say?"

He thought he was talking to hear himself talk. He thought Darr was avoiding him until he whipped his head around to his left. It was then he realized Darr was no longer present. Somehow, he figured the angel had managed to elude him without detection. Now, he was all alone and responsible for opening the scroll on his own, which he carefully went about.

"I see Darr's gone." Zutermier had returned alone. "What did he leave you?"

"It's another scroll." The Pope had replied without averting his eyes from the gold leaf paper. "Only this time, it contains a list of sinners and their sins, all of whom are clergymen of the Catholic Church."

"So what is to be done with this list of names?"

"The Lord wants them to be judged by man for their crimes."

The Pope had stared off into the day while pressing the scroll tightly against his inner thigh. "It looks as though we will be seeing Darr once again."

--THE END--